Praise for ...

"Fans of Llywelyn's mu... century Irish history will ... ning conclusion to the sag ... This series concludes a masterful fictional overview of the trials and tribulations of twentieth-century Ireland."　　　*—Booklist* on *1999*

"[Morgan Llywelyn's] strength comes from her extraordinary ability to place the story in the surrounding politics of the time. . . . Llywelyn's grasp of Northern Ireland's history is superb, and the immediacy of her writing is extremely gripping."　　　*—Irish Voice* on *1972*

"As the multinovel nears our own age, the reader draws more deeply into the flow of events and the characters. The years whistle by with joy and gunpowder."
　　　—Kirkus Reviews on *1972*

"Llywelyn is an astute observer of matters Irish and understands the passions that move the actors. *1972*'s ending is as tragic and inevitable as a tombstone, and as memorable as Swift's quip: 'The Irish have religion enough to hate, but not enough to love.'"
　　　—Richmond Times-Dispatch

"As part of Llywelyn's panorama of the Irish century, *1949* is gorgeously conceived and born, full of emotion, resonating with history, and fresh as tomorrow without a false note on any page."
　　　—Parke Godwin, author of Lord of Sunset

"A marriage of stories and truth that breathes life into history in a way a textbook never could. As one of the characters says, 'Sometimes you just have to claw at the world, you know? You have to make things right or die trying.' That theme is echoed not only throughout *1916* but in Llywelyn's entire body of work. It is her soul's song for Ireland, which is clearly the place of her heart."
　　　—Knoxville News-Sentinel

BOOKS BY MORGAN LLYWELYN

THE NOVELS OF THE IRISH CENTURY

1916: A Novel of the Irish Rebellion
1921: A Novel of the Irish Civil War
1949: A Novel of the Irish Free State
1972: A Novel of Ireland's Unfinished Revolution
*1999: A Novel of the Celtic Tiger and the Search
for Peace*

Bard
Brian Boru
The Elementals
Etruscans (with Michael Scott)
Finn Mac Cool
Grania
The Horse Goddess
The Last Prince of Ireland
Lion of Ireland
Pride of Lions
Strongbow

1999

A Novel of the Celtic Tiger and the Search for Peace

Morgan Llywelyn

A TOM DOHERTY ASSOCIATES BOOK
NEW YORK

NOTE: If you purchased this book without a cover, you should be aware that this book is stolen property. It was reported as "unsold and destroyed" to the publisher, and neither the author nor the publisher has received any payment for this "stripped book."

This is a work of fiction. All of the characters, organizations, and events portrayed in this novel are either products of the author's imagination or are used fictitiously.

1999: A NOVEL OF THE CELTIC TIGER AND THE SEARCH FOR PEACE

Copyright © 2008 by Morgan Llywelyn

All rights reserved.

A Forge Book
Published by Tom Doherty Associates, LLC
175 Fifth Avenue
New York, NY 10010

www.tor-forge.com

Forge® is a registered trademark of Tom Doherty Associates, LLC.

ISBN-13: 978-0-8125-7799-0
ISBN-10: 0-8125-7799-X

First Edition: February 2008
First Mass Market Edition: March 2009

Printed in the United States of America

0 9 8 7 6 5 4 3 2 1

For the bravest, who took the greatest risks

Acknowledgments

—◆◇◆—

The author gratefully acknowledges the innumerable contributions made to this book, and to the series of which it is the final volume, by people who were actively involved in the events depicted. There are far too many of them to list by name. Men and women from both sides of the political divide have given unstintingly of their records and their personal memories; memories which sometimes have contradicted the "official" version. Wherever possible the author has chosen to accept the word of the actual participants. Although this is a work of fiction every effort has been made to obtain historical veracity, and no historical event has been rewritten for dramatic effect.

A special thanks is owed to the Bobby Sands Trust for permission to use the quotes from the late Bobby Sands that are included in this book

Dramatis Personae —1999

Alice Cassidy and her husband, Dennis: Friends of Barry's from his days in Trinity College.

Isabella Mooney Kavanagh: Born in Dublin in 1923; elder daughter of Henry and Ella Mooney and sister of Henrietta Mooney Rice; widow of Michael Kavanagh.

Father John Aloysius: Catholic priest from Derry; an old friend of Barry Halloran's.

Winifred Baines Speer: Sister of Donald Baines (from *1921* by the same author); widow of Jonathan Speer and matriarch of an extended family in Belfast.

Paudie Coates: Automobile mechanic in Harold's Cross.

Brian Joseph (b. 1973), Grace Mary (b. 1976), and Patrick James Halloran (b. 1979): Children of Barry and Barbara Halloran.

Louise Kearney: A cousin of Henry Mooney who once owned a boardinghouse in Dublin's Gardiner Street, where Ursula lived as a child.

Paul Morrissey, his wife Eithne, their four sons and twin daughters, Dorothy and Eleanor: A farm family in County Clare.

Breda Casey Cunningham: Widowed nurse who helps take care of Ursula.

Michael Kavanagh: Barbara's deceased father.

Frederick Liggitt: Belfast businessman and leading member of the Orange Order.

Lewis Baines: Former lover of Ursula's and nephew of Winifred Speer.

Billy Keane and his family: Catholics living in West Belfast.

Historical Characters

Adams, Gerry (b. 1948): Belfast-born Irish republican and politician. First interned in 1972, he later took part in secret talks between the British and Irish governments; elected president of Sinn Féin in 1983 and won the seat for West Belfast in the British parliamentary elections; between 1988 and 1994 was involved in talks with John Hume towards establishing a peace process in Northern Ireland; was instrumental in arranging the 1994 IRA ceasefire; in 2005 it was Gerry Adams, together with Martin McGuinness, who convinced the IRA to decommission their arms and thus effectively end the war against Britain.

Ahern, Patrick "Bertie" (b. 1951): Dublin-born to a strong republican family; Fianna Fáil politician who became *taoiseach* on June 26, 1997.

Berners-Lee, Tim: Graduate of Oxford University; a principal computer research scientist at MIT; inventor of the World Wide Web.

Black, Christopher: IRA informer.

Blair, Tony (b. 1953): Became leader of the British Labour Party in 1994; prime minister 1997–2007.

Bradley, Fr. Denis (b. 1945): Born in Co. Donegal; enrolled in St. Columb's College and lived in Derry thereafter; administered last rites to three dying men on Bloody

Sunday; officiated at the wedding of Martin McGuinness; left the priesthood in the late 1970s to marry and raise a family; pursued twin careers in the media and in drug counselling; helped negotiate the 1994 IRA ceasefire by serving as a link between the IRA and the British government; later appointed vice chairman of the Northern Ireland policing board.

Bruton, John Gerard (b. 1947): Politician, landowner, member of Fine Gael, served as *taoiseach* 1994–97.

Carter, James Earl "Jimmy" (b. 1924): Thirty-ninth president of the United States 1977–81.

Clinton, William Jefferson "Bill" (b. 1946): Forty-second president of the United States 1993–2001.

Corrigan, Mairéad, and Betty Williams: Cofounders of the Northern Ireland Peace People Movement in 1976; recipients of the Nobel Peace Prize in 1977.

Cosgrave, Liam (b. 1920): Son of W. T. Cosgrave, revolutionary and cofounder of the Irish Free State. Liam Cosgrave studied law and practiced at the bar before entering the Dáil for Fine Gael in 1943; minister for external affairs 1954–57; became leader of Fine Gael in 1965; became *taoiseach* in the Fine Gael/Labour coalition elected in 1973; lost to Fianna Fáil in 1977 general election; retired from the Dáil in 1981.

Craig, William: Served as home affairs minister in the Northern Ireland Parliament at Stormont; launched a militant right-wing movement called Vanguard.

DeLorean, John: Entrepreneur and automobile manufacturer.

de Valera, Eamon (1882–1975): Born in America, raised in Ireland; joined the Volunteers at the founding of the organisation; a commandant in the 1916 Rising; elected member of Parliament for East Clare in 1917; in 1919 elected president of the first Dáil Éireann; resigned due to his opposition to the 1921 Anglo-Irish Treaty; formed Fianna Fáil political party in 1926; elected president of Ireland in 1959; reelected 1966.

Donoughmore, Lord (John Michael Henry Hely-Hutchinson): Born in England in 1902; educated at Oxford; served as Conservative MP 1943–45; steward for the Irish Turf Club; Grand Master of the Order of Freemasons in Ireland. Married Dorothy Jean Hetham, who became president of the Clonmel Flower Show.

Drumm, Máire: Sinn Féin vice president murdered in 1976 by members of the UDA.

Dugdale, Bridget Rose (b. 1941): Daughter of a wealthy English landowner and Lloyds underwriter, Lieutenant Colonel James Dugdale; studied at Oxford and earned a Ph.D. at London University; became a recruit to Irish republicanism as a result of Bloody Sunday and was involved in a number of arms smuggling operations amongst other exploits.

Ennis, Séamus (1919–82): Born in north County Dublin, the son of a piper, Ennis became the foremost exponent of the uilleann piper in Ireland and an expert in all aspects of traditional music.

Ervine, David (1953–2007): Born to a working-class family in East Belfast; joined the UVF at 19; arrested in 1974 for possession of explosives; sent to Cage 19, Long Kesh; released in 1980; stood in local council elections as a Progressive Unionist Party candidate in 1985; subsequently became leader of the Progressive Unionist Party and one of the architects of conflict resolution in Northern Ireland. Died on January 7, 2007, following a heart attack. Gerry Adams was one of the mourners at his funeral.

Faul, Fr. Denis (1932–2006): Campaigned for civil rights in Northern Ireland; chaplain at Long Kesh during the hunger strikes; subsequently elevated to Monsignor.

Faulkner, Brian (1921–77): Unionist politician and heir to a large shirt-manufacturing business; appointed chief of the power-sharing Northern Ireland Executive in January 1974; resigned within a matter of months when power sharing was brought down by a general strike.

Fennell, Desmond (b. 1929): Belfast-born journalist and author; lived in Connemara during the 1970s; lecturer in political science at University College Galway 1976–82; lecturer in communications at the College of Commerce in Rathmines, Dublin, from 1983.

FitzGerald, Garret (b. 1926): Born in Dublin, the son of Desmond FitzGerald, who was one of the founders of the Irish Free State. Educated at Belvedere and UCD; worked in Aer Lingus 1947–58; lectured on economics at UCD; entered politics in 1964; became a Fine Gael senator in 1965; became TD for Dublin Southeast in 1969; appointed minister for foreign affairs in 1973; became *taoiseach* of Fine Gael/Labour coalition in 1981.

Fitzgerald, Jim: Head groom at Ballymany Stud Farm, County Kildare.

Gadhafi, Muammar: Libyan dictator.

Gageby, Douglas (1918–2004): Journalist and editor of *The Irish Times* 1963–74 and again 1977–86. Gageby was also the son-in-law of Seán Lester, the last secretary-general of the League of Nations.

Gallagher, Eddie: IRA member from Ballybofey, County Donegal, and close friend of Rose Dugdale.

Gardiner, Luke: Self-made millionaire and property developer in the eighteenth century; appointed as deputy vice treasurer of Ireland and receiver general in 1725; surveyor general of Customs in 1745. Together with his son, also Luke Gardiner (1745–98), was responsible for planning much of Dublin.

Garland, Seán (b. 1934): Dublin-born of a working-class family; educated by the Christian Brothers; joined the IRA in 1953; joined the British Army in 1954 in order to infiltrate it and pass on information to the IRA; commandant of the Lynch Column during the Border Campaign of 1956; later chief of staff of the Official IRA; national organiser for Official Sinn Féin; chairman of the Workers Party.

"Gibraltar Three": Seán Savage, Daniel McCann, and Mairéad Farrell.

Gorbachev, Mikhail Sergeyevich (b. 1931): General secretary of the Communist Party of the Soviet Union from 1985 to 1991; president of the Soviet Union from 1990; awarded the Nobel Prize for Peace in 1990; presided over the breakup of the Soviet Union into individual constituent republics.

Goulding, Cathal (1927–98): Joined the republican movement as a young man; imprisoned and also interned for IRA membership; elected chief of staff of the IRA in 1962; after the split in 1969 became chief of staff of the Official IRA.

H-Block escapees: (in addition to Gerry Kelly) Rab Kerr, Tony McAllister, Brendan "Bik" McFarlane, Seán McGlinchey, Brendan Mead, Bobby Storey.

Haughey, Charles James (1925–2006): Born in Castlebar, County Mayo; a brilliant student; barrister; certified accountant; member of Fianna Fáil; married to Maureen Lemass, daughter of Seán Lemass; elected to the Dáil in 1957; became minister for justice in 1961; minister for agriculture 1964–66; minister for finance 1966–70; dismissed from cabinet in 1970, arrested and charged with conspiring to import arms into Northern Ireland, acquitted of all charges; as leader of Fianna Fáil he served as *taoiseach* in 1979 and again in 1982 and 1987.

Heath, Edward "Ted" Richard George (1916–2005): Conservative politician, writer, and prime minister of Great Britain from 1970 to 1974.

Hermon, Sir John "Jack" (1928–2008): Chief constable of the RUC 1980–89.

Higgins, Michael D. (b. 1941): Born in Limerick; author, poet, politician; educated at St. Flannan's College in Ennis, University College Galway, Indiana University and Manchester University; twice mayor of Galway City; chairman of the Irish Labour Party 1977–1987; Minister for Arts, Culture and the Gaeltacht 1993–1997; elected president of the Labour Party 2003; currently serving in Dáil Eireann as T. D. for Galway West.

Hilditch, Stanley: Governor of Her Majesty's Prison, the Maze, in 1981.

Hume, John (b. 1937): Leader of the SDLP—the Social Democratic and Labour Party in Northern Ireland.

Irwin, Stephen, and Torrens Knight: Members of the Ulster Defence Association convicted of the Greysteele Massacre in 1993.

John Paul II, original name Karol Wojtyla (1920–2005): The first Polish-born pope (1978–2005) in the history of the Roman Catholic Church.

Kennedy, Edward Moore "Ted" (b. 1932): Born in Brookline, Massachusetts; a prominent figure in the Democratic Party; elected to the U.S. Senate in 1962; became majority whip in the Senate in 1969; a leading advocate of many liberal causes and a strong voice for Irish America.

Kinsella, Thomas: Irish poet.

Lowry, Sir Robert: Northern Ireland judge.

Lynch, John Mary "Jack" (1917–99): Born in Cork; one of the county's most outstanding athletes, winning one All-Ireland Gaelic football championship and five All-Ireland hurling championships; qualified as a barrister while working in Dublin as a civil servant; elected to the Dáil in 1948; parliamentary secretary 1951–54; minister for education 1957–59; minister for industry and commerce 1959–65; minister for finance 1965–66; elected leader of Fianna Fáil and *taoiseach* 1966–73, 1977–79.

McAliskey, Josephine Bernadette Devlin (b. 1947): Born in County Tyrone; prominent member of the People's Democracy movement in Northern Ireland; took part in numerous civil rights marches and the Battle of the Bogside; sentenced to six months for riotous behaviour; became the youngest woman ever elected an MP in Westminster; seriously injured in a loyalist gun attack in

February 1981; a central figure in the H-Block Committee during the hunger strike that same year.

McAnespie, Aiden: Member of Sinn Féin, shot in the back by British security forces.

MacAirt, Proinsias (Frank Card) (1922–92): Officer in the IRA.

MacBride, Seán (1904–88): Volunteer, lawyer, politician, journalist, peace activist. The son of John MacBride, who was executed by the British for his part in the 1916 Rising, and Maud Gonne MacBride. Born and educated in France, MacBride was assistant to Michael Collins during the Treaty negotiations; later served for a time as chief of staff of the IRA; was called to the bar in 1937; in 1946 he founded the political party, Clann na Poblachta; served as a TD from 1954–57; chairman of Amnesty International 1973–76; received the Nobel Peace Prize in 1974; awarded the Lenin Peace Prize in 1977 and the American Medal for Justice in 1978; was one of those responsible for the European Convention on Human Rights.

McGee, Mary: Married woman living in Skerries, County Dublin.

McGuinness, Martin (b. 1950): Born in the Bogside of Derry, Northern Ireland; by the time he was 21 he was O/C of the Derry Brigade of the IRA; in 1972 was one of a seven-member delegation invited to London for peace talks with Willie Whitelaw; married his wife, Bernie, while he was on the run—the priest who married them was Fr. Denis Bradley; in 1973 McGuinness was arrested for membership in the IRA; in 1975 was director of operations for the Northern Command of the IRA; became chief of staff in 1978; resigned in 1982 to devote himself to republican politics; appointed as Sinn Féin's chief negotiator; elected MP for Mid-Ulster; served as minister for education in the Northern Ireland Assembly.

MacStiofáin, Seán (John Stephenson) (1928–2001): London-born and half-English; served in the Royal Air Force 1945–48; joined the IRA shortly afterwards; appointed director of intelligence in 1966; chief of staff of the Provisional IRA 1969–72.

MacThomáis, Éamonn (Éamonn Patrick Thomas) (1927–2002): Patriot, historian, writer, Dubliner. Joined both Sinn Féin and the IRA in the fifties; became treasurer of Sinn Féin; manager and contributor to the *United Irishman*; Dublin O/C at the start of the Border Campaign; arrested in 1957 and interned in Curragh Camp; released in 1959; became editor of *An Phoblacht* in 1972; arrested again in 1973; upon release was again editor of *An Phoblacht*; rearrested within two months and sentenced to fifteen months in prison for allegedly possessing an IRA press bulletin; author of numerous books about Dublin; creator and presenter of RTE series during the seventies on the history of Dublin; conducted numerous walking tours of Dublin; lecturer and Keeper of the House of Lords Chamber in the Bank of Ireland on College Green, Dublin, 1988–2002.

Macken, Eddie: Member of numerous Irish showjumping teams.

Magee, Patrick: Irish republican convicted of the Brighton bombing in 1984.

Major, John (b. 1943): Entered the House of Commons during the Conservative Party landslide in 1979; junior minister in 1986; in 1989 Prime Minister Margaret Thatcher appointed him to the cabinet post of foreign secretary; subsequently served as chancellor of the Exchequer;

on November 28, 1990, Major became leader of the Conservative Party and prime minister after Thatcher resigned.

Mallon, Séamus (b. 1936): Born in Markethill, County Armagh; schoolteacher; civil rights activist; SDLP spokesperson on law and order from 1982; deputy first minister of Northern Ireland 1998–99; deputy leader SDLP 1979–2001 MP for Newry and Armagh 1986–2005.

Mansergh, Martin (b. 1946): Personal and political adviser to Charles J. Haughey.

Maxwell, Sir John Grenville: British general who took command in Ireland after the 1916 Rising and ordered the executions of the leaders.

Mayhew, Sir Patrick: Attorney general in Northern Ireland; appointed secretary of state for Northern Ireland in 1992.

Meir, Golda (1898–1978): A founder of the State of Israel and its fourth prime minister, serving from 1969 to 1974.

Morrison, Danny (b. 1953): Volunteer; editor of the *Republican News*; national director of publicity for Sinn Féin in the eighties.

Mr. Justice Gannon: Appointed as a judge in Northern Ireland in the 1970s.

Mowlam, Mo (1949–2005): Lecturer at Newcastle University until 1983; senior administrator at Northern College, Barnsley, until her election as MP 1987; opposition spokeswoman on Northern Ireland 1987–89; opposition spokeswoman on trade and industry 1990–92; opposition spokeswoman on Citizens' Charter and

Women's Affairs 1992–93; shadow national heritage secretary 1993–94; shadow Northern Ireland secretary 1994–97; secretary of state, Northern Ireland 1997–99.

Newman, Sir Kenneth (b. 1926): Served with the British police in Palestine; a commander with the Metropolitan Police in London; then a deputy chief constable in Northern Ireland; was appointed chief constable of the Royal Ulster Constabulary in 1976.

Nixon, Richard Milhous (1913–94): Vice president of the United States 1953–61; thirty-seventh president of the United States 1969–1974.

Nugent, Ciaran: Member of the IRA and first of the "Blanket Men" in the H-Blocks.

Ó Brádaigh, Ruairí (Rory Brady) (b. 1932): Born in County Longford; graduated from University College, Dublin; taught school in County Roscommon; joined Sinn Féin in 1950; joined the IRA in 1951; Sinn Féin TD for Longford-Westmeath 1975; IRA chief of staff 1958–59 and 1961–62; when the republican movement split in 1970 became the first president of Provisional Sinn Féin; lost leadership to Gerry Adams in 1983; leader of faction that left Sinn Féin to form Republican Sinn Féin.

O'Callaghan, Sean: IRA informer.

Ó Conaill, Dáithí (David O'Connell) (1938–91): Schoolteacher from Cork; joined Sinn Féin in 1955; subsequently joined the IRA; second in command to Seán Garland in the 1956 Border Campaign; lost a lung to a bullet wound; member of the Army Council.

Ó Dálaigh, Cearbhall (1911–78): Born in Bray, County Wicklow; called to the bar in 1934; became senior counsel in 1945; supreme court judge 1953; chief justice 1961; elected president of Ireland in 1974.

O'Donnell, Mary: Noted Irish fashion designer born in County Donegal; trained with Mainbocher and with Sybil Connolly before going into business for herself in 1963.

Ó Fíaich, Cardinal Tomás (1923–90): Historian and cardinal of the Church; born in Crossmaglen, County Armagh, shortly after partition; ordained in 1948; lecturer in modern history at Maynooth 1953; professor 1959; college president 1974; named archbishop of Armagh in 1977; elevated to cardinal in 1979.

O'Hanlon, Feargal: IRA Volunteer killed during the Brookeborough raid.

O'Leary, Michael (1936–2006): *Tanaiste* under Garret FitzGerald.

O'Malley, Desmond (b. 1939): Politician who succeeded his uncle Donagh O'Malley as a TD for Limerick East; parliamentary secretary to Taoiseach Jack Lynch in 1969; minister for justice 1970–73; strongly anti-IRA, O'Malley introduced a special no-jury court to deal with militant republicanism. Appointed minister for industry and commerce in 1977. O'Malley was expelled from Fianna Fáil in 1985 for refusing to follow the party line and went on to found the Progressive Democrats.

Pahlavi, Mohammad Reza (1919–80): Shah of Iran 1941–79. The shah's efforts at modernisation produced strong economic growth that transformed his country; however his friendship with both the United States and Israel, and his support of women's rights, turned the religious fundamentalists against him. He appealed to the United States for help but it was not forthcoming; he was driven from power in 1979 and replaced by the Ayatollah Khomeini, who established a religious revolutionary regime.

Paisley, Ian Richard Kyle (b. 1926): Born in Armagh, the son of James Kyle Paisley, originally a Baptist minister, and his wife Isabella; eventually moved to the Reformed Presbyterian Church; at sixteen young Ian attended a fundamentalist college in South Wales. He was ordained as a Presbyterian minister in August 1946. Later he would found his own church, the Free Presbyterian Church of Ulster, with a strong separatist and fundamentalist theology. From the beginning Ian Paisley was dedicated to the condemnation of Catholicism. His fire-and-brimstone speeches won a wide following among working-class Ulster Protestants, and inspired an extreme, militant sectarianism calling itself "loyalism." Upon founding the Democratic Unionist Party, or DUP, Paisley led his followers away from the more moderate Ulster Unionist Party. After a lifetime spent in political manoeuvring, in 2007 Ian Paisley finally became first minister of the Northern Ireland Assembly at Stormont.

Prisoners identified by name in the Cages and the H-Blocks.

Reagan, Ronald Wilson (1911–2004): Radio sports announcer; film actor; president of the Screen Actors Guild; governor of California 1967–74; fortieth president of the United States 1981–89.

Rees, Merlyn (1920–2006): The son of a Welsh coal miner, Rees joined the Labour Party; named as shadow secretary of state for Northern Ireland in 1972; became secretary of state for Northern Ireland 1974–76; promoted to home secretary in 1976.

Reid, Fr. Alec: Redemptorist priest from Clonard Monastery who acted as mediator in various republican feuds; brought Sinn Féin and the SDLP together for talks in 1988; gave artificial respiration to two British army men who were dragged from their vehicle and killed after they drove into the funeral of Volunteer Kevin Brady in 1988; was one of the two independent clerical witnesses to the final act of IRA decommissioning in 2005.

Reynolds, Albert (b. 1932): Businessman and politician; member of Fianna Fáil; elected to Dáil Éireann as TD for Longford-Roscommon in 1977; minister for finance (1988–91); minister for industry and commerce (1987–88); minister for industry and energy (1982); minister for posts and telegraphs and transport (1979–81); eighth *taoiseach* of the Republic of Ireland 1992–94.

Robinson, Mary (b. 1944): Academic; barrister; civil rights campaigner; member of the Irish Senate 1969–89; elected Ireland's first female president in 1990.

Sands, Bobby (1954–81): Born in Belfast; during his youth loyalist harassment forced his family to move twice; Sands left school at fifteen to become an apprentice coach-builder; joined the IRA while still in his teens; arrested for IRA membership in 1972; sentenced in 1973 to five years' imprisonment in Long Kesh; studied Irish in prison; released in April of 1976; rearrested in October of that year for possession of a gun; sentenced to fourteen years; arrived in the H-Blocks in September 1977; wrote articles under the pen name "Marcella" for the republican press; first man to go on hunger strike on March 1, 1981; in the April by-election Sands stood for the British Parliament and won, defeating the Unionist candidate; died on May 5, his sixty-sixth day without food.

Shankill Butchers and victims: As named in text and according to police sources.

Spence, Gusty (b. 1933): Born in the Shankill area of Belfast; joined the Royal Ulster Rifles in 1957 and served in Cyprus; joined the UVF in 1965 as commanding officer of the Shankill unit; arrested in 1972 and imprisoned in the Maze; resigned from the UVF in 1978; in 1991 became commander of combined loyalist forces that declared a ceasefire in 1994.

Stalker, John (b. 1945): Served on the police force of Manchester, England, for over twenty years; in 1978 promoted to head of the Warwickshire CID; in 1984 named deputy chief constable of Greater Manchester.

Stephenson, Sam: Irish architect who designed Dublin Civic Offices at Wood Quay.

Stone, Michael "Flint": Loyalist gunman convicted of the murders of three men during a funeral at Milltown Cemetery in Belfast.

Tebbit, Norman: Secretary of state for trade and industry in the Thatcher government.

Thain, Ian: Private in the British army convicted of murdering a northern Catholic and imprisoned for life. Released after only two years and returned to his regiment.

Thatcher, Margaret Hilda, nee Roberts (b. 1925): Conservative British prime minister known as "The Iron Lady." Daughter of a grocer who had a minor career in the Conservative Party and eventually became mayor of Grantham. Margaret Roberts was educated at Oxford; worked as a research chemist; married Dennis Thatcher,

wealthy oil industry executive; read for the bar and specialised in tax law; elected to Parliament as a Conservative in 1959; became a cabinet minister under Edward
Heath 1970–74; succeeded Heath as Conservative leader
in 1975; became prime minister of the United Kingdom
in 1979; was Britain's longest serving prime minister in
the twentieth century before being ousted in 1990 and replaced as head of the Conservative Party and prime minister by John Major.

Twomey, Séamus (1919–89): Commandant of the
Belfast Brigade; succeeded Seán MacStiofáin as chief of
staff of the Provisional IRA.

Vidal, Gore (b. 1925): American novelist; born at
West Point; served in the Pacific in World War Two; his
works included *Williwaw, The City and the Pillar, Myra
Breckinridge, Washington, DC, Burr, 1876,* and *Julian.*

Widgery, Lord Chief Justice: British jurist who conducted the first tribunal to investigate Bloody Sunday.

Wilson, Fr. Des: Catholic priest from Gerry Adams'
parish of West Belfast who became involved early on in
conflict resolution in the north; in the 1970s he did much
work in the prisons.

Wilson, James Harold (1916–95): The son of an industrial chemist; educated at Oxford; member of the
Labour Party; elected to the House of Commons in 1945;
prime minister of the United Kingdom 1964–70, 1974–76.

Wright, Billy (1960–97): Known as "King Rat," Wright
was the leader of the Loyalist Volunteer Force.

1999

Prologue

**Excerpt from the Address of the Continental Congress
to the People of Ireland
on the eve of the American Revolution**

"Friends and fellow subjects. We are desirous of possessing the good opinion of the virtuous and humane. We are peculiarly desirous of furnishing the People of Ireland with a true statement of our motives and objects, the better to enable you to judge of our conduct with accuracy, and determine the merits of the controversy with impartiality and precision.

You have been friendly to the rights of mankind, and we acknowledge with pleasure and gratitude that the Irish Nation has produced patriots who have highly distinguished themselves in the cause of humanity and America. On the other hand, we are not ignorant that the labours and manufactures of Ireland, like those of the silk-worm, were of little moment to herself, but served only to give luxury to those who neither toil nor spin.

Accept our most grateful acknowledgments for the friendly disposition you have already shown toward us. We know that you are not without your grievances. We sympathize with you in your distress, and are pleased to find that the design of subjugating us has persuaded the English Government to dispense to Ireland some vagrant rays of ministerial sunshine. The tender mercies of the

British Government have long been cruel toward you.
God grant that the iniquitous schemes of extirpating liberty may soon be defeated."

July 28, 1775

(Signed) John Hancock

Chapter One

────◦◦◦◦────

LIKE candles blown out by a celestial wind, the last stars vanished.

The beam of headlamps swung wildly as the Austin Healey skidded on a patch of black ice. Barry Halloran turned into the skid and kept his foot on the accelerator. The green car fishtailed, teetered on the brink of a ditch, recovered and raced on.

Barry's anger was unstoppable.

He hardly saw the road. Other images clouded his vision like a double exposure. Unarmed civilians being shot down in the street. An injured man shot in the back at point-blank range as he lay writhing on the pavement. An old woman battered to the ground with the butt of a rifle. British soldiers sniggering while the still-bleeding bodies of their victims were tossed into trucks like sides of beef.

On the screen of Barry's mind the cinematic horror ran over and over again.

His knuckles were white on the steering wheel.

He had taken advantage of the better roads in Northern Ireland by driving south from Derry through Tyrone and Fermanagh. Avoiding the manned border crossing west of Enniskillen, he had entered the Republic of Ireland by a neglected byway, then angled southward again across Leitrim and Roscommon. Even when he reached County Galway very few lights were visible from the road. Much of the region was all but deserted. In the west of Ireland unemployment was endemic. Thousands of young men and women had "taken the boat" to England in search of jobs.

Signposts were notoriously unreliable. With nothing better to do, the local youngsters who remained behind often turned road signs to point in the wrong direction. The unwary driver could go miles out of his way before discovering his mistake.

Finbar Lewis Halloran needed no signposts to County Clare. The map was imprinted on the marrow of his bones.

By the time he turned into the country lane leading off the Ennis Road dawn was breaking. A sullen crimson dawn for the last day of January 1972. "Red sky at night, farmers' delight," Barry muttered to himself. "Red sky at morning, farmers take warning."

Take warning, his tired brain echoed

Ancient hedgerows of furze and whitethorn rose like walls on either side of the laneway. Deep ruts held automobile tyres to the track. Once committed, a driver had no choice but to follow the lane to the end.

After a few hundred yards it came to a substantial farmhouse flanked by barns and outbuildings. Within easy sight from the house a large paddock waited to receive the broodmares, heavy with foal, who would be turned out later in the morning.

Everything looks the same. Thank God, it always looks the same. Barry could feel knots loosening in the pit of his stomach.

Built of local stone in the eighteenth century, the original tiny cottage had been altered repeatedly by successive generations of Hallorans. The house now comprised two full storeys with a steeply pitched slate roof bracketed by brick chimneys. In a rare fit of domesticity, Ursula Halloran had built an extension off the kitchen to hold an array of modern appliances, such as a washing machine and a freezer chest. She never got around to buying them. The space had become a catchall for muddy boots and a haven for orphaned farm animals.

Ursula referred to it as "the nursery."

Barry slammed on the brakes and hurled himself from

the car like a giant spring uncoiling. He was very tall and the leg space beneath the dashboard was insufficient. The long drive had caused his damaged leg to stiffen. When he stood upright a spear of pain shot through the muscles.

A swift intake of breath. A momentary closing of eyes. Then it was over.

Two long strides carried him to the house.

A light was burning in the parlour to the left of the hall. As he ran past, Barry glimpsed the huddled figure of his mother in her favourite armchair, where she sometimes fell asleep listening to the late news on the radio. He took the stairs three at a time. Raced to his room, flung open the door. Threw himself on his knees beside the bed and fumbled beneath the mattress. Inhaled the dusty scent of feathers and ticking, and linen bleached in the sun.

Grasped the polished stock of Ned Halloran's old rifle.

A woman said from the doorway, "Thank God you're all right! When I rang your house in Dublin Barbara told me where you'd gone. What just happened in Derry is all over the news, RTE even interrupted its regular programming. I've been terrified."

The haggard man stood up with a rifle in his hands. "You've never been terrified in your life, Ursula." His deep baritone voice was hoarse with weariness.

"That's all you know. What happened?"

"I don't think I can talk about it, not yet."

"Please, Barry."

Reluctantly, he dragged out the words that made it all real again. "When the civil rights march formed up in the Creggan I was there with my cameras. A great opportunity for photojournalism, I thought. Images of hope in Northern Ireland after all these years. People came in the thousands, even from the Republic. Men and women, boys and girls; it was more like a huge picnic than a protest rally. They brought food, their children, even their dogs. There was a lot of laughter and optimism. By the time they moved out the marchers were singing."

His voice dropped to a harsh whisper. "When they reached the Rossville Flats area the British soldiers trapped them in those narrow streets and shot them down like dogs. At least thirteen were killed then and there. Scores of others were wounded. I saw it; I saw it all." Barry closed his eyes for a moment; swayed where he stood.

Ursula put out a hand to steady him. He brushed it away. "I'm all right," he insisted.

His mother sat down on the bed. Running up the stairs after him had left her short of breath. "They're already calling it Bloody Sunday," she panted. "Like the original Bloody Sunday in 1920, when British forces machine-gunned Irish civilians at a football match. That incident was pretty well hushed up, but what happened yesterday is a different story. Television around the world is carrying scenes from Derry."

"Bless the telly," rasped Barry. "For once the Brits can't pretend one of their atrocities never happened."

He leaned the rifle against the wall and slumped onto the bed beside his mother. Ursula waited. Slowly, inch by inch, his spine straightened. When he spoke again his tone was that of a professional observer. "When I went to Derry I didn't expect a massacre, Ursula, though maybe I should have. Maybe we all should have. Surely by now we know the imperial mentality.

"Remember when Martin Luther King gathered a quarter of a million people at the U.S. Capitol in support of civil rights for his people? What a splendid day that was. The whole world seemed new, as if chains were finally being broken and anything was possible. The Catholics in Northern Ireland took King's message to heart. They believed the same nonviolent protest could work for them.

"They were wrong.

"Yesterday they staged a peaceful march for their civil rights, and were shot in cold blood by the very army that was supposed to protect them. That's justice in the United Kingdom. In 1960 the American people elected a Catholic president. In 1972 Catholics in Northern Ireland can't even get a decent job." Barry's voice remained steady. Yet tremors of outrage ran through his body.

His mother longed to take him in her arms and comfort him. Theirs had never been that sort of relationship, however. His rumpled hair was the same red-gold it had been when he was a boy, but the sleeves of his coat were stained with someone else's blood.

He drew a long, deep breath. Exhaled slowly. Drew another. Sought the quiet pool at the centre of himself, which alone could armour a man against the shocks of life.

When he got to his feet, Ursula tilted her head back to look up into his face. Jutting cheekbones and aquiline nose; a wide, mobile mouth. Sharply etched lines that made him appear older than his thirty-three years.

In his deep-set grey eyes she glimpsed the flash of swords.

Barry Halloran looked dangerous.

"What are you going to do now?" she wanted to know.

"Go up to Dublin."

"Not now surely. You must be in shock, you need a hot meal and some sleep."

"I don't need either one, Ursula; I need to go to Dublin."

Total surrender was not in her nature. "At least take a cup of strong tea first. Wash your face, have a shave . . . and leave your grandfather's rifle with me. After yesterday, the Gardai* will be out in full strength. You could be stopped anywhere, and if they took Papa's rifle from you we'd never get it back."

"Don't worry, they won't stop me. I know every back road between here and Dublin, I'll be there by teatime."

So everything's already decided, Ursula thought. *I should have known it the moment I saw him holding the rifle.*

The rifle was a short magazine Lee-Enfield .303 made

---

*Short for *Garda Siochana*, Guardians of the Peace: the Irish police force.

during World War One, and fitted with a small brass plate proclaiming its place of manufacture: "Winchester Repeating Arms Co., New Haven, Connecticut." Ursula Halloran, who knew things, had a bad feeling about that weapon.

For years she had expected her beloved papa would die with the Lee-Enfield in his hands. Much to everyone's surprise, Ned Halloran had lived to die in his bed. Before age and his many wounds finally caught up with him he gave the rifle to his daughter and made her promise to pass it on to Barry when the boy reached his fifteenth birthday. When Barry later ran away to follow in his grandfather's footsteps and join the Irish Republican Army, he took the rifle with him.

"I really would feel better if you left Papa's rifle here this time, Barry," Ursula said. "For my protection."

He looked down at the small thin woman with her cap of silver hair. And her fierce, blue-grey eyes. "I'd pity anyone who was fool enough to attack you, Ursula. You're never unarmed. After I took up photography I gave your old Mauser back to you; I suspect it's under your pillow this very minute. And there's always the shotgun in the barn.* But I'm taking the rifle. After yesterday every Volunteer* in the country will be digging up his weapons. I'm sure Séamus has already retrieved his."

I should have known, thought Ursula. *Séamus. That's why he's in such a hurry to get to Dublin. Who else would he turn to at a time like this?*

Séamus McCoy had been Barry's training officer in the IRA. Barry had never known his father, who was killed in 1941 when German bombs were dumped on Dublin's North Strand. Séamus McCoy had never had a son. The experienced soldier had given the raw youngster an unspoken paternal affection. Their relationship answered a deep need in both men.

---

*Member of the Irish Republican Army.

In his youth Barry had dreamed of being a warrior in the ancient Celtic mould. He was a natural athlete with more energy than he could use; the IRA had provided an outlet for both. But the first time he saw men killed in front of him the gap between romantic imagination and bloody reality had shaken him to the core.

Eventually Barry had disengaged himself from active service. He never discussed the reason for his decision with anyone, even Séamus McCoy. Yet he remained committed to Irish republicanism. While other Volunteers struggled to keep the resistance movement alive by fighting skirmishes and throwing bombs—sometimes blowing themselves up instead of RUC stations*—Barry had turned to freelance photojournalism as a way of furthering the republican viewpoint.

"I like cameras," was his offhand explanation for his career choice, "because I'm good at fiddley things like adjusting f-stops." It went deeper than that. Photography suited his complex nature.

Barry Halloran had always been a puzzle to those who knew him. As a boy he was reckless and fun-loving, yet given to long silences. His nature combined a fiery temper with a sense of poetry. In a single day he might go from infectious gaiety to brooding melancholy and back again; even his mother was never sure what her child was thinking.

Maturity had taught him to keep a lid on his more extreme emotions. Photography provided a creative outlet for those feelings. An inspired moment behind the camera could give voice to the griefs hidden in Barry's heart, or expose an injustice that enraged him.

Photojournalism was in its infancy in Ireland, however, so in order to augment an uncertain income, Barry had borrowed enough money to purchase a boardinghouse. At

*Royal Ulster Constabulary; the police force of Northern Ireland.

the time he bought the house, in an area of Dublin called
Harold's Cross, there were eight boarders; unmarried men
with steady jobs who, for the most part, paid their rent on
time.

"I never thought I'd become a landlord, when the Irish
have hated landlords for centuries," Barry commented
wryly.

Then, when Séamus McCoy was diagnosed with cancer, Barry had taken him in. He saw his friend through
painful surgery and a long convalescence, then persuaded
him to stay on at the boardinghouse as manager. Harold's
Cross was a growing enterprise.

The other member of the staff was a vivacious young
American, Barbara Kavanagh, a granddaughter of Ursula's
beloved Uncle Henry. Barbara had been in Italy studying
to be an opera singer when her voice was damaged by an
overzealous teacher. Instead of returning to America she
had stayed in Europe and attempted to build a less demanding musical career. In her naïveté the girl was mer-
cilessly exploited. At last, angry and disillusioned, she
arrived in Dublin. Barry had offered her a safe haven until she got back on her feet.

Barbara was still in Harold's Cross, where she was now
the housekeeper to pay her way. There was no denying
she was an asset. She handled a multiplicity of tasks with
typical American efficiency.

Ursula was not fooled by the title of "housekeeper."
*Plenty of priests have housekeepers who take care of
more than the parochial house,* she reminded herself. She
had a dark suspicion that someday her son would marry
Barbara Kavanagh, and a darker suspicion that it would
be a mistake. A headstrong and egocentric young woman,
Barbara was far from the traditional model of an Irish
wife. And though he would never admit it, in his heart of
hearts Barry was a traditional man.

His mother was the rebel.

When she followed Barry outside she noticed that he was limping. "It's a long drive to Dublin," she said.

He patted his car as she would pat the neck of a horse. "Apollo will take care of me." He loved the car, which owed its nickname to the U.S. space programme. Space travel interested Barry. A lot of things interested Barry.

She watched him stow the rifle and two boxes of cartridges in the boot of the car and cover them with photographic equipment. The length of his folded tripods was sufficient to conceal a rifle barrel.

Barry slammed the lid of the boot and walked to the front of the car. "I'll see you when I see you," he said casually.

"What do you think will happen now?"

"Ursula, you know as well as I do the IRA won't take this lying down. The Army's not the force it once was, but the Brits can't shoot innocent Irish people and walk away. Not anymore." A muscle twitched in his jaw. "They'll pay for what they've done."

Ursula thought of all the things she wanted to say to him. She settled for, "Mind yourself."

"You too," he replied. He pressed the back of his hand against her cheek, just for a moment. Then he got into the car. A firm foot on the accelerator sent the Austin Healey roaring down the laneway.

Ursula stood watching until it was swallowed up by the hedgerows.

"I love you very much," she whispered into the empty space where her son had been.

Chapter Two

—◆—

As he raced through the small towns and villages that dotted the route to Dublin, Barry kept the car radio tuned to RTE. He did not need a news presenter to tell him that change was in the air. The sleepy backwaters of rural Ireland were coming awake and clusters of men were gathered outside every pub and post office, talking angrily, punctuating their conversations with fists shaken in the air. As he drove through Monasterevin, Barry shouted out the car window, "Up the Republic!" Reckless words to utter in public: a favourite slogan of the outlawed IRA.

They elicited a loud cheer.

Less than twenty-four hours had elapsed since the bloody afternoon of January 30, 1972, yet already Ireland was being transformed.

The energy and optimism of the 1960s had proved to be an exception. Afterwards Ireland had reverted to the sad grey decline it had endured since the end of World War One. Political patronage was endemic. The Dublin middle class, devoted to the type of bureaucracy inherited from Britain, ran the country. They turned their backs on both the world and the rest of Ireland. What the poet Patrick Kavanagh had derided as "the evil genius of mediocrity" was promulgated as the highest level of achievement to which an Irish person might aspire. Anything else was "getting above yourself."

The Hallorans had often displayed a propensity for getting above themselves.

Barry's showy little sports car screeched to a halt in

front of the yellow brick house shortly after four in the afternoon; a miracle considering the condition of Irish roads. With a twist of his hand Barry switched off the headlamps. Even at this hour the night was drawing in. The first of February—St. Bridget's Day—was officially the first day of spring in Ireland, but that was tomorrow, and tomorrow seemed very far away.

When Barry got out of the car his left leg refused to bear his weight at all. With a terrific effort he forced his body to his will. *Don't give in to it. Never let the bastards win.* One step, two; he was moving again. Moving through the pain and past it.

As he mounted the front steps he called, "Séamus! Séamus, are you here?"

The door opened to reveal a statuesque young woman wearing a blue cardigan and a woollen skirt. Her shoulder-length hair was the colour of dark bronze. Her expression was one of extreme disapproval. "Stop shouting, Barry! We're not deaf."

"Is he here or not?"

"Hello, Barbara," she said. "I'm glad to see you, Barbara. Have you a kiss for me, Barbara?"

He brushed past her into the house. In the cold blue dusk of February Barbara had turned on the overhead light fixture in the front hall, revealing the boldly patterned carpet that climbed the staircase into a realm of shadows. At the foot of the stairs, mahogany doors black with old varnish opened into the parlour and the dining room. To the left of the front door a tall clock ticked away the minutes; on the other side a wooden coat tree staggered like a drunk after midnight beneath the weight of a motley assortment of male outerwear. A curtain drawn across the far end of the hall created a private alcove for the telephone.

Barry went to the foot of the stairs and called, "Séamus? You up there?"

Séamus McCoy peered down from the first-floor landing. "Seventeen?"

"*Is mise,*"* Barry replied in Irish. "Come on down."

McCoy was a middle-aged man with a tidemark of grizzled hair around an otherwise bald head. He wore thick spectacles and appeared frail, but beneath his clothes was a wiry body of exceptional durability. McCoy had survived both a hard life in the IRA and a gruelling bout with cancer.

"You look like the backside of hell," Barry said when his friend reached the foot of the stairs.

McCoy squinted up·at Barry's unshaven face. "You're no oil painting yourself." Years spent in the south had not blunted his sharp-edged Belfast accent.

"That's what travelling on our bad roads will do for you," Barry said nonchalantly. "On the radio they claim the authorities are worried about anti-British demonstrations. I thought you might be in one today, Séamus."

"Not me, I've been waiting for you. Besides, Dublin's pretty quiet—for now anyway. People are still trying to get their heads around what happened."

"How did you know I wasn't one of the casualties in Derry? None of them have been named as far as I know."

"Not yet," McCoy confirmed. "But I wasn't worried about you, *avic.*† They couldn't kill you with an axe." He laughed a little too loudly.

Barry responded with a devil-may-care grin. "I'm glad to hear you acknowledge that I'm immortal."

"And I'm glad the two of you find this so amusing," Barbara snapped.

"You have to laugh or you'd cry," McCoy told her. "That's life in the real world." He took his shabby crombie overcoat from the coat tree and pulled a chequered cap from one of its pockets. "Seventeen, you too shattered to ramble down to the pub for a pint?"

"Let's go."

*It's me.
†My son.

McCoy dropped his gaze to the dried blood on Barry's coat sleeves. "You might want to change that first."

Barry shrugged out of the stained coat. Before he could take another from the coat tree Barbara stepped in front of him. "What about me?" she challenged.

A man had once remarked that she was spectacular when she was in a temper. Barbara never forgot it; she never forgot any personal remark about herself. Now she tossed her hair with a theatrically angry gesture and fixed blazing hazel eyes on Barry. "If you think you can come flying in the door and head right out again without so much as a by-your-leave, Barry Halloran, you have another think coming!"

He reached around her for a coat. "I don't have to ask your permission."

"But I thought we were . . ."

"Thought we were what, Barbara?" he asked as he put on the coat.

"Well. You know."

"I don't know. And this isn't the time."

"When is the time?"

Instead of an answer, Barry laid a hand on McCoy's shoulder and steered him out of the house.

Barbara slammed the door behind them.

She was trembling with an emotion she would never allow him to see. Deep down, she was afraid of Barry. Not afraid he would hurt her physically—he would never hurt a woman. But afraid he would see through her defiant facade to the insecurities and imperfections she tried to keep hidden.

So she challenged him over and over again to be sure her fortifications were intact.

"You'll pay for that later," McCoy warned Barry as they walked to the car. "The wee lass likes to be ignored about as much as a cat likes to get wet."

"I can't think about her now, Séamus. She'll have to be on the long finger for a while."

A cold wind was rising. The two men turned up their collars as they walked to the car. McCoy eased himself into the passenger seat and leaned forward to squint at the gauges on the dashboard. In the gathering darkness they were unreadable. "Is there enough petrol in this yoke?"

"I filled it on the way up from Clare."

"You went to the farm before coming here? You've had a hell of a long drive since yesterday afternoon, then." McCoy did not ask why Barry had gone so far out of his way. It was his custom to wait for people to tell him what they wanted him to know.

Before being swallowed up by Dublin, Harold's Cross had been a country village. It still possessed a village green and a baroque Victorian necropolis called Mount Jerome Cemetery. There were more pubs than churches; a ratio Irish men considered highly desirable. On this evening Barry bypassed the local pubs. He crossed the Grand Canal by the Portobello Bridge and drove the short distance to the Bleeding Horse instead.

The Bleeding Horse Pub occupied a two-storey brick building dating from the eighteenth century. Although it lacked the impressive antiquity of the Brazen Head Tavern, which had been purveying drink to Dubliners for seven hundred years, the Bleeding Horse had its own cachet. It was owned and managed by staunch Irish nationalists, and offered a place where like-minded men could exchange news and views without fear that a paid informer was listening.

Such informers were not necessarily British.

A dense cloud of cigarette smoke billowed out to meet Barry and McCoy when they opened the door. "Damn that smells good," said McCoy.

"You're off the fags for life, remember?"

"A man can dream," McCoy replied. "First shout's mine." He reached into his pocket as he headed for the bar.

Carrying pint glasses brimming with dark, creamy-headed Guinness, he and Barry made their way to a table at the back of the pub. Four other men sauntered over to join them. The youngest of these was considerably older than McCoy. The four had become "hurlers on the ditch"; commentators on a game they were no longer able to play.

"Aha," said McCoy. "The usual suspects." He acknowledged each man in turn. "Luke, Patsy, Brendan, Danny."

Childhood tuberculosis had left Luke with a hollow chest that he unconsciously protected by drawing his shoulders forward. He was stronger than he looked, however, and the little schooling he had received from the Christian Brothers had not been wasted. He could quote reams of poetry in both Irish and English and was much in demand late at night in the Bleeding Horse. "We heard you were in Derry," he said to Barry.

"I was in Derry." Barry was hoarse with weariness. The others leaned forward, eager to catch every word. Among these men Barry Halloran had a reputation.

"Was it as bad as they say?"

"Worse."

"Did any of the paras get a shot at you?"

First Barry allowed himself a deep drink of Guinness. His taste buds savoured the rich malt tempered with just the right degree of bitterness before letting it slide down his throat. *Like silk,* he thought, as he always did. He put down the pint glass and wiped the foam from his upper lip. "I was carrying my professional photographic gear, Luke, so they could tell I was a journalist. They left me alone just as they did the television news team that showed up. In fact, I think they were glad to see us." His lips curled in a sardonic smile. "My guess is, the soldiers believed we'd make them look heroic on camera."

"Heroic me arse," sneered Patsy, a stringy little man like a bantam rooster fallen on hard times. In his younger days Patsy had worked in a boning parlour. As the result of an accident—common enough in those establishments—while boning out a sheep's neck, he had lost the thumb on one hand. Now he obsessively stroked his jaw with the remaining thumb.

When he spoke Patsy's accent betrayed his native tenements of Summerhill in North Dublin. "I'm after watchin' the pitchers on the telly in me other local. Like a feckin' war it was. All them poor sods runnin' and screamin' and a priest bent over double wavin' a bloody handkerchief to keep the feckin' Brits from shootin' 'em while they carried a dyin' boy outta the road."

White-haired, bushy-browed Brendan—whom women still described as "a fine figure of a man"—spoke like the college professor he once had been, before his politics got in the way. "The level of outrage here is astonishing," he said, "given the apathy people in the Republic have previously shown to the suffering of their northern counterparts. The *taoiseach** has recalled our ambassador from London and declared February second as a national day of mourning."

"Jack Lynch must have made that announcement through gritted teeth," said Barry. "His government has done everything it could to prevent people in the Republic from knowing how much the Catholics in the north are being persecuted. What you call apathy, Professor, is ignorance more than anything else."

Luke bristled. "Aren't the Catholics up there Irish too? Half the people on this side of the border have relatives north of the border, myself included. I'll never understand how our government can abandon them."

"That's easy," said Danny. A burly, dark-visaged individual from the Kerry mountains, he walked with a John Wayne swagger that predated *The Quiet Man*. Danny never discussed his past and invariably sat facing the doorway with his back to the wall. If seating to his requirements was not available, he stood. "Lynch and his crowd are too cow-

---

*Chief; in Irish government, the prime minister.

ardly to stand up to the Brits," he said in a disgusted voice. "That's your answer."

Barry pushed his glass away. There was not enough anaesthetic in it to numb either the pain in his leg or the memories in his brain. "If only things were that simple," he responded. "But politics on this island have muddied the waters to the point where nothing's simple. Every politician has his own personal agenda we know nothing about."

Brendan said, "That's why Sinn Féin adopted a policy of abstentionism years ago. After the Treaty, Sinn Féin decided politics was too corrupt to be involved in anymore."

"They were probably right," Barry agreed. "Just look at who's attracted to politics these days. When whole Catholic neighbourhoods in the north were torched by loyalists in '68, Ian Paisley claimed the houses went on fire because they were loaded with petrol bombs. He said the Catholic churches were attacked because they were arsenals and the priests were handing out submachine guns to their parishioners.[1] Adolf Hitler proved a man can attract a big following if he peddles hatred loud enough and long enough. Encouraging sectarianism has built Paisley a political power base."

"Which Big Ian calls, with no apparent sense of irony, the Democratic Unionist Party," Brendan interjected. "But they're not unionists in the sense that unionism represents a legitimate desire to remain part of the United Kingdom. In university circles I have met some very decent unionists: well-educated and thoughtful people. I respect their feelings even if I don't agree with them."

Barry said, "Ian Paisley doesn't recruit his followers from the universities, he doesn't want people who've been taught to think for themselves. He targets the undereducated, working-class Protestants whose worldview is too narrow to allow for anything outside their own fundamentalist beliefs. They call themselves 'loyalist' to justify their blind hatred for Catholics."

"All Protestants aren't unionists," Luke commented. "And thank God all unionists aren't loyalists."

"All Catholics aren't nationalists, either. It's as much a mistake to make unionist a synonym for Protestant as to make nationalist a synonym for Catholic. Or Sinn Féin a synonym for the IRA," Barry could not resist adding. "I know plenty of Catholics in the Six Counties who have no particular interest in reuniting the island, whether through constitutional nationalism or militant republicanism. They just want an end to discrimination."

Patsy was overtaken by a jaw-wrenching yawn.

"What's the matter with you?" asked Luke. "Are the words too big for you?"

Patsy glowered at his friend. "I don't hafta sit here and be insulted. I could be home in the scratcher wi' me oul woman."

Luke laughed. "You forget, I've seen your 'oul woman.' You do have to be here."

Watching Barry from across the table, McCoy was not fooled by his apparent composure. *He's holding it all inside,* McCoy thought. *But for how long? The lad's a ticking bomb.*

The analogy was apt.

Barry was saying, "Lynch's Fianna Fáil* Party claims to be 'the republican party' when they're campaigning for election and pays lip service to a united Ireland, but as soon as the election's over they forget about it. Before any election promises are always thrown around like snuff at a wake. Fianna Fáil outlawed the real republicans years ago in order to keep themselves in office. It's not cowardice, it's political expediency, little different from Ian Paisley's self-serving bigotry.

"Fianna Fáil tries to pretend that Ireland is only the twenty-six counties we were left with after partition, because that's where their party has power. As far as they're

*Soldiers of Destiny.

concerned the stolen six counties in the north have nothing
to do with us. That way, they don't have to demand accountability from the British government for whatever
happens up there. Other political parties like Fine Gael and
Labour go along with the pretence because they aspire to
power themselves, and it's in their interest to maintain the
status quo. The only political party that wants to restore a
united Ireland is Sinn Féin."

"And they're outlawed!" Danny slammed a heavy fist
on the table, sloshing the drinks. "Same as the IRA's been
outlawed. That's what politicians do when they get in
power. Outlaw their opponents. Shoot 'em dead if they
think they can get away with it, the way the Free Staters
shot the republicans after the Civil War."

Brendan shook a finger in admonition. "Now be fair,
Danny, all politicians aren't like that. At least I hope not,
because Ruairí Ó Brádaigh, the president of Provisional
Sinn Féin,* has suggested that the only way out of the
morass in the north may be through political means.[2]
Logic dictates that we can never defeat the British mili-
tarily."

"We did once, Professor," said McCoy.

"Because Michael Collins was a genius at guerrilla
warfare and the British hadn't recovered from their losses
in the First World War. The situation's different now."

When Barry cleared his throat all eyes turned toward
him. *Make them wait for it,* he reminded himself. *If you
want people to remember what you say, make them wait
for it.* "I'll tell you something for nothing. Politics isn't
the answer. It's the problem."

Danny cried, "See, I told you! Halloran agrees with me,
the gun's the only thing the Brits will understand."

*Irish republican political party.

Chapter Three

——◈——

I N the parlour Barbara Kavanagh went from window to window, watching for the beam of headlamps.

She had spent hours arranging the parlour to reflect her own taste. There was no money for new furniture to replace the shabby tables and chairs dating from the thirties, but slipcovers and new curtains had brightened the place, and vases placed around the room were always filled with fresh flowers in season or artistic arrangements of leaves and branches.

Barry let her do what she liked, with one exception. He insisted on retaining a singular ornament that Barbara found appalling. A table to the right of the fireplace held a big glass dome atop a polished walnut base. Within the dome was a very large, rather damaged stone nose.

When she had tried to carry the ugly thing to the attic Philpott had stopped her. "You'd best leave that where you found it," he warned. "Barry'll never forgive you if you move Lord Nelson's nose. It's his trophy."

Warren Philpott was the small, wispy man from whom Barry had bought the boardinghouse. He was now employed to cook breakfast and the evening meal—which the Irish called "tea," a holdover from English occupation. On this particular evening he had come and gone, leaving a stack of dirty dishes for the housekeeper to wash. Eleven of the twelve men currently boarding in the house had retired to their rooms. The straggler had planted himself in the most comfortable chair in the parlour as he did every night, and was reading *The Irish Times* from back to front, beginning with the obituaries. There was no point in trying to talk to him.

Nor was Barbara in the mood for washing dishes. The anger that had been building up in her since Barry's return was in direct proportion to her fears about his safety while he was away, and had reached fever pitch. She paused long enough to glance at herself in the mirror above the mantelpiece. *Fool. You fool. What are you doing?*

The mirror reflected a striking face. Beneath dark, dead-level brows, Barbara's hazel eyes looked golden. Her creamy complexion was the envy of many women. But as far as she was concerned any chance of beauty was ruined by the heavy jaw she had inherited from her grandfather.

A deep jaw and a big-boned frame would have been assets to an operatic contralto. *If things had been different I might have been singing at La Scala. So why am I working as a housekeeper in Dublin?* Barbara Kavanagh silently asked the image in the mirror.

The answer was Barry Halloran.

At last she went upstairs for a bath, filling the room with the pungent scent of jasmine bath salts. After soaking until the water turned cold, she gave herself a manicure. The results disappointed her. Bright red nail varnish made her fingers look like talons dipped in blood. She stripped off the offending scarlet with swipes of remover and replaced it with a more subtle shade.

Shortly after the clock struck two she crawled into bed. Naked. Alone.

Barry's room down the hall was still unoccupied.

When Barbara entered the kitchen in the morning the kettle was already boiling on the Aga, the immense cast-iron cooker that dominated the kitchen and devoured quantities of turf. McCoy was loading a tray with jugs of milk and bowls of sugar to carry into the dining room. He was a man who did what needed to be done, whether it was his job or not.

"Don't tell me the boarders are already down, Séamus."

"Not at all. Philpott should be here any minute, though. And I've fed the Aga."

Barbara began taking dishes out of the press. "Where's Barry?"

"Still asleep, I reckon. Let the lad be, he's worn-out and he's going to need his strength." He lifted the tray and carried it through the door to the dining room.

Barbara followed him with a stack of plates. "What's Barry going to need his strength for? You two were out until all hours; what were you up to?"

"Just having a chin-wag with some pals." McCoy set the tray on the long dining table.

Barbara slammed the plates down with a force almost, but not quite, sufficient to crack them.

"Mind yourself there!" McCoy warned.

"I'll worry about the dishes; you tell me why you kept Barry out so late."

McCoy gave a sigh. "It was him keeping me out, more like. We had a few jars at the pub, and when they called closing time, we finished the conversation at Brendan Delahanty's place."

"You could have come back here."

"Brendan's was closer, he lives in Camden Street."

She pounced. "So you were at the Bleeding Horse! I knew it."

"It's our local," McCoy replied defensively. "An Irishman's morally entitled to drink at the pub of his choice and call it his 'local.' Could be you don't understand about that, coming from America."

She began setting the table. "I understand that the Bleeding Horse is an IRA hangout."

Barbara's directness sometimes made McCoy uncomfortable. Northern Protestants took pride in being painfully blunt, but most Irish people were more subtle. "To tell the truth," he said, "there's not a lot left of the IRA. The number on active service is mighty small these days. Most of the remaining Volunteers are old-timers like me who enjoy meeting and exchanging war stories, and where's the harm? If we were talking about World War Two you wouldn't object. The Americans were heroes in that war."

"I wish you'd stop talking about my nationality as if it were an intellectual limitation. I know more about this country than you think. My mother was born right here in Dublin. My father was born in America but he was an Irish republican because his father was an Irish republican. Dad raised money in America for the IRA. When I was a little girl he made his first trip to Ireland with a couple of his republican friends and never came home again. Being associated with the IRA got him shot dead in a place called Ballymena, in Northern Ireland. That's why I don't want Barry to have anything to do with them."

McCoy said, "I'm truly sorry for your loss. But what you don't realise is just how much we've lost over here. What eight hundred years of colonialism and domination by a foreign power has cost us. We thought it was almost over in 1921, but then the Brits . . ."

"I'm tired of hearing you blame the British for everything!" the girl flared. "That's one thing about you Irish, it's never your fault, it's always someone else's."

"I'd call that human nature, lass." *She's very young*, McCoy reminded himself as she vanished into the kitchen, *and she really doesn't understand. Who could unless they were born here?*

McCoy was well aware of Ireland's isolation in global terms. As a northern Catholic he had received little formal education but was a voracious reader, particularly of anything touching on Irish history. Over the years of their friendship Barry had filled in the gaps in McCoy's knowledge. Barry had learned Irish history from his grandfather, who had been a student of Pádraic Pearse.

Sharing a house with Barbara Kavanagh had enlarged McCoy's horizons in a different direction. She unwittingly had given him a sense of how her countrymen viewed Ireland. A small, impoverished island on the rim of the

Atlantic, Ireland was romanticised by Americans who believed it was caught in a time warp. They had no knowledge of the act of partition that had torn the country in two. To the average American Ireland was "quaint"; a dreaming emerald landscape of thatched cottages, priests, and drunkards. As for Europe and the wider world, "We're not even on their radar screen," Barry had once remarked.

With Bloody Sunday, Ireland had leaped into the international consciousness in an appalling way.

They probably think we've gone mad, McCoy thought. *Wonder if Barbara will stay here now? She could so easily go home to America.*

From time to time McCoy had dreamed of emigrating as so many thousands of Irish men and women had done before him, beguiled by the extravagance of optimism and opportunity that they believed America personified. In his heart he knew he would never go; not while Ireland was partitioned and the battle was yet to be won . . . and courage came out of a bottle. The Army was here and here he would remain.

The sound of male voices sidelined his train of thought. The first boarders were coming down the stairs, asking if the morning papers were in.

Barry slept until midafternoon. Several times Barbara went to the closed door of his room and raised her hand to knock, then turned away. While Barry slept she channelled her anger into window washing and floor scrubbing, then carried the rugs from the front hall out to the clothesline and gave them a thorough beating. *That's for you, Barry Halloran. And that, and that, and that!*

When Barry finally appeared she was wearing a fresh blouse and her best skirt. She pouted her lips for a kiss but he brushed past her. She could feel the tension he gave off like heat waves. Assuming the smile of a housewife in a television commercial, she said sweetly, "Do you want something to eat now, or shall I unpack for you?"

"There's no unpacking to do. All I had with me was a change of underwear and my shaving gear, and I brought them in last night. If you want to do something for me, how about a fry-up? I could murder a couple of eggs and some sausage."

Barbara put an apron over her clothes and made his favourite toasted ham and cheese sandwiches, then sat across the table from him while he ate. She arranged her hands on the table so he could admire her rose pink fingernails. When he did not appear to notice, she folded her hands in her lap and sat watching him. Expectantly.

Barry knew what she wanted. Barbara pleaded for compliments like a dog pleading for bones, but he would not respond with the effusiveness she craved. A man's feelings were best kept under control. He habitually compartmentalised the elements of his life. Saltpetre and sulphur should be kept away from coal dust; fuel oil and ammonium nitrate must be stored separately; if exposed to too much heat, kieselguhr decomposed.

The volatile Barbara Kavanagh was capable of unleashing powerful emotions Barry was not willing to risk when his focus was—must be—elsewhere. As soon as he finished eating he left the house.

Barbara found McCoy in the cubbyhole under the stairs that he called his office. He was lettering a new "Room and Board Available" sign. Black crayon on white pasteboard, with the word "available" underlined in red. "How's this?" he asked, holding it up for her inspection. "Jackson's leaving on the fifteenth so we need to replace him."

She scarcely glanced at the sign. "Where's Barry gone, Séamus?"

"Reckon he wanted to be by himself for a while. Walking, probably. He'll come back in his own good time."

"He could have asked me to go with him. He hardly spoke a word to me this afternoon."

"Don't let it bother you. Seventeen's a bit of a lone

wolf, he's had to be . . ." McCoy's jaws abruptly snapped shut.

"Why?"

"Because that's his nature, I guess," McCoy finished lamely. "Anyway, give him a wee bit of time. He'll talk to you when he's ready." He began putting his crayons back into an old cigar box.

Barbara lingered in the doorway. "Why do you call him 'Seventeen,' Séamus? Is it a private joke?"

"Aye." He smiled reminiscently. "First time I laid eyes on Barry was in 1956. He claimed to be eighteen and was hot to join the IRA. He was a great tall lad even then, but I could tell he was lying about his age. Turned out he was only seventeen. We accepted him because he was Ned Halloran's grandson. I started calling him Seventeen to remind him it was equally important to tell the truth."

"Barry lied to you?"

"Everybody lies sometimes, Barbara."

"Well I certainly wouldn't want to marry a liar."

"Then you'd best not marry at all," McCoy advised.

"Maybe I won't!"

What does she expect of the lad? McCoy wondered as she flounced away. *More to the point, what does he expect of her?*

Barry returned shortly after dark. When Barbara tried to engage him in conversation he gave her a noncommittal smile, went up to his room, and closed the door. He searched through his record collection until he found *Mise Eire,* Seán O'Riada's passionate paean to a free Ireland, and put it on his gramophone. Turning the volume up as far as it would go, he stretched out on the bed and closed his eyes.

Chapter Four

I N the short time since Bloody Sunday, information had leaked out of Northern Ireland like water from a sieve. It emerged that representatives of the British government had made private commitments to northern unionists regarding the civil rights march.

One or two southern newspapers dutifully reported that a Protestant prayer meeting organised by Ian Paisley's Democratic Unionist Party had been scheduled at the Guildhall Square in Derry on the twenty-ninth of January. A huge crowd had been expected to pour into the square, causing major disruption to the adjacent Catholic community. Worried civic authorities had cancelled the meeting to avoid heightening sectarian tensions.

In response, an angry statement had been issued by the Democratic Unionists: "We have been assured that the civil rights march scheduled for tomorrow will be halted by force if necessary. We are prepared to give the government a final opportunity to demonstrate their integrity and honour their promise, but warn that if they fail in this undertaking they need never again ask loyalist people to forfeit their basic right of peaceful and legal assembly."[1]

Word of the British intention to use force against the civil rights marchers, coupled with the DUP's threat If they did not get their own way, reached the Republic. The sparks of fury were ignited.

·　　·　　·

On the national day of mourning a green Austin Healey carrying two men left Harold's Cross in late afternoon and headed for the Baggot Street Bridge. Crossing the canal, they drove to that area of Dublin where, amidst government buildings and art galleries and large, grassy squares protected by wrought-iron railings, the professional class of Dublin occupied shabby-genteel Georgian terraces.

The streetlamps had been turned on. If this were an ordinary Wednesday their pale golden light would fall on men in suits returning from a day at the office, and smartly dressed women laden with purchases from the shops in Grafton Street. On this particular evening the normal pedestrian traffic was swelled by members of every social class who were pouring in from throughout the city. Some of them carried hand-lettered placards condemning the British. "Avenge the Martyrs of Derry!" one urged.

Ahead lay Merrion Square.

Already a large crowd had gathered outside the British Embassy on the south side of the square. The embassy occupied an immaculately maintained terrace of red-brick Georgian town houses. Four storeys over basement; elegant fanlighted doorways; tall windows luxuriously curtained. Polished brass flagpole flaunting a large Union Jack.

Facing the embassy from across the square was the hotchpotch of buildings that housed the Irish government. Collectively known as Leinster House, they centred around the slowly decaying former residence of the earl of Leinster, which was flanked by equally run-down neoclassical buildings badly stained with coal dust. The Irish tricolour that fluttered from the roof needed a good washing.

The crowd was growing larger every minute, threatening to overwhelm the unarmed Gardai. Dublin Fire brigades were being summoned to help control the protest. As Barry urged the car forward he saw men in IRA uniforms directing traffic. *This is where they should be. This is where we should be.*

When the Austin Healey was tucked into the last available parking space in Stephen's Lane, the two men got out. Barry put the car keys in his pocket, then hesitated. Went back to the boot. Hesitated again, shook his head, joined McCoy.

"Forget something?"

"Nothing that won't keep, Séamus. Come on."

There was no mistaking the mood of the crowd. It growled like an angry animal. The lights were on in the embassy but the curtains were closed. Barry saw someone on the second floor pull the heavy draperies aside and look down into the street, then hastily let the curtain fall again.

Others observed the gesture too. "Yuh bastards, yuh filthy bastards!" screamed a woman's voice. "Come out here and let us see yez!"

The curtains remained closed.

A single stone, hurled by an angry arm, was followed by a veritable fusillade of stones and bricks that clattered against the front of the embassy.

"Bloody murderers!" a man shouted.

The crowd roared in agreement.

People emerged from the side streets and laneways that surrounded the square, bringing more missiles. Barry and McCoy were handed bricks by a hot-eyed teenaged boy whose face was wet with perspiration in spite of the cold. He stayed with them to join in the attack.

Inside the embassy a possible evacuation order for all personnel was issued. A telephone call requested that an airplane be put on standby.

With an accuracy perfected in his boyhood by throwing thousands of stones at wasps' nests along the banks of the Fergus, Barry hurled a brick at the fanlight above the door of the embassy. Glass and timber shattered. The boy who had given Barry the brick cried gleefully, "Kill 'em, kill 'em all!"

At those words Barry's flashback returned. Ten terrible minutes in Derry that had seemed to last a lifetime. Again he saw the civil rights campaigners—a three-hundred-yard stretch packed with marchers—approaching Free Derry Corner, singing "We Shall Overcome" and holding their banners aloft.

Once more Barry watched, frozen with horror, as hundreds of heavily armed troops from Her Majesty's Parachute Regiment One swarmed into the no-go area marked out with portable barricades. The paras were shouting encouragement to one another and profanities at both the marchers and the spectators who had gathered to cheer them on. Then from one of the paras came a shocking, adrenaline-charged cry: "Kill 'em, kill 'em all!"

And the shooting began.

Blood. Fountains of blood, rivers of blood.

Women and children screaming.

Bodies falling.

SÉAMUS McCoy had to shout to be heard above the crowd. "You reckon they're evacuating the embassy by a back door, Seventeen?" When Barry did not answer, McCoy turned towards him.

He was not there.

McCoy swivelled around, craning his neck. The streetlights surrounding the square flooded the area with light. Barry was a head taller than the average man; with his bright hair he should be easy to spot.

Yet he had vanished.

Séamus McCoy had been a soldier for too long to condone recklessness; the sort of wild and crazy courage that could make a man a hero—or get him killed. Barry Halloran had that sort of recklessness. This, McCoy feared, was the sort of situation to bring it out.

Shortly after joining the IRA Barry had taken part in the Border Campaign, intended as the first step toward forcing the British out of Northern Ireland. In January 1957 he was part of a small company of Volunteers assigned to attack the Royal Ulster Constabulary at Brookeborough, County

Fermanagh. Because of his inexperience Barry had been posted as a lookout, but when his comrades came under sustained gunfire he had abandoned his safe position and rushed through the hail of bullets to be with them.

His best friend, Feargal O'Hanlon, had died in his arms.

Séamus McCoy was aware of the lasting effect the incident had on Barry. Almost overnight he had changed from a spirited boy to a deeply, quietly angry and unpredictable man.

Unpredictability was what made him dangerous.

"Damn it, Seventeen," McCoy muttered under his breath, "where the hell are you?" He recalled Barry's hesitancy at the boot of the car. *Could be he went back for his cameras. Or . . .*

Barry drove straight from Derry to his mother's farm, when he could have assured her he was safe with a phone call. There was only one thing at the farm he would want bad enough to go so far out of his way.

"Damn it, Seventeen!" McCoy exclaimed aloud. "There's hundreds of police here. Don't be daft!" He tried to push his way through the crowd, hoping to intercept Barry in time. He made little headway. The mob was focussed on the British Embassy and oblivious to anything else. They surged back and forth like a tide, carrying McCoy with them in spite of all he could do.

In his mind's eye he pictured Barry running back from the car, carrying the rifle. As furious as he had been at Brookeborough; as out of control. Perhaps he was already in the laneway behind the embassy. If he shot a British diplomat . . .

A fog of despair enveloped Séamus McCoy. Some things were beyond a man's control. If he had been a religious person McCoy might have said they were in God's hands, but his faith had faded away over the years. He had seen too many crimes committed in the name of God.

God.

Clinging to the word, he tried to recover the God of his

Catholic childhood. The loving, omnipotent Father. Would it be possible at this late date to make a bargain with Him? *Take me, not Barry.* McCoy tried to think of a persuasive enough prayer, but nothing came.

"Look! The flag!" a voice cried.

Almost as one, the crowd looked.

They saw a man scrambling along the brass flagpole. His bright hair was unmistakable in the light from the street-lamps.

Barry Halloran tore the British flag from the pole and flung it to the cheering throng below. Within seconds the Union Jack had been ripped to shreds.

A man close beside McCoy said, "That was worth the walk all by itself."

McCoy craned his neck, trying to keep Barry in sight. "Where'd you walk from?"

"Swords."

"Helluva long way to go for a stroll."

The other man said, "There's demonstrations going on all over the country. Factory workers in north County Dublin downed tools at two this afternoon and met up in Swords. Some of the lads had hammered a coffin together, and we draped it with an Irish flag and marched through Swords carrying it on our shoulders."[2] The man's voice rang with pride. "Swords isn't much more than a village, but every person in town turned out to cheer us. We brought that coffin all the way here, it's over in the square if you want to see it."

"Good on you!" said McCoy. "Here, let me shake your hand."

A few minutes later Barry, looking flushed and triumphant, appeared. The crowd parted in respect to let him through. "Did you see it, Séamus?" he asked eagerly. His eyes were shining.

McCoy pretended to be looking in the opposite direction. "See what? Oh, there you are, Seventeen. I wondered where you'd got to."

"You knew bloody well where I was, you must have seen me with the flag."

"I did of course, you great eejit. I thought you'd gone for your . . . cameras. You took me by surprise."

Barry noticed the slight hesitation. "I took myself by surprise, Séamus," he admitted. "When my mother was young she tore down the British flags that had been put up in Grafton Street to celebrate the birthday of King George. This evening I decided it was important to keep family traditions alive. Would you not agree?"

"With a heart and a half," McCoy replied.

The crowd continued to grow, overflowing the streets around Merrion Square. They broke open the padlocked gates of the fence that protected the square from "undesirable elements," and filled that too, while the police watched helplessly from the sidelines. Some members of the Gardai were not above throwing a stone or two themselves.

Then the first petrol bombs appeared.

Chapter Five

February 2, 1972

BRITISH EMBASSY IN DUBLIN BURNED BY ANGRY MOB

OIL portraits of the English nobility fed the fire as readily as did the costly antique furniture. When the blaze was at its height a number of spectators expressed regret for the destruction. Although some left, the majority lingered until well after midnight.

By dawn on the third of February "the little bit of Britain" that had occupied the south side of Merrion Square was reduced to ashes and rubble.

BARRY Halloran did not take the photographs of the burning embassy that would appear in the newspapers. When the first television cameras arrived McCoy had insisted on going back to Harold's Cross. "Tomorrow the government's going to try to put the blame for this on someone, and you don't want your face all over the telly, Seventeen. It was one thing to be caught by accident in Derry; it'd be something else entirely to be seen as part of a mob burning the British Embassy. How many times have you told me that a journalist has to appear objective?"

"What about you, Séamus? Do you not want to see the place destroyed?"

McCoy cast one long, deeply satisfying look at the burning building, then turned away. "Reckon I've seen enough."

BY six o'clock it was pitch-dark and bitterly cold. In the kitchen at Harold's Cross Philpott was preparing a casserole, sending the aroma of meat and onions and Bisto gravy wafting through the house. The boarders returning from work sniffed appreciatively. One by one they drifted into the parlour to listen to the evening news on the large cabinet radio while they waited for their meal. There was no television in the house. Barry's most recent expenditure had been to have his red Austin Healey painted Irish green.

Just as Barbara entered the room to summon the boarders to table, a news reader announced, "We have been informed that the demonstration at the British Embassy is out of control. A crowd estimated by police to be over fifty thousand has set fire to the embassy, and the building has been evacuated."

The boarders responded with expressions of alarm or approval, depending upon their politics. Their overriding concern was the hot meal waiting for them in the dining room.

Barbara did not follow them to the table. She remained in the parlour, staring at the radio. Neither Barry nor McCoy had mentioned where they were going when they left the house, but she felt certain they were part of the crowd that was out of control.

Barry's taking this whole Derry business too seriously, she told herself. *What did it have to do with him anyway, aside from a chance to take pictures? I know he talks to Séamus about it, so why won't he talk to me? We used to tell each other everything.*

At least I did, she mentally amended.

The first time she saw Barry Halloran she had been ten years old and he eighteen. He and his mother had come to America to attend the funeral of Barbara's grandfather, Henry Mooney. Barry had not paid much attention to Barbara then, but she promised herself that someday he would.

And he had.

Soon after their affair began she had remarked, "You're awfully sensual for a Catholic."

"Catholics are as sensual as anyone else," he had replied. "You certainly are. But maybe it's stronger in the Irish because we have to keep the lid on it. In this country the Church tries to repress any sexuality outside of the marriage bed. When I was sixteen my parish priest began asking me if I ever had any bad thoughts." Barry laughed. "I was sixteen! I had nothing *but* 'bad thoughts.'

"Dances were held almost every weekend somewhere around Ennis and I loved to dance, but being so close to a girl invariably gave me a huge erection. It was a common problem among young lads. We tended to stay on the other side of the room from the girls because we couldn't bear to be embarrassed."

"But you're not embarrassed now," she had said. Reaching for him.

ABANDONING the parlour to the boarders, Barbara went to her room to write a letter to Isabella Kavanagh.

Dear Mom,

I'm sure I must have a few clothes left at home, in spite of the package you sent at Christmas. I need them all, I'm desperate. The stores in Dublin have no idea of quality. There's no silk lingerie available, not even good rayon. Neiman Marcus wouldn't let anyone through the front door wearing the cheap cotton that passes for ladies' underwear over here. Worse yet, it only comes in white. Please buy half a dozen bras, two pettislips, and a dozen pairs of panties for me, in black, with lace. Send everything air mail. I'll pay you back in June when I get my next check from Grandpapa Mooney's trust fund. Don't wait until then though, send them immediately. This is urgent.

Barbara reread the letter before putting it into an envelope. *That's terribly shallow. Those people who were shot on Sunday wouldn't think it was urgent to have fancy underwear.* She tore the paper into tiny bits and threw them into the wastepaper basket.

When she heard the front door open she ran out onto the stair landing. The voices of two men carried up to her.

"Are you not going to bring your gear inside, Seventeen?"

"My cameras are safe enough where they are. They'd be safe around here even if I didn't lock the boot."

"I wasn't talking about your cameras. I meant the rifle."

"What makes you think there's a rifle in the car?"

McCoy gave a snort. "I didn't come down in the last shower, Seventeen. Not just a rifle, *the* rifle; the one you called to the farm to collect."

Barbara shouted down the stairs, "You're not bringing a rifle into this house, Barry Halloran!"

He turned abruptly and went outside.

Séamus McCoy bolted for the parlour. *Sometimes a man has to keep his head below the parapet.*

Barry came back carrying the Lee-Enfield. Barbara was waiting in the hall with her fists on her hips. "I told you I don't want that in here."

"This is my house and I do want it here. For sentimental reasons."

She eyed the rifle as if it were a rattlesnake. "How could anyone be sentimental about a gun?"

Barry propped the weapon in the corner behind the coatrack, out of her sight. Drew a deep breath; organised his thoughts. Began his campaign. "Barbara, I once asked if you knew a rebel song called 'The Old Fenian Gun.' "

"And I'd never heard of it. Why, is it important?"

"This rifle belonged to my grandfather, Ned Halloran. He called it his Fenian gun, though strictly speaking it wasn't a Fenian weapon; the Fenians as such predated the First World War, which is when Granda's rifle was manufactured. But he carried it in the IRA and even took it with him when he went to fight on the republican side in the Spanish Civil War. Ned Halloran's 'Fenian gun' is a big piece of history, Barbara. It's my legacy from him. That and his notebooks and—"

"What sort of a legacy is some old gun?" she interrupted.

"One beyond price. Can you not understand?"

There was no mistaking the passion in his voice. Barry's potential for passion attracted Barbara more than anything else about him. Yet whatever volcanoes raged within him—and she was certain they were there—never came to the surface with her. He was tireless in bed, tender and demanding by turn, yet she always sensed he was holding something back.

Until he lost all control and became the primal male of her secret fantasies she could not have the satisfaction of taming him.

As he spoke of his grandfather, Barry had displayed deep emotions to which Barbara had never been given access. She was eager for more. "I'm trying to understand; really I am," she said. "But . . . well for a start, I don't even know what 'Fenian' means."

Barry prided himself on his knowledge of Irish history—another legacy from Ned Halloran. "The word comes from '*fianna*,'" he explained, "a band of heroic warriors in Ireland in pre-Christian times. In 1858 a secret society was founded in America with the goal of establishing an independent Irish republic. Borrowing the name of those ancient warriors, the new group called themselves the Fenian Brotherhood. When they organised in Ireland they became known as the Irish Republican Brotherhood, or IRB. The role of the Fenians in America would be to provide funds and weapons; 'the sinews of war.'[1] In Ireland the IRB was to organise and field an army to put an end to foreign domination once and for all."

Barbara widened her eyes. "Are you saying the Irish Revolution originated in America?"

"To a certain extent, it did. The first Fenians were Irish-born men who fled to the States after yet another failed attempt to overthrow British rule here. A number of prominent Irish Americans joined their organisation and pumped money and enthusiasm into the project. A Fenian bombing campaign in England caused certain notoriety, but nothing conclusive.

"Then early in this century the IRB infiltrated Sinn Féin, which was a small, nonmilitant political party that had an intellectual following. It was also a good place to recruit philosophical republicans. The IRB was behind

the founding of the Irish Volunteers in Dublin in 1913. The
Volunteers were a direct reaction to the rise of a heavily
armed Protestant militia in the north called the Ulster Volunteer Force. The UVF are still around, as a loyalist paramilitary organisation.

"In 1916 the Irish Volunteers and James Connolly's
Citizen Army joined together for the Easter Rising. Their
commanding officer was Pádraic Pearse—a member of
the IRB. But it was Connolly who named the combined
force the Irish Republican Army. The IRA exists to this
day because the island of Ireland still hasn't won total
freedom." Barry lowered his voice. "It's unfinished business. *My* business, Barbara." His whole body vibrated with
those words.

To her dismay, she realised there was a wider chasm
between them than she had suspected. She knew that both
Barry and McCoy were, or had been, members of the
IRA, but months ago she had explained to Barry that Irish
republicanism in all its forms was anathema to her. She
had thought he understood. She believed he had "given
all that up" for her sake.

*I was wrong. Barry's telling me he and the rifle are in-
separable. Take one and I take the other.*

A T the final count, fourteen innocent civilians died as a
result of being shot by members of Her Majesty's army
on Bloody Sunday. British prime minister Edward Heath
and his government became the targets of international
opprobrium. The carnage in Derry could not be swept
under the rug; the world had seen. Something must be
done to make it appear that the government was taking
swift and decisive action—though not against its own
army.

As if a line had been drawn in the sand, Bloody Sunday changed the island of Ireland irrevocably.

It changed the IRA overnight.

In the early 1940s the Irish Republican Army had seen itself as a resistance movement in the mould of the French Resistance during World War Two. Bolstered by this heroic self-image, many of the older Volunteers seemed content to let the corps fade into history.

The sense of injustice refused to fade.

In the late forties the IRA had undertaken to reinvent itself. Most of the senior staff with their wealth of experience were gone. Their successors were too young to have fought in the Civil War, much less the Easter Rising. The noble ideals that had inspired the leaders of 1916 were perceived to be outmoded. Two world wars had changed perceptions about the glory of battle.

The IRA tried to reinvigorate the unfinished revolution but could not gather enough support in a country that was struggling to survive hard times. So the Army had limped along, outlawed, reviled, striking at the British whenever possible. Every company had to raise money for itself, often through illegal means. The weapons acquired were as various as their sources. Handguns were smuggled into Ireland from supporters in the United States. A limited number of new 303s from New Zealand were bought through a Canadian gun dealer. Another provider was found for the MI carbine, but the rifle was notoriously difficult for a left-handed man to use because the clip could hit him in the eye. A few men who had previously worked in construction put their experience to use in making explosive devices.

But no ambush, no skirmish, no booby trap, was sufficient to persuade the British to withdraw from Northern Ireland. The IRA was simply too small and underequipped.

Then came Bloody Sunday.

Within days there was a huge upsurge in young people, both male and female, clamouring to join the Irish Republican Army. In private houses, in schools and shops and pubs, in quiet country laneways, they gathered to repeat in determined voices, "I do solemnly swear . . ."

Across the Republic people of every age and background told one another, "We're all IRA now."

THE atmosphere in the boardinghouse was strained. Having made his position clear, Barry left the next step up to Barbara. In that part of his mind where his emotions were being held under lock and key, he knew he was in love with her. But his position was nonnegotiable. *I am what I am, what my ancestors and circumstances have made me. If she can't accept that, we don't have any future together.*

Barbara vacillated between demanding a showdown over his IRA membership or accepting it. *If I insist on a showdown I'll lose him. If I accept without a struggle I'll still lose. He'll never take my feelings into consideration after that.* In desperation she adopted the policy she had heard described as "an Irish solution to an Irish problem." She did nothing and hoped the problem would somehow go away on its own.

Following the burning of the embassy the Irish government cracked down on anti-British protests—very cautiously. Feelings about Bloody Sunday were still running high. If the government was seen to be taking a pro-British stance at such a sensitive time the political repercussions could be dire.

On the sixth of February a defiant group of civil rights campaigners held a march in Newry, County Down. Unrequested, several IRA recruits appeared to act as a guard of honour. Newry was strongly unionist, a town dedicated to maintaining a British identity and remaining within the United Kingdom. It was also home to a number of loyalists, the extreme and very militant right-wing branch of unionism. The sight of IRA Volunteers on the streets of Newry raised northern tensions to fever pitch.

William Craig, former home affairs minister in the Northern Ireland Parliament at Stormont, launched an extreme right-wing movement called Vanguard. Its purpose was to function as a pressure group within the Ulster Unionist Party. The first of a series of large-scale rallies was held in Lisburn, County Antrim, on the twelfth of February.[2]

Ursula Halloran, who subscribed to newspapers both north and south, read with mounting indignation the report of Craig's arrival at the Vanguard rally complete with a motorcycle escort. Hundreds of loyalists in paramilitary uniforms had been paraded for his inspection. According to the newspaper account, Craig had read the Vanguard pledge aloud, then asked his audience to endorse the movement by raising their stiffened right arms and shouting "I do!" three times.

Ursula threw the paper down. "Welcome back to the Nazis!" she said in disgust. "Don't people ever learn?"

I N the Republic February saw the return to political prominence of Charles J. Haughey.

The Arms Trials of 1970 had been a shock to the nation. When a wave of sectarian violence erupted in the north in 1969, the IRA had been secretly promised weapons by the Irish government under Jack Lynch.[3] The guns were to be imported from abroad and used to aid northern Catholics in the defence of their homes. Loyalist paramilitaries already were importing tens of thousands of weapons from Britain and the continent.

Dublin had reneged on its promise at the last moment. Two government ministers, Charles Haughey and Neil Blaney, were hung out to dry; deserted by their colleagues and left to take the blame. Charged with illegal gun-running, they eventually were acquitted. Blaney had retired from politics soon after. Haughey was a different sort of man. A brilliant student in school, a barrister, a certified accountant, and a man of enormous energy and ambition, he had bided his time, quietly building up a network of valuable supporters. Being married to the daughter of a former *taoiseach,* Seán Lemass, did him no harm.

Now he was back from the political wilderness and pursuing the leadership of Fianna Fáil with obsessive vigour.

BECAUSE of McCoy's poor eyesight, Barry no longer allowed him to drive the car. "If you crashed Apollo I'd be stuck, Séamus. A car's a necessity for my kind of photographer."

McCoy often walked to the Bleeding Horse at lunchtime for a pint and a sandwich. One afternoon he returned to find a letter addressed to "S. McCoy" waiting on the hall table.

The house was empty for the moment. Barbara had gone to a matinee at the cinema with Alice Cassidy. Alice and her husband Dennis had been at Trinity College with Barry, and Alice had been Barbara's first female friend in Dublin. Barry himself was in Arklow for the day on a photographic assignment, and the boarders were still at work. There was no one to look over McCoy's shoulder. Yet he took the plain white envelope to his room and closed the door before opening the letter.

The message was brief, with neither salutation nor signature.

"You are needed."

He dropped the single sheet of paper on his bed.

James Andrew McCoy had been born and raised in West Belfast. The Northern Ireland capital was a grimy industrial city in a lovely setting, with a winding river and a vista of mountains. The beauties of the landscape were small consolation for the conditions under which many were living. Following World War Two heavy industry, the backbone of Northern Ireland's prosperity, had collapsed. Working-class Protestants found themselves in a situation only marginally better than that of Catholics who had never been allowed to have decent jobs.

The latter, including McCoy's parents, lived in ghettos in areas like West Belfast. Decaying tenements, where two rooms might contain families as large as twelve or fourteen, leaned against one another to keep from falling down. The inhabitants shared a communal toilet in the yard and the expectation of lifelong poverty.

Séamus McCoy had never possessed a home of his own. He had never even lived in a room as well appointed as the one in which he now stood. The chest and wardrobe were old but of excellent quality. Clean curtains hung at the windows; a rug made a pool of bright colour on the floor. The air retained a spicy hint of the aftershave Barbara had given him for Christmas. His treasured books, a battered collection heavily slanted toward recent Irish history and military biographies, overflowed a bookcase beside his bed. His other personal possessions were scattered about like territorial flags.

A sudden spattering of sleet rattled the windowpanes, but within the yellow brick house was comfort and warmth.

So peaceful, McCoy thought wistfully. *A man could spend the rest of his life here without getting his feathers ruffled.*

When Barry returned from Arklow McCoy told him about the letter.

"I've been expecting them to send for you, Séamus. The Army must have its hands full with so many joining up at once. A good training officer will be worth his weight in gold, but you're not able for it and you know it."

"I'm in great form, Seventeen!" McCoy retorted hotly. "But even if I was on my deathbed I'd go, and not just because of Bloody Sunday. The Army has other problems."

"What are you talking about?"

"Until now we always insisted that a recruit come from a known republican background and be of good character. But these newcomers—there's no way the Army can investigate every one of them before they take the oath.

We could wind up with thugs and thieves and God knows what. You know what cancer is, Seventeen? An unrestricted growth, that's what the doctors told me. I reckon unrestricted growth could be mighty bad for the Army. I'd be surprised if some of these lads aren't joining up just to get weapons in their hands, and I'd be just as surprised if a lot of the loyalists haven't joined Ian Paisley's new Ulster Volunteer Force for the same reason. There's always some men with a criminal streak. Becoming paramilitaries gives them an ideal opportunity."

Barry said reassuringly, "You and I both remember when the IRA was robbing banks to fund itself, and not so very long ago, either. That didn't turn the Army into a gang of criminals."

"Not then," McCoy agreed, "but it set a precedent—is that the word? These young ones coming along may think it's okay to break the law whenever and however they want. It don't take much for a crowd of hotheaded lads to start running wild. That's why I'm going back; I have to do what I can to keep 'em in line. You want to go with me?"

Chapter Six

━━━━◦≪◈≫◦◦━━━━

On February twenty-first Richard M. Nixon became the first United States president to pay a state visit to China, opening up direct communications with the People's Republic of China after a twenty-one-year estrangement.

The following day a bomb planted by the Official IRA at the headquarters of the British Parachute Regiment in Aldershot, England, killed seven people including an army chaplain.

At a Vanguard rally in Belfast's Ormeau Park in March, William Craig addressed an audience of almost a hundred thousand. A significant number of the men present were wearing masks and carrying cudgels. Craig told his audience they must do whatever was necessary to preserve their British traditions and way of life. "We must build up dossiers on those men and women in this country who are a menace to this country," he said, "because one of these days, if and when the politicians fail us, it may be our job to liquidate the enemy."[1] To make doubly sure he was not misunderstood, he concluded, "God help those who get in our way."

The loyalists got the message.

O N the ninth of March four young and inexperienced Volunteers were killed when a bomb they had been preparing exploded prematurely.

S ÉAMUS McCoy often spoke of "going up the road" by which he meant returning to the armed struggle. As the month of March wore on he was still in Harold's Cross, but he had his overcoat mended and bought a new pair of boots. He was spending a lot of time in the Bleeding Horse.

Within Barbara's hearing Barry never said anything about going with McCoy. He exhibited an almost glacial calm—which might have been interpreted as indifference—whenever Bloody Sunday or the resurgence of the IRA was mentioned.

Barbara was not deceived. She had long since discovered that Barry's facade could be in inverse ratio to his deeper feelings.

It was unbearable that so much of him was locked away from her; unbearable to think there might be a different life he desired more than life with her. Had her rival been another woman she would have fought with all the wiles she possessed.

How can one woman fight a whole army?

She and Barry were polite with each other. They did not discuss politics or anything else that might be construed as serious. Sex, which had been frequent and passionate on both sides, had ceased abruptly after Bloody Sunday. Barry no longer instigated lovemaking and Barbara was too proud to ask why, or make the overtures herself. She existed in an emotional limbo she felt powerless to end. *He'll go when McCoy goes, I know he will.*

Well I won't sit here and wait for you with folded hands, Barry Halloran!

Philpott kept a small radio on the kitchen windowsill. When she was alone in the kitchen Barbara turned it on and sang along with the music. She did not bother to change stations when the news came on. After the initial expressions of outrage, she noticed that Bloody Sunday swiftly disappeared from the news programmes.

"People in the streets are still talking about it," she said to McCoy, "but it's not mentioned on the radio anymore. Isn't that odd?"

"RTE is owned by the state, lass. What do you expect?"

"You mean the news is censored?"

"Not exactly. But that shower of villains in Leinster House has made it plain they don't want anything to do with Northern Ireland. No news programmer who values his job is likely to defy government policy."

"That's shocking!" she cried. "Thank God nothing like that could happen in America. We have freedom of the press; I think it's guaranteed in the Constitution or something."

T H E Irish government announced that for the second year in a row there would be no Easter Monday military parade commemorating the 1916 Rising. A huge celebration in

1966 had set the tone for years to follow, but in 1971 it had been impossible to put together a large enough contingent to hold a parade. Too many members of the national army had been needed to man the border with Northern Ireland, where tensions were mounting.

A year later tensions were higher than ever.

Walls in loyalist areas of Northern Ireland were decorated with huge, elaborate murals of Protestant domination. They were as much a part of the landscape as the Union Jack fluttering from thousands of unionist windows. Following Bloody Sunday, hastily painted admonitions to support the IRA had appeared on walls and hoardings. Within a matter of days they were augmented by murals depicting armed members of the IRA wearing balaclavas and looking every bit as menacing as their loyalist counterparts.

Catholic women showed their support for the republicans by hiding weapons for them. "The wee woman with the guns under her mattress" became a heroine. Instead of cowboys and Indians their sons played at being Volunteers and Oranges—making sure the Volunteers always won.

These developments made no headlines in the Republic of Ireland, but the rapid growth of republicanism was duly noted by members of the international press corps who had remained in the north. In their reports they chose to ignore any positive aspects of Belfast and Derry. The pictures they transmitted to the outside world were of nervous British army patrols, furtive IRA Volunteers darting from one street to another, rolls of barbed wire, bombed-out buildings, cruising armoured vehicles, and heaps of rubble. Focusing narrowly on those elements created an image of total war: photogenic and highly dramatic. The vast majority of northerners, the decent people on both sides of the divide who abhorred violence, were left out of the equation entirely.

Northern Ireland became the newest stop on the media crisis tour—Vietnam, the Middle East, Latin American guerrillas, and Euroterrorists[2]—that kept people glued to their televisions and advertisers buying more airtime.

ISABELLA Kavanagh's voice crackled down the telephone line. "You come home right now, Barbara, as soon as you can get on a plane. I won't have my only child living in a war zone."

"Don't be ridiculous, Mom; Ireland's no such thing."

"I know what I'm talking about, young lady. Night after night on the nine o'clock news they show . . ."

"What's happening in a very small area in six counties that call themselves part of the United Kingdom," her daughter interrupted, unaware that her phraseology unconsciously reflected the influence of Barry Halloran. "If a couple of towns in New England were having riots you wouldn't call America a war zone."

"But everyone knows how violent the Irish are, they're always fighting in bars. That's why I want you here with me."

"You never wanted me with you before," Barbara countered.

"Of course I did, you're my daughter."

Barbara began to shiver. The little alcove at the end of the hallway was the coldest part of the house, with the pervasive chill of dead air. "Be honest, Mom. Most of the time we don't even like each other."

"That's a dreadful thing to say. I don't know how you can be so cruel when I'm . . ."

"So sweet and kind to everyone?"

"Don't be sarcastic, Barbara, it's unattractive in a woman. I'm only trying to help. Give me one good reason why you won't listen to—"

"I'll give you a damned good reason!" Barbara shouted at her mother. It was the only way to make her listen. "I'm not going back to America because I'm marrying Barry Halloran!"

"Should you not wait to be asked?" drawled a voice from the other side of the curtain.

A n assignment for *An Phoblacht** had taken Barry into the city that morning, following a restless night. Even through closed doors he could hear McCoy coughing in his room. A deep, rasping cough; frighteningly familiar.

At the newspaper offices Barry had told his friend Éamonn MacThomáis, "I'm worried about Séamus. He has a hell of a cough and no colour in his face, but the man's as stubborn as a boulder in a muddy field. If the cancer has come back he'll never admit it. He's determined to go north if it kills him and there's no way I can stop him. One morning soon, I'll wake up to find he's gone."

MacThomáis was a dozen years older than Barry, a small man with bright eyes and an elfin smile. He was the sort of person others liked at first sight. He was also a patriot; a republican to his fingertips. "I know how you feel," he told Barry, "but I can understand why Séamus wants to get back in the war. I'd go myself, except I've been told I'm more valuable where I am. It looks like I'm going to be made editor of the paper."

"Éamonn, that's great news! No better man."

"It's not official yet but you can expect the announcement soon. Now, what about Séamus? Maybe you're imagining things. He always did smoke like a chimney and that makes a man cough."

"He's not supposed to touch cigarettes anymore. Doctor's orders."

"Who obeys those? Séamus could have cigarettes stashed everywhere the way a secret drinker stashes whiskey. And if he looks pale it's because a man can't get a sunburn in Ireland. Stop mindering him. Going back on active service could be the best tonic for the man."

---

*The Republic; monthly newspaper of the republican movement.

"I'm sure you're right," Barry said with a total lack of conviction.

MacThomáis was a perennial optimist who anticipated rainbows where others saw rain. It was one of the qualities Barry liked most about the man. But he remained convinced that McCoy was ill. *If Séamus goes back to the Army he won't take proper care of himself. Even as a training officer he'll be on the run a lot of the time and out in all weathers. Based on past experience, he won't seek medical care until it's too late.*

Have to keep him here. Have to.

Shortly after noon Barry headed for Harold's Cross. Most Dublin restaurants were closed at midday; a peculiarly Irish custom. Pubs offered only a limited assortment of toasted sandwiches and the ubiquitous pickled eggs, so Barry preferred to eat at home. Cooking was Philpott's passion and he always left something good in the Aga. Today it was a casserole. Barbara made a fresh pot of tea and joined Barry and McCoy at the table.

The older man declined the food.

"It's beef and potatoes," Barbara urged. "Your favourite."

"Tea'll do me."

Barry furtively scanned his face for signs of illness.

"Why do you keep looking at me like that?"

"Ducks' meat,* Séamus."

McCoy knuckled his eyes. "There. You happy now?"

"Happy enough. If you're not going to eat your food, pass it over here, will you? Thanks. What are you doing this afternoon?"

"Thought I'd ramble around town for a while. Get some air."

"Pull the other one, Séamus, it has bells on," Barbara said. "You're going to the Bleeding Horse." She stood up, rigid with disapproval, and headed for the kitchen.

McCoy gave a chuckle. " 'Pull the other one, it has

---

*Dried mucus in the corner of the eye.

bells on.' I'll say this for the girl, she's learning to talk like us. She still has the American twang, though."

"Not when she sings," said Barry.

After lunch he retired to the darkroom he had fitted out in the former pantry. The windowless room was small and stuffy, but its proximity to the kitchen meant Barry could listen to Barbara singing while she washed the dishes.

The first time he heard her sing was in 1964. She and her mother had visited the Hallorans on their way to Italy—and to the teacher who would destroy the girl's prospects for an operatic career. Barry would never forget Barbara's rendition of Adalgisa's aria from *Norma*. Standing beside a paddock at the Halloran farm, she had sung in a rich contralto, *"Deh! Proteggimi, o Dio!"*—the impassioned plea of a woman begging the gods to save her from a fatal love.

If amber could sing, Barry had thought then, *it would sound like Barbara Kavanagh*.

The voice was a little husky in the lower register now, a bit roughened in the high notes, but its power over him was undiminished. Of all her physical attributes, her voice was the most truly Barbara.

Barry was about to put the last roll of film in the tray of developer when he heard the double ring of the telephone. He wiped his hands and headed for the hall.

Outside the curtained alcove, he paused.

Ursula Halloran was an inveterate eavesdropper, a habit her son lamented. But when Barbara shouted at her mother it was impossible not to hear.

Barry stood absolutely still.

I n the Bleeding Horse, McCoy was saying earnestly, "Barry Halloran can think faster than any man I ever saw. He may limp a wee bit if he's tired, but sure, we all have our war wounds. A gang of loyalist thugs gave him his. They beat him half to death when he was unarmed, but his injuries had no effect on his skill. He's still the best in the business."

"We could certainly use him," replied the man on the other side of the table. "It's a bonus that he's well educated. Our new recruits are mostly young Catholics from the ghettos with minimal education and no job experience, so they desperately need training in a whole range of areas. Do you think Halloran would be interested?"

"He's halfway there now," McCoy averred. "All he needs is a wee push, and I can . . ." he broke off, coughing.

"I don't like the sound of that cough, Séamus."

"Don't worry about me, I'm as tough as new rope. I've been smoking too many fags lately, that's all."

The other man looked puzzled. "That's odd. I can't remember the last time I saw you with a cigarette."

"Ah sure, I smoke all the time, what else can a man do when he's bored? The Army's been my life; now it's up and running again nothing can keep me away. And the same's true for Barry."

S HOULD you not wait to be asked?"

Barbara flung back the curtain. When she saw Barry she flushed an angry red. "How dare you eavesdrop on me!"

He assumed a lazy, heavy-lidded smile, screening his eyes with his lashes. "I'm only going to say this once, Barbara, and that's it, full stop."

"Are you giving me an ultimatum? I don't take ultimatums."

He was, he congratulated himself, finally learning how to handle her. *Never fight fire with fire.* Leaning forward, he softly murmured, "Will you marry me?"

"Who're you talking to?" Isabella shrilled from the phone.

Barry plucked the receiver from Barbara's suddenly numb fingers. "Mrs. Kavanagh? Barry Halloran here," he said crisply. "I've proposed to your daughter and . . ." Looking at Barbara, he raised one quizzical eyebrow.

This isn't the way I pictured it, her mind protested. *He's supposed to offer me a ring and I'll make him wait for an answer and even then I might say no. I don't want to spend my life running a boardinghouse.*

Yet she could not tear her eyes away from his. Many men were more handsome, but none had his compelling presence. Barry Halloran was more vividly alive than anyone else she knew.

"Yes," she whispered. Then, louder, "Yes, I'll marry you."

". . . and she's agreed," Barry told Isabella Kavanagh. "All we have to do is set the date, which I hope will be very soon."

"Don't tell me you've got my child pregnant!"

Barry responded with the clear, boyish laugh of someone who had trained himself to appear convincingly innocent—even in the guiltiest circumstances. "I respect your daughter far too much for any carry-on of that sort, Mrs. Kavanagh. We plan to have a family someday, but let's begin with the wedding. You're the first person we've invited."

Barbara shook her head violently. Barry ignored her. "You will come, Mrs. Kavanagh? Barbara will be so pleased," he purred into the phone. "And of course I'll call you Isabella. Thanks for asking."

McCoy had been rehearsing his speech. *You're building a pretty good life for yourself, Seventeen, but wouldn't you rather do something that will make a difference to the whole of Ireland? I've just been talking to a pal of mine from GHQ, and he thinks there might be a place for you there. If Barbara's what's holding you back, you'll have to sit her down and explain that the Army will always come first. You owe it to the girl.*

As McCoy approached the house he noticed the lights were still blazing, though the hour was late. The old familiar prickle of tension ran up his spine and across his scalp. *Something must be wrong. Barbara's always careful with the electrics.*

He dropped his hand to his side and fumbled for a weapon that was not there. *Damn.* He silently eased the front door open and crossed the hall on the balls of his feet.

A number of voices could be heard in the parlour. Still walking on tiptoe, McCoy peered through the open doorway. He saw a dozen boarders with glasses in their hands eddying around Barbara while Barry stood to one side, looking bemused. "You're just in time to join us in a toast, Séamus," Barry called upon catching sight of him. "There's Jameson's on the sideboard, let me pour you one."

McCoy heaved a sigh of relief. "Dee-lighted." As Barry handed him the drink he asked, "What're we drinking to?"

"The wedding."

"What wedding?"

"Barbara's and mine," said Barry.

McCoy stopped with the glass halfway to his lips.

"We've set the date for the first of May and there's a lot to do between now and then," Barry continued as if unaware that his friend was suddenly paralysed. "Barbara's mother is coming over from America and she and Ursula will be staying here, so we'll have to move some of these lads around to make room for them. Plus we'll have to do those repairs we've been putting on the long finger. Everything'll be down to you and me, Séamus, but together we can manage. If we start first thing in the morning we . . ."

"We've got to draw up a guest list and have the invitations printed," Barbara interrupted. "Not to mention booking the church and a priest. And having my dress made. It must be absolutely gorgeous. And white. Mom will go into convulsions if I don't wear white at my wedding."

McCoy finished raising his glass and drained it in one long swallow. *But Barry and I are going back to the Army!*

Then Barry said, "Séamus, I'm counting on you to be my best man."

Chapter Seven

———••⧟••———

SPURRED by brutal assaults on northern Catholics and in particular the burning of entire neighbourhoods by loyalist mobs, in November of 1969 the seriously depleted IRA had made a desperate request for weapons from the KGB.[1] Shortly after the request was made the IRA had split in two: the Officials under Cathal Goulding and the Provisionals led by Seán MacStiofáin. With the Irish propensity for nicknames, the Officials became the Stickies and the Provisional IRA, the Provos.

The political party called Sinn Féin soon split along similar lines.

The sympathies of the KGB were wholly with the Officials, who had a decidedly Marxist slant, rather than the Provisionals. But the weapons the Russians had promised failed to arrive.

The IRA learned to improvise.

The emotions engendered by Bloody Sunday were about to boil over.

URSULA made an earnest effort to sound pleased when Barry telephoned her with the news. "You both have my blessing," she assured him.

"You *are* coming to the wedding, aren't you? We want you to stay here with us."

"Of course I'm coming. I shall have to do something about my weirdrobe, though."

"Meaning you think your wardrobe is weird by ordinary standards," Barry interpreted.

"Well, it is. There's nothing but jodhpurs and jumpers."

"Don't try to tell me that. Since you never throw anything away, I'm sure you still have that beautiful dress Mary O'Donnell made for you. Remember? The one you wore when I took my degree from Trinity."

"It's a tweed suit, Barry," his mother said in exasperation. "Years out of fashion and certainly not appropriate for a spring wedding." No one, especially her son, would ever know how she had scrimped and saved to pay for that suit.

"Then come to Dublin in time to have her make something else. That way you'll already be here when Isabella arrives. She's a formidable woman as I recall; I'd be glad to have you at my side."

As she hung up the phone, Ursula's eyes were sparkling with amusement. *Formidable? Isabella Kavanagh? We'll see about that.*

Formidable was not a word she took lightly.

O n the twenty-fourth of March the British prime minister, Edward Heath, announced the suspension of the Northern Ireland Parliament at Stormont. Stormont was to be the sacrificial lamb, taking all the blame for letting "the unfortunate situation" develop that had led to Bloody Sunday. Thenceforth the province would be governed by direct rule from London. Willie Whitelaw would become the first secretary of state for Northern Ireland. Any semblance of autonomy for the Six Counties was gone.

The IRA, led by Seán MacStiofáin, claimed credit for

driving Stormont out of existence through its ongoing campaign against the British. But with the demise of Stormont any lingering chance there might have been for improving the conditions of Catholics in Northern Ireland through constitutional means was gone as well.

The imposition of direct rule on Northern Ireland ostensibly brought fifty years of unionist domination to an end. In actuality, however, it opened the door for worse to come. In the outburst of violence that followed, both loyalists and republicans established no-go areas: a harbinger of all-out war.

T H E wedding date had been Barry's suggestion. He had expected Barbara to argue; it was her nature to argue about almost everything, but to his surprise she acquiesced without a murmur.

In Ireland the first of May was laden with symbology. *Bealtaine* in the ancient Celtic calendar, meaning the feast of brilliant fire, May Day marked the beginning of summer. Since pre-Christian times young women had washed their faces in the dew on that particular morning to enhance their beauty.

In Catholic Ireland, May Day was dedicated to the Virgin Mary. Children heaped altars with flowers in honour of Our Lady and took part in religious pageants throughout the country, their young voices raised in celebration of the Queen of the May. The touchingly innocent custom was fading in 1972, to Barry's regret.

He was pleased when Barbara, who only attended Mass sporadically, was willing to be married in the church where he and McCoy—and most of the residents of the boardinghouse—went to Mass every week.

Instead of the local parish priest, Barry wanted to be married by a priest from Northern Ireland. "When I was hammered by the gang in Derry that broke my leg, Father

Aloysius found me and took care of me," he explained to Barbara. "I might not be alive today if it weren't for him."

"We'll have whoever you want," Barbara said meekly, looking up at him from under her eyelashes.

He did not question her uncharacteristic compliance. He was too busy thinking up more ways of keeping McCoy close to hand, which involved assigning countless tasks to him—but none that were beyond the ability of a man with damaged lungs.

The following morning McCoy assembled the necessary tools to replace some chipped floor tiles in the second-floor bathroom. *I should be training recruits in Belfast by now,* he fumed to himself as he climbed the stairs. *Why in hell did I hang around here after Bloody Sunday? My own stupid fault. Once he says, "I do," I'm going up the road. That girl will keep him so busy he'll never miss me.*

The black and white tiles were arranged in a vivid zigzag pattern that made McCoy's eyes water. When rubbing did not help, he sat down on the lid of the toilet seat and closed his eyes.

Aaah, that's better. Maybe I need new spectacles. Always some damn thing. His thoughts began to wander. *Seventeen getting married. Shouldn't call him Seventeen anymore. A lot of the boy left in him, though. Once in a while I catch a glimpse of the rascal.*

Wonder how that girl will handle him? Women always try to handle men. Still it might not be so bad, having a wife. A plump and pretty lass. Or thin and quick, I'm easy. Long as she's someone I can talk to. And laugh with. Have to laugh.

Behind closed eyes, McCoy lost himself in a reverie about the life he would never enjoy.

Later that morning he put up a new clothesline for Barbara, then lingered to help hang the washing. "I have to say, I never thought the two of you would get married," he admitted as they stretched a damp sheet between them.

She took three wooden clothes pegs from her apron pocket and deftly fastened the sheet to the line. "I'm a bit surprised myself. One day we were barely civil to each other, and the next day we were engaged. I don't know if he'd planned to propose to me all along or if it was a sudden impulse." She gave a wistful little sigh. "I do wish I understood him better, Séamus."

McCoy pulled another sheet from the laundry basket and gave it a final wring. "I can tell you this much: he's decent through and through, front to back, top to bottom. There's not many you can say that about. I'd take a bullet for Barry." McCoy's expression hardened like cement setting. "And I'd put a bullet into anybody who hurt him."

Barbara theatrically pressed one hand to her bosom. "Well *I* certainly won't hurt him!"

O n the second of April Radió na Gaeltachta began operations with a two-hour evening broadcast, on medium wave only, from the Connemara Gaeltacht in West Galway. The idea had been promoted by Desmond Fennell, a journalist who had moved to the Gaeltacht. Fennell was astonished to discover how alien RTE's "national" radio service appeared to local people. RTE broadcast in English. The people who lived in Ireland's Gaeltacht areas spoke Irish.

On the third of April Ursula Halloran went into Limerick and bought a new radio. One capable of receiving medium wave transmissions.

Then she purchased a train ticket.

M c C o y lay snoring on his bed with his mouth ajar like an open gate. He was startled awake by Barry's voice from the doorway. "I'm off to Heuston Station to collect Ursula, Séamus. Want to come along?"

He sat up abruptly and struggled to find his spectacles, which had slipped behind the pillow. "I reckon I'll wait here. Your car won't be big enough for three people and your mother's luggage too."

Barry laughed. "You don't know Ursula, then; she travels light. You might as well come with me, you don't look very busy anyway."

They drove along Clanbrassil Street past three- and four-storey red brick buildings dating from the Victorian era and earlier. Some still bore Dutch architectural influences traceable to the victory of William of Orange at the Battle of the Boyne. One of Barry's pet projects involved wandering around Dublin with his cameras, compiling an archive of the ancient city's medieval architecture.

He had several archival collections already. Family and friends, politicians, historic locations throughout the island. And fellow republicans.

After the Austin Healey had turned into Merchants Quay he remarked, "You haven't said a word since we left the house, Séamus. Come to think of it, you've been mighty quiet for days now. Is something on your mind?"

The older man replied with an inarticulate grunt.

"I see. There is something on your mind."

Another grunt.

The car continued west along the quays. "My marriage, is that it? I thought you liked Barbara."

"I do like Barbara, but you know my feelings about Volunteers marrying. It's not fair to the woman. When you go back to the Army . . ."

"Who said I'm going back?"

"Bloody Sunday, for God's sake! I saw your face when you came home afterwards. What can either of us do but go back? Besides, Seventeen, you love the Army. You were made for it."

"If you mean I was made to kill other men, I can't accept that."

"What about those four youngsters who got themselves killed last month, Seventeen? They might still be alive if they'd had someone to teach them properly. The Army needs you, damn it."

"Heuston Station coming up," Barry announced, putting an end to the conversation. "Keep an eye out for my mother while I find a parking space."

Ursula Halloran recognised the car before Barry could park it and walked briskly towards them. True to her son's prediction, she carried one small suitcase. Both men jumped out to help her with it.

She laughed. "I'm not used to such gallantry. Hello, Barry. And you, Séamus, it's been a long time since we last met. I'm glad to see you again."

Barry gave his mother a perfunctory kiss on the cheek. McCoy, suddenly self-conscious, settled for a handshake.

Before getting into the car Ursula stole another quick look at her son. In maturity Barry had become a serious man, though his grave demeanour occasionally was lit by the lightning flash of a reckless grin. She knew the little boy was still in there somewhere; a belief he confirmed by giving her a surreptitious wink.

When they reached the house Barbara was waiting at the door. She threw her arms around her soon-to-be mother-in-law. Unused to such effusiveness, Ursula briefly resisted, then forced herself to return the hug.

A few minutes later they were settled in the parlour. Barbara disappeared into the kitchen and returned carrying a tray laden with tea and fruitcake. The slices of cake were fanned artistically on the plate. Beside the teapot was a pitcher of milk and a bowl of sugar cubes complete with newly purchased silver tongs. The spoons had been polished to a high lustre that very morning. Instead of paper serviettes Barbara provided tiny linen napkins, ironed to perfection.

She waited for Barry's mother to shower her with compliments.

Thanks to the generosity of Henry and Ella Mooney, Ursula had attended a finishing school in Switzerland. She was at ease with more formality than Barbara could imagine. She declined the fruitcake, drank her tea black—and made no comment about the carefully prepared collation.

On the ledger in Barbara's mind a black mark appeared opposite Ursula's name.

Barbara dropped two lumps of sugar into her tea and turned it almost white with milk. "It's too bad your father won't be here," she said to Barry. "But I think it gives us a special bond, don't you? Both of our mothers being widows, I mean."

Barry deftly changed the subject.

He had never told Barbara the truth about his origins, allowing her to assume, as most people did, that his mother had married a man with the same surname. On an island the size of Ireland it was not uncommon.

In this case it was untrue.

Barry's father was Finbar Cassidy. Ursula had never married Finbar Cassidy—or anyone else. As a young woman in the 1930s she had despised the powerless servitude of wives in Catholic Ireland. When she found herself pregnant she had taken a job in Switzerland with the League of Nations. If she had remained in Ireland her child would have been taken away from her by the Church as soon as it was born, to be raised in an orphanage or given to strangers. Wealthy Americans were willing to give the Church hefty contributions in return for being allowed to adopt "pretty Irish babies."

Finbar Lewis Halloran had escaped this fate by being born in Geneva, where Ursula had acquired a Swiss passport for him. She liked to think of her little son as a citizen of the world. By the time she felt it was safe to take him to Ireland, Finbar Cassidy was dead. Killed by a German bomb that fell on Dublin's North Strand.

Defying both the patriarchal Church and the crushing weight of social convention, Ursula Halloran had raised

her son by herself. She did not tell Barry the true story of
his paternity until he was a grown man.

He never told anyone else. There are secrets of conscience and secrets of the heart, and this was both.

Chapter Eight

O N the nineteenth of April a tribunal headed by Lord
Chief Justice Widgery, which had been established to
look into the events surrounding Bloody Sunday, issued
its report. The tribunal fully exonerated the British army
and laid sole blame on NICRA, the Northern Ireland
Civil Rights Association, for organising the march.

Eyewitnesses to the event joined relatives of the victims
in claiming the tribunal had been a whitewash. The British
government ignored them. Northern Catholics rightly interpreted the government's attitude to mean that they could
expect no support from the state. As usual, they were on
their own.

No British soldier was ever convicted or even disciplined for his actions on Bloody Sunday.

The IRA stepped up its campaign of violence against
the British army in Northern Ireland.

T R Y as he might, Séamus could not guess how old Ursula was. *Funny,* he thought, *once you reach a certain age
the years don't matter so much but the generations do.
Ursula and I must be almost the same generation; we remember the same music.*

He was unaware how often his eyes followed her about the house.

In her one small suitcase Ursula had made room for a well-worn paperback novel. McCoy found her curled up on the couch in the parlour, totally absorbed.

"What are you reading?" he wondered.

She glanced up; smiled. "A favourite of mine, an historical novel called *Julian*, by Gore Vidal, an American writer. Fascinating if you're interested in Roman history."

"I'm interested in Irish history. But I don't read novels."

Keeping a finger in the book to mark her place, Ursula sat up. "Listen here to me, Séamus. History—whether Irish, English, Russian, or Chinese—is about people, and all people have something in common. A good historical novel gives you access to their feelings as well as to the events that shaped them, so you can understand the whole picture better. For example, this book tells the story of Julian the Apostate, who tried to swim against a mighty tide of change. Do you know anything about him?"

"Can't say I do."

"Here, sit down by me." She patted the couch. "Julian was the nephew of Constantine the Great, the emperor who converted to Christianity and made it the state religion of Rome. When Julian himself became emperor in A.D. 361 he set about trying to reverse the process. Vidal gives you a fascinating look at the two belief systems, pagan and Christian, from Julian's point of view. Seen through his eyes the 'religion of the dead Jew' was absurd, contradictory—and not at all original. Many of its tenets were taken directly from the ancient cult of Mithras. Listen to this . . ." She riffled through the pages, found the passage she wanted, and began to read aloud.

They did not realise how much time had passed until the afternoon light began to fade. Ursula put the book aside. "How about a drink, Séamus?"

"Delighted." McCoy followed her to the kitchen. He hid

his disappointment when she began the time-honoured ritual of brewing tea, and said gallantly, "That's just what I
need, I'm a divvil for a hot brew."

Ursula gave him a cup of tea.

Then she poured herself a whiskey.

She felt she needed it in order to face another boring
evening when little was discussed but plans for the wedding. Many of the details were not at Barbara's instiga-
tion but at Isabella's; the result of numerous transatlantic
telephone calls from Texas.

During the meal Barbara complained, "Mom says I
have to write a personal letter to Cousin Winnie in
Belfast to include with her wedding invitation. Since I've
never met the woman, Mom says a 'nice letter' to introduce myself is called for. As if I don't have enough to do
already."

Barry reached for the butter. "Who's Cousin Winnie?
You never mentioned having relatives in Belfast."

"Oh yes, there's a whole batch up there. I don't know
any of them, but they're all related in various ways to my
grandmother Ella. Winifred's the matriarch, she's older
than God. Now let me see if I have this straight." Barbara
began ticking facts off on her fingers. "Winnie's maiden
name was Speer and she married Ernest Mansell, my
grandmother's first cousin."

Ursula's eyes began to glaze over, as they always did
when someone listed their familial connections.

Barbara continued headlong. "After Mansell died Winnie married another cousin of my grandmother's. He was
a widower who lived in Belfast but had extensive holdings
in Canada; Toronto, I think. According to Mom, Donald
Baines left Winnie an absolute fortune when he died."

Ursula snapped to attention. "Did you say Donald
Baines?"

"Yes, did you know him?"

"In Ireland everyone knows everyone else, or knows

someone who does. Many years ago I was acquainted with a man whose surname was Baines."

Barry slanted a look in his mother's direction. "I didn't know you'd ever been to Belfast."

"I have never been to Belfast. I met Mr. Baines here in Dublin when I was working for Radio Éireann during its early years. There was some mix-up about his doing an interview for us."

"Mr. Baines? Donald?"

"Not Donald," Ursula said in clipped tones, slamming the door on the subject. "Please pass the butter if you've finished with it."

That night she could not sleep. Looking for another book to read she wandered downstairs, then into the kitchen to make a cup of tea. She noticed the red light burning over the pantry door.

"Barry? Are you still working this late?"

"Be right out," he called. In a few moments the red light went off and he emerged, looking bleary-eyed. His mother was already preparing a cup for him too. They sat side by side in the kitchen like two old friends, drinking their tea and talking about this and that.

It seemed a night for confidences.

Barry remarked, "I've always wondered why you called your father 'Papa.' It's not an Irish term."

Ursula took another sip of tea. "I couldn't very well call him Da because he wasn't my real father."

Barry could not have been more astonished if the law of gravity were repealed. "What are you talking about?"

"Human life is a search for identity, Barry. Some people think they know theirs from the beginning. Others are forever wondering who they are."

Ursula smiled at the bewilderment on her son's face. "It's grand to be my age," she told him. "When I was young I said whatever I thought, but with maturity I learned to be more circumspect. There were secrets to keep and feelings to spare; you understand. Now I'm old enough to talk straight again and it's wonderfully liberating.

"I don't know who gave birth to me, but I was approximately four years old in 1914. That's when Ned Halloran found me wandering in a Dublin street. I couldn't tell anyone who I was or where I came from. The only name I'd ever heard myself called was 'Precious.'

"My mother, whoever she was, took advantage of the chaos surrounding the Bachelor's Walk Massacre* to abandon me. She was probably destitute, a woman of the tenements on the north side of the city. When Ned found me I was undernourished and in shock. He took me to Jervis Street Hospital, where the nuns gave me the name 'Ursula Jervis' so they would have something to put on their records. When I was strong enough they sent me to an orphanage. But I was one of the lucky ones; Ned and Síle rescued me a second time and raised me as their own. For a long time they continued to call me Precious. I always called them Mama and Papa."

Barry was stunned.

Ursula went on, "Thanks to Church and State illegitimate is the worst label one can apply to a child in Ireland. The Irish Free State was illegitimate, the forced mating of British guile with Irish expediency. The current Republic of Ireland is a bastard too, a con trick that's a far cry from the Irish Republic we fought for in 1916. That's why I continue to support the IRA."

"I think I need more than tea," Barry told his mother. "How about a whiskey?"

"I thought you'd never ask."

DRESSED in the latest American fashion—with sturdy corsetry underneath—Isabella Kavanagh arrived at

*See *1916* by the same author.

Dublin Airport in the morning. Her short, tightly curled grey hair was tinted an improbable shade of lavender, resembling an exotic moss. She had brought two oversized Pullman cases, two slightly smaller matching suitcases, a fitted bag holding six pairs of shoes, an Italian leather vanity case, and a brown-and-white-striped hatbox. Isabella rode to Harold's Cross in the Austin Healey with Barry and Barbara. A taxicab had to be hired for her luggage.

Isabella was strict with her face. She allowed it no expression that might cause lasting lines. Upon first seeing the boardinghouse she conveyed her disapproval by a momentary narrowing of her eyes. "You'll want to buy something nicer now," she told Barry as she got out of the car.

Ursula opened the front door. "You're very welcome, Isabella," she said with a smile.

"You ought to take better care of your complexion, Ursula," the other woman answered. "I hardly recognised you. Of course I haven't seen you since we were over here in '64, on our way to Italy for Barbara's opera training. A woman can age dreadfully in eight years if she's not careful."

Ursula struggled to keep smiling as she reached for Isabella's vanity case. "Here, let me carry this upstairs for you."

"I'll take it myself. If you drop it you'll break something and my entire Elizabeth Arden collection's in there." Isabella noticed Séamus McCoy standing behind Ursula. "Are you the porter?"

McCoy was startled. "I'm . . . a friend."

"Oh. Well, you look like a porter. Get those suitcases, will you?"

Barry interposed himself between McCoy and the luggage. Taking the handle of a Pullman case in each hand, he hefted the two with no apparent effort. Isabella watched as he carried the heavy suitcases up the stairs. "My," she remarked, "he's very strong, isn't he? I had forgotten he was a farm boy."

"My son's a university graduate. And a successful professional photographer," Ursula added. The smile was but a memory.

"You'd never know it to look at him," said Isabella. "Of course I don't know what a 'professional photographer' is supposed to look like. Some sort of Bohemian, I suppose."

The initial few minutes would set the tone for Isabella Kavanagh's entire visit. She trailed criticism like cigarette smoke, finding fault with everything. Her opinions were absolute; incapable of change.

That afternoon Barbara was recruited to help her mother unpack. Isabella began by taking an embroidered silk pouch from her vanity case and handing it to her daughter. "Your grandmother Ella's pearls," she explained. "They'll be your 'something old,' but not borrowed. She would want you to keep them but you must take very good care of them, Barbara; they were the most expensive jewellery Pop-Pop ever gave her. A family heirloom, you understand, never to be sold under any circumstances."

Next Isabella flung back the lid of a Pullman case to reveal a wedding gown nestled in layers of tissue and complete with train and veil.

"I wanted to choose my own!" Barbara wailed.

"Nonsense, dear. The least you could do is let me supply your gown. I didn't have one for my wedding because we ran away to get married. In those days I thought an elopement was romantic." She gave a sniff. "We live and learn." She unfolded the dress and held it up. "Anyway, this is the gown I never had. Isn't it luscious?"

Barbara gazed in dismay at a voluminous white satin confection smothered by tiers of tulle and lace.

When she went downstairs she found Ursula reading in the parlour. "Disaster," Barbara groaned as she sank into a chair. "Absolute disaster."

Ursula looked up. "What is?"

"Mom's brought a wedding gown that looks like a huge wedding cake. She purposely bought something that will make me seem positively obese, so she'll look skinny standing next to me in the wedding photos."

"I can't believe Isabella would do that," Ursula said with a total lack of conviction.

"Oh yes, she would. She has. And there's no arguing with her, it just makes her more stubborn. What can I do?"

Ursula carefully closed her book. "You can go with me to see Mary O'Donnell. She's making my dress for the wedding and she can make yours too. One you will like."

"Mom will never allow it."

Ursula's eyes danced. "Leave her to me."

That evening she casually remarked, "I'm having the first fitting of my dress for the wedding tomorrow. Early in the morning, as soon as the shops are open. I would invite you to join me, Isabella, but I'm sure you're exhausted after your journey."

Isabella had a distasteful mental image of a poky little Dublin shop, draughty and badly lit, smelling of cheap fabric. "Absolutely exhausted," she agreed. "I'll have to stay in bed tomorrow or I'll be a wreck. I think I'll go up now, in fact."

"Quite wise," said Ursula. "You always have had good sense."

Isabella started toward the door.

Ursula turned toward Barbara and raised her voice slightly. "My dear friend Mary O'Donnell is making my frock herself. I'm sure you've heard of her; Mary trained in New York with the great Sybil Connolly . . ."

Isabella paused at the doorway.

". . . and now she's the foremost designer in Ireland," Ursula continued. "Barry's done some fashion photography for her, it's in all the magazines."

Isabella turned around.

"The cream of Belfast society come down to Dublin to have Mary design clothes for them. I expect your cousin Winifred is a client of hers," Ursula concluded.

The following morning Barry drove his mother and his

fiancée to Mary O'Donnell's atelier. Barbara could hardly contain her glee. She twisted around to say to Ursula in the backseat, "What fun that was last night! My mother actually begged you for an introduction to your friend. And then you deliberately misunderstood her and thought she meant me."

"Deliberate is the key word," said Ursula. "I knew she wouldn't insist on anything for herself if she thought you could have a wedding gown that would impress the Belfast relatives."

"My mother's a great negotiator," Barry said. "You should see her trading livestock in the Ennis Mart. Ursula invariably gets the best of the deal, but she makes the other fellow think he has. She's the most amazing woman in Ireland." He took his eyes off the road long enough to cast a fond glance over his shoulder at Ursula.

Barbara's lips tightened imperceptibly.

Barry parked the car in a nearby street while the two women went to meet with Mary O'Donnell. He had a number of things to do in the city but first he sat alone in the car for a while, staring at the long-fingered hands splayed out on the steering wheel.

The dedicated effort that went into training those hands. Those reflexes. Practicing, practicing till my fingers bled.

What was it all for?

Chapter Nine

———— ·⧡· ————

I<small>N</small> the editorial offices of *An Phoblacht*—a single cramped room overflowing with precariously balanced stacks of newsprint, typewritten pages, hastily scribbled notes, photographs, books, and miscellaneous flotsam organised according to a scheme only Éamonn MacThomáis could understand—MacThomáis was dialling his home telephone number. On the cluttered desk before him was an expensively engraved pasteboard square. Beside the invitation was a half-empty flask of black coffee, tepid now, which his wife had prepared for him earlier.

"Rosaleen?" he said when she answered the phone. "I have news for you. Barry Halloran's going to be married." He chuckled at her surprise. "I'm not codding you, he really is. To that American girl. He just dropped our invitation in.

"I'd best warn you the police may be watching the church. Someone from Special Branch,* probably. Through cleverness and sheer good luck Barry's never been charged with membership in the IRA, but some of his guests have. Now don't worry, Little Girl, the police will be wearing civilian clothes, you won't even know who they are. It's just a shame, that's all. His new wife will have to learn to cope. I only hope she's half the woman you are."

Two days before the wedding Winifred Baines arrived with a small entourage of well-dressed Speers and Mansells. They displayed the mixture of curiosity and

---

*Detective wing of the security forces.

apprehension common to people visiting an exotic foreign country for the first time. Isabella met them at the train station. As she was leading them to the taxi rank, a Speer whispered to a Mansell, "Is Mrs. Kavanagh one of us or is she RC?"

"I hope she's one of us," the other replied. "How could we tell our friends we've been to a Catholic wedding?"

Isabella took them straight to the Russell Hotel, where she had booked rooms for them. She insisted Barry and Barbara come to meet the cousins there, rather than in Harold's Cross. On the following day she planned to take them on a tour of the "better areas" of Dublin. The wedding reception would also be held at the Russell. By this stratagem Isabella hoped to keep the Belfast cousins from ever seeing the boardinghouse.

When Barry returned from meeting them he told Ursula, "Cousin Winnie's about eighty years old, bowlegged and back-bent, and gives off a powerful smell of dogs. Her clothes look as old as she is. No jewellery. Lace-up shoes. As you can imagine, Isabella's attempts to impress the old dear fall flat. She does seem to like Barbara, though; she invited her to come to Belfast and see her kennels. She raises King Charles spaniels."

Ursula raised her eyebrows. "Flat-faced dogs. They sniffle."

Later that evening Barbara knocked on the door of Ursula's room. "I've been wondering," she began hesitantly, "if . . . well . . . is what we're doing legal?"

"What on earth are you talking about?"

"I mean, just how closely are Barry and I related? I know my grandfather Henry was your uncle."

Ursula laughed. "He wasn't really my uncle, that was just a courtesy title. I began calling him Uncle Henry when I was five years old, just as he called me Little Business. Henry and Papa were best friends."

Barbara looked relieved. "That's all right then. I wish I knew more about Barry's ancestors."

"Ancestors." Ursula rolled the word around in her mouth, tasting it as if it were a foreign substance. *Meeting her Belfast relatives must have started this train of thought.*

The girl went on, "He did tell me his grandfather was in the IRA, but that hardly constitutes a family tree." She fixed Ursula with an enquiring gaze.

Ursula hesitated. *This wedding is certainly stirring up the mud. Maybe that's what weddings do; I wouldn't know.* "My parents—they're both dead now—were Ned and Síle Halloran," she said. "They were both born in County Clare; her maiden name was Duffy."

"Do you resemble them very much?"

Ursula hesitated again.

"Well, do you? I'd like to have an idea what my children may look like."

"Is it so important? Surely you'll love them no matter what."

"Of course I will, but I still want to know."

She's going to worry this like a dog worrying a bone, Ursula told herself. *And I suppose she has the right.* In a matter-of-fact voice she said, "I don't look like either Ned or Síle because I wasn't born to them. One of my parents must have had good teeth, though. Mine are excellent and you know how uncommon that is in Ireland."

Barbara had only heard the first sentence. Her eyebrows shot upward. "You were an orphan?"

"I was a foundling."

"Were you illegitimate?" Barbara blurted.

"I have no idea."

"How could you grow up without knowing who you are?"

Ursula said firmly, "I know exactly who I am, Barbara. It takes a lifetime for any of us to learn that, but I have."

O n the eve of the wedding Father Aloysius was invited to dine at the yellow brick house. Leaving the dining room to the boarders, Barbara prepared the parlour for a private party. "There'll be six of us eating in there," she explained. "Barry and me, our mothers, and Séamus and Father Aloysius."

Isabella's lips narrowed to a thin line. "Are you sure you want outsiders at such an intimate family occasion?"

Barbara refused to give ground. "Father Aloysius is no outsider, he'll be marrying us tomorrow. As for Séamus, well . . . he is family."

McCoy could not hide his pleased smile.

That evening Barbara assiduously sought to steer the talk away from politics. The men kept steering it back. As soon as the meal was over Isabella went up to bed, pleading a headache. Barbara promptly settled herself on the couch next to Barry and rubbed her cheek against his shoulder. A small, proprietary gesture.

Father Aloysius—John to his friends—was stoop-shouldered and almost completely bald, with a deeply furrowed face. Barry had described him to Barbara as "born to look worried." In actuality he was an engaging man with a wealth of amusing anecdotes. "The best man usually tells the naughty stories on an occasion like this," he said to McCoy, "but I'd like to usurp the privilege if I may."

"Feel free. I don't know any anyway."

"I doubt that, Séamus. I'll expect to see you in confession for telling a lie. Anyway, here's a true tale which may be, ah, rather appropriate.

"Some years ago I was visiting a parishioner in Alt-nagelvin Hospital. He told me that the man in the next bed was the biggest troublemaker on the ward. He complained constantly, drove the nurses crazy. His private parts had undergone surgery for some medical condition, I don't know what, and he wanted everyone to be as miserable as he was. But the nurses found a way to get even.

"Picture this: the head of the malcontent's bed was directly in front of a window. In order to raise the window blind every morning a nurse had to stand close to the bed and stretch across him. So the nurses started coming in with no knickers on. The poor fellow couldn't resist trying to look up their skirts as they reached above him, and every time he did the inevitable happened. He made little tents with his sheet. And howled with pain."

Ursula threw back her head and laughed as heartily as Barry and McCoy. After a moment's hesitation—and some shock at discovering that a priest would tell such a story—Barbara laughed too.

The levity did not last long. Soon the conversation returned, inevitably, to the situation in the north. Father Aloysius said, "A friend of mine is Father Alec Reid, who belongs to the Congregation of the Most Holy Redeemer—they're known as the Redemptorists, Barbara. When the loyalists burned Bombay Street—"*

"Aided and abetted by the RUC," McCoy interjected.

"I wouldn't know, I never see a constable in the confessional."

Barbara asked, "Why not?"

"They dig with the other foot," McCoy told her.

"What does that mean?"

"Protestants," Barry said succinctly.

"Anyway," the priest continued, "Alec was in Belfast at the time. He was baffled because until then the city had seemed relatively peaceful. He asked a man in the street, 'When did all this start?' The answer he got was: 'The first time the English set foot on this island.' Alec returned to his order and reported, 'This is going to be very bad.' "[1]

Pressed against Barry's shoulder, with the scent of him in her nostrils and the feel of him tight against her body, Barbara closed her eyes. *I won't let the damned north ruin my wedding. I won't I won't I won't!*

*See *1972* by the same author.

O N May Day Barry was up and dressed while the rest of
the house was still asleep. Raw energy was bursting from
the pores of his skin. Energy that had been building up
since Bloody Sunday. He and Barbara were still not sleeping together, but the reason for abstinence had changed.

"I want to come to our wedding chaste," Barbara had
said after accepting his proposal. "As chaste as possible,"
she amended when Barry laughed. "Besides, I wouldn't
feel right about sneaking around with our mothers under
the same roof. Once we're married, though . . ." Her voice
had trailed away, leaving the rest up to his imagination.

In the predawn gloom, Barry wandered aimlessly
through his house, wondering what a man was expected
to think about on his wedding day. *The wedding night,
maybe? Is that why I'm marrying her? Be honest, Halloran. Is it sex?*

*Well, yes. Partly. I've never suffered from a shortage of
women, though,* he admitted to himself. In spite of the
stern inhibitions imposed upon generations of Catholic
men by generations of Irish priests, Barry Halloran had
enjoyed a relatively active sex life. *I'm marrying Barbara
because I . . .*

Love her?

He was suddenly impatient with himself. *Of course I
love her. She's the most exciting woman I've ever met.
Only a fool would let someone like that get away. I proposed because the timing was opportune, but I would
have done it anyway.*

Sooner or later.

The air in the house was stale with last night's cigarette
smoke. Barry stepped outside. As the front door closed
behind him he caught his breath in wonder.

Flung across a sapphire sky were swirls of cloud like
skeins of pink silk. Reflecting the first rays of the sun,
they painted the land with light.

Ireland through rose-coloured glasses.
He hurried back into the house for a camera.

S É A M U S McCoy waited with Barry Halloran below the altar. The older man was uncomfortable in his hired suit; he ran a finger around the inside of his collar to pull it free from his neck. *What if Barbara doesn't show? She might not. Anything could happen with that one.* He looked up at Father Aloysius for reassurance. The priest smiled blandly. *Do they teach them that in seminary?* McCoy wondered. *An all-purpose smile, useful for everything but funerals.* He glanced at Barry, noting a thin film of sweat on his friend's forehead. *Guess I'm not the only one who thinks she might not come.*

When the organ music began Barry and McCoy turned as one. Alice Cassidy, a plump and pretty blonde who was Barbara's only attendant, appeared in the arched doorway. She was halfway up the aisle before the bride made a solo entrance. Barbara had refused to have anyone give her away. "I belong to myself," she insisted. "If anyone's giving me to Barry, it's me."

On her wedding day she made no effort to appear demure. Throwing back her head, she paced up the aisle like a queen. Her gown was a narrow sheath of ivory silk, elegant in its simplicity. Instead of a veil, a Juliet cap nestled in her upswept hair. Around her throat was a single strand of large, perfectly matched pearls, their lustre emphasising her glowing complexion.

A sigh of admiration swept the church. "She's absolutely gorgeous," Rosaleen MacThomáis whispered to her husband. Paudie Coates, the garage owner from whom Barry had bought the Austin Healey, started to stand up for a better look. His wife tugged at his coattails. "Sit down!" she hissed. "What will people think?"

To Barry's dazzled vision Barbara first appeared as a luminous flame.

He narrowed his eyes to adjust the focus and the flame became a living woman. He automatically studied her the way he would study any photographic subject: seeking the truth behind the image. And the artist in him detected something the man had not. Barbara's posture was not proud but haughty. Her smile was that of a conqueror.

Barry's stomach clenched. *I'm making a dreadful mistake.*

He was struck by the profound conviction that there had been another occasion long ago when he realised the same truth about the same woman. *It's just déjà vu. Happens to everybody.*

McCoy's elbow dug into his ribs. "Come out of your trance, Seventeen. Father Aloysius has cleared his throat twice. Let's get on with it."

BECAUSE they had a long automobile drive ahead, the newlyweds left the reception after a token appearance. "Séamus and I will stay here until the last guest leaves," Ursula assured them in the hotel foyer. "And don't worry, I'll take Isabella to the airport myself. We'll book a taxi in the morning."

When Barbara attempted a farewell hug Ursula seemed unaware of her. She was gazing past the girl with a distracted expression.

Barry said, "A farthing for your thoughts, Ursula."

She snatched herself back from a faraway place. "You're going to have three children. Two boys and a girl."

Barbara stared at her. "What on earth are you talking about?"

"Ursula knows things," said Barry.

"Well, she can't possibly know how many children we're going to have, because I've decided I don't want any. I'm not the motherly type."

For the first time since agreeing to marry him she was throwing down a challenge.

Barry recognised it for what it was. *Oh no, you don't, my girl.* "I do want children," he said quietly. Firmly. "I'm the fatherly type." He began pulling names out of the air. "We'll call them Brian, Patrick, and . . . Grace."

His new wife folded her arms across her chest. "We most certainly will not!"

They would spend their honeymoon in the seaside village of Lahinch, in the west of Clare. "You're going to love it," Barry promised Barbara. "The county was always musical; everyone was expected to be able to sing or at least lilt, or maybe play a squeeze box. But trad is making a big comeback now and . . ."

"Trad?"

"Traditional music."

"Like 'When Irish Eyes Are Smiling'?"

"That's not traditional," Barry told her. "It's not even Irish, it's a Tin Pan Alley tune."

She replied frostily, "I defer to your superior musical knowledge, Mr. Halloran."

Best avoid this subject for a while, Barry warned himself.

They arrived long after dark, as he had planned. The only hotel was best seen in a dim light; it was shabby with the accumulation of too much history. Yet the old building had a certain glamour. It possessed a fine staircase from the Victorian era, and a faint, characteristic fragrance of vanilla.

Time stood still in Lahinch. The perfect place for a honeymoon.

On their wedding night Barry paused at the foot of the stairs. Reading his intention in his eyes, Barbara said, "I'm a big girl, you can't possibly carry me up those."

He could and did. To the top of the stairs, to the end of the hall, into their room, and across to the bed. Their lovemaking was more passionate than ever, fuelled by the hidden, simmering rage Barry could control but not expunge.

Barbara attributed his intensity to her erotic power.

She slept late the next morning, and every morning

thereafter. Room service was an unheard-of luxury, so Barry paid the owner extra to have a breakfast tray carried up to her. She did not come downstairs until noon at the earliest.

Barry spent his mornings wandering around Lahinch and along the seacoast. Alone with his thoughts. To his regret, they did not centre on the woman waiting for him in the hotel.

When he committed to the marriage he had resolved to give Barbara as much of himself as he could. For years he had cultivated a certain remoteness until it became an essential part of his character, but he knew it was an acquired characteristic. For Barbara's sake he must try to find his way back to the warm, open boy he once had been. For their honeymoon at least he would keep the world at arm's length.

Yet like weeds growing through pavement, the political situation was pushing through to poison the atmosphere. The desk clerk in the hotel was talking about it. The owner of the newsagency was talking about it. Even the fishermen on the pier were talking about it.

In Clare, the Banner County, which had a long history of republicanism, everyone was talking about the resurrection of the IRA.

I can trust Séamus to stay in Harold's Cross to keep things ticking over until we get home. Then I'll have to convince him he's absolutely essential to the ongoing operation of the boardinghouse.

But how the hell am I going to keep me *out of it?*

The turbulent Atlantic with its constantly changing moods made a perfect backdrop for Barbara. Barry took countless photographs of her on the beach. Watching the long rollers come sweeping in, or silhouetted against a flamboyant sunset.

"It's like being at the end of the world," she said.

"Over here we say the next parish is Boston," he replied.

Lahinch was far off the tourist trail. Most visitors were

Irish families who rented battered caravans parked in the salty grass at the edge of the beach, and joined a transient community of swarming children and barking dogs and harassed parents who fled to the comfort of the nearest pub. They had no money for expensive souvenirs, so the village had no gift shop.

On the last day of their honeymoon Barry presented his wife with a glossy, trumpet-shaped seashell, a beautiful exotic washed up from some faraway land. *Like Barbara herself,* he thought.

"Where did you buy this?"

"I didn't buy it. The sea gave it to me."

Her face fell. "Oh." Wrapping the shell in soiled clothes, she tossed it into the bottom of her suitcase.

When they returned to the yellow brick house she put the shell on a shelf in the top of her wardrobe. She sometimes took it out and held it to her cheek. But never when Barry was in the room.

Chapter Ten

ON the tenth of May a referendum on joining the European Economic Community was held in the Republic. 1,041,890 voted in favour, 211,891 opposed.

That night in the Bleeding Horse Brendan told the Usual Suspects, "It's something to cheer about, I tell you. Being part of the European Community will make such terms as unionism and republicanism redundant, because both parts of the island eventually will be subsumed into a United States of Europe. People living across the water already refer to themselves as English or Scots or Welsh. The only

people who loudly proclaim British identity at every opportunity are the unionists in Northern Ireland. I feel confident that a united Europe will make no allowances for their
petty provincialism."

McCoy squinted at him through a pall of cigarette
smoke. "You ever actually been in the north?"

"I have been in the north. I once gave a series of lectures at Queen's University."

"Lectures. In university." McCoy curled his lip. "You'd
want to take a walk down the Falls Road. Or through the
Shankill, for that matter. The problem's not in lecture
halls, Professor, it's in heads and hearts on the street."

LIFE in the yellow brick house resumed its familiar
rhythm. A new bedroom was available for boarders because Barry and Barbara were sharing one. "When I go
north you'll have two vacancies," McCoy said.

Barry was ready for him. "You can't run out on me yet,
Séamus. I was up in the attic yesterday and there's a lot of
water seeping down from the roof. We'll need to do some
serious repairs straightaway. Can I count on you?"

McCoy reluctantly agreed. Although Barry pretended
to divide the work equally, he made sure to do the strenuous part himself. "You could have got Barbara to hand
roofing nails to you," McCoy grumbled.

"My Barbara? You must be joking."

When the roof was done Barry announced that the
long-abandoned mews at the rear of the property must be
rescued before it finished falling down. "Barbara's had a
brilliant idea. We can turn it into two, maybe even three,
self-contained flats. I'll draw up the plans myself."

McCoy was less than enthusiastic. "Doesn't picture-
taking keep you busy enough?"

"We need more income. My mother says we're going
to have three children."

McCoy's bark of laughter became a racking cough.

When he recovered he said, "By that time our boys will have run the Brits out of the north for good."

"You sound optimistic."

"I am optimistic. But it'll happen a lot faster if you're with us."

Barry thrust his hands deep into his pockets so McCoy could not see his tightly balled fists. Self-control took all the strength he possessed. Yet he kept his voice gentle. "I have too many commitments here now."

McCoy squinted up at him. "Is there something you're not telling me, *avic*?"

"I'm telling you the truth of the situation. That old mews will be a valuable asset, but rebuilding and fitting it out will take months. It needs wiring, plumbing, everything. My photographic assignments have to be given priority, so I can't do the work myself. I can hire the labour but without someone trustworthy to supervise them we could be robbed blind. See why I need you?"

"I see you've become a bloody capitalist," McCoy growled, "willing to exploit the working classes. But if you're going to be pigheaded about it, I'll hang around and help. Only for a wee while, mind."

McCoy was well aware of his cough; the occasional pain in his chest; the occasional taste of blood in his mouth. *It's an old scar that keeps tearing open,* he told himself. *If I take it easy for a few more weeks it'll heal on its own. Maybe by then I can persuade him to go with me.*

TOGETHER with the Special Powers Act, which allowed internment of suspects without trial for an open-ended period, Bloody Sunday fed a burgeoning radicalism among the Catholics in Northern Ireland. Centuries of enforced servility in order to survive had made them timid; they had forgotten how to fight back.

They were relearning.

In the Northern Ireland Office a policy document entitled

"The Future of Northern Ireland" flatly stated that the most salient feature of the Northern Ireland Parliament for more than half a century had been its virtually complete concentration in the hands of a single political party, the Ulster Unionists.[1] With the dissolution of its parliament the control of what was often called "the province" had reverted to London. Unionists were alarmed. As the IRA gathered adherents, they felt themselves under siege on not one but two fronts.

In drawing up the Government of Ireland Act in 1920, under which a separate parliament had been established for those northeastern counties where Protestants were in the majority, the British government had stated its preference for an Irish union. Subsequently partition had been established with a democratic proviso: it was to remain in effect as long as the majority agreed. Implicit in that phrase was the understanding that if and when the majority in the north wished to reunite the island, they would be allowed to do so.

Unionist politicians were terrified that their hegemony in the Six Counties would not coincide with the long-term plans of London. Publicly they declared their allegiance to the Crown loud and long; privately they feared the British government would sell them down the river.

Throughout the summer the Army continued to expand. True to McCoy's prediction, many recruits did not come from a republican background. Some entered the IRA through left-wing politics; others simply gravitated towards militarism. Some of the latter, infuriated by the failure of the civil rights movement, had been operating freelance. Then one day a car would draw up and a smiling man lean out the window. "You boys really want to do something? Come join us."

As always there were a few men and women who were in love with revolution for its own sake. Had the problems in the north not existed they would have sought and found

other revolutions elsewhere in the world, and given them
the same fanatic devotion.

The secretary of state for Northern Ireland insisted that
the Ulster Defence Association was not as vicious as the
Provos. However, the shooting of Catholic civilians by
loyalists was taking place at an average of four a week.

ONE evening Barbara was aglow with excitement. While
shopping in Dublin that afternoon she had wandered into
a pub in Baggot Street that featured Irish music, the traditional sounds of pipe and bodhran. "It's absolutely brilliant!" she enthused to Barry. "I'm thrilled I've discovered
it."

Obviously she had forgotten what he told her about traditional music on their honeymoon. It was typical of Barbara, her husband observed to himself, that nothing
existed unless she was personally acquainted with it.

He told her, "I've known about Irish music all my life.
In the late forties Ursula and I used to listen to Séamus
Ennis on Radio Éireann, when he was touring the country
collecting the old songs for the Irish Folklore Society.
Séamus Ennis was the greatest piper Ireland's ever produced, in my opinion. He did some of the first mobile
radio broadcasts ever heard in this country, and educated
us all. In those days the music was still vibrant and alive
in many parts of the island."

"Oh, but it's vibrant and alive now!" Barbara cried. "I
can't imagine why you ever stopped listening to it."

"I didn't stop, as you put it. Let's just say my interest
was superseded by a passion for classical."

Barbara would not give him an inch. "You know as much
about classical music as a pig knows about a holiday."

For a while she flung herself headlong into Irish music
with the rabid devotion of the new convert. She bought
stacks of records; she tuned the radio to any station that

would play her new passion. At first she could not tell the good from the mediocre, or the original from the merely derivative. By the time she could, she was losing interest and looking for something else.

On the twenty-first of July the IRA set off twenty-two bombs in Belfast. Eleven people were killed; 130 injured. Within hours newspaper headlines proclaimed Bloody Friday. Ten days later three car bombs exploded in County Londonderry and six more died.

The Irish, who had been the victims of attack but never attacked another country, had become the aggressors. This was diametrically opposed to the British sense of order.

In a hastily arranged cabinet meeting the British government considered several radical proposals for handling the situation in Northern Ireland. Among these was the possibility of realigning the border to isolate Catholics from Protestants altogether. Almost half a million people would have to be relocated. Catholics would be pushed into southern and western enclaves, leaving Belfast a totally Protestant city in a tiny Protestant state.[2]

The idea was abandoned for fear it would cause another international outcry and bring up Bloody Sunday again. Instead the British government began spending millions in a vain attempt to counter the "cowshed technology" of the IRA.

The rejuvenated Army was delighted. "Now that we're in the war," newcomers boasted, "Ireland will be put back together in short order." Old hands warned, "That's how people felt after partition. Everyone said it couldn't last, an island as small as Ireland couldn't be divided, it wasn't economically viable. But it's still divided."

"And costing Britain a fortune," the young ones countered. "They'll be glad to be rid of it. All we have to do is put on sufficient pressure."

. . .

IN March of 1973 the U.S. withdrew its last ground
troops from Vietnam, but pledged to continue bombing
and napalm attacks. The world gasped at the photo of a
badly burned naked girl running down a road. The child's
small face, deep in shock, looked strangely remote.

MARY McGee of Skerries, County Dublin, had four children and suffered from high blood pressure as well as
having had a stroke. Her doctor strongly advised her
against having any more children. Contraceptives were
taboo in the Republic, forbidden by both Church and State,
so Mrs. McGee sent to England for them. Upon its arrival
in Ireland the package was seized by the postal authorities
and its contents destroyed.[3]

ON the seventeenth of August *An Phoblacht* moved from
its offices at 2A Lower Kevin St. to Kevin Barry House, 44
Parnell Square, and Éamonn MacThomáis took over as
editor from Coleman Moynihan. When Barry called in
looking for an assignment, Éamonn MacThomáis enlisted
his help to transport the last load of books and files.
"How's married life treating you?" he asked as they loaded
boxes into Barry's car.

"Married life's fine," Barry said automatically.

"And Séamus? How's he doing?"

"Not so good. He hasn't collapsed, which is what I
halfway expected by now. Without having a doctor look
at him I don't know what his situation is. The mews conversion should be finished by the end of autumn, and then
I don't know how I'll keep him here."

"He's still talking about going back on active duty,
then?"

"Every day," Barry said glumly. *I wish to God he*

*wouldn't. Always bringing it up, reminding me, prodding
me, making it so damn hard.*

"Frankly," said MacThomáis, "I thought you'd have gone
by now yourself."

"I'm up to me oxters in work here," Barry replied.
"The photography's really taken off."

It had, but that was not his real reason.

MacThomáis soon began making major changes in *An
Phoblacht*. A passionate, outspoken man, he had no hesitation about using his editorial powers to condemn British
policy in Northern Ireland. He referred to the infamous
1919 Amritsar Massacre in India as an example of the savage reprisals the British used for keeping "the natives" in
line.

He also reported the words of John Taylor of the Ulster
Unionist Party who stated, "We should make it clear that
force means death and whoever gets in our way, whether
republicans or others, there will be killings."[4]

I don't know why we have to live in Harold's Cross,"
Barbara pouted one evening as she and Barry were getting ready for bed. "No one who's anyone lives here."

Barry said, "I like to think I'm someone."

"If you were we'd live in a better neighbourhood."

Barry recognised the start of one of her campaigns. "If
we had a television . . ." spoken like a child pleading for
sweets meant "If I don't get a television immediately I
will make every single day a misery."

Barry was proud of having made a success of the
boardinghouse and he liked living in Harold's Cross.

He intensely disliked being pressured.

Barbara bought an assortment of British magazines
portraying luxurious homes and left them in prominent
places around the house. She also began reading adver-
tisements of property for sale aloud.

Barry pretended not to notice, but everyone else did.

McCoy said, "God love the woman, Barry; is there no satisfying her?"

With a flash of the jaunty grin that had fluttered many a girlish heart before his marriage, Barry replied, "There's one way I can always satisfy her."

A crimson tide rose from McCoy's collar and crept up his leathery neck.

"Why, Séamus! I think you're blushing."

"I never blush," he growled.

I N September the Olympic Games took place in Munich, the first time they had been held in Germany since 1936. In repudiation of the so-called Hitler Olympics these were billed as "The Games of Peace and Joy." All of Ireland celebrated when Mary Peters from Northern Ireland won gold in the Women's Pentathlon. Mark Spitz of the U.S. captured seven gold medals in Swimming; tiny Olga Korbut won four in Gymnastics for the U.S.S.R.

The peace and joy of the Games were shattered when a group calling itself Black September, an extremist faction of the Palestinian Liberation Organisation, invaded the Olympic Village. Bursting into the Israeli compound, they killed a wrestling coach and a weightlifter and took the remaining athletes hostage. Their demands included the release of more than two hundred Palestinians being held in Israeli prisons, and safe passage out of Germany.

Israeli prime minister Golda Meir said to her cabinet, "I don't know where these animals come from."

A rescue attempt by trained hit team ended in a shoot-out that killed all nine hostages, five members of Black September, and one German policeman.

B A R R Y ' S record collection had expanded from its classical origins to embrace American jazz, the Irish folk group called Planxty, the Swedish foursome Abba who won

Eurovision in 1974 with "Waterloo," and the Mamas and the Papas. Barry loved the voice of Mama Cass—though Barbara dismissed her as "not technically correct." Barry suspected she was jealous.

Barry and Barbara argued about music as they argued about many things. She was an ardent fan of Elvis Presley. Barry preferred the Beatles, whose Liverpool accents she claimed were incomprehensible. "Presley doesn't even write his own music," Barry said. "The Beatles do."

"Yes, but it takes four of them to put on a performance while Elvis can do it all by himself."

Barbara's favourite ploy for initiating an argument was to say something derogatory about the IRA. When the most recent IRA shooting in the north made headlines in the newspapers, she said with contempt, "They're nothing but a gang of terrorists."

Barry said, "There's something you need to understand, Barbara. Violent reaction on behalf of a minority who are suffering intolerable oppression can't be compared to murders committed by loyalist death squads organised and condoned by representatives of the United Kingdom. That's state-sponsored terrorism."

His measured, articulate statement made little impression on Barbara. The next time she was bored and wanted excitement she again accused the IRA of terrorism.

This time Barry allowed himself to lose his temper—just a little. "The whole point of war is to out-terrorise your enemy! I don't suppose a woman like you can understand, so I'll make it easy for you. Hiroshima was the ultimate act of terrorism, and who perpetrated that?"

At the height of a quarrel Barbara was given to shouting and door slamming. Barry rarely raised his voice. He tried to keep their rows private; she preferred an audience.

An embarrassed McCoy told the boarders, "They just fight for the fun of making up." Privately he thought, *I don't need this, I'd rather have a real war. I'll be damn*

*glad when we finish the new flats. But it's just one delay
after another. Where does Barry find these lazy arseholes?
They bring the wrong materials, they stop for tea every fifteen minutes, the plumber leaves in the middle of the day
and doesn't come back for a fortnight . . . at this rate it'll
be almost Christmas before we're done. After the holidays
I'm definitely going up the road. Nothing's going to stop
me this time.*

One of the Hallorans' worst quarrels resulted from a
remark Barbara made during the evening meal, in front
of everyone: "The problems in the north would end tomorrow if Ireland simply rejoined the United Kingdom.
It was stupid to leave in the first place. The Irish are incapable of governing themselves, the IRA proves that."

For once Barry's response was not tempered. In the face
of his icy rage the dining room swiftly emptied of boarders. This time it was Barry who slammed the front door on
his way out.

When McCoy helped Barbara clear the table, he noticed that her hands were shaking. He said, "I could have
warned you not to make Barry really angry."

"I wasn't trying to do that."

"The only reason you said what you did was to get up
his nose."

"Well what if it was? He's so damned smug, so
damned certain that what he calls 'physical force republicanism' is the only way."

"Wait until you talk to an Orangeman. And by the way,
you should know that Barry doesn't like women swearing."

"Why, because his mother doesn't swear? I'll bet Ursula curses like a sailor when no one's around. Given her
background," Barbara added.

McCoy looked blank.

He doesn't know, she realised. She was pleased to be in
possession of such a potent secret. It delighted Barbara to

think of Ursula as her social inferior; a child of the tenements. The squalid, decaying tenements that still existed throughout Dublin, releasing their fetid breath to contaminate the streets of the capital.

What a lovely weapon to hold over your mother-in-law.

I N the sixties and seventies every town of any size in Ireland had at least one ballroom. Aside from the Church, they were the primary social focus for young people. The showbands who performed in the ballrooms were immensely popular. They toured the island and were equally welcome north and south. The most famous was the Dublin-based Miami Showband—often referred to as "the Irish Beatles." Its members came from both sides of the border and from both the Catholic and Protestant traditions. Showbands were not about politics or religion; they were about entertaining people. They also helped set the fashions. Like many men in Ireland Barry was wearing long sideburns. His hair swept his collar.

Barbara thought he was amazingly handsome and wished she had more opportunities to show him off. When she saw an advertisement for the Miami Showband's next Dublin appearance she begged him to take her dancing.

"I don't dance anymore," he said. "My left leg . . ."

"It's not reliable, I know. But I've noticed it doesn't keep you from doing anything you really want to do."

"Barbara, I have to be up before dawn tomorrow and drive to Kinsale for a sunrise photo shoot with Mary O'Donnell. I already told you about it."

Barbara subsided into silks and sulks. But the matter was not forgotten.

In November an interview with the chief of staff of the Provisional IRA, whose identity was not revealed, created an uproar when it was aired on radio. The government promptly sacked the RTE Authority for allowing the broadcast. Later that month Seán MacStiofáin was given a six-month prison sentence for membership in an illegal organisation, and the reporter who had interviewed him was sentenced to three months for refusing to identify MacStiofáin as his interviewee.

On the night of December first a car bomb exploded close to Liberty Hall in Dublin, injuring thirty citizens of the Republic and causing extensive damage. Within twenty minutes a second car bomb exploded in Sackville Place, just off O'Connell Street. This time two men were killed and ninety other people injured.

Only minutes before the first explosion an anonymous telephone caller had rung the *Belfast Newsletter* with a warning—giving incorrect locations and issued too late to prevent the bombings. No one was ever arrested. No charges were ever brought against the perpetrators.

Among the regulars in the Bleeding Horse there was no doubt where the blame lay. The Usual Suspects shared the consensus opinion. "The loyalists did it. And British agents helped them."

The attacks on Dublin marked the turning of a corner. The IRA determined to carry the war to the enemy.

It would not be the first time. Fenians had undertaken a bombing campaign in Britain in 1880, and the IRA in 1920. The tradition would continue.

Chapter Eleven

THE conversion of the mews into two self-contained flats—or "apartments," as Barbara called them—proved a great success. When Barry put an ad in the classified section of the newspapers the telephone began ringing almost at once. In less than a week a retired couple had taken one flat, and a widower and his two nearly grown sons had taken the second. The older son planned to study for the priesthood. His proud father said, "My uncle was a priest and both my sisters are nuns."

SHORTLY before Christmas the government of the Republic removed the reference to the "special position" of the Catholic Church from the Irish Constitution. But no amount of legislation could remove it from the Irish psyche.

CHRISTMAS sneaked up on Barry. It was the twenty-third of December when he realised he had not bought a present for his wife. He slipped away from an assignment at Leinster House to walk the short distance to Brown Thomas in Grafton Street. When she saw a label from Dublin's most expensive department store, Barbara would criticise him for being extravagant. But she would be unbearable if he gave her anything less than the best.

Buoyed by the thought of added income from the flats, Barry wandered through the various departments until he discovered a cashmere cardigan as tawny as her eyes. The price surpassed his worst expectations. He left the store in a slight daze and made his way back toward Leinster House.

As he turned into Dawson Street a hand was placed on Barry's shoulder from behind. A voice he recognised said, "Halloran."

"How're you keeping?" he asked without looking around.

"Not so bad. But we could use you."

"You're doing pretty well on your own."

"We could do better. Explosives aren't like anything else, you know. Volunteers who say they'll do anything back off fast when we mention explosives. Compared to the IRA the loyalists are still at a primitive stage in building bombs, but they're getting a lot of help to close the gap. If we hope to stay ahead of them we'll need the best possible engineers. That means you, Halloran."

Still Barry did not look around. He was listening to a younger version of his own voice asking, "Was my father killed by a bomb?"

His mother had not answered, but her eyes filled with anguish.

"Just yes or no, Ursula. Was he?"

"Yes," she had whispered.

Barry squared his shoulders. Out of the side of his mouth he told the man behind him, "Nelson's Pillar was my last bomb."

"Is that definite?"

"You have my word on it."

O N New Year's Day, 1973, Taoiseach Jack Lynch signed the Treaty of Rome. The Republic of Ireland officially joined the European Economic Community. In their rush to gain the benefits of the Common Market for their economically hard-pressed country, government officials had overlooked much of the fine print to which they were agreeing. They gave away the majority of Ireland's fishing resources—an act of monumental myopia for an island nation—in return for allowing farmers, and particularly large farmers, huge financial windfalls from the Common Agricultural Policy.

As a beneficial result of Ireland's entry into the EEC, the infamous "Marriage Bar" was lifted. At last women would be allowed to remain in salaried employment after marriage. Originally applied to the civil service, the ban had been extended with the full support of the Church to include both the public and private sectors, covering such diverse occupations as the nursing profession and in the Guinness Brewery.

THE year began bitterly cold. Howling gales pursued one another in swift succession across Ireland.

And Barbara discovered she was pregnant.

She was dismayed. "How could this have happened?" she wailed to Barry.

"In the most natural way in the world," he said. "You haven't been trying to prevent it, have you?"

"Where would I get contraceptives in Catholic Ireland?"

"Women must know other ways of preventing conception."

Barbara gave a hollow laugh. "Oh, I tried the usual methods—Alice Cassidy advised a vinegar douche—but here I am anyway. Up the spout. A bun in the oven. What am I going to do?"

"What's so terrible about having a baby? I'm over the moon about it."

"You would be," she said sourly. "You don't have to carry it for nine months and be swollen all out of shape."

"I'll love you just the same. More."

"Well, I won't love me. And I won't love changing dirty diapers, either, or having to get up for a squalling baby in the middle of the night."

"We call them nappies over here, and I'll change them if you don't want to," he promised. "I'll get up in the middle of the night too."

"You're just saying that, you don't mean it."

"I always mean what I say, Barbara." His voice was very low, very soft. But the skin tightened around his eyes.

SINCE the beginning of the twentieth century tens of thousands of Irish women had "taken the boat" to England for an abortion. They were not all young single girls in trouble; many were married women. Due to the Church's insistence on a total ban on contraception, a wife might bear her husband a huge number of children over the years of their marriage. Some had twenty or more. If even half of these survived, the burden on the woman could be crushing. Backstreet abortionists flourished. Women who could not afford to take the boat felt they had no other option.

I could go to England without telling him I was going, Barbara thought to herself. *But he would never forgive me. I'm stuck with this.*

Damn the Church, damn sex, damn Ireland!

BARRY seized on the opportunity to tell Séamus, "You can't leave us now. Someone has to be with Barbara when I'm off on an assignment."

"She's as healthy as a horse, Seventeen; she doesn't need a minder."

"Anything could go wrong at any time. You know how women are when they're pregnant."

McCoy's shoulders slumped. "It looks like I'm about to learn."

"I think I've got it sussed out," he told the Usual Suspects later. "Barry'll use any excuse to keep me from going back to the Army."

"Why'd he want to do that?"

"It isn't him, it's that girl he married. She hates anything to do with republicanism."

Patsy stopped stroking his jaw long enough to say, "That explains why Barry don't come in so much anymore. She's got 'im tied to her apron strings."

"I'm missing something here," said Brendan. "First you claim it's Barry who's keeping you in Dublin. Then it's his wife. I'm a bit confused. Do you mean they're conspiring together against you?"

McCoy bristled. "I never said that."

"Well, is there a conspiracy or not?"

"Pick up any rock on this island and look under it and you'll find a conspiracy," McCoy said testily. "In Northern Ireland the RUC and the loyalists are as close as two fingers on one hand. On this side of the border Special Branch conspires with the pro-Brits. Our politicians conspire against each other and the government conspires against everybody. We're up to our knees in conspiracies. That's not what I'm talking about!"

Brendan made soothing gestures with his age-spotted hands. "There's no need to get shirty with me, Séamus. I was only trying to understand your problem."

"My problem is, I need a drink and it's your shout. Make mine a double, will you?"

When the drink arrived McCoy spent a long time staring into its amber depths. *Maybe I haven't fought hard enough. If I just walked out the door neither one of 'em could stop me.*

Maybe I don't want to walk out the door.

Maybe the cancer's come back and I'm afraid.

He stayed in the pub until closing time, then got a ride to Harold's Cross with the barman. He was not in the mood for a long walk.

• • •

O N the twenty-fourth of January Dr. Rose Dugdale, accompanied by three men, hijacked a helicopter in Donegal. Dr. Dugdale was a devoted Irish republican in spite of the fact that she was English by birth and came from a prosperous family. She and her companions used the helicopter to drop three milk churns containing bombs onto the Strabane RUC station.

The bombs failed to explode.

A T the end of January two White House aides were convicted of breaking into Democratic Party Headquarters in the Watergate Building in Washington, D.C., the preceding year. They had been charged with conspiring to spy on President Nixon's opponent during his reelection campaign.

A general election in the Republic of Ireland in February saw a Fine Gael/Labour coalition led by Liam Cosgrave oust Fianna Fáil from power after sixteen years. The new coalition was decidedly right-wing in spite of its Labour component. However, Conor Cruise O'Brien, minister for posts and telegraphs, made a bombastic speech in the Dáil denouncing tax loopholes and all those who would avail of them.

February in Northern Ireland marked the arrest of the first two loyalists to be detained under the Special Powers Act. The Loyalist Association of Workers responded with a one-day strike. Loyalists also attacked Catholic homes and businesses, leading to a gun battle with the British army that resulted in five deaths.[1]

Two car bombs exploded in central London in early March. One was outside the Old Bailey, the other at the

Agriculture Ministry. One person was killed and over two hundred injured. Police, fearing it signalled the start of a republican bombing campaign, arrested ten men who were waiting to board a plane for Belfast. They were accused of being members of the IRA but it was difficult to prove. The men had no police records in either England nor Ireland.

The IRA was recruiting unknowns for its campaign.

An Phoblacht, under the editorship of Éamonn Mac-Thomáis, became a weekly paper with a circulation of forty thousand copies per issue. It also became a target for increased harassment by the Garda Special Branch.

The colossal twin towers of the World Trade Center in New York City were dedicated in April. As he studied the photographs in the newspapers, Barry Halloran remarked, "I like the Chrysler Building better. It has more character."

T HERE was no Easter Rising Commemorative Parade in 1973, either. The IRA claimed to be the legitimate heirs of the Rising and they were committing acts of violence of which many people disapproved.

T H A T year a new radio programme burst onto the Irish scene like a thunderclap. *Hall's Pictorial Ireland* was a weekly satire that took no prisoners. Ireland did not engage in political cartooning to the extent the British did, but possessed an ancient and honourable tradition of satire. In pre-Christian times a satirist could bring down a king. "Hall's Pictorial" played a large part in achieving the same thing by depicting the current crop of Irish politicians as an unsavoury and unattractive lot. The public loved it.

N O matter how much Barbara wanted to keep politics out of the house in Harold's Cross, it kept intruding. Like

the rifle—hidden out of her sight but always there—
politics played a part in Barry's life. He had first achieved
international recognition as a photographer with a haunting candid portrait of Eamon de Valera. Eight years later
politicians were eager to pose for his lens.

But his favourite subject was Ireland. The land could
not be killed; would not disappear. Was safe to love.

Her beauty revealed itself to his artist's eye in sweeping
panoramas and intimate vignettes. The faded elegance of a
decaying Georgian streetscape; an emerald fern bowing
over a spill of rubbish; a ruined castle with empty windows
looking for a lost kingdom.

"Why do you take so many sad pictures?" Barbara
asked her husband.

"Sadness is part of what makes Ireland beautiful," he
said, "just as the pathos of songs like 'The Minstrel Boy'
makes them unforgettable."

J O H N McCormack, a married Catholic with three young
children, died in a Belfast hospital on the fourteenth of
May. He had been shot five times in the head by members
of the UVF as he walked along Garnet Street.[2] McCormack was a social security officer whose only crime was
being caught on the street in a Catholic neighbourhood.

In the Republic the Cosgrave government made it obvious they intended to ignore the situation in the north in
hopes it would go away. McCormack's murder went un-
reported by the media, with the exception of a few lines
in the *Cork Examiner* that attributed the deed to "Protestant extremists."

One of Barry's boarders was from Cork, and routinely
bought the *Examiner*. After reading the article he wondered aloud, "How can people do such awful things?"

"They learn by example," Barbara spoke up, "when
they're very young. When it all seems innocent and they
don't know any better."

Barry was impressed by her perception.

In Northern Ireland he had seen young children watching enraptured as their fathers and uncles marched in the Orange parades. Small boys with shining eyes were eager for the day when they would strut behind the banners, bang the drums, be part of the pageantry, the glory! Accepting hatred as the price of membership in something larger than themselves.

Not knowing any better.

Chapter Twelve

W ITH the support of her husband Shay, her family, and her doctor, Mary McGee of Skerries had taken a case against the government of the Republic. She had argued that the Criminal Law Amendment Act, which banned the importation of contraceptives, breached her constitutional rights.

When she was thrust into the media spotlight she heard from a number of people who agreed with her, mostly women, and many who disagreed, mostly men. One of the latter condemned her actions in the strongest terms and stated that he himself had eighteen children. Mrs. McGee replied, "You did not have eighteen children. Your wife did."

Mary McGee had lost her case in the High Court but went on to the Supreme Court, where in 1973 she obtained an historic decision in her favour. A woman had taken on the State and won.

A ripple of shock ran through Ireland—though not enough to shake the granitic foundations of the Church.

Catholic women were still forbidden to prevent pregnancy
by any means other than the so-called rhythm method. Or
abstinence.

IN June a loyalist group calling themselves the Ulster
Freedom Fighters shot two Catholics—one a seventeen-
year-old boy—in Belfast, then telephoned the *Belfast Telegraph* to boast, "We gave him two in the back and one in
the head! There will be more."

The IRA retaliated by shooting a civilian who provided
sandwiches to the British army, and a Unionist candidate
for the upcoming elections.

Since the partitioning of Ireland in 1922 most murders
in the north had been committed by Protestants killing
Catholics. But the pendulum had begun to swing.

A song called "Feel the Need" topped the Irish charts.
Radio stations throughout America played "Tie a Yellow
Ribbon Around the Old Oak Tree" as peace negotiators
struggled to agree to terms in Vietnam.

IN Northern Ireland people went to the polls to vote on an
Assembly to replace the old Stormont government. After
suggestions for a power-sharing executive consisting of
both Protestants and Catholics had emerged, loyalists were
vociferous in their condemnation of the arrangement.

The new Assembly was in for a rocky time.

ÉAMONN MacThomáis was arrested in July. He was
charged with IRA membership on the strength of a sworn
statement by a member of Special Branch, and certain
papers found in his office—such as the newsletter of the
National Union of Journalists. Douglas Gageby, editor of

The Irish Times, was mystified. "Why didn't they arrest me?" he wondered. "I have the same material on my desk that Éamonn has on his. So does every newspaperman in Dublin."[1]

Before the trial Barry visited his friend in a holding cell at the Bridewell. MacThomáis was unabashed by his predicament. "The judge will realise it was all a mistake and send me home," he said cheerfully. "In the meantime, keep an eye on Rosaleen for me, will you?"

"I will of course. I can take her around to the shops in my car."

"Now don't go spoiling my Little Girl, Barry. In a few days I'll be taking her to the shops myself. I'm eager to get back to work, there's a lot bubbling under the surface right now." He tapped his finger against the side of his nose.

"Will you have an assignment for me?"

"Not this time."

"A camera can explain things words could never convey."

"Not this time," MacThomáis reiterated. "Any photograph would be counterproductive. I can't write about the subject at all, in fact. You see, the number of informers in the IRA is multiplying. The Army doesn't know how they're being recruited, but they suspect MI5, the British Intelligence agency. When our lads find an informer he's summarily executed, and not too gently, either. Some are tumbled into unmarked graves where they'll never be found."

Barry shook his head. "Brutal killings, unmarked graves—we're in danger of becoming the very thing we're fighting."

"We won't," MacThomáis assured him. He clapped Barry on the back. "We're going to turn things around; you, me, all of us working together, we're going to get our country back the way it should have been."

Afterwards, Barry told Séamus, "I went to see Éamonn to cheer him up, but he cheered me up instead."

"That's why I read *An Phoblacht,*" McCoy said. "No matter how bad things look, it reminds me that plenty of others feel the way I do about Ireland. Éamonn's right. We'll get our country back."

Rosaleen MacThomáis was shocked when her husband was found guilty. "I can't believe someone from Special Branch would lie like that!" she said to Barry after the trial. "The man was under *oath!*"

MacThomáis was sent to Mountjoy Jail; one of a growing number of republicans being held in the Dublin prison. Governments both north and south were making an effort to put as many as possible behind bars. But the violence continued to escalate. Feeding on its own heat.

AUGUST brought a languid, sodden softness to the air, and a hint of amber and saffron to the wilting trees in O'Connell Street. Children abandoned breakfast tables to run outside and play the last wonderful games while there was still time. Their harried mothers anxiously consulted the family finances with an eye to buying clothes for school.

Dublin stretched, yawned, gathered herself for change.

IN Northern Ireland Patrick Duffy, an unemployed Catholic man with seven children, was shot dead. His body was placed inside a coffin that was left in a car abandoned at the border. On the seventeenth of August the IRA put a notice in one of the local papers, saying that Duffy had been executed for giving information to the RUC Special Branch.

THE Usual Suspects were amused at the uproar caused by the incident.

"I admit the Provos can be brutal to informers," said Luke, "but since the IRA's being branded as a terrorist organisation, why should people be surprised by the methods they use?"

"They follow well-established precedent," Brendan added. "The Army believes its struggle is a legitimate war against an occupying force, so informers are, ipso facto, traitors. After the Civil War, the victorious pro-Treatyites executed over seventy republicans—their former comrades in arms during the War of Independence—as traitors. How's that for setting an example?"

T H E hospital waiting room contained fifteen battered chairs, a wooden table decorated with ring marks, piles of disarticulated newspapers, ancient issues of the *Catholic Digest* and *Ireland's Own*, and a single dog-eared *National Geographic* that automatically fell open at a colour photograph of bare-breasted women in Borneo.

"A lot of history's been made in and around the Rotunda Hospital," Barry said. "Did you know the Irish Volunteers were founded in these very grounds?"

"I did know," McCoy replied patiently. "That's the fourth time you've told me today."

"I must be nervous, I'm talking too much."

"That's the second time you've said that. I'm a wee bit nervous myself, Seventeen, and she's not even having my baby."

"I should hope not. I was hoping for a handsome son."

"What makes you so sure it's a boy?"

"Ursula said it would be."

"You talk to her recently?"

"I rang her shortly after we brought Barbara in. She's coming up to Dublin as soon as she can." Had he been less distracted Barry might have noticed the sudden light in McCoy's eyes.

Hours crawled by with all the speed of time spent in a dentist's chair. Countless cups of tea grew cold on the table. McCoy read the same newspaper article twice before he realised it was about women's fashions. At last a beaming nurse beckoned to Barry from the doorway. "You have a son, Mr. Halloran. Nine pounds six ounces and a full head of hair. If you listen you can hear him; he has a great pair of lungs. Wait, Mr. Halloran, you can't go in there yet, you can't . . ."

Barry pushed past the woman and strode into the delivery room. When more nurses and a beefy obstetrician tried to block his way he brushed them aside like gnats.

There he is! That little red squirming creature is a brand-new person and this is his first day in the world.

Barry's brain had been prepared for the moment; it took his heart by surprise.

I have taken life; now I've given life.

Thank God.

He felt a powerful urge to fall on his knees and pray.

Instead he fell in love with his son.

B ACK in her room, Barbara was exhausted but proud. "The doctor called him splendid, Barry."

He looked at the flushed face, the dishevelled hair, the seeping breasts wetting the front of her hospital gown. *You're splendid,* he thought. But did not say.

Brian Joseph Halloran was christened in the church where his parents had been married. The Cassidys were his godparents. Séamus McCoy stood beside Ursula Halloran for the ceremony, and glowed with pride when someone mistook him for the baby's grandfather. That night he drank far too many toasts to wet the baby's head. Barry had to carry him upstairs.

From the beginning Brian was a lusty, demanding boy. "He's going to be as big as his father," Ursula predicted.

"How can you tell?"

"Look at his hands, they're huge. Puppies who have outsized feet grow up to be very big dogs."

"My son," Barbara said sharply, "is not a puppy."

"He's my son too," Barry reminded her. *I need not have worried about her being a good mother,* he told himself. *She's like a tigress with her cub.*

Ursula stayed in Dublin until the infant and his mother were well settled in the new routine. Barry was surprised by her skill with the baby. "I never thought of you as a maternal person, Ursula."

"I don't know why not. I reared you very carefully."

"Funnily enough I seem to remember growing up wild, like some sort of wild animal roaming the countryside."

"I suppose you were," Ursula agreed, "until Séamus took you by the scruff of the neck and taught you military discipline. But I taught you to be brave and independent. If that's not being a good mother, I don't know what is."

"Reckon your mother's good at everything she does," McCoy remarked to Barry.

The following evening, after an argument with Barbara over something trivial that assumed gigantic proportions, McCoy suggested Barry accompany him to the Bleeding Horse. "The new adjutant of the Belfast Brigade is in Dublin visiting GHQ for a couple of days, Seventeen, and there's a chance they'll bring him along to the pub tonight. I'd like to meet him."

"You mean you'd like to give him a chance to recruit me."

McCoy looked offended. "It never crossed my mind."

The pub was surprisingly empty when they arrived. Of the Usual Suspects, only Luke and Danny were seated at one of the tables. McCoy went to the bar for a round of drinks. While he was out of earshot Barry asked the other two, "Have you seen Séamus smoking lately?"

"Can't say I have. And even if he was," Danny added with a wink, "I'm not one to inform on a pal."

Luke said sharply, "Don't joke about that."

Barry's senses were on instant alert. "What's wrong?"

"Nothing's wrong."

"Be straight with me, Luke. Has something happened?"

Luke studied his fingernails. "We, ah, had some visitors a couple of hours ago. That is, the pub did."

McCoy set the drinks on the table. "The young adjutant from Belfast Brigade? You mean we missed him? Damn it all anyway."

"Not him," Luke said. "Three middle-aged men; hard men from the look of them. Dundalk accents. I never saw them in here before and they didn't stay long this time. Just long enough to take a good look around."

"What did they want?"

"Didn't say. They ordered one drink apiece and passed a few words with the bartender, all very casual. Too casual if you ask me." Luke glanced over his shoulder, then dropped his voice. "Personally, I think they were looking for an informer."

There was a sudden chill in the air. Danny looked alarmed.

"I just sat in the corner and read my newspaper," Luke went on. "It was nothing to do with me."

"Did you question the bartender after they left?"

"He's of the same opinion I am, Barry. Nothing specific, you understand. Just a feeling."

McCoy asked, "What about you, Danny?"

"I wasn't here," the Kerry man said quickly.

Business was bad in the Bleeding Horse that night. The regular customers came in, stayed long enough to hear what had happened, looked appraisingly at those around them— or avoided looking at them—and left earlier than usual.

"I doubt if the new man from Belfast will call in now," Barry told McCoy. "Word gets around fast."

"Aye."

"We might as well do our drinking at home then."

"Aye," McCoy agreed with a sigh of resignation.

Barry drove home slowly, lost in thought until he realised that McCoy was talking to him.

"You believe that, Seventeen? One of the pub regulars could be an informer?"

"What? Oh . . . it's a possibility. There've been informers in this country since the first Queen Elizabeth began bribing the Irish to betray one another. The question is, how should we deal with them?"

"There's no question about it," said McCoy. "Suppose you found out tomorrow that a man you'd been drinking with tonight had informed on you—or on me. The IRA's not a democracy, Seventeen, it's an army, and the troops take orders. They may come with a hand on the shoulder or a word in the ear, but they're orders and there's no arguing. Volunteers do as they're told. It's our greatest strength."

Chapter Thirteen

⸺⸺◆⸺⸺

URSULA was troubled by the tension she felt in the house. *So much arguing can't be good for the baby. People think they don't understand anything at that age, but they do. They're like animals, they pick up on everything.*

"I think it's time I went back to Clare," she told Barbara. "You're under a strain, having your mother-in-law in the house."

"I enjoy having you here," the young woman protested. Her eyes contradicted her words.

"That's very kind of you, Barbara," Ursula said, "but I've been away from my horses too long. I must start training up the youngsters for sale next spring."

"Surely you don't still ride!"

Ursula's eyes flashed. "Of course I still ride."

"I mean, well . . . a woman in her early sixties . . ."

". . . is a woman in her early sixties," Ursula snapped. "Neither helpless nor dysfunctional, as you will find out for yourself someday, God willing."

Barbara had a gift for saying insulting things in an innocent way, as if she did not know they were insulting. But she knew when she was caught. "I thought you hired people for that sort of thing," she said sulkily.

"I employ farm labour, but I prepare my own horses. I can't afford to pay an expensive trainer, and besides, I love them and they know it. Every living thing responds to love," Ursula added, hoping Barbara would get the message.

Love my son. Give him what he needs.

Barry took his mother to the train station. He did not try to dissuade her from leaving, but he was sorry to see her go. When they were together he was aware there were things unsaid between them, things that should be said. Yet he did not know what they were or how to start the conversation.

As he waited with her on the train platform she asked abruptly, "Do you still have Papa's rifle?"

"I do of course."

"But you've never gone back to active service."

"I have not."

She knew there was no point in asking him for an explanation. Like herself, Barry kept his own counsel.

Ursula Halloran had been an Irish republican for as long as she could remember. She had actively served in the cause of the Republic; she had been worried and upset and enormously proud when her only child ran off to follow in her footsteps. She had fully expected that the rage she saw in him following Bloody Sunday would erupt into violence. Her only concern had been for his safety. When he appeared to do nothing Ursula had been surprised. And relieved. And disappointed.

Since the Civil War Ireland had been fractured in many ways. So had the island's inhabitants. Partition was an outward symbol of a deep inward divide. In both north and south many people gave lip service to the politically acceptable line while feeling very differently in their hidden hearts.

I N September the body of James Joseph Brown, a Catholic from Derry whose wife was expecting their first child, was found dumped in the Foyle Road. The IRA issued a statement alleging Brown had attempted to infiltrate the organisation, and had been passing information to the British since 1971. It was further claimed that Brown had received a total of 120 pounds sterling, a considerable sum, for his information.

The following month Ronald Fletcher, a Protestant from East Belfast, was killed when a bomb planted by the Ulster Defence Association—or the Ulster Freedom Fighters, depending on who one spoke to—exploded in the doorway of Wilson's Bar on the Upper Newtownards Road. Fletcher, an innocent bystander, was killed when the wall collapsed on him.

On Halloween the IRA hijacked a helicopter and forced the pilot to land in the exercise yard of Dublin's Mountjoy Prison. Three leading Provos were snatched to freedom in an operation planned to the split second.

In November a Catholic pensioner called Francis McNelis was killed by a UVF bomb in the Avenue Bar, close to Belfast city centre. Almost every day that month someone was murdered. Catholic or Protestant, civilian or paramilitary or member of the security forces, no one in Northern Ireland was exempt from a sudden, violent end.

During a meeting of the Northern Ireland Assembly on the fifth of December fighting broke out in the chamber. Four moderate Unionists were physically attacked by members of Vanguard and the DUP. Police eventually removed the attackers to the accompaniment of jeers from the crowd gathered outside.

The Assembly was close to collapse.

On the sixth, at an English civil service college called Sunningdale, a conference was held between representatives of the British and Irish governments. An agreement was drawn up stipulating that the unification of Ireland could only take place with the consent of the majority in Northern Ireland. In addition, a Council of Ireland was to be established to promote north-south economic cooperation.

The mere mention of cooperation with the Republic evoked paroxysms of anger among loyalists.

O N the first of January 1974 a new power-sharing Northern Ireland Executive took office at Stormont, led by Brian Faulkner—a relatively moderate Unionist politician who had justified internment by saying, "We are, quite simply, at war with the terrorists and in a state of war many sacrifices have to be made."[1]

The Usual Suspects were not impressed by the new regime. "It won't make no difference," Patsy said. "You can change the label on a tin of beans but it's still beans."

"Amen," agreed McCoy.

"Apart from being a supporter of Ian Paisley, Faulkner seems like an intelligent man," said Brendan. "Perhaps we should give him a chance before we pass judgement."

Danny responded with a derisive sneer. "We don't have to give him a chance. He's a politician, and we know what they are. We got plenty of that breed down here. All mouth and no trousers."

T H E Usual Suspects were not alone in their view of the new Executive. A fresh outbreak of violence followed its establishment. The death toll mounted. By 1974 Northern Ireland was firmly labelled in the minds of news editors abroad as "reliable." If nothing more exciting was happening one could always count on the Irish situation to provide a hard news story or dramatic photographs.

The credit on some of the most stark photos was "Barry Halloran."

Several times a week that year Barry put his cameras, tripod, and a couple of holdalls into the boot of the Austin Healey and drove north, to Belfast or Newry or Derry. He never crossed the border without first stopping in a hotel in Dundalk and taking certain precautions. To his knowledge no constabulary possessed a photograph of him, since he had never been arrested, yet there were those in the north who would remember him from days long past.

Barry made certain that the tall red-haired man who stood out in any crowd in the Republic was never seen in Northern Ireland. He travelled with several sets of clothing that ran the gamut from a nearly new three-piece suit to a torn sweater and dingy dungarees. The grooming kit that held his razor and aftershave also contained materials to change the colour of his hair, rolls of cotton to fill out his cheeks, bits of wax and spirit gum, and three pairs of spectacles with different frames, but plain glass lenses.

To augment his disguises he borrowed freely from the Usual Suspects, assuming Danny's wide-legged swagger, or Luke's rounded shoulders, or Patsy's habit of rubbing his thumb along his jawbone. He could even alter his posture so that he appeared shorter than he really was.

When he left the hotel in Dundalk he might be any of half a dozen different men—none of them resembling the real Barry Halloran.

His extensive knowledge of Northern Ireland served him well. He knew the hot spots, the flash points, instinctively. The Orange marches, when loyalists in their thousands paraded through nationalist neighbourhoods in acts of blatant triumphalism, attracted trouble like a magnet. But so did the crowded pubs—Protestant or Catholic—on a Fri-

day night, or the lonely streets in a poor neighbourhood—
Catholic or Protestant—where discontent sowed seeds of
violence.

Attempting to cover the war in Northern Ireland—and
this was a war; only the wilfully uninformed believed
otherwise—was a near impossibility for print journalists
and photojournalists alike. There was never time for reflection. Things that made no sense from any rational perspec-
tive were everyday occurrences. Violence erupted out of
nowhere and then melted away before anyone could determine its actual cause or the identity of the protagonists.
Ensnarled in chaos, Barry ran, crouched, scrambled over
walls, was alternately terrified and furious, reloaded the
camera, flattened himself into doorways, observed bar-
baric cruelty on both sides and occasional moments of
touching heroism as well, swore aloud, beat an impotent
fist against a closed door, slept in his clothes, accepted a
cup of tea from strangers, strove day after day to tell the
story with some degree of objectivity. Knew that he failed
far more often than he succeeded. But he tried.

That's all any of us can do. Try.

Barry was not alone in attempting the impossible. War
correspondents with experience in conflicts from the former U.S.S.R. to Afghanistan and Lebanon were being
sent to Belfast now. Male and female alike, many arrived
complete with helmets, flak jackets, and their own pre-
conceived ideas about "Ireland."

The north quickly disabused them.

At the end of the day Barry often joined some of them
in a hotel bar, or one of the dark little pubs frequented by
the "old hands." For a few hours he could recapture the
sense of camaraderie that had so appealed to him in the
Army. He and his fellow journalists belonged to a confra-
ternity that comprehended both more and less of what
was going on than the combatants in the eye of the storm.

Sometimes—always without success—the newcomers

tried to make sense of the situation in Northern Ireland to one another. The old hands, Barry among them, did not even try.

It was too frustrating.

When the number of Protestants killed began to exceed that of Catholics, Barry's photographs reflected the change in statistics. He made no attempt to disguise the brutality of either side but let the pictures speak for themselves.

His lens captured the stern immobility of two men in black balaclavas flanking the open coffin of a third man whose rosary was strung through his fingers. The shocked expression of a little girl crouching beside a pile of rubble from which a thin stream of blood trickled. The agonised grimace of a Protestant man helping to carry his best friend's coffin. Bypassers studiously ignoring the fact that armed British soldiers were questioning a terrified woman while her small son clung to her hand. The pathetic vulnerability of two naked feet visible from beneath the sheet that covered a body dumped on the side of the road.

In March Barry took a candid portrait of Merlyn Rees, the newly appointed secretary of state for Northern Ireland. Barry tellingly photographed Rees surrounded by members of the Ulster Workers Council, which had been founded the year before. The UWC was vehemently opposed to any sort of power sharing. Their grim expressions did not bode well for the future.

Barry, complete with two days' growth of stubble and a beer belly swelling beneath his clothes, slipped among them to take "snapshots" of the occasion. Many UWC members were doing the same thing. One or two even offered to buy him a drink later. He cheerfully bought his share of rounds in the nearest loyalist pub while condemning the IRA in a voice distorted by the strip of wax inside his lower lip.

His Merlyn Rees photographs were purchased by all the international news services.

Barbara was not happy about Barry's time across the border. "Surely there are enough subjects for you here in the Republic, and you'd be a lot safer."

"I'm safe as long as I do my work and mind my business."

"Why does your business have to be violence?"

"Those are the pictures editors want," he told her.

One night Barry returned from South Armagh very late to find Barbara still awake; lying naked on their bed in a provocative pose. She had worked hard to regain her figure since the baby was born and was proud of it. She wanted him to notice; wanted to see her success in his eyes.

"I've been waiting for you," she said throatily.

Her blatant sexuality startled Barry. Since Brian's birth he had carried a mental image, unlikely though he knew that image to be, of Barbara as madonna.

"Would you like to photograph me?" she invited.

He swallowed hard. "I must have a hundred pictures of you already."

"From our honeymoon! Take some of me now. Like this."

"I don't need to. I have only to close my eyes to see you in living colour in any pose I like."

She leaped from the bed, ran to her dressing room, and slammed the door. "I hate you, Barry Halloran, I *hate* you! You don't care about anything but your stupid war!"

ON the eleventh of March Keith and Kenneth Little-john, who had been convicted of membership in the IRA, escaped from prison. The subject was a matter of intense discussion among republicans. "Rumour has it," McCoy told the Usual Suspects in the Bleeding Horse, "that they both work for MI6." He added darkly, "Infiltrators. Informers."

In the United Kingdom the newly elected Labour prime minister, Harold Wilson, was beginning to exercise his power. April saw free family planning made available on the British National Health Service. Women in the Republic looked enviously across the border.

B ARBARA Halloran was not among them. She thought giving birth was the most wonderful thing that had ever happened to her. Her son was complete and perfect in every detail, like a great opera of which she was both creator and producer. Barry might be preoccupied but she always had Brian.

For a time she became oversolicitous. She insisted Brian's cot be placed next to their bed so she could check on him again and again in the night. Long before he could walk she bought an elaborate safety gate for the stairs.

"How are the boarders supposed to go up and down with that contraption?" McCoy queried.

"Well, they can step over it, can't they?"

McCoy complained to Barry. "I don't know what's got into the woman, but we can't block the stairs in a boardinghouse. Say something to her, Seventeen."

He did. Barbara accused him of not caring about his son's safety.

Once again the argument was loud and long, but in the end the gate was put away.

O N the night of April twenty-sixth Rose Dugdale rang the doorbell of Russborough House, an elegant mansion outside of Blessington in County Wicklow. The owner of Russborough was Sir Alfred Beit, a multimillionaire financier and renowned art collector. Sir Alfred was at home that evening. When the butler opened the door four men rushed out of the darkness and knocked him down. The gang then took Sir Alfred, Lady Beit, and the household staff into the library, and tied them up with nylon stockings.

The gang left with a massive haul: nineteen paintings,

some of them virtually priceless, including a Vermeer, three Rubenses, a Goya, and two Gainesboroughs.[2] The subsequent ransom demand included the release of republican prisoners in the north, but was never met.

B ARBARA invited her mother-in-law to a celebration of their second wedding anniversary. She did not invite her own mother. "I know Mom puts up a big front," she told Barry, "but she really can't afford to fly over here for every little thing."

"If our wedding anniversary is a 'little thing' why are you arranging such a big party?" he asked. "You've invited everyone who came to the wedding and the world and his wife as well. I don't know how we're going to fit them all in."

"We could if we had a larger house," Barbara replied airily.

Ursula travelled to Dublin a couple of days early to combine business with pleasure. A wealthy man from Wicklow who was interested in buying young hunters was driving up to meet her, and she planned to take him and his wife to dinner. To the delight of Séamus McCoy, she asked him to join them. "A dinner party goes much better with four than three," she explained. "They're landed gentry, they probably vote Fine Gael. But no one else has any money."

"I'll hold up my end," McCoy promised.

He hurried to Arnott's Department Store to buy a new suit.

Barry teased him unmercifully. "Some republican you are. Giving yourself airs just because you're going to dinner with the gentry."

But Barbara assured him he looked "very nice indeed" in his new suit.

The dinner was a success. While Ursula and the husband talked horses, McCoy noticed that the wife looked a little lost. *She talks like Brendan,* he thought, *so she must have had a fancy education.* Turning toward her, he said, "I'm not much into horses myself. Books are more my line."

She brightened at once. "Oh, really? What do you read?"

Anything about war or the IRA but I'd better not say that. "All sorts," he replied nonchalantly. "In fact, I collect old books." A wild exaggeration; only four or five of his battered assortment predated the twentieth century. But it was enough. The wife began telling him about the extensive library she had inherited. "You really must come down to us sometime," she enthused, "and spend a few days browsing. Do you know, we have some signed first editions of Dickens!"

Once or twice Ursula glanced across the table at the dedicated republican and the daughter of the Ascendancy deep in conversation. *There's more to that man than meets the eye,* she told herself.

After dinner she and McCoy took a taxi back to Harold's Cross. Ursula was in a buoyant mood. The man from Wicklow had arranged to meet her at the farm the following weekend—chequebook in hand. "I really need that sale," Ursula admitted. "For years I've been hanging on by my fingernails, like most people are. Now things seem to be going right at last. Little Brian, Barry, and Barbara . . . although just between us, Séamus, there was a time I would not have given tuppence for their marriage lasting one year, never mind two."

McCoy had entertained similar feelings, but kept them to himself. "Why not?" he asked.

"They're too different in some ways. And too much alike in others."

"You have that right. They're as stubborn as each other."

"I know. They're both incapable of compromise and compromise is essential for a good relationship. Of course, what do I know about relationships," Ursula added with a self-deprecating laugh. "I've never been married."

This was news to Séamus McCoy. *Seventeen never*

mentioned that little detail. She must have loved someone sometime, though, because she had his son. And reared the boy all by herself! He was filled with admiration for her courage.

On the first of May Barbara not only produced a lavish anniversary party but starred in it as well, holding centre stage with accomplished ease. At Barry's request she sang two Thomas Moore songs and a selection of jazz numbers. She received numerous compliments on her voice and went to bed that night in a radiant mood.

"I think 1974 is going to be our lucky year," she whispered to her husband. In the dark she reached out for him.

In the dark he tangled his fingers in her hair.

Chapter Fourteen

THE Ulster Workers Council and a number of Unionist politicians combined with loyalist paramilitary groups, such as the UVF and the Ulster Defence Association, in an attempt to undermine the Sunningdale Agreement. Prominent among the enemies of any form of power sharing was the Vanguard Party. At the forefront was Ian Paisley.

On the fourteenth of May the UWC called a general strike for Northern Ireland. Paramilitary intimidation was employed to force working-class Protestants to take part. Masked men in camouflage jackets appeared around the Northern Ireland Office. There were rumours that MI5, the British internal intelligence force, was supporting the anti-Sunningdale faction. When the British army refused to break the strike the hand of the extremists was strengthened.

Brian Faulkner and Merlyn Rees seemed powerless to handle the situation.

In London Harold Wilson's government began secretly drawing up a Doomsday Scenario in readiness for a possible British withdrawal from the north of Ireland.[1]

T H E man from Wicklow bought all six of Ursula's three-year-old hunter prospects. She hired a horse van and delivered them herself, then drove up to Dublin to tell her family, "He never blinked at the price!" Her eyes were dancing. "It means we'll be able to put a new roof on the big barn now."

Barry persuaded her to remain at Harold's Cross through the weekend and get a bit of rest before driving the van back to Clare. Barbara was still in a good mood from the success of her party. The two women chatted like old friends; Ursula even helped her daughter-in-law with the washing-up.

The seventeenth of May was a mild, occasionally showery day in Dublin, with long spells of radiant sunshine. After lunch Ursula expressed a desire to go into town to buy a present for the baby. *And something nice for Barbara too,* she decided.

There was a bus strike in the city, so in midafternoon Barry transported his mother in the Austin Healey. At her request he left her in O'Connell Street. "Get your messages,"* he said, "and I'll collect you in front of Clery's around six. Until then I'll be taking photographs in the Phoenix Park."

Ursula stood watching until the little green car was swallowed up by traffic, which was heavier than usual due to the strike. Mention of the Phoenix Park had struck a responsive chord in her. *The last time I was in the park was*

*Do your shopping.

*with Finbar Cassidy. Can it really have been more than
forty years ago? So much has happened since then. My
years with Radio Éireann. Switzerland and the League of
Nations. Barry. The Second World War.*

She gave herself a mental shake. *Stop maundering and
get on with it, Ursula. Look to the living.*

Others might patronise the fashionable shops in Grafton
Street, but Ursula preferred the north side of the city.
Prices were lower because the residents were poorer. Yet
there was a yeasty flavour to life north of the Liffey; a
stubborn zest for living in spite of hardship. Northsiders
spoke a colourful language of their own, peppered with
profanities so wittily crafted they did not sound profane.

As she went from shop to shop Ursula listened for the
word play that had inspired her own creativity with language. Sadly, it was getting harder to find. The language
of the streets was coarsening; degenerating into unimagi-
native vulgarity. *Every other word seems to be fuck,* she
thought in disgust. *If the people were poor at least their
speech was rich. What are we losing?*

She was no longer certain she remembered being rescued by Ned Halloran and she recalled nothing of her life
before then, neither the tenements where she had lived
nor the mother who had abandoned her. But the grimy,
littered streets captured her feet the way the ruts in the
farm laneway captured automobile tyres.

How well she knew this place!

The mingled smells of cheap clothing and homemade
cigarettes. Red-faced men drinking quantities of porter.
Mothers pushing shabby prams their infants had out-
grown, now piled high with coal or pawnable goods to exchange for enough money to feed their families this
week. Thin children in hand-me-down clothes.

And the colourful cries of the women selling fish and
fruit in Moore Street. *When I worked in Radio Éireann I
had a furnished room above the greengrocer's shop in*

Moore Street. There was a faded blue door, and a gaslight. One night Finbar and I climbed those stairs together . . .

Finbar Cassidy. Dead all these years, yet today he had walked back into her mind. Once or twice she even glanced around, half expecting to see his warm brown eyes smiling at her.

Is there still a greengrocer in Moore Street these days? With flats above? Is the door painted blue? With an effort she resisted the temptation to enter Moore Street. Instead, when her shopping was completed, Ursula went to the Venezian Café in Parnell Street for a cup of tea. On a sudden impulse she ordered a scone as well. *Louise made such wonderful scones at Number Sixteen.*

Louise Kearney, Henry Mooney's cousin, had once owned a boardinghouse at Number Sixteen Gardiner Street. A little girl called Precious had lived there with Ned and Síle Halloran.

Ned and Síle. And Uncle Henry.

Gathering up her parcels, Ursula left her cup of tea going cold on the table.

Does everyone look backwards with such longing? she asked herself as the door of the café closed behind her. *Why do we not appreciate the time we're in? The future is the problem. We keep looking ahead instead of looking around.*

She began walking. Following familiar pavements.

If only I could return to the Dublin I knew with Ned and Síle; Dublin dear and shabby and innocent in a way that no city is innocent now.

Does it all still exist somewhere like a gemstone set in a ring? If I follow the ring all the way around will I come to the stone again?

She walked down O'Connell Street toward Clery's Department Store, joining a heavy stream of pedestrian traffic. It was Friday afternoon and the shops were closing. People were eager to go home.

So was Precious.

When she came to the corner of North Earl Street she

could see the big clock in front of Clery's. *Not yet five-thirty. There's enough time, then.* She turned left into North Earl Street, which became Talbot Street and would take her to Gardiner Street. Her steps quickened.

The past seemed very close now. She could almost reach out and touch it.

Talbot Street was busy from the bus terminus at one end to the train station at the other. Pedestrians thronged the pavement and a number of cars were parked along the kerbs. As Ursula approached the junction with Gardiner Street she heard a huge *thump* in the distance; somewhere behind her, she thought. Glancing around, she saw nothing out of the ordinary. Some of her fellow pedestrians hesitated. A woman with three children turned and started back toward O'Connell Street.

Ursula resumed walking toward Gardiner Street.

She thought she heard a whistle followed by a thunderous roar. Then past and present collided, and the wall beside her exploded into a deadly rain of bricks and mortar.

THREE bombs exploded almost simultaneously in Dublin with no warning given. The first and largest was in a car parked in Parnell Street. Another car bomb was left in South Leinster Street beside the perimeter wall of Trinity College. The third was in Talbot Street. Their combined death toll would be twenty-six; over three hundred were injured. The dead and dying, intermingled with building wreckage and unidentifiable human remains, lay on both sides of the Liffey.

Ninety minutes later another bomb exploded in the town of Monaghan, close to the border with Northern Ireland. Seven more people died. May seventeenth would prove to be the bloodiest single day in the bloody history of the Troubles.

·   ·   ·

B ARRY enjoyed his afternoon in the Phoenix Park. The deer that roamed the park allowed him to come quite close as they grazed. Curious fawns stared at him with big bright eyes, unconsciously posing for their portraits. He followed them on a long ramble across rolling meadows and through sun-dappled woods, taking numerous photographs. He could not remember when he had felt so peaceful, so at one with the universe.

Barbara can't call these pictures sad. Maybe we'll frame the best of them to hang in Brian's room.

He was about to return to his car—and cursing himself for having wandered so far, because his bad leg was aching—when he heard the first bomb.

Barry knew instantly what it was. The explosion came from north of the Liffey, probably somewhere around the GPO. He began to run.

He was halfway back to the Austin Healey when he heard the next bomb go off.

By the time he reached his car the city's rarely used alarm bells were ringing. At the park gates he discovered that traffic was already jammed along the quays. Refusing to back down for anyone, Barry nosed the Austin Healey into the mass of automobiles and lorries headed towards O'Connell Bridge.

Dublin's main hospitals were already on standby. The first ambulances were on the road sixty seconds after the alarm bell was sounded, and off-duty staff was being recalled to help with the dead and injured. Following the second explosion Dublin's one-way street system was abolished. The Dublin Fire Brigade and the Stillorgan Ambulance Service arrived at the bomb sites within minutes. Makeshift emergency centres were being set up around the city. A decision was made to take victims from Talbot Street to the dancehall in the basement of Moran's Hotel, which was within yards of the blast.[2]

Barry was able to drive no farther than the Ha'penny

Bridge. From there on, nothing was moving. He swung his little car onto the pavement at the foot of the bridge, leaped out, and sprinted to O'Connell Street. Dublin's main thoroughfare was thronged with frightened, hysterical people. Looking over their heads, Barry could see the major congestion appeared to be around Clery's.

He began working his way toward the big department store. *She must be there somewhere. Maybe she was already waiting out front when it . . . when the bomb . . .* He slammed a door on the mental images. He could do nothing if he surrendered to them.

Uniformed members of the Dublin police were forcing the milling crowd back in order to let ambulances through. Barry tried to get information from someone; anyone. "Did you see a small grey-haired woman in front of Clery's? Do you know what happened to her?"

Too many people were asking similar questions. No one had answers.

At last a harried policeman paused to tell Barry, "There was a bomb in Talbot Street. Call to the hospitals. If she was injured she'll probably be sent to Jervis Street or the Rotunda, they're nearest."

"Jervis Street," Barry repeated numbly. *Is that an omen?*

"If she's dead," the policeman continued, "sooner or later they'll take her to the—"

"I know." Barry interrupted the man before he could say "morgue." Taking advantage of his towering height, Barry forced his way through total chaos step by step. Until he entered Talbot Street.

And saw what the bomb had done.

PHILPOTT was growing a little deaf. He turned up the radio in the kitchen to a level Barbara found almost unbearable. She warned him he would wake the baby sleeping upstairs but he paid no attention; perhaps he could not hear her. Exasperated, she stopped peeling potatoes and turned down the volume herself.

"Did you hear that?" she asked suddenly.

"Sorry?"

"It sounded like a fire alarm."

"I didn't hear anything. Are you ready with those potatoes? I need them for the stew." He turned the radio up again.

Barbara suffered in silence for a few minutes, then lowered the volume until it was almost inaudible. "Now leave it," she ordered.

When the six o'clock news came on she only heard snatches of the newsreader's voice, but enough to alarm her. Reaching past Philpott, she spun the volume to full on.

He protested, "I thought you said . . ."

The voice blared into the room. "We repeat, there have been several large explosions in the centre of Dublin within the last half hour. We will give further details as soon as we receive them. Meanwhile people are being urged to avoid the areas around O'Connell Street and Trinity College."

Barbara gave a shriek and covered her mouth with both hands.

McCoy berated himself for not accompanying Ursula into the city. "Thank God you didn't," said Barbara, "I need you here." She had run upstairs to get the baby and was holding him tightly clamped against her breasts. Too tightly; little Brian wriggled valiantly in an attempt to gain his freedom.

For Barbara's sake McCoy kept his worries to himself. "Whatever's happened, Seventeen'll deal with it. He's mighty altogether in an emergency. They'll both be home soon, he told me they'd be here for tea." He forced a smile. "You and Philpott best get the meal ready."

But Barry and Ursula did not come home.

As the first boarders straggled in one reported, "Dublin

looks like Berlin in the last days of the war." Another elaborated, "There's wreckage all over the place, and the ambulance drivers are picking up body parts."

Barbara caught him by the arm. Her urgent fingers would leave bruises. "Did you see Barry down there?"

"Didn't see anyone I know. Or if I did, I didn't recognise them. You can't imagine what it's like."

She couldn't, but McCoy could. *Barry,* he kept thinking. *Ursula. Ursula!*

The boardinghouse was one of the few in the neighbourhood that had a private telephone. Soon people were coming to the door and pleading to ring the hospitals. "It's no use," McCoy had to tell them. "I've already rung all of them and they aren't giving out information yet."

For those waiting desperately for some news of their loved ones, the evening of May seventeenth lasted for a hundred years. A police cordon around the Talbot Street area did not prevent a huge crowd from entering the Pro-Cathedral to pray.

That night Taoiseach Liam Cosgrave appeared on RTE to say, "I want to express the revulsion and condemnation felt by every decent person on this island at these unforgivable acts." Then he solemnly promised the country his government would do everything possible to see the culprits brought to justice. The minister for justice held a press conference at government buildings to announce the Gardai were launching a huge manhunt. Within an hour the Gardai issued their own statement, reporting the RUC had established that two of the cars used in the bombings had been hijacked in loyalist areas of Belfast that same morning.

It was the last report on the matter that the Irish government would release to the nation.

However, the British government received a report from the British ambassador to Ireland, Sir Arthur Galsworthy, in which he commented with satisfaction that the bombings had hardened attitudes against the republican movement,

and given the Irish people an insight into the views of
northern Protestants.

The ambassador concluded, "I think the Irish have
taken the point."[3]

Chapter Fifteen

O N May eighteenth RTE informed viewers and listen-
ers that the Dublin death toll was the largest for any single
incident since World War Two, when German bombs
dropped on the North Strand had killed forty-three people.

The *Evening Press* described the scene at Dublin City
Morgue. Hundreds of distraught relatives had viewed the
bomb-mutilated corpses, hoping they would not find a
beloved face.

Several papers carried a quote from Sammy Smith, the
press officer for the Ulster Workers Council: "I am very
happy about the bombings in Dublin. There is a war with
the Free State and now we are laughing at them."[1]

On the nineteenth of May Merlyn Rees declared a state
of emergency and flew to Chequers to talk with the British
prime minister.

A new song was making its way up the charts. From the
hit musical *Joseph and the Amazing Technicolor Dream
Coat* came "Any Dream Will Do."

F A R , far, far away, bees were droning in the clover. It must
be summer then. Summer on the farm. Aunt Eileen would

be gathering the honey. If she was a very good girl she would be given a piece of honeycomb.

Ursula smiled in her sleep.

The droning grew louder; turned into a mumblevoice. Disturbed her pretty dream. "Go away," she thought she said.

The irritating mumblevoice turned into intelligible words. Words pulling Ursula away from the fragrant fields in spite of all she could do, dragging her into a tunnel of roiling clouds where she soared and spun helplessly until she was tumbled onto something solid.

When she opened her eyes she saw only a haze. Then her vision cleared.

She gasped. "You can't have him!"

Father Michael bent down. The head on the pillow was swathed in gauze, all he could see were two grey-blue eyes. Young eyes. "Have who, my child?"

"My baby. He's not ill . . . illegitimate," she said with an effort. Pain had seized her; was shaking her in relentless jaws. "I'm not illegitimate. We are . . . legitimate human beings."

"I'm sure you are, my child." The priest straightened up. Turning to the doctor who had summoned him, he said, "Last rites may be premature."

"That's good news for her son."

"Where is he?"

"Asleep on a bench in the waiting room."

"His relatives must take him home at once!" said the priest. "One can't have infants sleeping on benches in the waiting room."

The doctor gave a weary chuckle. "Some infant. He's six and a half feet tall with the constitution of an ox. This is the first time he's slept since we brought her in. I was going to waken him once you'd given her last rites."

"Let him sleep a bit longer," the priest advised.

After an hour a nurse woke Barry to tell him his mother had regained consciousness. He rushed to the ward she shared with five other victims of the bombings. Ursula was in the bed at the far end of the room, immobilised in a co-coon of plaster and bandages. Only one hand was free. It lay atop the sheet like an injured bird. When Barry took it in his, her eyes rolled toward him.

"I'm right here, Ursula, and I'll be here as long as you need me. Don't try to talk now, just get better." Without relinquishing her hand he sat down in a chair beside the bed. She gazed at his face until she fell asleep again—a natural sleep, the nurse assured him.

He left Ursula's side long enough to use the nearest telephone. McCoy answered on the first ring. Barry's re-lieved voice rang down the line. "She's regained con-sciousness, Séamus!"

Barbara and McCoy took turns visiting the hospital so one of them would always be in Harold's Cross with little Brian. Barbara came by taxi and brought fresh clothes for Barry. "You should have phoned me Friday night," she scolded; not for the first time. "I nearly went crazy worry-ing about you."

"I was looking for Ursula," he explained yet again.

"You could have stopped long enough to get to a tele-phone."

"Everyone was fighting for telephones, there was no point. Besides, I thought they would take her to Jervis Street so I kept going back there. It was Saturday morn-ing before I learned she was here in the Rotunda. That's when I rang you."

Barbara was not really listening. "I was terrified, I imagined the most awful things had happened to you."

Barry put his arms around her and rested his chin on top of her head. "I'm all right, sweetheart. Don't you re-member? They couldn't kill me with an axe."

When McCoy arrived he told Barry, "Paudie Coates lo-cated a duplicate key, so he took me to collect your car. We found it right where you said, with your cameras still in the boot."

"I don't even remember putting them in. Where's Apollo now?"

"Parked out front. I'm driving it." McCoy braced himself for an argument.

"That's all right then," Barry said absently.

"Any chance of me seeing Ursula?"

"Not yet, Séamus. Right now they won't allow any visitors but me."

WHILE Ursula fought for life in her hospital bed Northern Ireland underwent its own crisis. The UWC strike paralysed the province and temporarily destroyed its economy. Men marched up and down the streets brandishing placards; other men shouted vehemently into microphones and television cameras. The climax came when extremist politicians, loyalist paramilitaries, and trade union activists from the Harland and Wolff shipyard joined a vast parade of farm machinery to clog the great avenue leading up to Stormont.

Unwilling or unable to face down such intransigence, the British discarded the power-sharing initiative. The Sunningdale Agreement, which had offered so much hope only five months earlier, collapsed.

URSULA'S first coherent question to her son was not about her own condition. "Is the baby all right?" When he assured her little Brian was fine, she said, "What about my horses?"

"Don't worry, I've already contacted Paul Morrissey. He's going to manage the farm until you're home again."

"Paul Morrissey?"

"You remember him, Ursula," Barry said patiently. "He owns the farm just north of yours. Four big strapping sons. Horse-crazy twin daughters."

She forced herself to concentrate. *Forget the pain. Wipe*

it away. Think. Think! "Dorothy and Eleanor. They're . . . fourteen."

"They are."

Ursula gave a satisfied sigh and went back to sleep.

The next time she awoke Father Michael was at her bedside. When she saw the dog collar she closed her eyes again. The priest stayed where he was.

A dark presence hovering. Like death. Well, I'm not ready. "I don't want you," she said aloud.

"You need me," he assured her.

"I need a doctor."

"My concern is not with your bodily health, but your immortal soul."

"My soul's fine," she said peevishly.

"Are you in a state of grace, my child?"

"I seriously doubt it."

The priest frowned at her chart. "You *are* a Catholic, are you not?"

· Her reply shocked him. "I believe in the creator of the universe. I don't believe in organised religion."

Barry rented a furnished room within yards of the Rotunda. He used it for sleeping; the rest of the time he was at the hospital. He never went out, and he had no desire to photograph the devastation the bombs had caused. The camera had served as a filter between himself and many dire scenes, but it could not filter out his imagination. He knew he would see his mother lying in the rubble.

The anger was growing in him again. Growing, and growing.

T H E Ulster Volunteer Force denied any responsibility for the bombings, yet within hours of the events reliable informants had reported that two cells of the organisation had been involved. One group had driven down from Belfast to attack Dublin. Others, from nearby Cavan, were responsible for the bombing in Monaghan.[2]

The sophistication of the four bombs far exceeded the technology of the loyalist paramilitaries. Experts in the Republic had realised very quickly that the bombings could not have been carried out without collusion on the part of the RUC—and possibly elements of British Intelligence as well. To make such a claim would be to accuse Britain of having bombed another sovereign nation. Under international law, that was an act of war.

When notified by the British authorities that several suspects were being held in custody in Northern Ireland, the Irish government did not react. The RUC invited members of the Garda Siochana to come north and sit in on interrogation of the suspects, but they declined.

Instead of bringing the full force of the law to bear in finding the murderers and bringing them to justice, the Fine Gael/Labour coalition set out to use the atrocity to further its own anti-republican agenda. Conor Cruise O'Brien, minister for posts and telegraphs, blamed republicans for "provoking" the loyalists.

The bombings disappeared from the media headlines. Few of the victims' families were even offered condolences by their local politicians. No national day of mourning was announced. The national flag was not flown at half-mast. No fund was set up for the dependents of the murder victims, nor was any support or counselling offered to them.

The Department of Justice files on the bombings went missing, never to surface again.

In a reverse of the IRA slogan, "One bomb in London is worth a hundred in Belfast," the loyalists had proved that one bomb in Dublin was worth a hundred in Belfast. The Irish government was so frightened by the events in Dublin-Monaghan that they would turn their collective backs on the north for years, preferring to act as if the Six Counties and their problems did not exist.

.   .   .

Ursula hated hospitals and everything to do with them. Most of all she hated being helpless. *Trapped in a plaster mummy case!* When she sneezed and a nurse enquired, "Do we need to blow our nose?" Ursula replied coldly, "I wasn't aware we shared a common nose, but if you need to blow yours, go ahead. It's big enough."

On Wednesday night the Usual Suspects met in the Bleeding Horse.

"Every dog and devil knows it was the UVF what done it," said Patsy.

Luke added, "This is one atrocity they don't dare beat the drum about, though. It might turn their supporters in Whitehall* against them."

"Unless Whitehall had a hand in it," Danny muttered darkly.

"The bombings made the international papers," said Brendan. "I usually purchase *Le Monde* at the news agency across from Trinity, but with the streets blocked off I had to walk for half a mile to find a copy. They're calling this 'a Protestant backlash.' "[3]

Danny was clenching and unclenching his big fists. The gnarled knuckles resembled the roots of some ancient oak tree pushing up from the earth. "If I was five years younger I'd go north tomorrow and give 'em the same as they gave us."

"We already have," Brendan reminded him. "It was called Bloody Friday. We bomb and shoot them and they shoot and bomb us. Where is it going to end?" He shook his head wearily. "Where is it going to end at all?"

Ursula begged her son for news of the outside world. "They won't let me have a radio," she complained.

"They're trying to keep you quiet for your own good. Listen here while I tell you about Brian instead. He's amazing; not yet a year old and he's trying to stand up. Barbara says he's precocious."

*British government buildings.

"Talk to me about Talbot Street, Barry."

"Absolutely not!"

"I can't believe it happened again," she said, with wonder in her voice.

He wished he could see the expression beneath her bandages. "What do you mean 'again,' Ursula?"

"British artillery blew Dublin to pieces in 1916. Síle was holding my hand and we were trying to get away." Her breathing grew laboured but she was determined to go on. "I heard a strange whistling sound, then everything went black. I heard the same sound in Talbot Street, Barry. The *same sound*," she stressed.

"Ursula, the bomb in Talbot Street used gelignite; I could smell it. Believe me when I tell you it couldn't have made a whistling noise."

"But I heard it. I heard it!"

When McCoy arrived as he did every day, Barry said, "Will you stay with her while I have a little chat with her doctor? Don't be surprised if she rambles a bit, Séamus, she took a frightful knock on the head."

He found the doctor he sought in another ward, surrounded by anxious relatives all trying to talk to him at once. Barry waited with barely controlled impatience until he was able to get the man's attention. "My mother seems confused today."

"Ah . . . yes. We need to talk, Mr. Halloran." Taking Barry by the elbow, the doctor steered him into the corridor and around a corner. "Your mother's mental state is due to her concussion and the medication she's on. There is a more serious problem. We're able to deal with her lower-body injuries, but she also has suffered damage to the spinal cord."

"Can you operate?"

"Not in this case. We simply don't know enough about spinal cord injuries."

"Will it heal on its own?"

The doctor allowed his professional mask to slip just

enough to reveal the human beneath. "I wish I could say yes, but that would be giving you false hope. I'm afraid your mother will never walk again."

When Barry returned to the ward McCoy glanced up. "Your face is as long as a wet winter, Seventeen."

Barry gave a tiny nod to indicate he wanted to speak to him outside. Ursula's sharp eyes noticed the gesture. "What's wrong?"

"Nothing's wrong," Barry assured her. "It's just some business about the boardinghouse."

McCoy followed Barry into the corridor. He listened with his head down and his arms folded across his chest; as stolid as an ox waiting for the axe to fall. "You sure you got it right, Seventeen? Maybe you didn't understand the medical jargon."

"I understood him, I just can't take it in." Barry struggled to keep his emotions under tight control. "Some people flinch their way through life, Séamus, but Ursula strides through hers. I can't imagine her any other way."

"Oh Christ. Oh Christ." McCoy stared at the floor. *They didn't care who she was or what she was, they just ruined her life.* "The fuckin' Orange bastards," he said in a guttural monotone that did not sound like him at all. "Ye fuckin' planters' shit, may you and all your breed roast in hell."

What the hell can I do for her now?

What the hell can I do?

McCoy did not notice when Barry left him to return to the ward. He had forgotten about Barry, the boardinghouse, everything else. The only job he had left was becoming clear. He was being steadied and aimed like a rifle to carry out his sole objective. His sacred duty.

When Barry sat down by his mother's bed Ursula asked anxiously, "What's wrong?"

When did she start sounding anxious? He hated lying

to her, but this was one time when he must. "Nothing's wrong," he said calmly. Taking a book of poetry out of his pocket, he began reading aloud. His eyes and lips co-ordinated the endeavour; his mind was somewhere else. More than an hour passed before he realised McCoy had not returned. It was unthinkable that he would leave without telling Ursula good-bye. "I'll be back in a minute," Barry said.

McCoy was not in the corridor; not at the nurses' station; not in the lobby nor the coffee shop.

Not in the hospital.

When Barry went outside there was no sign of the Austin Healey anywhere. He returned to the lobby and rang the boardinghouse. "Is Séamus there, Barbara?"

"He came in a little while ago and got that old pack of his, then he went out again."

"Did he take my car?"

"No, it's still parked outside."

Barry's next phone call was to the Bleeding Horse. "Is Séamus anywhere around?" he asked the bartender.

"Not a whisker of him, Barry. Why, did he go missing?"

"I don't know yet. Who else is in there? The Professor?"

"Only Patsy, propping up the bar. But he's always here, you'd think he had no home to go to."

"If Séamus does come in tell him I'm looking for him, will you?"

O n the twenty-eighth of May Merlyn Rees announced, "There is now no statutory basis for the Northern Ireland Executive." Brian Faulkner resigned as chief executive. The UWC had won. The Sunningdale Agreement was brought down; power sharing in Northern Ireland was consigned to the scrap heap of history.

·   ·   ·

Barry read selected items from the newspapers to Ursula. One reporter had described the Ulster Workers Council as "A plucky little band of Ulstermen who have brought London to its knees."

"Plucky little band indeed!" Barry said sarcastically. "All they had in their arsenal was the British army, the RUC, a half-dozen power stations, an airport, a ferry terminal, and four-fifths of the civil service. Not to mention the BBC, which was happy to broadcast any information the loyalists fed them—power blackouts, surgery cancellations, petrol shortages—anything that would keep people in a state of anxiety. Like his ancient namesake, this Merlyn's waved a magic wand. And made democracy disappear."

"What does Séamus have to say about it?" Ursula's voice was querulous. "Why doesn't he come to see me anymore?"

"I'm keeping him too busy these days," Barry replied. With practice it was getting easier to lie to his mother. "We had a lot of projects planned for this spring and summer and we have to take advantage of the good weather while it lasts."

Though he would continue the search for several days, he knew it was futile.

Séamus McCoy had gone up the road.

Chapter Sixteen

I<small>N</small> June six members of the IRA serving time in English prisons were on hunger strike, protesting the appalling conditions in which they were being kept. Two young women who had been convicted of bombing the Old Bailey, Marion and Dolours Price, attracted the most media attention. But some of the men were nearer death. When Michael Gaughan died on the third of June in Parkhurst Prison the IRA responded immediately.

A bomb exploded on the seventeenth in Westminster Hall, injuring eleven people. However, another story was still in the headlines: the IRA kidnapping of Lord and Lady Donoughmore.

The wealthy British peer owned an eighteenth-century mansion, Knocklofty House, in County Kildare. On the day following Gaughan's death a rogue IRA unit had been driving around the Irish countryside, guided by a copy of *The Stately Homes of Ireland,* looking for someone prominent to kidnap to force the British to end the stalemate over the remaining hunger strikers. When the elderly Lord and Lady Donoughmore returned home in full evening dress from a night out, they were violently seized and carried away.

The initial violence did not last. While they were being held in a safe house, Lord Donoughmore later related in his diary, the leader of the gang, a Belfast man called Eddie Gallagher, personally cooked a traditional Irish fry-up for his hostages with the best eggs they had ever tasted.

While the couple waited to know their fate—listening

to news on the radio and working crossword puzzles—six hundred people met at a rally in the nearby town of Clonmel to demand their release.

On the seventh of June the Price sisters went off their hunger strike in Brixton Jail as a result of negotiations with the British; negotiations that had nothing to do with the kidnapping of the Donoughmores, who were not nearly as prominent in British society as Gallagher's gang had believed. In an early example of the so-called Stockholm Syndrome, the Donoughmores had grown genuinely fond of their captors. They felt only gratitude when on Saturday they were driven to Dublin and released unharmed at the Parkgate entrance of the Phoenix Park.

The negotiations that did not concern them had taken place in Northern Ireland between senior British officials and members of the republican leadership, including Seán MacStiofáin and Dáithí Ó Conaill of the Dublin IRA, Séamus Twomey the Belfast commandant, Martin McGuinness from Derry, and Sinn Féin's Gerry Adams, who had been released from Long Kesh to take part.

On the twenty-second of June the IRA announced a ceasefire. Further talks were to go ahead in London on the seventh of July.

The loyalists promptly stepped up their assassination campaign against Catholics in the north.

A t the end of the month Ursula's plaster mummy case was removed. Her wizened, shrunken body horrified her. "Don't let my son see me like this," she pleaded. Using chocolates Barbara had given her, she bribed a nurse to purchase two voluminous flannel nightgowns that would cover her from neck to toe.

I n July Gerry Adams went to London with the IRA contingent meeting British representatives to discuss "a way forward" in the north. The talks disintegrated into a show of temper on both sides. The republicans felt the British had no intention of ameliorating their position, and would always side with the unionists to the detriment of northern nationalists.

All bets were off. The republicans flew home.

ÉAMONN MacThomáis completed his prison sentence that month and resumed his duties as editor of *An Phoblacht*.

In the British House of Commons Merlyn Rees announced vague plans to phase out internment gradually. Amorphous promises for the unspecified future were not enough, however. The IRA responded by setting off bombs in Birmingham, Manchester, and the Tower of London. The bomb in the Tower killed one person and injured a number of others.

ACTING "as a matter of conscience,"[1] Taoiseach Liam Cosgrave voted against his own government's bill proposing the regulation of contraception. On July sixteenth the bill was defeated by seventy-five votes to sixty-one.

PORTLAOISE Prison in County Laois was a prime example of the Irish government's attitude toward the IRA. The *taoiseach*'s father, William Cosgrave, had been a leader of the victorious Free State side in the Civil War. His son Liam's motto was, "We did it before and we'll do it again."[2] Under his administration Portlaoise had become infamous for denying basic privileges to republican prisoners, fights, beatings, and torture beyond the usual rough treatment accorded prisoners by their guards.

On the eighteenth of August 1974, nineteen republicans blasted their way out of Portlaoise. A member of the republican "escape committee" had noticed a breach in security near the laundry house, a small door that opened onto the street outside. The republicans then set themselves to making imitation guards' uniforms that fooled the real guards long enough to allow them to plant a small bomb to blow open the door and make good their escape.

S PINAL injuries are tricky, we simply don't know enough about them," Ursula's doctor told Barry. "We've done all we can for your mother in hospital. With assistance she's able to sit up for brief periods, and her bladder and bowels are functioning satisfactorily. Because she insists her pain has reached a tolerable level we've reduced her medication. I hesitate to recommend sending her to a convalescent facility, however. I doubt if a woman of her spirit would thrive in that environment. Will you be able to care for her at home?"

"The farm?"

"Oh no, she needs to be close to a major hospital where a doctor can examine her at least every few months. I meant your home here in Dublin."

Barry did not anticipate a pleasant conversation with Barbara that afternoon. To his surprise she met him at the front door. Before he could speak she said, "This letter just came in the post. It's addressed to me, so I opened it. But it doesn't make any sense." She handed Barry a small, grubby envelope, containing a single cigarette paper folded in half.

Written in pencil on the small scrap was, "17. Been lifted. In the Kesh."

There was no signature.

"I thought it must be for you," Barbara said, "because of the 17. But what does lifted mean? And what's the Kesh?"

"Séamus has been caught and sent to Long Kesh. It's a prison in Northern Ireland."

"Prison! Oh, Barry, that sweet man—and he is a sweet man, I didn't realise it until now." Her eyes began to glitter with tears. "What a terrible year, first your mother and now Séamus. It's like God is angry with us."

"God had nothing to do with this," Barry said grimly. He gathered her into his arms and rested his chin on her head.

Against his chest, she said in a muffled voice, "You didn't want him to go north, why wouldn't he listen to you?"

"Séamus is his own man, Barbara. He did what he thought is right."

She pulled back to look up at him. "You think seeking revenge is right?"

"Did you never want revenge for your father's death?"

"That's different."

"It is not different, it's the same emotion."

"Maybe," she conceded. "But I didn't do anything about it."

"Because you had no way to. Séamus did."

"And look where it got him! What are we going to do, Barry? Can we pay his bail or something?"

"I doubt it. He's probably been interned, which means they can hold him as long as they like without bail or trial."

"That's ghastly!" She began to sob in earnest.

"That's British law."

While Barbara was agonising over McCoy Barry told her, "At least there's one bright light in all of this. We're going to have Ursula with us. The doctor said I can bring her home as soon as we can get things ready for her."

LONG Kesh, "the long bog," was the site of a former World War Two air base some eight miles from Belfast. Prisoners were housed in metal-roofed Nissan huts.

Clusters of four or five huts were enclosed by a steel mesh fence, forming what was accurately called a Cage. The prison compound contained over twenty Cages that were enclosed within a twelve-foot-high steel mesh fence topped by two double rows of razor wire. The entire area was overlooked by guard towers manned by soldiers equipped with searchlights and orders to shoot to kill.

On the other side of the fence was a no-go zone with British soldiers encamped.

Brian Faulkner had once remarked that the place looked like a German concentration camp; an accurate description.

A number of IRA Volunteers—invariably described as terrorists in the media—were interned in Long Kesh. Following Bloody Sunday the British government had granted the republicans Special Category Status in recognition of the fact that they were fighting for a political cause.

Within Long Kesh there were loyalist paramilitaries as well. They were not called terrorists. Nor did they have Special Category Status.

THE full import of Ursula's impending arrival struck Barbara when a van with "Hospital Rentals" on the side pulled up in front of the yellow brick house. She watched with growing dismay as a very large mechanical bed and a commode chair were unloaded.

"Where do you want these, missus?"

"We're going to use one of the downstairs rooms for now. I just hope that bed will fit in there. Come, I'll show you the way." *I'll have to be a full-time nurse. Plus taking care of Brian, plus running this house . . . damn you, Séamus McCoy! How could you run off and leave us like this? Don't you ever think of anyone but yourself?*

Later that afternoon she was standing at the front door

with Brian in her arms—*Let him see how much I have to do already!*—when the Austin Healey pulled up to the kerb. Barry gently lifted his mother out of the car and carried her to the house.

"Didn't you bring a wheelchair?" Barbara asked him.

Ursula said sharply, "I'm not a cripple!"

With Barbara following behind, Barry carried his mother to her room. "Where's Séamus?" she asked him. "Why isn't he here to meet me?"

"I'll explain later, Ursula, let's get you settled first."

"Tell me now," she said as he laid her on the bed. "Whatever it is, tell me now. Where is Séamus McCoy?"

"Give me a chance, will you? Barbara, put Brian down for a minute and help me here."

Ursula caught her son's wrist in one frail hand. "*Now,*" she said.

Barry knew that tone. No further dissembling would be allowed. "Séamus has been arrested," he said.

Ursula blinked. "For what?"

"I don't know the details yet."

"When was he arrested?"

"I don't know that either; it happened some time after he left here."

"Séamus left here? Of his own accord? When?"

Barry was finding the conversation increasingly painful. "After we were told you would never walk again."

"So you've been lying about him all this time, when you know how I feel about lying!"

Unnoticed by either of them, Barbara carried Brian out of the room. She did not enjoy scenes unless they were of her own making.

"Séamus went back to active service," Barry told his mother. "I think it was because he wanted revenge for what happened to you."

The little bit of colour that had returned to Ursula's face vanished.

When Barry came out of his mother's room a few

minutes later, Barbara ambushed him. "Why did you order such a big bed? Wouldn't a single one do?"

"She needs to be as comfortable as we can possibly make her. She's used to a full-sized bed on the farm so I want her to have one here."

"How am I supposed to take care of a bedridden invalid and Brian too? It's crazy, Barry, I can't do it. Séamus is gone and Philpott's no use, he knows nothing about children and he's scared to death of women."

"Keep your voice down, she'll hear you and she has enough on her plate right now. The news about Séamus hit her very hard."

"That's right, worry about Ursula. Worry about everybody but me, I'm just your wife, your slave."

"Don't be ridicu—"

"One thing I'm not is a trained nurse. That commode chair, for instance. I don't even know how it's supposed to work."

"It's quite simple," he said. "Ursula sits in the chair and when she's finished, you empty the bowl underneath the way you'd empty a chamber pot."

Barbara was indignant. "I've never used a chamber pot in my life."

"By you, I meant one of us."

"How is she going to get into the chair?"

"One of us will have to lift her in."

Barbara's voice grew more strident. "I cannot possibly lift your mother."

"Ursula's nothing but skin and bone," Barry said. "You won't have any trouble, you weigh almost twice what she does and you're a strong young woman. Please, sweetheart, don't let's row about this. The only way Ursula can make further progress is if she's at home with the people she loves around her."

"How long will that take?"

"I don't know."

"Well, what did the doctor say?"

"He doesn't know either." Out of fairness, Barry was forced to add, "He doesn't think she'll ever get much better."

Once again Barry found himself facing a furious woman. "Well, that's just wonderful, isn't it?" Barbara cried. "That's just God damned wonderful!"

Chapter Seventeen

⸻◈⸻

August 9, 1974

U.S. PRESIDENT RICHARD NIXON RESIGNS TO
AVOID IMPEACHMENT

In spite of her condition Ursula tried to be a participating member of the family. She urged Barbara to leave little Brian with her while she was busy elsewhere in the house.

"You can't possibly look after a toddler," Barbara said as she propped the older woman up on her pillows. "He'll be away in a minute and into all sorts of trouble."

"Put him on my bed," replied Ursula, "and give us a chance."

"But he'll hurt you."

"He won't hurt me. Please."

With reluctance, Barbara set her squirming son on the bed beside Ursula. The child immediately began to crawl onto the interesting range of hills beneath the covers. "Not there, Brian," Ursula said. "That's my territory." Taking his small face between her hands, she looked squarely into his eyes. In the calm, confidant voice used for her horses, she said, "Now you and I must agree on your territory."

"For God's sake, Ursula, he's only a baby, he doesn't know what you're talking about."

Ursula ignored her. "Brian, you can go anywhere on this bed that's flat." She patted the flat part to demonstrate. "That's your territory."

He stared at her solemnly.

"Your kingdom," Ursula elaborated. "Where you can do what you like. Do you know what a king is?" He watched in fascination as she took a sheet of paper from the bedside locker and folded it into a little cap. Placing the cap atop his head, she pronounced, "I crown thee King Brian!"

Brian looked toward his mother. When Barbara broke into laughter he laughed too. "Cwow?" he enquired, reaching up to touch his head.

"That's your crown and I am your Nana," said Ursula.

"Nana," he repeated with a broad grin.

He spent the better part of an hour on his grandmother's bed, chattering away in his own language while she talked to him in hers.

That night an amused Barbara told Barry, "I'd swear they understood each other."

The next time Brian was left with Ursula he set out to explore her room. She made the same arrangement with him, pointing to various things. "That's your kingdom, you can go there. That's my kingdom, leave it alone."

Amazingly, the scheme worked, though elsewhere in the house the boy was into everything. Barbara was exhausted running after him.

She found a brief respite in brewing tea and carrying a tray into Ursula's room. While the two women drank their tea Brian pottered contentedly around them. "I don't understand it," Barbara remarked. "When you say 'no' he stops whatever he's doing. I shout at him until I'm blue in the face and he ignores me."

"Precisely," said Ursula.

She was always glad to see the little boy but did not particularly enjoy his mother's company. Barbara was too self-absorbed; she had to be the central feature of every conversation. When Ursula made an effort to introduce a more interesting topic, the resignation of the U.S. president, Barbara said, "I don't know anything about it, I'm apolitical."

"But one has to care about politics. It affects every aspect of our lives."

"Not mine," Barbara insisted. "Mom wrote to our congressman I don't know how many times, trying to get me into one of the best music schools in New York, but he never answered."

"That's no surprise," said Ursula. "Politicians are designed for transmission, not reception."

Privately she thought the same applied to her daughter-in-law.

BARRY offered to buy a small television set for his mother's room but Ursula declined. "I don't even need a radio," she said. "I'll get well sooner if I have a little peace and quiet. When I was growing up we may have had opinions but we kept them to ourselves. Some people didn't even dare to think for fear the priest would find out about it.

"Now every crank and critic not only has opinions, but broadcasts them far and wide. We are treated to interminable discourses on anything from the latest rock music to British royal scandals to traffic problems in Dublin. Spare me for a while."

But she could not lie alone in a silent room day after day, Barry told himself. Not Ursula, who had led such an active life. She must have company as well as medical care, so he hired a private nurse to come to his mother two days a week. In order to meet the added cost he began working longer hours in the darkroom, and accepting assignments that took him farther and farther afield. He did not like leaving the women alone and did not want to ask the boarders to keep an eye on them, so he asked Philpott to stay in the house when he was away. The little man agreed—provided he was allowed to use the bedroom and private sitting room he had occupied when he owned and ran the boardinghouse himself.

That would mean temporarily relocating one of the better-paying boarders, who might leave if he had to accept reduced quarters. The loss in income could be substantial.

"There's an easy solution," Barbara told her husband. "Stay with us yourself."

"I can't do that and work too."

"Then give up photography."

"It's my career, Barbara. I've spent years building it up, you can't expect me to walk away." But Barry knew photography was more than his career. The camera had become his weapon in the unfinished revolution. Pictures could demonstrate more clearly than words the reasons behind the ongoing struggle of the IRA.

Barbara thrust her jaw forward belligerently. "I gave up my singing career for you!"

"You didn't give up your career, it gave you up." Barry tried to hold his temper but she was pushing him too far. Pushing him into another lie. "I gave up the Army for you."

"You never did! If you had your way you'd be in the north with Séamus right now. And here's something else I know: as soon as your mother gets a little stronger you'll abandon us in a flash and leave me to cope with everything alone!"

That last accusation was so unfair it left Barry speechless.

Ursula knew they were fighting; knew it was about her. *If I wasn't here I suppose they would row over something else*, she told herself. The presents she had purchased that fateful day in Dublin had vanished, together with the handbag she was carrying. Fortunately she already had cashed the cheque from the sale of the horses and hidden the bulk of the money in the lining of her suitcase. Early in life Ursula had learned the importance of having cash put by.

"If money's a problem," she said to Barry, "perhaps I can help."

"You need what you have for the farm. We have to keep everything ticking over down there until you can go home." He said the words though he did not believe them.

Ursula did. *Until I can go home.*

WITHIN six weeks of being released from prison Éamonn MacThomáis was arrested again—on the same charge. His wife was warned he could receive as much as five years. MacThomáis was convinced they had to release him; being tried for the same offence on which he had completed serving his sentence was ludicrous. At his trial in the Bridewell he shouted to Rosaleen in the gallery, "Get steak and onions, I'll be home for dinner."

MacThomáis was found guilty and sentenced to three more years in Portlaoise Prison. When he heard the verdict he visibly crumpled. Paddy Cooney, the minister for justice, later told him, "You took *An Phoblacht* from a monthly to a weekly and we were afraid you were going to make it a daily. You had to be stopped."[1]

ON the twelfth of September supporters both of jailed republicans and of loyalists demonstrated in Belfast, protesting the poor quality of food in the prisons and the lack of parole.

In Belfast four days later a judge and a magistrate were killed by the IRA.

·   ·   ·

T H E nurse whom Barry hired was a middle-aged widow, a big woman with a generous spread of lap. She walked with her toes pointing toward eleven o'clock and two. Her sons and daughters had emigrated to London and Liverpool and Manchester; to New York and New Jersey and New Zealand. To Ursula's relief she did not use the imperial "we." She spoke in a whispery voice that prompted her new patient to ask, "Were you ever a nun?"

Breda Casey Cunningham laughed. "Oh dear, Mrs. Halloran, I was never a nun, I couldn't be that good for five minutes."

Before the day was over they were calling each other by their Christian names.

One morning the nurse and the postman arrived at the front door at the same time. He handed Breda the day's post, which she carried inside and put on the hall table—with one exception. Barbara was busy upstairs, so she showed the questionable envelope to Ursula. "Is this for anyone here?"

The envelope was addressed in pencil to "F. L. Halloran."

Finbar Lewis, Ursula thought. *How many people know that's Barry's full name? Or have to do their writing in pencil?* She opened the letter.

Here I am again, Seventeen. This is a great place for a holiday. I can write to you and you can write to me. Address below.

Just to fill you in, I was seized on suspicion and interned for an indefinite period. Some loyalists have been interned the same as republicans, but the two groups are kept in separate Cages for the sake of their health. The Oranges are classified as "detainees" while we are "internees." The rest of the Cages are occupied by sentenced prisoners, whether they are republicans, loyalists, or ODCs—that's Ordinary Decent Criminals to you.

When they checked me into this hotel they searched me from my ears to my tail. The screws—prison guards—made me bend over naked while one of them called "the stargazer" squatted behind me and shone an electric torch up my arsehole. He didn't find anything because I'd had no time to hide anything. Some of the boys have really clever ways of hiding things, but that's another story.

The Belfast Brigade of the IRA has four battalions. Three are on active service. The Fourth Battalion comprises the Volunteers in Long Kesh. We are organised along military guidelines with the usual chain of command. Every republican Cage has its own O/C* and adjutant, and because we are political prisoners our leadership meets with the prison authorities on a regular basis.

A Cage holds between seventy-five and eighty men divided amongst four or five huts. The doors of the huts are opened at seven-thirty in the morning and don't close until ten at night. During that time we can walk around outside, but inside the Cage. We tend to walk anti-clockwise. I don't know why.

We're not just serving time in here the way the Oranges are. In addition to military drill—we carry dummy rifles carved out of old timber some of the guards gave us—we do a lot of reading. Those republicans who didn't get much education on the outside are making up for it now. We have lectures on Irish history, revolutionary politics, and how to escape from prison. Under international law every POW has a duty of escape.

On the football pitches—we have a big one and a smaller one, interconnected by gates—we can talk with Volunteers from the other Cages. I've come across old friends and made some new ones. There's

*Officer Commanding.

one in particular I'm impressed with, the O/C in Cage Eleven. He's thirty years younger than me and doesn't have any more education than me, but his mind goes clickety-click all the time. Men like Gerry are the future of republicanism.

There are some advantages to my situation that you would not expect. Example. We all get the same lousy prison grub, but detainees and ODCs get a slice of Dawn margarine cut from a long roll. Republican internees get real butter. I told you it was a great place for a holiday.

Also, as prisoners of war we can wear our own clothes. Some of our lads even have uniforms consisting of Italian army coats and berets. There are layers upon layers of rules in the Kesh but a lot of them are broken for us because of our political status. A whole rake of Provos who never thought about politics before are seriously interested in the subject now. The authorities are beginning to be afraid we'll politicise the ODCs, especially the blacks. We suspect they're trying to plant a spy in every Cage. If we catch one I leave the rest to your imagination.

I envy the boys with Italian army coats. All I have are the clothes I was lifted in, and it's cold here even on warm days because the place was built on a bog. Damp, windy, misty, miserable. The men with wives and girlfriends on the outside get them to smuggle sweaters in by wearing them. They also smuggle cigarettes and razors and so forth in their knickers. God love the women.

Yours,
Séamus

Ursula sat holding the letter in her hands. *God love the women.* She was motionless for so long the nurse began to worry. "Is it bad news? Here, let me help you lie down for a while."

"Not bad news, Breda; just a message from a friend. A dear friend." Ursula briefly brushed her hand across her eyes as if to remove a stray wisp of hair. "In that wardrobe over there you'll find some clothes. If there are any woollen jumpers, wrap them up in a parcel for me, will you?"

REPUBLICAN women were as active, and as dedicated, as their men. With a condom—available in the north but not the south—a cigarette pack and some sulphuric acid, it was possible to construct an incendiary weapon. A woman could try on a coat in a unionist-owned shop, leave the small bomb unseen in a coat pocket, and walk away. When the acid burned through the condom it ignited the paper. The resulting fire was highly destructive.

ON the fifth of October bombs planted in the Horse and Groom Pub in Guildford, England, left five people dead and over fifty injured. Two more were killed in a pub bombing in Woolwich. Subsequently four men accused of being members of the IRA were arrested and jailed. Their pictures were prominently displayed on television, identified as "The Guildford Four."

Speaking in Parliament, Prime Minister Harold Wilson promised to fight the IRA with the full resources of the United Kingdom.

TEN days later republican prisoners set fire to the Cages in Long Kesh.

November sixth brought further violence to the prison. Thirty-three republicans successfully tunnelled their way out, but were discovered as they ran toward freedom. One man was shot and killed; the rest were recaptured.

ON the twenty-first of November two pubs in Birmingham were bombed, killing a total of twenty-one people.

Six suspects were arrested. Almost overnight they became "The Birmingham Six."

Speaking for the Provos in an interview shown on British television, Dáithí Ó Conaill denied both the Guildford and Birmingham bombings. "We strike at economic, military, political, and judicial targets," he stated.

IN the first week of December Barry received a letter from McCoy.

> Reckon you've heard about the fun we've been having up here. The fire was in protest against the lousy food and the restrictions on visitors, plus the governor of the prison had made some demands we simply could not accept. When he refused to withdraw them, every company burned its own Cage. We managed to burn a couple of the loyalist Cages too, and corralled them in a third. It was some party, Seventeen. You wouldn't see the likes of it in Dublin on a Saturday night.
>
> While the black smoke was boiling up some of the lads started going "over the wire" and legging it. Our O/Cs ordered us to assemble on the roadway as soon as possible. Meanwhile a Volunteer got on the phone to the control centre. The major in command thought he was talking to a screw. Our lad assured him everything was under control and all the prisoners had returned to the compound. The major said, "Jolly good, this is the first accurate report I've had since the trouble started." But the phone call had to be cut short when the hut went on fire and our lad made a hasty exit.
>
> After a while the loyalists cut themselves free with wire cutters (divvil knows how they got them) and gave first aid to some of the injured IRA men. Many loyalists are no better or worse than us, I guess. They think they're right just like we think we are. I wonder how God can be on both sides at once.

The Brits sent squaddies* by helicopter to try to control us but our lads were too well organised for them. We didn't give in until we were too tired and hungry to keep fighting. The Kesh looked like the underside of hell by that stage. We slept on the football pitch for a month, until they sent the army in to rebuild the huts. The quality is not near as good as the originals. There's a rumour going around that a bigger prison will be built soon. Something we can't burn down. I'll keep you posted.

The letter was dated before the escape attempt. "Séamus might have been involved in that too," Barry warned his mother. "One man was killed."

"Not Séamus," said Ursula. "I would have known."

IN classic republican tradition, Sinn Féin suffered another split on December eighth when a dissident group broke away to form the Irish Republican Socialist Party.

Máire Drumm, a vice president of Provisional Sinn Féin, had arranged a meeting between six Provisionals and a group of northern Protestant clergymen. The expressed hope of the clergymen was "to try to strengthen the doves in the Army Council."[2] The meeting began on the ninth of December in Feakle, County Clare. Dáithí Ó Conaill and Ruairí Ó Brádaigh, the president of Provisional Sinn Féin, were amongst those present.

The meeting encountered numerous difficulties, but by the tenth they were making solid progress. Then an IRA courier arrived with urgent information. Dublin Castle had learned about the meeting and was sending Special Branch to arrest Ó Conaill, described as the most wanted man in the British Isles. He made a hasty departure. The meeting continued until the arrival of Special Branch forces brought it to an abrupt end, but the negotiations bore fruit.

*Members of an army squad.

The banner headline in *An Phoblacht* proclaimed, "IRA Declares Christmas Ceasefire!"

On Christmas Day an intermediary for the British government paid a visit to Ruairí Ó Brádaigh in his home to discuss extending the ceasefire into the New Year. Ó Brádaigh told the man, "There is no war as far as we're concerned, though of course the IRA reserve the right to defend themselves."[3]

Chapter Eighteen

—◦◦◦◦◦◦—

On the first of January Ireland took over the rotating presidency of the EEC for the first time. The IRA ceasefire was still in effect but 1975 would be a year of mixed blessings. The Fine Gael/Labour coalition was beset by severe problems at home. The stagnant Irish economy was in a cul-de-sac, with inflation hitting twenty percent and the highest unemployment rate in the EEC. "Hall's Pictorial" satirised "the Minister for Hardship."

Not to be outdone, Ursula quipped during dinner, "We're suffering from stagflation."

She had given in on the matter of the wheelchair. Eating meals on a tray in her room was intolerable. "It makes me feel like a pariah," she told Barry. When the wheelchair arrived she discovered that she rather enjoyed being ceremoniously wheeled through the house to the dining room, like a queen arriving in a sedan chair.

She could not endure the chair for long. As soon as the meal was ended she had to go back to bed. She lay there hating the prison of her body.

· · ·

THE IRA ceasefire had not received unanimous approval from republicans. There was strong disagreement between those who thought the truce offered a way into meaningful negotiations, and others who believed the military campaign was the only hope for ever getting the British to withdraw.

Opinion among the Usual Suspects was divided. Brendan was guardedly optimistic. "If the IRA proves it can be trusted, Britain may be willing, step by step, to begin withdrawing from the north."

Luke was less hopeful. "Maybe, but only if withdrawal is in their own best interests."

"It is of course. Maintaining Northern Ireland is costing the rest of the United Kingdom a fortune. It's an artificial economy, you know; quite unsustainable in the real world. With the ongoing shrinkage of heavy industry since World War Two almost forty percent of all employment in the north is in the civil service. If you were a taxpayer in Kensington would you be happy paying for that?"

Danny argued, "More's at stake than money. Britain hangs on to the north to save face. Ireland was their first conquest, the first place they colonised. Now their damned empire's dying on its feet, Ireland's gonna be the last holding they release."

"Only way to get them out is to blast them out," Patsy asserted. "If Séamus was here he'd tell you the same."

"Any news of him lately?"

"Not since Barry was in here the other night."

"Now there," said Danny, "is the man you need to blast them out."

EARLY in the new year the Irish Republican Socialist Party set up a military wing called the Irish National

Liberation Army, which attracted a number of disaffected Provos.

The ceasefire ended abruptly on the twenty-seventh of January. Four bombs attributed to the IRA went off in London. No one was killed, but nineteen people were injured by another bomb in Manchester.

Meanwhile top-secret meetings were being held between representatives of the British government and the Provisional IRA with an eye toward establishing a permanent truce. The Provos presented twelve points in their negotiations; the British responded with sixteen. Ostensibly the British were interested in resolving the outstanding problems. In actuality they hoped to drag matters on and on until the IRA lost its support base altogether and gave up the struggle. "Play the Provos along" was the British policy as expressed by Merlyn Rees, the secretary of state for Northern Ireland.[1]

R ELATIONS between Dublin and London grew increasingly strained. Liam Cosgrave's government suspected the British were negotiating with the IRA about pulling out of the north. Should that happen, massive violence was predicted. Cosgrave and his cabinet began secretly planning to accommodate up to fifty thousand of the refugees they expected to flood south across the border.[2] At least twice that number were anticipated, but the Republic simply did not have enough resources for them.

Nor did the Irish government want them. The incomers could have a dramatic effect on the political landscape. If enough of them were Irish nationalists they would want no part of Fine Gael, whose founders had backed the treaty that partitioned Ireland.

The IRA announced a new ceasefire to go into effect on the tenth of February. Seven incident centres manned by Provisional Sinn Féin were opened to monitor the ceasefire in cooperation with British officials.

• • •

T H E Irish possess an irrepressible wild streak that the English have never understood. Centuries of exercising imperial control have left them unable to recognise an unfettered spirit.

In Long Kesh this spirit expressed itself through imaginative pranks and mordant humour. "Being in Long Kesh is like being in the Army, only different," McCoy wrote, "in that none of us volunteered for this and we are doing our damnedest to get out. As long as we're here, though, we manage to have some fun. The screws are baffled by what we get up to. (It don't take much to baffle them, they are not hired for their brains.) When they get mad enough they hammer us. I have some new scars but I'm tougher than I thought I was. We all are."

I N February Margaret Thatcher, wife of a wealthy businessman, became the first female leader of a political party in Britain. Taking the reins of the Conservative Party at the age of forty-nine, Mrs. Thatcher said simply, "I beat four chaps. Now let's get down to work."

O N the first of March Seán Garland of the Official IRA was ambushed on his way home by members of the newly formed INLA. He spent four months in hospital.

B A R R Y bought all the major Irish newspapers, including those from the north. As he explained to Barbara, "I never know where I might find the next story to tell with my camera."

"Television cameras tell lots of stories every day," she replied. "If only we had a telly . . ."

Until that moment Barry had been considering pur-
chasing a television at last.

He changed his mind.

If he wanted to see the news on television, there was
always the set in the Bleeding Horse. Grainy black-and-
white pictures of a world created for drunken comment.

Since McCoy's arrest Barry had been visiting the pub
more often, though he rarely had more than one drink.
When he returned home Barbara usually made her resentment obvious. Yet at the most unexpected times she would
urge him to go. "It'll do you good to talk with those bud-
dies of yours," she said.

When she bothered to think about it she knew how
much her husband missed Séamus McCoy. She missed
him herself, and wrote to him every week or so—usually
after Brian was asleep. Most of her missives were in the
form of postcards. She had a huge box of postcards given
to the Hallorans by a company for whom Barry took scenic photographs.

McCoy's most frequent correspondent was Ursula. She
filled empty hours by composing long, amusing letters,
spiced with word games or quotes from books she was
reading. In the evenings she scoured the day's newspapers
for articles she thought McCoy would find interesting.
Everything was grist to her epistolary mill, from reports
charting Brian's development to the employment situation
of the boarders and the current gossip in Harold's Cross.

In her letters Ursula never mentioned McCoy's imprisonment, however. Or her illness.

Illness. I'm not ill, I'm broken.

The word "broken" rang like an alarm bell in her brain.

*I'm not broken! In spite of everything that happened to
them Papa and Mama were never broken. Pearse and
Connolly were never broken. Papa used to say, "You have
not lost the battle until you lay down your arms."*

.   .   .

THE fall of Saigon at the end of April resulted in tens of thousands of South Vietnamese trying to flee the city as communist forces swept in. Television relayed unforgettable images of Americans being rescued from the U.S. Embassy by helicopter. After fourteen years, the Vietnam War was over.

BARBARA enjoyed ambushing Barry. She met him as he came in the front door with, "What did you bring me?"

"What do you mean? Was I supposed to bring you something?"

"If that isn't just like a man! You forgot all about our anniversary, didn't you?" While Barry's brain raced across the known calendar, trying to catch up, she went on, "Now you're trying to play innocent because you don't have a present for me. I didn't expect much, just some little token, a tiny thing to show you still love me." She sounded wistful.

He took a deep breath. "Barbara, our anniversary isn't until next week."

"Oh," she said.

And walked away.

WHEN the IRA ceasefire continued to hold, loyalists launched the greatest assault on Catholic civilians in recent memory.[3]

WEEKS elapsed before another letter arrived from McCoy. The envelope showed signs of having been opened and resealed.

I may never get out of this place, Seventeen. Example. A member of the INLA was arrested and charged with stealing his brother-in-law's car. While awaiting trial he was put in our Cage because we have a couple of other INLA men here. When he got to court he beat the charge. The estranged wife had secretly given the car to her boyfriend. So he returned here to collect his things. When he left an RUC man was waiting for him at the front gate. "Back you go," says the constable. He grabbed the poor sod by the shoulder and marched him back into the Kesh as an internee. You can't win.

There's a young lad in this Cage who's something of a poet. We call him Madra Rua.* (Almost everyone in the Cages has a nickname. I won't tell you mine.) He loves animals anyway and he's forever rescuing birds that fly into the wire and are injured. In the morning he goes out before anyone else does to walk around the compound and smoke his pipe. One morning this fella rescued a seagull. Now most of us cherish our sleep in the early mornings and I was still in bed. When he brought it into the hut the seagull flapped away from him and onto my bed and covered it with birdshit. I was really mad. Madra Rua kept the gull and made a pet of it.

It's still here and so am I.

Séamus

THE British government erected an additional prison at the Long Kesh site to accommodate the burgeoning population. Based on a German model from World War Two, the new facility consisted of eight immense, flat-roofed prison blocks built in the shape of a giant "H," together with an assortment of auxiliary buildings and a prison hospital. The four legs of the "H," called wings, contained twenty-five cells each. The cells had been built for single occupancy but could easily hold two.

The centre bar of the "H," although rectangular in shape, was called the Circle. It was locked off from the wings with barred steel doors. The Circle contained the warders'

*Red Dog.

offices, storage closets, a medical treatment room, a communications room, toilets, and two games rooms for the
prisoners. There was an officers' mess just off the Circle—
as well as a padded cell for prisoners who were deemed
to be a danger to themselves. The cell was six feet square
and contained nothing but the "padding" on the walls. This
consisted of one thin layer of wallpaper pasted on bare
concrete.

All construction was of concrete, iron, or steel. Nothing flammable; nothing yielding.

Each H-Block was enclosed by a high fence topped with
razor wire, with more wire strung across the top to thwart
helicopter rescue. The entire H-Block compound was surrounded by a concrete wall seventeen feet high and over
two miles long. A corrugated iron wall further separated
the Blocks from the Cages. The perimeter boundaries of
the combined prison consisted of more iron walls augmented by wire fencing. The result was a prison within a
prison within a prison, like nested Russian dolls but without the pleasant connotation.

As part of the upgrading, Long Kesh officially was renamed Her Majesty's Prison, The Maze. The H-Blocks
were designated as The Maze (Cellular), while the Cages
were The Maze (Compound). Most people, however, continued to refer to the overall prison complex—which now
covered 630 acres, more area than Belfast city centre—as
Long Kesh.

The British claimed H.M.P. The Maze was the most
luxurious prison in Europe.

Before the first prisoner arrived in the H-Blocks, the
Sunday Times revealed that files on visitors to republican
prisoners in Long Kesh had been given to loyalist paramilitaries by members of the Royal Ulster Constabulary.[4]

B A R R Y drove to Clare as often as he could. Each time
he went down Ursula asked him to collect something for

her, like the pillow from her bed or her favourite books. The best thing he brought his mother was peace of mind. He was able to report that Paul Morrissey had been the perfect person to take over management of the farm. An honest, hardworking man, Morrissey was as conscientious about caring for Ursula's property as his own. "Clare people look after each other," he told Barry.

Morrissey also maintained good relations with the farm labourers, local men who had been with Ursula for years. They did not resent his supervision—or if they did, they did not show it. With typical Irish begrudgery they may have complained about him at their own firesides, but they did their work at the farm. Livestock was tended, buildings and fences were maintained. The wife of one of the men came every week to sweep and dust the empty house.

No matter when Barry arrived at the farm, he would find at least one of the Morrissey twins—leggy, dark-haired girls with gummy smiles and identical giggles— with the horses. Ursula's beloved animals had never been more thoroughly groomed.

"Some of the brood mares are used to being ridden," Barry said to Dorothy and Eleanor on a bright day in early summer. "Why don't you take my mother's saddle out of the tack room and have a ride around the fields?" They did not have to be asked twice. Within minutes Dorothy was mounted on a placid bay mare while Eleanor sat on the fence, swinging her feet as she waited her turn.

Barry watched them for a while, then ambled away with no particular destination. And no awareness of time.

He enjoyed the same sense of peace he had felt that afternoon in the Phoenix Park. The smell of the earth, the green of the fields, the soughing of the wind, all contributed to easing his troubled spirit. As long as he was at the farm he could believe all things were possible.

When he drove away down the lane the world began to close in on him again. By the time he reached Dublin peace seemed very far away, like a fairy tale heard in one's youth.

Barbara was waiting for him with a new list of complaints. "Something's wrong with the washing machine, two of the boarders haven't paid their rent yet, I can't find the tax information for last year . . ."

At some point Barry stopped listening. In his head he went back to the farm.

That evening Barry opened a bottle of wine he had been saving—an exotic beverage in seventies Ireland. He hoped it would lighten the atmosphere. "The twins were really chuffed about being allowed to ride," he told Ursula as he filled her glass. "We need another saddle so they can go out together."

His mother laughed; the first time he had heard her laugh in weeks. "Do you not think one of those girls was riding bareback by the time your car reached the main road?"

Towards the end of the meal she began to reminisce about the Morrissey family. "A generation ago there was a huge tribe of them just across the fields," she told Barbara. "When Barry was seven or eight he used to march the young ones up and down the lane while he shouted orders. Not Paul, of course; he was grown by then. But poor Eithne was always with them. I can still see her little bare feet and her runny nose."

"Who was poor Eithne?"

Barry answered Barbara's question. "Eithne Walsh. She used to play with the Morrissey children."

"Her people were poor even by the standards of the day," Ursula interjected. "Lord love them, they had neither 'in' nor 'on.' But when Eithne grew up she married Paul Morrissey. Everyone said he was a great catch, but Eithne was the great catch." The unaccustomed wine was making Ursula giddy. "Who would have thought that sickly-looking girl would bear four huge sons and two daughters and never a sick day amongst any of them? And she's a wonderful wife to him. Next to Uncle Henry and Aunt Ella, the Morrisseys are the happiest couple I ever saw."

"What's their secret?" Barry wondered.

From observation Ursula believed there was only one area where Barry and Barbara had no problems. Feeling herself on safe ground, she replied, "Perhaps they have a wonderful sex life."

Barbara put down her spoon. "Sex," she said. "A subject men know nothing about."

Barry raised his eyebrows. "Sorry?"

"Well, they don't. I mean they can *do* it, but they really have no comprehension of what's going on. At least as far as women are concerned. Have you read *Ulysses,* by James Joyce? Particularly the ending?"

"I have read *Ulysses,*" Barry assured her, "but I'm surprised you did."

·   "That's what I mean, you just proved my point. Men have all these notions about women that come entirely from their own heads. Of course I've read *Ulysses,* I've read lots of books, Mr. High-and-Mighty Halloran. But how could you know that? When did you ever ask me?"

"I'm talking about the final chapter when Molly Bloom is thinking about sex, letting it run on and on in her head with lots of asides and no punctuation. It's been cited as one of the most erotic passages ever written—cited by men, that is. I wonder how many women think so?

"James Joyce was depicting the way he thought women were. Men want to believe women have exactly the same sexual thoughts and responses they do. But we don't; ours are different. And men are too arrogant to notice.

"A man thinks he's a great lover if he asks the woman what she wants. If she actually tells him, he may even do it; once. Then he'll go back to doing everything his way. He'll be absolutely convinced, in spite of anything she might have said, that she's feeling just what he feels and is turned on by what turns him on. And he's so wrong!"

Ursula was staring at her daughter-in-law in astonishment.

"Are you trying to tell me you don't like the way I make love to you?" Barry said.

"I'm not trying to tell you anything. I never *have* been able to tell you anything."

Ursula murmured, "You really shouldn't be having this conversation in front of me."

"If I try to have it in the bedroom your son will get mad and turn his back to me. If I try to have it anywhere else he'll tell me it's not the right time or place. What am I supposed to do, Ursula? Suffer in silence?"

"Women of my generation did."

"Did *you*?" Barbara shot back.

Barry stood up and left the room.

A few days later Ursula told Breda Cunningham, "I very much fear my son and his wife are in a deteriorelationship."

"What's that when it's at home?"

"A relationship that's deteriorating. It's not my fault but I feel responsible in a way, because I've seen it coming and didn't do anything."

"What could you have done?" asked the nurse.

"I don't know. I feel so helpless now."

"If you were in the whole of your health it wouldn't make any difference. Husbands and wives row all the time, it's nature. Are you ready for your sponge bath?"

Ursula ignored her. "Barbara has never learned that happiness is a condition we create in ourselves. She expects someone or something else to do it for her."

"Well, you can't, missus," Breda said firmly. "So turn this way and I'll get on with the washing."

                    •   •   •

VIOLENCE in the north continued to increase. Bullets and bombs were daily events. Protestant and Catholic alike were victims. Merlyn Rees claimed it was due to internal feuds within the paramilitary organisations on both sides. He insisted the truce was still holding.

Chapter Nineteen

July 31, 1975

MIAMI SHOWBAND SHOT DOWN BY UVF IN
NORTHERN IRELAND

THE Miami Showband had been performing at the Castle Ballroom in Banbridge, where they entertained between four and five hundred young people. At two the following morning the band was travelling back to Dublin when they were halted by what appeared to be a police checkpoint near the town of Newry. The musicians were ordered from their coach at gunpoint by members of the UVF wearing the uniforms of the Ulster Defence Regiment. The loyalists searched the vehicle, then started to put a bomb inside.

The bomb exploded prematurely. The blast killed two UVF men, Harris Boyle and Wesley Somerville, and blew the showband's saxophonist, Des Lee, into a nearby field.

The UVF immediately opened fire on the rest of the group, killing lead singer Fran O'Toole, Brian McCoy, and Tony Geraghty outright, and inflicting serious chest wounds on Stephen Travers.

After the loyalists sped away, Des Lee, in spite of an injured leg, made his way to the road and succeeded in flagging down a passing motorist who took him to the Newry police station.

The massacre of the Miami Showband ended the showband era in Northern Ireland. Musicians would no longer travel across the border.

H o w could anyone do something like that?" Barbara asked Barry. "They were entertainers, for God's sake! Young men without a thought in their heads except to make music."

"You've never experienced the atmosphere that produces extreme violence," he told her. "In Northern Ireland prejudice is endemic. It's a disease no medicine will cure. There are only two responses: derision or extermination."

"Why doesn't someone just sit them down and talk calmly to them?"

Like you and I discuss our problems? "Outsiders always ask that question," he said aloud. "Those who think hatred should be amenable to reason don't understand the nature of hatred. Nor do they understand the nature of the human male—usually underprivileged and undereducated—who has more energy than peacetime outlets can absorb. He's bored and he's angry and he doesn't even know why. If he finds a leader, or a cause, he can become a lethal weapon."

"Is that what happened to you?"

The luminous grey eyes looked past her, gazing down the haunted corridors of memory. "I was neither underprivileged nor undereducated," Barry said.

F I V E people were killed in a bar on the Shankill Road on the thirteenth of August when it was attacked by members of the Provisional IRA. The bar was widely believed to be a UVF hangout.

· · ·

O N the twenty-ninth of August Eamon de Valera, founder
of the Fianna Fáil Party, former *taoiseach,* former president
of Ireland, principal author of the Irish Constitution—and
the last republican commandant to surrender in 1916—died
peacefully at the age of ninety-two.

I N October Jane and Peter McKearney, the parents of
five children, were in their home in Moy, Northern Ireland, when someone came to the house. Mrs. McKearney
opened the door to find herself facing a masked gunman
armed with a Sterling submachine gun. She was shot
eleven times; her husband, eighteen times. Both died at
the scene, the victims of loyalist gunmen.[1] The McKear-
neys' only crime was being Catholic.

In November loyalists exploded a bomb in Dublin Airport, killing one man.

That same month Lenny Murphy, a member of the Ulster Volunteer Force, read details in the Belfast-based
Newsletter of the shooting of four British soldiers by the
IRA. That night Murphy summoned three other members
of the organisation: a man from his own unit called Archie
Waller, a carpet salesman known as Benjamin "Pretty
Boy" Edwards, and William Moore, a former meat plant
employee who now drove a taxicab. Murphy specifically
requested that Moore bring the butcher's knives he had
used in his former employment. The four spent the evening drinking together until after midnight, then went
hunting a *taig.**

Murphy already had a nasty reputation. While imprisoned in Crumlin Road Jail he had murdered a fellow prisoner and was considered extremely dangerous—yet he
had been released in 1973.

---

*Pejorative for Catholic.

The quartet drove to the Antrim Road in a Catholic area of Belfast. They found their first victim in Francis Crossan, a man they did not know and had never seen before. Crossan had spent the evening at a club and was on his way home. A new home, at least to him, since his family had been intimidated into leaving their former home the previous year. Crossan's route took him past the spot where his brother Patrick, a bus driver, had been the victim of a sectarian shooting several years earlier.

Moore stayed with the black taxicab while the other three leaped out and hit Crossan over the head with a wheel brace. When he sagged to the ground, they dragged him into the backseat and sped away. His abductors kept battering Crossan with the wheel brace until the taxi came to a stop in an alley off the Shankill Road—the Protestant district. The four men dragged their unconscious victim into an alleyway. Using one of Moore's butchery knives, Murphy hacked at Crossan until he was covered with blood and his head was nearly severed from his body.[2]

After the murder Murphy cleaned the knife and returned it to its owner.

Crossan's killing was grisly even by Northern Ireland standards. The overworked detectives of the RUC's C Division made a serious effort to find the killers, but in a year that would see thirty-four murders and 153 attempted murders they made little progress.

The incident was not mentioned in newspapers in the Republic.

Barry only learned of it when he went to Belfast to do a photo essay on Catholic families who had been driven out of their homes by loyalist threats. A middle-aged woman told him of the terrible death of one of her neighbours: Francis Crossan.

"He was a nice man, a quiet man," she said wistfully. "Never hurt nobody. When they chased him and his family out of their last place the police wouldn't do nothin' about it. Now this. And who benefits, I ask you. Who benefits?"

She cast a nervous glance up and down the street, then retreated into her own home and bolted the door.

Barry sought out Crossan's former residence and took photographs of the little rented house with its broken door and boarded-up windows. It had been a pitiful enough hovel when occupied. Empty, it stood as a silent condemnation.

ON November fourth Merlyn Rees announced that republicans taken into custody after the first of March, 1976, would not be granted Special Category Status. A month later Rees announced the end of internment. In future republicans would receive a trial in special courts known as "Diplock" courts, with specially appointed judges, many of whom were members of the Orange Order, but no juries. In a Diplock court republicans could be convicted on the basis of either written or oral statements, or the word of a member of the security forces.

BETWEEN August 1971 and December 1975 a total of 1,981 people had been indefinitely detained without trial. Only 107 were loyalists. The rest were republicans—but not only men. Republican women, equally as dedicated, were being beaten and abused in Maghaberry, Armagh, and prisons in England as well. When they attempted to complain to the authorities they were accused of having deliberately injured themselves to denigrate their guards.

TUESDAY was laundry day. As Breda Cunningham started to change Ursula's pillowcase her hand encountered cold metal. She straightened up with a start. "What do you call this?" she demanded.

"A Mauser semiautomatic," said Ursula. "It used to belong to my mother. And don't wave it around like that, it's loaded. It may be old but I keep it in good working order. Here, give it to me."

The nurse surrendered the weapon as if it were hot to the touch. "Why was it under your pillow?"

"It's comforting to me," Ursula replied, "so I had Barry bring it up from the farm. I've kept a weapon within arm's reach for most of my life, Breda. A woman alone needs protection. I remember the Black and Tans,* you see."

Breda was horrified. "That was fifty years ago! You're perfectly safe now and you have no need for that . . . that thing. Have your son put it away somewhere."

"I will not be treated like a helpless old woman who doesn't know what she's doing." While Breda watched, Ursula deliberately put the Mauser back under the pillow.

After that Breda insisted that Ursula change her own pillowcases.

SINCE August the O/C of Cage Eleven, Gerry Adams, had been writing a weekly column for the *Republican News.* The articles, written under the pen name of "Brownie," had to be smuggled out of the prison.

It was not possible to subscribe to the *Republican News,* which could only be obtained by avidly watching the newsstands. Whenever he was able to get his hands on a copy, Barry brought it home to Ursula. She quickly became a fan of the Brownie articles.

Some of them were lighthearted and wryly humorous, a tribute to fellow prisoners making the best of their predicament. In others Adams was setting out his own theory for building the Republic that Patrick Pearse and the men of 1916 had fought and died for. Time in prison had meant

---

*British irregulars recruited after World War One; notorious for their brutality in Ireland.

time to read, and think. Adams had come to believe that political structures would have to be developed to go hand-in-hand with the armed struggle.

Ursula cut out all of the Brownie articles and kept them in a tin box that once held Jacobs' Biscuits.

W HEN a UVF booby trap blew up under his car on the sixth of September, Michael O'Toole, a Catholic, was fatally injured. Five thousand mourners attended his funeral in the town of Larne, at which his brother, a former wing commander in the Royal Air Force, said the family did not want revenge, but justice.

On the twenty-second of September a Catholic woman, Margaret Hale, who was married and the mother of five children, lost her life in a UVF bomb and gun attack on McCann's Bar. The Catholic-owned public house was located between Loughgall and Portadown. Mid-Ulster was the UVF stronghold, based around Portadown and Lurgan.

F OLLOWING the death of Mrs. Hale towns all across the Six Counties were jolted by IRA bomb blasts.

On the second of October four members of the UVF were killed when their car blew up two miles from the town of Coleraine. An inquest found that the car had contained between three and five pounds of commercial explosives. A car bomb was being armed in the front seat when it exploded prematurely.

A wave of UVF attacks would see a total of twelve northern Catholics killed on that same day.

Sometimes the violence reached across the border. In December two civilians in Dundalk, County Louth, died in the explosion of a loyalist bomb.

·　　·　　·

ALL four Hallorans signed the Christmas card they sent to Séamus McCoy. Holding a pencil in his chubby little fist, Brian signed with a lopsided figure he called a star. The card arrived in Long Kesh together with a package containing yet another woolly jumper and a tin of Philpott's incomparable Christmas cake.

Since his first complaint about being cold McCoy had received an embarrassing number of sweaters, all in brown paper packages addressed in Ursula's handwriting. Trusting she would forgive him, he traded the latest woolly jumper for items he needed more.

LENNY Murphy continued his bloody work as self-appointed executioner by putting together a firing squad composed of Archie Waller, Sam McAllister, and William Green.[3] The gang seized three local men who had been accused of various petty crimes and ordered them to kneecap each other. When they tried to resist, one—a fellow member of the UVF—was shot dead by Archie Waller. The other two were shot in the knees and left writhing on the ground while Murphy's gang strolled away.

The UVF did not hesitate to dispense its own justice. Within a matter of days Archie Waller was dead.

The internecine war that followed resulted in several more murders and deflected Murphy's campaign of vengeance against Catholics. But only temporarily.

BARBARA announced she wanted a flocked Christmas tree. "A white one," she added, which further mystified Barry.

"What's that when it's at home?" he wondered.

"A tree that's been sprayed with cotton fibres and white paint, of course. They're very stylish."

"In America maybe, but not in Ireland."

"Nonsense," Barbara said firmly. "All you have to do is look."

Curiosity as much as the desire to please his wife propelled Barry on an expedition in search of a white-flocked tree. No one knew what he was talking about. A farmer selling Christmas trees by the side of the road in South Dublin summed things up. "I don't hold with heathen ideas," he told Barry. "My trees are the way God made them."

Barry took a detour on the way home and stopped in to the Bleeding Horse for a drink.

The Usual Suspects laughed when he told them what he had been doing. "You might as well go in search of the Holy Grail," said Brendan. "Where does the woman get such ideas?"

Barry felt he had to defend Barbara. "From her description, it could be beautiful."

"Did you buy a tree at all?"

"I did not buy a tree, though I must have looked at a hundred. But I did . . ." Suddenly he put down his glass. "I did have an idea," he told his friends. Leaving the drink unfinished, he drove to Harold's Cross for his cameras.

Barry spent two days taking pictures of opulent, symmetrical pines and sparse, lopsided pines. He stopped looking at them as objects and recognised them as individuals, spending as much as half an hour on a single tree, walking around it, studying it from every angle and in changing light, seeking to capture its unique personality before it succumbed to the slow death already decreed by the axe.

On Christmas Eve he very deliberately purchased a forlorn little tree no one else would buy, and took it home to be lavished with love.

Barry's photographic essay entitled "The Great Christmas Tree Search" earned more money than any single item of his political work that year. Barbara's response was, "It's time you did something worthwhile with your photography."

At that moment Barry hated her. He imagined putting his hands around that full white singer's throat and squeezing. Hard.

Yet he loved her.

Barbara was not the woman he had imagined her to be. In some ways she was more intelligent, in other ways less. A facade of naïveté concealed a devious mind. She delighted in demonstrating an encyclopaedic knowledge of trivia, often adding—with feigned astonishment—"You mean you didn't know that?" Yet Barry's attempts to impart information were dismissed with, "You just got that out of some book," as if book knowledge were of no value.

At the beginning of their relationship Barry had been charmed by capricious behaviour that he mistook for a facet of femininity. In time it wore thin. He could never be certain of Barbara's mood; walking into the house was like walking into a minefield. His wife never asked how he felt, or how his day had been, yet if he failed to make these enquiries of her she was mightily offended.

She took a positive delight in one-upmanship. Any area in which he excelled, she denigrated. Any subject in which he expressed an interest she dismissed as boring, though she might discuss the same subject animatedly with a perfect stranger. If Barry made a flat statement she invariably expressed the opposite view. When he pointed this out she took affront. "Am I not allowed to have my own opinions?"

With the passage of time Barry had realised that his love for Barbara had little to do with sex. The act of sex was one of overwhelming physical sensation but did not touch the well of tenderness at his inmost core. The tenderness a man must keep hidden, or be thought less of a man.

Yet for all her faults, Barbara constantly evoked tenderness in Barry. When she lifted their little son and laughed into his laughing face. When she snored in her sleep; little stuttering bursts like Apollo's motor on a frosty morning.

When she sang.

ON the fourth of January, 1976, five Catholics were killed by loyalists in two separate incidents near Whitecross in County Armagh.

The following day ten Protestants were shot dead in an ambush by republicans at Kingsmill, County Armagh.

On the ninth of the month Lenny Murphy struck again. He ordered his confederate William Moore to acquire a "clean" gun—one that could not be traced to the UVF—from a member of the Ulster Defence Regiment. The Walther pistol was used in the small hours of the following morning to shoot and kill a random victim, Ted McQuaid, in the Cliftonville area of Belfast.

MCCOY'S Christmas presents for the Hallorans did not arrive until the last day of January. They consisted of a wallet made in the prison craft shop for Barry, a coin purse from the same source for Barbara, and a tiny, beautifully carved wooden bird for Brian. Ursula received a slightly larger version of the same bird, with a note in its beak.

The note read, "This is me."

Chapter Twenty

ON the sixth of February two teenage members of the Provisional IRA ambushed and shot two policemen who were patrolling the Cliftonville Road. One of their victims died instantly, the other two days later.

When news of this latest killing reached the bar where Murphy, Edwards, and Moore were drinking, it did not take long for the black taxi to be on the road again. They stopped long enough to pick up a like-minded individual called Robert "Basher" Bates, then went *taig* hunting.

This time the victim was a small, inoffensive fifty-five-year-old man called Thomas Quinn, who worked as a road sweeper. He was savagely beaten and repeatedly attacked with a butcher's knife before being dumped on a grassy bank close to the road. There the knife was wielded again, cutting his throat through to the spine.

The Belfast *Sunday News* received a telephone call announcing where the body of a "militant republican" could be found, and claiming the act was in retaliation for the shooting of the constables.

The following Monday Murphy looked forward to slaughtering a whole truckful of *taigs*. He had learned that a crew of Catholic workmen stopped at a little shop on the Shankill Road every weekday as they passed through the Protestant neighbourhood. With the aid of several confederates, a Thompson submachine gun, and a MKI carbine, Murphy hijacked a Ford Cortina belonging to a postman.

The gang parked the stolen car in front of the shop and

took up their positions. Soon a lorry arrived and parked on the opposite side of the road while its occupants went inside. When they came out again, Murphy's gang opened fire. A horrified witness realised what was happening and shouted, "They're Prods, they're Prods!" but it was no use. The lorry was sprayed with eighteen rounds before the attackers sped away in the Cortina.

Two Protestant men died and two more were seriously injured. None of them had a connection with any paramilitary or political organisation.

When a BBC broadcast on the atrocity made clear that the victims had been Protestant, Murphy "went berserk" according to later testimony from Moore, and vowed to kill twice as many Catholics.

It was a vow he kept many times over.

The gang the press labelled the Shankill Butchers went on a mass murder spree unprecedented in the bloody annals of Northern Ireland. Catholic and Protestant alike fell prey to them; the total number of innocent men and women they shot, bludgeoned, and hacked to death may never be known. All the murders had one thing in common: extreme savagery.

This was killing for its own sake, feeding an irrational, sadistic bloodlust arising from educational and emotional deprivation coupled with a societal atmosphere where sectarian murder had been the norm for centuries.

WHEN the Shankill Butchers made headlines the London tabloids wanted pictures, and the more gruesome the better. Every freelance photographer with connections in Northern Ireland was approached. Barry already had seen enough horrors to last a lifetime, and had a marked distaste for sensationalism for its own sake. He declined the assignment until the money was too big to turn down.

Dear Séamus,
I may be in your neighbourhood soon. I've accepted an
assignment in Belfast and am applying for permission
to visit Long Kesh while I'm there.

Barry did not tell Barbara exactly what the northern assignment was, nor did she ask, once he told her the sum
he had been offered. She said, "We'll be able to have a
damp-proof course installed before this house falls down
around our ears. If you were going to buy a place at all
you should have bought one built on a concrete slab."

"Our climate and soil are not like those of America.
Our construction is adapted to . . ."

Barbara shrugged dismissively. "If you insist on doing
things the way they've always been done, this will always
be a banana republic."

He fought to keep his temper. "Copying someone else
is not necessarily improving."

"It is if they have a better way."

A muscle jumped in his jaw. "If you think America's
so wonderful I'm surprised you're not still there."

"How can you say that?" She burst into tears and ran to
her room.

Barry headed for his car.

THE leadership of the Provisionals had begun talking
amongst themselves about calling off the campaign altogether. They were forced to admit something they had been
avoiding for far too long: the British government had no
real interest in solving the problems in the north—and the
republicans did not have enough manpower or gun power
to force the issue.

Then on the twelfth of February Volunteer Frank Stagg
died in England's Wakefield Prison while on a hunger
strike. The British government had refused to transfer

him to an Irish jail. There was rioting in West Belfast the
following day.

The campaign was back on.

B ARRY Halloran arrived in Belfast in time to take photographs of the riot. When he rang Dublin that night he told
Barbara, "I shall be here for a while, maybe even several
weeks. There's so much going on right now that I'm spoiled
for choice when it comes to covering stories."

"I still don't like you being so far away."

He laughed. "Belfast to Dublin is no distance at all. If
you need me you'll always have a phone number where
you can reach me, and in the meantime I've given Philpott
strict orders to take good care of you."

"Thanks for nothing," said Barbara, slamming down the
receiver.

There were a number of people with whom Barry might
have stayed in Belfast, from dedicated republicans to Barbara's Protestant cousins. Instead he always chose the
sort of cheap, off-the-main-street hotel frequented by
travelling salesmen. A place where no one asked questions as long as you paid your bill and spoke with the sort
of vaguely neutral Northern Irish accent he had perfected
long ago.

WITH Britain in economic difficulties and the pound
floundering on the international money markets, on the
sixteenth of March Harold Wilson unexpectedly resigned
as the British prime minister. Although Wilson had been
able to steer Britain into EEC membership, his time in
office had seen no appreciable improvement in the running sore that was Northern Ireland.

On the seventeenth of March, St. Patrick's Day celebrations in the Hillcrest Bar in a Catholic area of Dungannon
ended in tragedy when the UVF car-bombed the bar. The

bomb was packed into a green Austin Healey parked just outside. When the car exploded at 8:20 that evening, fifty-seven-year-old Joseph Kelly died inside the bar. Andrew Small, aged sixty-two, was walking past the bar with his wife. He also died, as did a couple of children who were playing in the street nearby. Another patron of the bar, Patrick Barnard, died in hospital the following day.

BARRY did not take pictures of the wrecked bar; he was viewing the latest victim of the Shankill Butchers. Tom Madden had been stripped naked, hung upside down from a beam in a lock-up garage, and slowly skinned alive. After hours of agony he had died of strangulation. Hardened detectives turned their heads away, unable to look at the sight.

Barry did not photograph the body. Instead he photographed the shock and revulsion on the faces of the detectives.

Obtaining permission to visit a nonrelative in Long Kesh had proved to be a long, tedious process. The bureaucratic mind, pathologically obsessed with trivia, was the same everywhere. Barry had to submit identical documentation to a number of different offices that obviously did not share information with one another. He was called in for questioning several times—always expecting to have "Refused" stamped on his application.

But at last he was driving up the long, bleak stretch of the Bog Road that led to chained and padlocked gates and manned guard towers. The sky above was grimly grey.

So was the prison.

Barry had been in combat. He knew how it felt when someone was trying to kill him. That kind of fear could trigger an adrenaline rush that was, in its own way, exhilarating. There was no adrenaline rush to be had in Long Kesh. The prison was designed to shrink the human soul to insignificance.

As a visitor to the Maze (Compound) Barry was kept far away from the Maze (Cellular). All he could see of the new H-Blocks were the high concrete walls enclosing them.

Anything could be happening behind those walls, he thought with an eerie presentiment.

Barry was directed to a guard box where he presented his identification and stamped permission form. Two guards scrutinised them, peered intently at him, then looked at the documents again. When they were satisfied, he was taken to a windowless cubicle and searched. He endured the process in silence, with a clenched jaw and icy eyes that stared unblinkingly toward an invisible horizon.

Those eyes unnerved the guard who searched him. The man later remarked, "That big tall bastard made the hair stand up on the back of me neck."

When the search was concluded Barry was escorted to a low shed furnished with a few grimy plastic chairs. Two were a faded turquoise colour, the rest were orange. No other amenities were available. No tables, no magazines, no urn of tea, no pictures on the walls.

Barry sat down on one of the turquoise chairs. It was not only hard, but too small for a man of his height. He had to decide between sitting with his knees halfway to his chin or stretching his legs out in front of him for others to stumble over.

Because there already were four women and two young children in the waiting room, Barry chose the former posture.

While the children tried to find something to play with, the women chatted in working-class Belfast accents. Any semblance of normality was impossible. Soon they gave up and just sat, staring blankly at the blank walls.

Time passed. Everyone waited. As a matter of self-discipline Barry refrained from looking at his watch. The wan light coming through the smeared windowpane gave no hint of the location of the sun in the sky—if there was any sun.

Eventually a guard informed three of the four women that they would not be allowed to see their men that day. No explanation.

With a resigned sigh, the youngest stood up and removed the pink scarf she had worn at her throat to lend a little colour to her pale face. She tied the scarf over her hair like a bandana, beckoned her children to her, and followed the other two from the room. The fourth woman, older, sagging in her chair, continued to gaze at the wall.

I could take a portrait of her that would wring your heart. Is she someone's wife, someone's mother? How often does she come here? How often is she sent away without seeing him? What is her life like between visits? What is his?

A voice from the doorway startled Barry out of his reverie. "You Halloran?"

"I am."

"You here for James McCoy?"

"I am."

"He don't get many visitors," the guard commented. "Follow me."

The room set aside for visits was as bland and uncomfortable as the rest of the prison, equipped only with a few metal tables and the ubiquitous plastic chairs. A British soldier stood rigidly at guard just inside the door. When Barry entered two prisoners were already there, talking with their female visitors. Suddenly one of the men threw back his head and laughed. A great roaring laugh, filled with delight.

The soldier at the door stiffened; for a moment he looked frightened in spite of the sidearm he wore.

McCoy entered, accompanied by a prison guard. He was a little greyer, his squint more pronounced, but otherwise he looked the same as always. When Barry reached out to shake his hand the guard said, "No touching the prisoner."

Barry's hand fell to his side. "How're they treating you?"

"Can't complain."

The two men sat down facing each other across one of the narrow tables. Barry stretched his long legs to the side to avoid kicking his friend.

"What about your cough?" he wanted to know.

"Stop minderin' me, will you? In the Cages a man is obliged to keep himself in shape. The O/C has us doing sit-ups and squats and all that class of thing. I'm stronger than I was the last time you saw me," McCoy claimed proudly.

As long as the guard was near enough to hear them they spoke only of safe subjects. "How's your mother, Seventeen? Is she in any pain?"

"If she is, she never tells me. But some days she's pretty damned cranky."

"I don't blame her," said McCoy. "I'm getting pretty damned cranky myself."

Barry lowered his voice. "You haven't been hurt or anything, have you?"

"Nothing permanent," McCoy replied. His mouth twitched.

The precious minutes allotted for the visit were racing past. When the arrival of another set of visitors distracted the guards, McCoy said hurriedly, "We hear everything in here, sooner rather than later. IRA engineers are copying U.S. claymore mines now. DuPont in the States is the world's leading explosives manufacturer but the stuff's expensive and tricky to import. We're beginning to replace unstable explosives like nitrobenzine and ammonium nitrate with Semtex from the Czech Republic.

"Every company's struggling to get its own supply. Of course some companies are better at self-finance than others," McCoy said with a quiet chuckle. He swept the room with his eyes. No one was paying any attention to them.

"We have a few major arms dumps and a lot of transit dumps scattered throughout the country," he continued. "The main staging point is Dublin, but that could change if the situation changes. The IRA network's spread pretty thin from Tyrone to Kerry, which is a shame because there's a hell of a lot of coastline and the British can't watch all of it.

"I've been having a wee think, Seventeen. If the Army had someone with connections in the west of Ireland and America too, a very special man who knew a lot about explosives . . ." McCoy did not finish the sentence. It was not necessary.

Barry felt a drum beginning to beat inside him.

"I haven't mentioned this to anyone else yet," McCoy went on, "because I wanted to talk to you first." Barry saw the pupils of his eyes dilate suddenly. "I have a couple of those pictures right here," he said in a totally different voice.

Barry did not have to look around to know a guard was approaching. He willed his taut body to relax. "Great. Let's see them, Séamus."

McCoy forked two fingers into his shirt pocket and extracted several black-and-white snapshots. "One of the boys had a camera smuggled in," he explained as he handed Barry the photographs. "For holiday snaps, like I said."

The pictures showed a handful of grinning men lounging in front of a Nissan hut. They might be any high-spirited young lads, mugging for the camera. Unless you looked closely at their eyes.

"None of that now," said the guard. He reached for the photographs.

B ARRY knew he would not sleep that night.

Before going to his room he bought a small bottle of whiskey. He left it unopened on the locker beside his bed. *"Ní bhíonn an rath ach mar a mbíonn an smach,"* he reminded himself, quoting an old Irish proverb: "There is no luck except where there is discipline."

He stretched his long body diagonally across the lumpy bed and threw one forearm over his eyes. It would be a long time until dawn.

He paid one more visit to Long Kesh before returning to Dublin. Again it was difficult to speak openly, but he managed to tell McCoy, "I'm afraid I can't do that favour you asked of me."

If the older man was disappointed he did not show it. "Any particular reason?"

"There is one, but I can't go into it now. Maybe when you're out of here."

McCoy gave a hollow laugh. "For all I know that won't be until they carry me out in a box."

W H E N Barry returned to Harold's Cross Ursula was eager for news of McCoy. "Same old Séamus," he told her. "He's holding up pretty well—better than I expected, in fact. In a way he's lucky he was lifted when he was, because that means he'll stay in the Cages. Men arrested since the opening of the H-Blocks are going straight into them."

"The newspapers claim the H-Blocks are the last word in penal modernity," said Ursula.

"Perhaps they are, but if I were a fanciful man I would say those buildings are evil. I could feel it."

"I'm in charge of presentiments around here," his mother reminded him.

Barry's "Shankill Horror" series was snapped up by the tabloids. Barbara lodged the cheques in the bank and ordered damp proofing for the house.

"Get something pretty for yourself," Barry suggested.

"Why? When do you have time to look at me?"

"That's not true, sweetheart, I'm looking at you right now." Although he had a hundred other things to do Barry let the world wait for a couple of hours while he proved he was not ignoring her.

JAMES Callaghan became the new British prime minister in April of 1976. One of his first official acts was to order a change in the administrative ranks of Northern Ireland. The province was a seriously hot potato. A number of people had suggestions for dealing with the problem, but they were facing a stone wall. Two stone walls.

Republicans demanded the British army leave, to be followed by power sharing and ultimately a united Ireland.

Ian Paisley said No.

ON the fourteenth of April a four-hour peace vigil was held in St. Anne's Cathedral, Belfast. The names of 1,289 victims of the violence in Northern Ireland were read aloud. Men and women fingered their rosaries; some wept silently.

Four days later Gerry Adams, in one of his "Brownie" articles, addressed a message to the Volunteers on the eve of the sixtieth anniversary of the Easter Rising. "Active Republicanism means hard work, action, example . . . It means fighting. It's hard to write that down because, God knows, maybe I won't fight again and it will be cast up at me."[1]

In the Republic the Fine Gael/Labour coalition completely ignored the anniversary of the Easter Rising until the Sinn Féin Party announced its own commemoration, to be called "Reclaim the Spirit of 1916." The government banned the event. But over ten thousand people gathered at the GPO to hear a number of speakers. Nora Connolly, the daughter of James Connolly, one of the signatories of the Proclamation of the Republic, was amongst those prosecuted for defying the government's ban.

The Irish government then staged its own hasty wreath-laying at the GPO, unannounced and unattended by the public. Barry was invited to photograph the event but he was too disgusted to attend.

"I thought the politicians liked having you take their pictures," Barbara said. "You'll lose business if you act like that."

He set his jaw and did not answer.

O N the first of May Kenneth Newman, a dapper, slightly built pipe smoker and one of two deputy chief constables in Northern Ireland, was appointed chief constable of the RUC. Earlier in his career Newman had served with the police in Palestine and seen action during the violent campaign against the British policy of excluding the Jews.

Under the new chief constable new internal guidelines, known as the Walker Report, were issued. A policing culture was instituted that centralised decision-making power in the hands of the RUC Special Branch,[2] effectively making the Branch above any law but its own.

On the fifth of May nine republican prisoners tunnelled their way out of one of the Cages in Long Kesh. They had set up an ingenuous false wall at the rear of their Nissan hut, so that guards looking into the hut believed everything was normal. In actuality the wall concealed the soil they were digging out and the deepening hole.

A young recruit was assigned the role of lookout. His job was to stand at the front of the hut holding up a plate if the guards were coming, and lowering it as an all-clear. On the final day of tunnelling he was so excited he gave the wrong signal. Guards seized the men before they could make good their getaway.

On the day following the attempted breakout eight members of the SAS* were discovered in the Republic of Ireland. They claimed they had crossed the border by mistake.

---

*Special Air Service, a branch of the British army.

$\bullet$ $\bullet$ $\bullet$

A brief note from McCoy informed the Hallorans, "We had a wee bit of excitement here a couple of weeks back. The seagull almost flew away."

In the first week of June Barry had news of his own.

Dear Séamus,
Patrick James is on his way! The doctor tells us he could be a Christmas baby. I hope you approve of his name—Barbara suggested the "James" and Ursula and I heartily concur.

Chapter Twenty-one

IRELAND sweltered in a three-month heat wave that summer. Temperatures were in the seventies. Chemists sold salt tablets to their customers.

A new day dawned in aviation when the spectacular Concorde was launched.

Swedish pop group Abba hit the charts with "Money, Money, Money."

For an undisclosed sum former film star Grace Kelly, now princess of Monaco, purchased her ancestral home in County Mayo; thirty-five acres with a two-room cottage.

"GOOD enough for some," Barbara sniffed. The heat combined with her pregnancy was making her irritable. "With all that woman's wealth I don't know why she'd want to buy a hovel in the back of the beyond."

"She's Irish," Barry replied.

"I don't see what that has to do with it. She's not going to live there, she has that gorgeous palace in Monaco. It probably even has air-conditioning. If I had a home like that . . ." She left the thought hanging in the air.

Barry had become accustomed to the disparaging remarks she made about the house in Harold's Cross. *Isabella probably puts her up to it,* he thought. *Wants her princess to live in a castle. But castles are no place for Irish republicans, even if we could afford one.*

Yet he found himself eyeing property that bore "For Sale" signs. Large old Georgian houses in a sufficient state of dilapidation to be affordable. Dublin was filled with them.

It would be quite an adventure to buy a place like that and restore it. And a good investment, too—if Ireland ever becomes prosperous enough to have a strong housing market.

Which seemed highly unlikely.

F R O M the twenty-eighth of June there was a bank strike in the Republic. When people ran out of cheques they wrote them on scraps of paper and even paper napkins. Shopkeepers extended credit for food and other essentials; barter replaced the pound note as currency.

When the banks finally reopened on the sixth of September all cheques were honoured and debts paid. There was no report of anyone having lost money.

T H E fourth of July 1976, marked the bicentennial of the Declaration of Independence and the birth of the United States of America. Huge celebrations were held throughout the nation. A number of Irish Americans sent for their impoverished relatives "in the Old Country" to spend a holiday sharing the fun. Men and women and wide-eyed

children from Waterford and Galway and tiny farms in
Kerry wandered along the streets of New York and Boston,
staring at wonders they had never dreamed existed.

Meanwhile in Northern Ireland loyalists shot and
bombed and bludgeoned Catholics and the IRA ambushed
British soldiers and members of the RUC and planted
bombs along lonely roadways frequented by the security
forces.

And ordinary Irish men and women struggled to keep a
roof over their heads and food on the table.

WE'RE going to have to raise our prices," Barbara told
Barry. "We can't afford to keep feeding the boarders on
what they're paying us."

He said, "They're doing the best they can, same as everyone else."

"If the Irish had any gumption they'd stop meekly accepting whatever fate dishes out and make some changes.
Isn't there any fight in you at all?"

*Isn't there any fight in you at all? Oh, Barbara. If only
you knew.*

LOUTH man Séamus Ludlow was murdered while
hitchhiking outside of Dundalk, and his body dumped by
the roadside. The day after the body was found the Gardai claimed the IRA had killed Ludlow because he was an
informer. The claim split his family in two—particularly
after Special Branch tried to implicate some members of
Ludlow's family in his murder.

Four days after Ludlow's death a group of heavily armed
SAS men carrying weapons not associated with the British
army and wearing civilian clothes were detained in nearby
Omeath. Local people suspected they had been involved in
a number of recent killings along the border, but they were
released without charge after the Irish minister for foreign

affairs, Fine Gael's Garret FitzGerald, intervened in the investigation.[1]

For over twenty years the Gardai would continue to insist the IRA had killed Ludlow. Then massive pressure from families of the victims of the Dublin-Monaghan bombings caused a private inquiry into state-sponsored collusion to be undertaken. Justice Henry Barron, who headed up the enquiry and issued a report that has never been challenged by either the Irish or British governments, named and identified four loyalist paramilitaries as Ludlow's killers.

Liam Cosgrave, who had been *taoiseach* at the time of the Dublin-Monaghan bombings, refused to cooperate with the enquiry.

CHRISTOPHER Ewart-Biggs, the British ambassador to Ireland, was killed in Dublin on the twenty-first of July when an IRA land mine exploded under his car. Taoiseach Liam Cosgrave declared, "The atrocity fills all Irish people with a sense of shame."[2]

Eight days later Merlyn Rees told the House of Commons that there had been no discussions between Provisional Sinn Féin and the British government since early in the year.

Speaking at a republican rally on the anniversary of internment, Máire Drumm demanded the reinstatement of Special Category Status for republican prisoners. "If it is necessary," she said, "Belfast will come down stone by stone."[3]

THE summer grew hotter.

ON the tenth of August an IRA getaway car went out of control when the driver was shot and killed by a soldier in the Andersonstown area of Belfast. The car mounted the pavement and crushed Anne Maguire and her three young children. Two of the children died at the scene; the third died later. Mrs. Maguire was seriously injured.

Within forty-eight hours a thousand women gathered in Andersonstown in a spontaneous demonstration calling for peace. An even larger crowd attended a second rally on the fourteenth. A week later Mairéad Corrigan, an aunt of the dead children, and local woman Betty Williams addressed twenty thousand women, both Catholic and Protestant, in Ormeau Park. The Peace People Movement was born.

WHEN a woman called Rosaleen O'Kane was found in Cliftonpark Avenue on the seventeenth of September, the condition of her naked, badly burned corpse was such that the pathologist could not determine the exact cause of death. The police suspected she was yet another victim of the Shankill Butchers.

MORE than two years had passed since the bomb exploded in Talbot Street and Ursula was still an invalid.

Invalid. The word burned inside her like an ulcer. *I hate that word. In valid. Not valid.*

Among the things she had asked Barry to bring her from the farm was the treasured, well-worn dictionary Henry Mooney had given her so many years ago. She kept the book on her bedside locker. Looking up the definition for "valid" she read: "sound, defensible; legally acceptable."

When Barbara came to her room to say lunch was ready, Ursula greeted her with a defiant, "I may not be sound but I am legally acceptable!"

"What on earth are you talking about?"

"My status."

"I didn't know it was in question."

"It is in question."

Humour her, Barbara told herself. "You're Barry's mother and Brian's grandmother and my mother-in-law, so that's your status."

Ursula reached for the dictionary. "Status . . . status . . . here it is: 'rank or social position; relative importance.'"

Barbara laughed. "Well, you're an important relative all right. As for the other—of all the people I know, you care the least about rank and social position. You're the exact opposite of my mother in that respect." She began folding up the quilt at the foot of the bed.

Because of her advancing pregnancy Barbara no longer lifted Ursula. With fierce determination the older woman had learned to manoeuvre her upper body from the bed into the wheelchair unaided—as long as the wheels were locked. She could wheel the chair as well, and took pride in the speed she was able to obtain up and down the length of the front hall.

But it was not enough; not as good as being free.

"Every sentient being has a sense of status, Barbara," she said as she settled herself in the chair. "Hens have a pecking order, bees have queens and drones. And look at the northern unionists. They're determined to remain part of Britain because they think it confers some sort of superior status."

Barbara followed her out of the room. "Is this going to be another monologue about politics? Don't you Hallorans ever want to talk about anything else?"

"Don't you ever want to talk about anything but yourself?" Ursula retorted.

In angry silence broken only by the creaking of the wheelchair, the two women made their way to the dining room.

Barbara slammed a bowl of soup onto the table in front of Ursula.

"What's this?"

"Potato and cabbage."

"I don't want it."

"Suit yourself," Barbara said coldly. She went into the kitchen and began the washing-up. *I should be more patient with Ursula,* she told herself as she worked. *She's old and crippled and life must be miserable for her, especially since she was always so active.*

There was no sound from the dining room. Ursula was still sitting at the table.

Opening the fridge, Barbara noticed a bowl of hardboiled eggs. She quickly shelled two and chopped them up with a bit of celery, stirred in a generous dollop of Philpott's homemade salad cream, arranged the result on a bed of lettuce, garnished the salad with a fan composed of thin slices of fragrant fresh tomato, and carried the pretty result to Ursula. "If you don't want the soup try this."

Ursula glanced at the offering and looked away. "I hate eggs. You know I hate eggs."

"Well, damn it, I hate waiting hand and foot on somebody who doesn't show an ounce of appreciation!"

The two women glared at each other for a long moment.

Ursula wheeled her chair around and went to her room.

As part of their campaign against the IRA the British government determined on a policy of criminalisation to obscure the historical and political causes of the problem in Northern Ireland. Henceforth no vestige of political status would be granted to any aspect of the republican movement. Volunteers, no matter what their crimes—or what unproven crimes they were accused of—were officially felons. British authorities spoke of "squeezing the IRA like toothpaste." Referring to current paramilitary activity, they launched an advertising campaign that announced "Seven Years Is Too Much."

IRA responded with a campaign of its own: "Seven Hundred Years Is Too Much."

When he entered the H-Blocks on September fifteenth Ciaran Nugent, the first convicted IRA prisoner to be denied Special Category Status, refused to wear a prison uniform. He explained to his guards that he was a political prisoner and under the Geneva Convention was not to be treated as a common criminal. They would "have to nail the prison uniform on his back," he said. Rather than go naked he wrapped himself in the blanket from his bed.

Nugent's act of defiance resonated through the Blocks. First one, then another man went "on the blanket."

F R O M his darkroom Barry could hear Barbara singing along with Thin Lizzy on the radio in the kitchen. Their latest hit was "The Boys Are Back in Town."

I N Armagh Women's Prison a handful of republican women began a protest in sympathy with the men on the blanket in the H-Blocks. Their prison, which stood in the centre of Armagh town and looked like an old warehouse, was notorious for its lack of facilities—and lack of common decency. Prisoners routinely were harassed and abused by their guards.[4] After joining the H-Block protest the republican women lost the very few basic privileges they had, but they held their ground.

O N the fifteenth of October two brothers from the Ulster Defence Regiment were jailed for thirty-five years each in connection with the massacre of the Miami Showband. Seventeen months before the Showband killings they had faced charges of being involved with a loyalist bomb attack, but had been allowed to continue serving with the Regiment.

It was proved in court that Thomas Raymond Crozier and Rodney Shane McDowell were also members of the Ulster Volunteer Force, but they were not given additional sentences for belonging to an illegal organisation.

AFTER being refused a visa to travel to the United States for badly needed eye surgery, Sinn Féin vice-president Máire Drumm was admitted to the Mater Hospital in North Belfast. Two members of the paramilitary Ulster Defence Association, dressed in white lab coats, walked into the ward where Mrs. Drumm was recovering from her operation. They shot her dead at close range. Jim Craig, a leading member of the UDA who also was widely reputed to be working for Special Branch,[5] was arrested for the murder. Subsequently all charges against him were dropped.

Mairéad Corrigan and Betty Williams of the Peace People declared, "We do not equate the vicious and determined terrorism of the republican and loyalist paramilitary organisations with the occasional instances when members of the security forces may have stepped beyond the law."[6]

In the Bleeding Horse, the Usual Suspects were incensed by the Corrigan-Williams statement. Luke said, "Let me see if I have this right. Those women think it's okay for the police to shoot us, but not for us to shoot them?"

"The State—any State—has the monopoly on legalised violence," Barry responded. He sounded bitter.

Patsy lurched to his feet. "We gotta do something about that." He cast a bleary eye over the other men gathered around the table. "I'll get the drinks in."

MANY in Northern Ireland shared the reaction of the Usual Suspects. The Peace People Movement began to lose support.

B Y late autumn there were a handful of "blanket men" in
the H-Blocks, both Provos and members of the INLA. As
punishment for refusing to wear prison uniforms they were
kept locked in their cells twenty-four hours a day, seven
days a week, and deprived of all privileges including reading material. The cells contained no furniture aside from
thin mattresses laid on the bare concrete floor—and chamber pots. The blanket men were not allowed to use the flush
toilets outside the cells. Shivering in their icy cells, naked
except for a blanket, they naïvely hoped their symbolic
act would persuade the British to restore Special Category
Status.

Instead it elicited the opposite response.

Interrogation procedures grew more brutal. Young men
who genuinely believed they had been fighting for Irish
freedom suffered sustained beatings of calculated cruelty.
Truncheons were held between their ankles so that both
inside ankle bones (a more sensitive area than the "funny
bone" of the elbow) could be battered at one time. Muscles were torn and joints dislocated with no medical assistance given afterwards.

The protestors in the H-Blocks refused to bow to the
policy of criminalisation because it would mean they accepted the authority of the state—the British state, the
"conquerors"—and by extension accepted the partition
Britain had enforced on Ireland and British right to occupy Irish soil. Every one of the republicans understood
this in the marrow of his bones.

In spite of inhumane treatment they fought to remain
human. Their unshakable camaraderie was the secret envy
of their guards. They lifted one another's spirits by singing
rebel songs or love songs or even ancient working songs,
their voices echoing down the dismal corridors. Men stood
at the doors of their cells and shouted whatever came into
their heads: anything that might possibly interest or enter-

tain fellow prisoners. In this way the Blocks learned about fishing on Lough Neagh and the construction of a bootleg radio; the medieval Gaelic poets and the manufacture of *poitín*; last year's World Cup lineup and Napoleon's campaign in Russia.

The republicans were under almost constant scrutiny during the day but the night was theirs. After the last bell check at eleven o'clock, it was story time.

The storyteller pushed his mattress close to the door of his cell. In the H-Blocks sound travelled. When Bobby Sands shouted "the book at bedtime," he had a large and enthusiastic audience.

During Sands' first imprisonment in Long Kesh he had been in Cage Eleven with Gerry Adams, though he lived in a different hut. A bright-faced young man with a mane of wild red hair and an insatiable appetite for learning, Sands was popular with his fellow prisoners. He was a tough opponent on the football field, read voraciously, studied and became fluent in Irish, would talk to anyone about anything, and had a gift for poetry.

After being released from the Cages Sands was soon rearrested on the most convenient charge, possession of a firearm. This time he was sent to the H-Blocks. There he began keeping a diary of his prison experiences, written on toilet paper and smuggled out. Writing had become central to his understanding of himself.

When I was growing up I heard my mother talk about 1916 mostly in terms of James Connolly, and his fight for the rights of the working man. It didn't mean much to me then. I believed the RUC and the British Soldiers were the good guys, like in the westerns. Then came 1969, and the B-Specials poured into our neighbourhood to smash and burn and kill right along with the loyalists. That changed everything for me. By Easter of '71 I wanted nothing so much as to be part of the Provos, the people's army of resistance. At eighteen

and a half I joined the IRA. Since then I've been ha-
rassed, brutalised, and on the run, but at least I was
fighting back. A lot of my friends from my schooldays
were my comrades in arms.

I was arrested in 1972 but refused to recognise the
authority of the court. I spent three and a half years as
a POW with Special Category Status. When I was re-
leased I went back to the struggle—and here I am
again.

"The republican movement has given me an educa-
tion I never had. In school the only history we were
taught was English history, but I'm Irish! Now I can
read my own language and I know who my people are.
Me and the rest of the Volunteers would do anything for
them, same as they'll do anything for us. No matter
how much the Brits beat and batter us now, our revenge
will be the laughter of our children.[7]

In his nighttime storytelling Sands specialised in tales
in which the hero was an underdog who set himself
against the establishment. A favourite subject was the
American Indian chieftain Geronimo. Bobby also recited
from memory his versions of such politically based novels as *Trinity* and *Doctor Zhivago*.

Lying in the dark, listening with their eyes closed and
their minds fully engaged, the prisoners escaped Long
Kesh. For a while they became free spirits successfully
rebelling against all the injustice of an unjust world.

During the day the sanitation issue became a particular
bone of contention. A disposal trolley was supposed to
visit each cell once or twice every day to empty the
chamber pots. Then the authorities stopped sending the
trolley around.

With no way to dispose of their contents, the pots overflowed. It was only a matter of time until there was urine
and excrement all over the floor. When the prisoners tried

to hurl their faeces out the window the warders wired up the windows.

The desperate men began smearing it on the walls.

The Blanket Protest became the Dirty Protest.

THE Usual Suspects were outraged. "Those lousy Prod scumbags!" Patsy cried. "How can they treat our boys like that! Them guards ain't human. They're filthy maggots what oughta be ground under the heels of real men."

Barry said, "Insulting the other side is a coward's way to fight. There's nothing honourable about it. The concept of honour may be old-fashioned now, but it was intrinsic to the men of 1916. It is to me too."

"What else can we do *but* call them names?" Luke wanted to know. "We're not like you, Barry; young and strong. You could be back in the fight tomorrow."

Barry gave Luke a sombre look. In the depths of his grey eyes, banked fires smouldered.

Getting to his feet, he went to the bar and started ordering double whiskies. When the mood was on him he could drink an awesome amount and still appear to be sober, but he rarely indulged. One thing he never allowed himself was to get out of control.

On this night he almost did. At the last moment he bade the Usual Suspects good night and headed for home.

When someone switched on the light in her room, Ursula fought her way out of a tangle of dreams to see Barry standing in the doorway; or rather, leaning against the doorway.

"I need to ask you a question," he said. "Was my father a good man?"

Ursula blinked. "Your father?"

"Finbar Cassidy. That was his name, was it not?"

"It was his name."

"Was he a good man?"

"What do you mean by 'good'?"

Barry peered at her owlishly. "I don't know." Ursula realised he was drunk. "Kind, I guess." He paused; considered. "Or gentle."

The lines bracketing her mouth softened. An impartial observer might have glimpsed the young woman she once had been. "Your father was the kindest, gentlest man I ever knew."

"Ah." Barry turned around very carefully, like a man unsure of his balance, and started for the stairs. Then he turned around again and came back.

"Thank you," he said with formal politeness.

"Go to bed, Barry," his mother told him.

The following morning at the breakfast table she chose a moment when no one else was listening. "Why did you ask me if your father was a good man?" she asked in a low voice.

Barry did not swing his gaze towards her but turned his entire upper body in her direction. Slowly. Giving the headache no excuse to roll thunder through his skull. "Just pub conversation. Last night we were discussing nurture versus nature."

"That doesn't sound like pub conversation to me."

"How would you know? Ladies don't go into pubs."

"I am not a *lady*," Ursula said with disdain. "I am a *republican*."

BREDA Cunningham now only came once a week to the yellow brick house. Ursula claimed she did not need a nurse at all, but she looked forward to Breda's visits. Occasionally there was pain she admitted to no one else, which the nurse could alleviate with a hypodermic needle. More importantly, Breda eased her loneliness.

"Sometimes it feels like I'm stranded on a raft in the ocean," Ursula confided one day when the pain threatened to swallow her whole. "The sharks are circling and I'm helpless."

"Now don't talk like that, you're a lot stronger than you used to be."

"Only upper body strength," Ursula said dismissively. "Basically I'm still helpless. And Barry's wife hates me. Oh, she hides it most of the time. She's too intelligent to start an open war, but not intelligent enough to realise I'm not her enemy. Before my accident I didn't realise how she felt because we were never alone together for any length of time. When I came up to Dublin Barry was always here. And Séamus, of course."

Breda pursed her lips as she put the hypodermic needle back into its blue velvet case. "Every time you mention Séamus McCoy I hear something in your voice. You'd best tell me about him."

Ursula searched for a brief summation that would satisfy her inquisitor. "Séamus can do anything he turns his hand to, he's as useful as a little pot."

"That's not a man you're talking about," the nurse said, "it's a convenience. Tell me about the man."

"He's been like a father to Barry."

Breda gave her a searching look. "And? Is there something wrong with him? Does he have two heads? Two wives? Does the poor fella snore?"

Ursula's eyes twinkled. "I wouldn't know about that— the snoring, I mean. But he's not married and he's quite presentable."

"So everything's grand for the two of you except he's in prison."

"You read too many trashy novels, Breda."

When the new baby came Barbara would have her hands full, so Barry offered Warren Philpott the job of housekeeper. The little man's initial response was negative. "I sold the boardinghouse to you in the first place to be rid of all that."

"I could hire someone else, Warren, but you know the place better than anyone else. Suppose I offer you double what I'm paying you to cook, and . . . the old couple in the mews has decided to move in with their married daughter. You can have their flat when they leave."

An avaricious glint appeared in Philpott's eye. "As a sitting tenant? And for a nominal rent?"

Barry did some quick calculations in his head. "Very well, but the arrangement's just between us. You'll be keeping the books so my wife doesn't need to know."

Warren Philpott was mightily pleased with himself. When he sold the house to Barry in 1963 he had felt guilty about relinquishing property that had been in his family for generations. Now he had some of it back again. His status as a sitting tenant would mean in twenty years, if he lived that long, the mews flat was as good as his.

For good historical reasons, Irish law no longer favoured the landlords.

W HILE the children were small and boiling with energy, Barry often took the morning paper and searched for a temporarily uninhabited corner of his house where he could peruse it in peace.

Barbara hunted him down.

She stood in the doorway, arms akimbo, and said, "Why are you so grumpy all the time?"

He looked up. "I'm not grumpy."

"Yes you are, and it's awful. Look at you now with your long face. I don't know why you can't at least be pleasant."

"I thought I was being pleasant. Besides, I'm trying to read the newspaper and I rarely smile and laugh at what I see in the papers."

"You could at least make an effort," she said.

And walked away.

IN November the Peace People held a rally on the Falls
Road, the Catholic heartland of West Belfast. The Falls
was also Sinn Féin heartland. Party speakers usurped the
rally. Loud cheers greeted the remark, "Any call for peace,
regardless of the sincerity of those involved, which singles
out republican violence and which ignores the nature of the
society in which we live, is doomed to failure."

Writing from Long Kesh, Gerry Adams stated, "Republicans must ensure that our cause and methods remain
within the bounds of our own conscience. Revolutionary
violence must be controlled and disciplined, a symbol of
our people's resistance and the spearhead of their desire
for a peaceful and just society."[8]

THE Dirty Protest had no more effect on the authorities
than did the Blanket Protest, but it provided the enemies
of republicanism with fresh ammunition for denigrating
the IRA. "Filthy animals," was the mildest epithet.

Through his contacts in the international press Barry
Halloran was given an assignment to cover the story. It
would make him one of the few photojournalists ever to
enter the H-Blocks. He was assured there would be no
delay in obtaining the necessary credentials; the authorities wanted to display "IRA bestiality" to the world.

Barbara's reaction was predictable. "I don't want you
to go."

"It will only be for a couple of days, and I'll be able to
visit Séamus too."

"You'll be away when I go into labour, I know you
will."

"You're not due yet," Barry reminded her, "and I just
told you, I'll be back in a couple of days."

"But I'll be alone until then!"

"Not a bit of it. You'll have the boarders and Philpott and my mother, and if it will make you feel better I'll ask Mrs. Cunningham to stay here with you until . . ."

"So there's another room that will be costing us money instead of making money," Barbara complained.

T H E visitors' entrance for the H-Blocks was on the opposite side of the prison from the entrance to the Cages. Barry had to show a visitor's pass to get into the car park and produce his full documentation at the front gates, then again at a guard box just inside. The sentry on duty placed a phone call. Within a couple of minutes a prison official wearing civilian clothes arrived. He had a sallow complexion and wore a precisely knotted tie. He did not give Barry his name. No one involved with the prison cared to have their names known in the outside world. It was too dangerous.

After scrutinising Barry's papers at some length, the official looked up and scrutinised his face. "So you're a photojournalist."

"I am."

"We don't see many of those here. We've been told to accommodate you. Follow me." Turning smartly, he led Barry to a pair of corrugated iron gates in the towering cement wall that surrounded the H-Block compound.

Barry felt the weight of unseen eyes watching him from the observation posts.

At a curt nod from his companion, a uniformed guard opened a door in one of the gates and Barry got his first look at the H-Blocks.

There was something inherently menacing in the architecture of the Maze (Cellular). The massive, flat-topped grey Blocks crouched against the boggy earth like poisonous toads restrained within a labyrinth of wire and metal.

They were too big to photograph, Barry realised. The only way to take a picture of one would be from a helicopter, and from that distance the image would lose much of its impact. *They wouldn't let me bring a helicopter within an ass's roar of this place anyway.*

He was conducted to a featureless room in a small cement building, where he was searched by two guards while a third, ostentatiously armed, watched the procedure. *Screws,* Barry said to himself, mentally slipping into prison slang. The three men spoke to one another. No one spoke to Barry. He endured the search stoically, trying to imagine the effect this would have on someone's wife; someone's mother. His cameras and equipment also were searched. He had no faith that the guards knew anything about cameras, but everything was returned to him in good order.

The prison official rejoined him as he left the building. Two uniformed guards fell in behind them. From the moment Barry passed through the front gates at least one guard had always been within three paces of him.

If I had never done anything wrong in my life I would be feeling guilty by now, he thought.

"We're taking you to H-Three," his guide said. "There are protestors in Blocks Three, Four, and Five, but one example should satisfy you. I don't want you to get the wrong impression of the Maze, Mr. Halloran. We take excellent care of our prisoners. In every Block there's a library for the prisoners and a hobby room where they can play cards, shoot billiards, and so forth. They can also take part in arts and crafts, we even supply the materials. Plus we show a film once a month for those men who are on good behaviour. The first film we showed was *The Great Escape,* in fact."[9]

Suspecting this was a bizarre joke, Barry turned to look at him. The man was absolutely serious.

The entrance to Block Three was a featureless steel door set in a featureless cement wall. Beyond was a cement anteroom—cement floor, walls, and ceiling—that led to a narrow corridor blocked by another steel door. A barred door, this time. The chief warder, the principal officer in the Block, came forward to unlock the door.

Barry's guide left him abruptly. The two uniformed guards stayed at his back.

There was a whole series of barred doors. Each had to be unlocked and relocked after the party passed through, before the next could be unlocked. Progress seemed painfully slow in the claustrophobic passageway. The air was dead.

At the end of the passage was a wall of noise. The slightest sound was endlessly amplified by the hard surfaces, bouncing back and forth to become part of an ambient roar. One sound in particular would haunt Barry for years: the nerve-wrenching scream of the iron slider bolts in the heavy doors. A thousand fingernails screeching their way across a thousand slates in hell.

The air in H3 was not dead. It was chokingly thick with the stench of rotten food and urine and excrement. And anger, most of all.

Harsh fluorescent lighting overhead was an assault to the eyes. The few windows were divided by vertical bars of concrete that made any view of the horizon impossible. Narrow observation slits were fitted into the cells so that a man could be watched at any hour of the night or day.

The place was ruthlessly efficient in a way calculated to destroy not only the will, but the soul.

People should run out of here screaming, Barry said to himself. *Not just the prisoners, the guards too. This is a womb to make monsters.*

The chief warder directed him to the first cell. Barry fought down the urge to vomit. One of the guards sniggered. "Stinks, don't it? But they love it, animals love the smell of their own stink." He unlocked and opened the steel door.

The man stood in the middle of the cell. He was naked except for a thin blanket wrapped around his shoulders and as much of his body as possible. He might have been a boy or a man; his features were lost in a bush of untrimmed beard. The tips of his fingers were bloody where he had attempted to wear down his overgrown fingernails by scraping them on the concrete.

He might have been anyone.

Anyone's brother, anyone's son.

The cell measured 2.25 metres by 2.75 metres and contained no furniture; no fittings. The single lightbulb in its wire cage had been removed. The walls were smeared with swoops and swirls of excrement. Some had dried to a crusty blackish brown. Some was fresh. A mural of desperation painted with the raw materials of a human body.

Barry met the man's eyes. Amidst the filth they were clean and unafraid.

Barry turned to the chief warder. "Can I go in and take photographs?"

"It's what you're here for, isn't it?"

"Am I allowed to talk to him?"

"If you want, but we'll be watching. We watch 'em all the time," he added unnecessarily. "Like animals in a zoo, they are."

The prisoner turned to watch Barry enter. His features were concealed by his beard but his eyes were wary. He had learned to expect anything and nothing.

"I am Barry Halloran," Barry said, holding out his hand. "I'm a photojournalist, and I've received permission to document what you're doing here."

The prisoner hesitated as if expecting a trick. Barry gave him a reassuring smile. The man submitted to a perfunctory handshake before his fingers scurried back to reclaim the blanket that was sliding off his body. For a brief moment Barry glimpsed the extensive pattern of old bruises that mottled his flesh.

He gave his name and prison number, adding, "I am not a criminal."

Barry tried to keep the emotions he was feeling out of his voice. "Would you be willing to talk to me about yourself and how you came to be in here?"

"I am willing." But the eyes were still wary.

Barry started to put down his camera so he could take his notebook out of his pocket. Then he realised there was no surface upon which he dared set an expensive camera. "Will you hold this for a minute?" he asked the prisoner.

From the doorway the warder said, "I'll take that for you." He backed out of the cell with Barry's camera in his hand and closed the door.

The awful finality of a prison door closing behind him was one Barry had avoided all his life. Hearing it now, in this place, made him think of clods falling onto a coffin.

"I'm not a criminal," the prisoner repeated, "but I'm here because of criminals. Where I grew up people lived in dread of the Orangeys"—he gave the nickname the Belfast pronunciation. "Loyalists could do whatever they liked and the RUC wouldn't lift a finger. So me and a bunch of the lads set out to provide our people with protection."

"You joined the IRA," Barry said.

"They joined me, more like. We had to do something, it was our homes and our women and kids who were suffering. You don't know how bad it was."

"You're wrong about that," Barry said softly. "I know exactly how bad it was."

The prisoner squinted up at him. "Say . . . have we met someplace before?"

Barry shook his head. "We've never met before."

But I know you. And you know me.

Chapter Twenty-two

HE ain't there," said the guard on duty at the main gate to the Cages.

"What do you mean he's not there?"

With a tobacco-stained forefinger, the guard stabbed the request form Barry had filled out. "This says you want to visit prisoner 413, Company B, Cage Sixteen. He ain't there. So you can't visit him," the man added with irrefutable logic.

"Are we both talking about Séamus McCoy?" Barry asked.

The guard consulted a prison roster, muttering to himself as he turned the pages. "James Paul McCoy, it says here."

"That's the Anglicised version of his name, but he never uses it."

The guard scowled at Barry. "Is his name James or not? If it ain't, you can't see him at all."

"So he is here!"

"Not in Cage Sixteen he ain't."

"I've visited him before with that information."

"Maybe some other guard didn't pay attention to the Cage number you wrote down. But me, I'm thorough. McCoy ain't in Cage Sixteen so I'm not sending nobody to fetch him."

Barry knew stubborn when he saw it. Throttling his voice down to a tone of infinite patience, he said, "Can you tell me which Cage he's in?"

"If you don't know you got no business seeing him."

"But he has been moved?"

"Long time ago. Prisoners get moved around for a lot of reasons. Sometimes troublemakers have to be separated."

"Is that what happened with Séa . . . with James Mc-Coy?"

The guard looked indignant. "How should I know? The gov'nor don't discuss his decisions with me, all I have to do is make sure the forms are filled out proper. This one ain't. You get it right, you can come back and try again."

Obtaining McCoy's correct address was not difficult, but like everything to do with the prison system, getting a new visitor's pass issued took time. Three days passed before Barry again presented himself at the gates of Long Kesh.

A different guard admitted him with only a cursory glance at his documentation.

Barry's first question to McCoy was, "Why did you not tell me you'd been transferred?"

"Oh, that," he said nonchalantly. "That was a while back. I wrote your mother and gave her the new address."

"She neglected to tell me. Why were you moved?"

"I wanted to learn more Irish so I applied for a transfer to Cage Eleven, where they have a Gaeltacht hut with fluent speakers teaching the other lads. Since I'd managed to stay out of trouble—as far as the screws knew—since the fire, my request went through. The opportunity to study Irish is the best thing about the Kesh. Once we have the language, we're free.

"The men in Cage Eleven have a great spirit. I'm proud to know all of 'em. Not just Gerry Adams, but 'Cleaky' Clarke and Jim Gibney and Gerry Kelly and a pal of mine called Bobby Sands, who was released some months back. We may see him in here again, though. Getting released doesn't mean one of us is free, they'll lift him again as soon as they can—on charges of belonging to the IRA if for no other reason."

For a moment McCoy sounded bitter, then he made himself smile. "Enough of my moaning, Seventeen. How're you keeping?"

"All right."

McCoy studied his face. "If you say so. And your mother, how's she?"

Barry silently shook his head.

"Hell of a thing, isn't it?" said McCoy. "Life, I mean. No matter what you think it's going to be, it turns out to be something else. Your mother should be down in Clare training up a pony for little Brian to learn to ride on. And I should be back in the war. Instead . . . I could just about stand being a POW, but criminalisation is the nastiest trick the Brits have come up with since they sent the Black and Tans over. Instead of being freedom fighters, they've put us on the same level as rapists and child abusers. It's just another bloody way of humiliating the Irish.

"Seventeen, you and I both know that not every Volunteer is an altar boy. Out of any thousand men, whether they're labourers or priests or members of the IRA, there'll be a few who are twisted. The majority try to be decent skins and make a pretty good fist of it. But if you treat men like criminals sooner or later they're going to act like criminals. No wonder the screws are scared of being shot when they go home at night. I don't personally know of any man in the Cages who's marked some screw's card for him, but it happens. It happens in the Blocks too—probably more often. They're suffering more over there."

Barry nodded grimly.

His recent experience had made him acutely aware of the differences between the two parts of Long Kesh. The Cages were still a prison and security measures had been tightened since his last visit, but there was open air and natural light. The Cages were in the real world and so were their occupants.

The Blocks were a nightmare world of their own.

When the guard came to take McCoy back to Cage

Eleven his parting words to Barry were, "Patrick James Halloran. That has a powerful ring to it!"

Barry had checked out of his hotel before going to visit McCoy. He wanted to drive straight back to Dublin from Long Kesh, so he could develop his photographs as soon as possible. As he headed south he kept thinking about the images burned onto the film. The stark and sombre H-Blocks. The pathetic dignity—or was pathetic even the right word?—of the blanket men. The self-inflicted horror of their condition.

The splendid new billiards table in the games room—which he learned was paid for out of the prisoners' own funds—with its immaculate green felt. The only touch of green in the Maze.

He decided he would include no text with the photographs, just simple captions. That way neither side could accuse him of propagandizing.

The camera would do that for him.

Fyodor Dostoyevsky, the author of *Crime and Punishment,* once observed, "The degree of civilisation in a society can be judged by entering its prisons."

The roads north of the border were well paved and signposted. They should be. Northern Ireland, with its population of slightly over a million people, was costing the British taxpayer almost one billion pounds annually. Its internal economy, based on dying industries, was very far in the red. Without massive support from the rest of the United Kingdom the province would be bankrupt. Tenacious lobbying by the unionists kept the money rolling in, and it showed.

As soon as Barry drove across the border a drastic change occurred. The main artery between Belfast and Dublin abruptly turned from a modern motorway into a country road paved with disintegrating tarmacadam and scarred with potholes.

Under his breath he muttered to himself, "Why would

the unionists want to become part of the Republic anyway?"

When Barry reached Harold's Cross Philpott met him at the door. "They've taken her to hospital," the little man announced with the delight peculiar to people who enjoy giving bad news.

"Who? My mother?"

"Your wife."

"Sweet Jesus, mercy," Barry said automatically. "What happened?"

"I'm not sure, it was this morning and I'd gone to the shops for fresh veg. When I came back the ambulance was just pulling away. Mrs. Cunningham went with her. I rang your hotel in Belfast but you'd already checked out."

Barry ran to his mother's room. "Do you know what's wrong with Barbara?"

"She seemed perfectly fine at breakfast," Ursula told him. "Then this afternoon suddenly she announced she wanted to go to the hospital, so off they went."

The hospital lobby already had a tree decorated with multicoloured lights. Barry did not see it. He was fixed like a bullet on one target. At the front desk he asked his wife's condition and demanded to see the consultant in obstetrics, all in one breath.

The chief of the obstetrical department sought to retain a professional distance because being accosted by anxious fathers was part of his everyday experience. But Barry Halloran was very big and very intense. Not the sort of man one could easily handle.

Sweat broke out on the consultant's forehead. "I'm trying to tell you, Mr. Halloran, your wife insisted on the procedure. We don't like to do it except as a matter of absolute necessity because there are certain risks involved. But Mrs. Halloran was so overwrought I deemed it wiser to give in rather than letting her reach a state of hysteria."

Barry loomed over the man. "But she is all right? You're absolutely sure?"

"Perfectly all right, they both are. The infant was only a couple of weeks early and as well developed as a full-term child. We had an incubator ready and waiting but it wasn't necessary."

"Can I see him?"

The consultant relaxed enough to smile. "Him? You mean her. You have an exceptionally strong little girl."

Barry went to the nursery first. He wanted time to get control of his emotions before confronting Barbara.

The attending nurse lifted a tiny bundle of blankets out of a cot and brought Infant Halloran to the window for her father to see. Little red face, little red fists clutched close to chin. Then the eyes opened. Dark blue. Although Barry knew she could not focus on anything yet, he was willing to swear she looked right at him.

Hello, Grace Mary. Welcome to the world. Welcome to Ireland. It's in a bit of a mess right now but it's going to get better. I promise.

Barbara was still groggy, but as soon as he entered the room she said peevishly, "You should have been here, Barry. You let me down when I needed you most."

He balled his fists at his sides. "The doctor tells me you demanded to have labour induced even though there were risks involved."

She opened her eyes wide. "I was already *in* labour and they wouldn't acknowledge it!"

"You put our child in danger so you would have something to use against me as emotional blackmail."

"I did no such thing! Oh, Barry, how could you say that?" She turned her face into the pillow and began to sob.

Icily furious, he stalked from the room.

He found Breda Cunningham in the hospital café drinking a cup of tea. Barry slumped into a chair beside her.

Suddenly he felt very tired. "Thank you for staying with my wife, Breda," he said. "Tell me, was she really in labour, or not?"

The nurse set down her cup. "You must understand, I've had no training in obstetrics. She was sweating and appeared to be in pain so I didn't take any chances. I rang for an ambulance right away."

"That was the right thing to do," he said automatically.

She smiled. "You have a beautiful little girl, so there was no harm anyway."

W E shall have to wait a while for Patrick James," Barry wrote to McCoy. "Grace Mary decided to come first."

I N his next letter McCoy wrote, "Ask Patrick James to have the decency to wait until I'm out of here before he puts in his appearance. I'd like to attend the christening."

He was always eager for letters from the Hallorans, but the pleasure was bittersweet. They made him aware of life going on without him. When other men spoke of their wives or their girlfriends McCoy told himself, *I don't regret a thing. The Army's my life, and it'll be there for me when I get out.*

He thought he understood what impelled priests to make a lifelong commitment that excluded all other forms of commitment. In an uncertain world, unwavering dedication bestowed emotional serenity.

Yet sometimes, in the darkness before dawn, he thought of Ursula Halloran.

W H E N they brought the new baby home the house in Harold's Cross underwent a dramatic transformation. Brian, an energetic but well-behaved little boy, had for the most part adjusted himself to the adult rhythms of the house. Grace Mary made no such concessions. She was the centre of the world and everyone would have to adjust to her.

As if to make her point, on her very first day in the Halloran household she screamed ceaselessly. For a new-born baby she had amazing lung power. Even when nestled in her mother's arms, well fed, snugly wrapped in fresh blankets and wearing a dry nappy, she shrieked in a voice that could be heard to the top of the house.

Barbara was baffled. "What am I supposed to do now?" she asked her husband.

Barry had no suggestions.

Barbara stood up and walked, sang, patted, sat down, rocked, walked again, sang again, and patted some more. The baby went on screaming.

Finally Barry took the squalling infant to give her mother a few minutes of relief. During the transfer the blankets in which the child was cocooned became dislodged, and fresh air reached her hot little body.

She stopped crying. In the blink of an eye Grace Mary changed from a squalling fury into a cooing bundle. One tiny hand celebrated its newfound freedom by reaching towards her father's face.

That hand clutched Barry's heart.

"I've fallen in love again," he confessed to Ursula. "With my own child."

"She's not your anything," his mother averred. "She's her own person. She will grow up to be more separate from you than you can possibly imagine right now, but that's how it should be."

"That's years and years away."

"I assure you, it's closer than you think."

Barry was besotted with his daughter but less than pleased with her mother. Believing Barbara had wilfully chosen to induce the pregnancy—in spite of possible risk to the baby's life—he was as cold to her as he was warm to

Grace Mary. He spoke to Barbara in monosyllables when he spoke to her at all. At night, in their bed, he turned his back on her.

Barbara tried to coax him out of it but he was unresponsive. The frost had set in; deep. At last she asked Ursula to intercede on her behalf. "I really was in labour but he doesn't believe me. He'll believe you, though; tell him for me."

"I can't, Barbara. I was in my room when you decided to go to the hospital; I didn't see you. I don't know if you were in labour or not."

"Well, I'm telling you I was! I've had one baby already, I know what it's like. I felt a sudden clamping feeling in my stomach as I was going up the stairs. I waited for a moment until it eased off. A few minutes later there was another one. The pains were quite regular for a while—not hard, but enough to be noticeable. I thought I had plenty of time, so I went to our room to pack a suitcase for the hospital. When I reached up to take the case off the top of the wardrobe I felt the most awful pain rip right through me. I was afraid something had gone wrong, so I ran to the head of the stairs and called Breda and she came up to me at once. By then the clamping feeling had stopped, and that frightened me still more. I was terrified the baby would be damaged if labour stopped midway!"

"I'm not the one you have to convince," said Ursula.

Barbara tried, but there never seemed a good time to talk to Barry. If he was at home he was either in the darkroom or with the children. She had to admit he was wonderful with the baby. No matter how loudly Grace Mary was crying she would stop if her father picked her up.

"I suppose I should be jealous," Barbara remarked. "She likes you more than she likes me." She meant to flatter him; she meant it as a joke. She expected Barry to deny it.

He did not.

Barbara again appealed to her mother-in-law. "Barry said you're a great negotiator. Won't you negotiate between the two of us; persuade him to listen to my side of the story?"

"Why should I?"

Barbara was disconcerted. "Because . . . well, I mean . . ."

This time it was Ursula who did the interrupting. "Let me explain the first rule of negotiation: to get something you must give something. Take us, for instance. If you have an offer that will induce me to help you, let's hear it. But before you speak, remember that by your own choice you and I are not friends. I am not obliged to give you my support."

"Wherever did you get the idea we're not friends, Ursula? Why, I love you! You're Barry's mother and . . ."

". . . and no fool. Forget the wide-eyed stare, stage dramatics don't impress me. I'm willing to talk to the real Barbara but I won't waste my time with a phony."

Barbara lowered her elevated eyelids. "You're very direct."

"It prevents misunderstandings."

Barbara was torn between her desire to reply in kind— what a wonderful relief that would be!—and her fear of losing face by admitting Ursula was right. She chose the latter. "I don't have to stand here and be insulted," she said frigidly. Leaving the room, she slammed the door behind her. *That prissy old woman. Prissy old illegitimate woman. How dare she!*

Brian and Grace Mary kept Barbara busy for the rest of the day, while at the back of her head she carried on a running dialogue with Ursula Halloran. She thought of all the things she wished she had said: the biting, terribly clever remarks that would have cut the other woman to the bone. By teatime the energy of anger had drained away. Barbara stole a few moments' respite by sinking into a chair in the temporarily unoccupied parlour.

I need more help in this house.

She gazed vacantly around the room, noticing a thin layer of dust on the tabletops.

What I really need is a wife.
Everybody needs a wife.
All I have is a husband and he's never here, damn it.
But if I lost him . . .

I don't want to lose Barry, God knows I don't. Perhaps I should have held my temper and listened to Ursula. What was that she said? You have to give something to get something. But what can I offer him? It's too soon after the baby for sex. What else could he possibly want that . . .

Her eye fell on the unusual artefact that held pride of place in the parlour. A statue's nose with a large nick in it, the result of a well-placed rifle shot from the roof of the GPO in 1916.

Barbara had overheard Barry tell Séamus McCoy, "Blowing up Nelson's Pillar was the best thing I've done since I joined the IRA." *How can he be proud of an act of vandalism?* she wondered.

She sat up abruptly. *That's what I can do! I can make a real effort to understand the things that mean so much to him.*

She waited until the children were asleep and the boarders had retired to their rooms, then took up watch outside the darkroom door. Barry worked very late that night, as he did most nights. When he came out and saw her the skin around his eyes tightened. "What do you want?"

"What makes you think I want anything?"

"You always want something. I'm tired, Barbara; will it not wait?"

"This is very small, it won't cost money and it won't be any trouble. But now that the children are here . . . well, I think I should know more about your side of the family, so I can tell them when they're older. You once mentioned your grandfather's notebooks. Do you still have them? I'd love to see them. Maybe it would help me understand . . . well, more about you."

It was the last thing Barry had expected. "Do you mean it?"

"Absolutely," she said solemnly.

He wanted to believe her.

The next day was Sunday. After Mass Barry went up to the attics. Covered with a layer of velvety dust were broken bits of furniture, chipped chamber pots, an old dressmaker's dummy with a wasp waist, stacks of yellowing newspapers, and an assortment of packing cases that had not been opened since Philpott sold the house to Barry. "Most of that stuff belonged to my family and I've never even looked at it," he had told Barry. "I'll come back for it later and get it out of your way." He never kept the promise. Although Philpott was back, his detritus was still in the attics, together with contributions by more recent residents.

Carefully concealed beneath an old canvas horse rug in a far corner under the eaves was Ned Halloran's old canvas backpack. Once the buckles had been rusty and difficult to open, but diligent applications of metal polish over a number of years had them gleaming like new. Barry smiled to himself as he opened the pack.

Memory made manifest.

The marriage certificate of Edward Joseph Halloran and Síle Duffy. A folded square of paper with "Síle" written on it, containing a curl of russet-coloured hair. Two thick bundles of school copybooks tightly bound together with twine.

A dangerous treasure trove.

Chapter Twenty-three

BARRY took Barbara to his darkroom—which she was never invited to enter—closed and locked the door, and turned on the overhead light.

She gave a nervous laugh. "Why all the secrecy?"

"Nobody knows about these notebooks and I want to keep it that way."

"Nobody? Not even Ursula?"

"If my mother knew I had them she'd want them for herself, and I couldn't refuse. Granda originally trained to be a schoolteacher, which may be why he used ordinary school copybooks for his journals. He put everything into them; his personal experiences, his philosophy, even a bit of poetry. There's a lot of information about his time in the IRA too. You might not like that part, but it's in his authentic voice.

"I found these by accident years ago. After I read them I would have given anything to be able to talk with Granda again, but by then he was dead. I could never tell him what a remarkable man he really was. Perhaps people have to die before we love them fully, before our understanding can encompass their faults as well as their virtues and we can cherish them entire."

"I know what you mean," Barbara chimed in. "I feel the same about my grandparents. When Mom gave me my grandmother's pearls I began wondering what Ella Rutledge was like as a young woman and what her married life was like. They always seemed so happy together; I wish I could ask them what the secret was."

Barry said, "Would you listen if they told you?"

"Perhaps not. I guess every generation has to learn the same lessons all over again. No wonder we never make any progress."

The honest regret in her voice touched his heart.

We'll make progress, Barbara, he vowed silently. *Somehow, we will. Maybe this is a start.*

He stood with folded arms, watching as she bent over the notebooks. She picked up one after another and gently · turned the brittle, yellowing pages. He saw her lips move as she read one passage; he saw her smile at another.

"What's this?" she asked abruptly. "This jumble of numbers?"

Barry peered over her shoulder. His breath was warm against her cheek and she felt the familiar thrill.

"That's code," he told her. "When Granda's sister Kathleen emigrated to America she joined an organisation called Friends of Irish Freedom that raised a lot of money for the IRA. Those are Granda's records of donors and amounts."

"Can you read the code?"

"It took me a long time to decipher it, but . . ."

"So you know the names of the people who gave money?"

"I do. It's one reason for keeping these books secret. If those names became known even today there might be reprisals against their descend . . ."

In a small, tight voice, Barbara said, "Was one of them Michael Kavanagh?"

With a jolt, Barry realised it had been a serious mistake to show her the notebooks. *You damn fool, how could you have forgotten about her family history?* "There was a Michael Kavanagh," he conceded. "Of course there must have been a number of men with that name in Ameri—"

"Do those records show anything more than the names?"

"Addresses."

"And what address for that particular Michael Kavanagh?"

They had passed the point where lying was an option. Reluctantly, Barry said, "Saratoga Springs in upstate New York."

Barbara closed the notebook she was holding. She was trembling. When she spoke her voice was very faint, dragged up from the depths. "My father was named Michael Kavanagh. His father was a chauffeur for a wealthy woman in Saratoga Springs. That's where my parents met; where they lived until he was killed here in Ireland, chasing some insane dream. Now I have his death warrant in my hands." She had gone very pale. "Thank you for sharing it with me."

Walking out of the room, she left Barry with nothing to say.

SECTION 31 of the Broadcasting Act was being invoked specifically to prohibit members of the republican movement from speaking on radio or television in the Republic of Ireland.[1] The government in power that had brought this legislation into being saw no irony in its existence. The gag order covered both the IRA and Sinn Féin—a constitutionally organised political party and therefore legally entitled to speak on issues such as trade union matters involving its constituents. Section 31 made it impossible for either group to defend itself publicly against whatever charges the Irish government, the British government, or anyone else cared to make. Countless events were never filmed or recorded, denying future generations a priceless historical record.

As a freelance photojournalist Barry Halloran did not fall under the purlieu of Section 31. With his camera he could say what he pleased, as long as he had an audience for his work.

After the unfortunate incident with Barbara he relocated his grandfather's notebooks to an even safer hiding place. He could imagine her throwing the books on the fire, and they were irreplaceable. The ideals they expressed were central to his life. Written on the final flyleaf, in Ned Halloran's beautiful copperplate hand, were words from the Proclamation of the Irish Republic:

"We declare the right of the people of Ireland to the ownership of Ireland and to the unfettered control of Irish destinies, to be sovereign and indefeasible."

I N January of 1977 six members of the British defence forces were killed by IRA snipers and ambushes.

And Michael McHugh, a Catholic living in Castlederg, County Tyrone, received an unsigned letter:

> Dear Michael,
> Just a few lines to let you know that your name has been added to our list. By our list we mean our vermin extermination list.[2]

Within days McHugh was killed by the Ulster Freedom Fighters, a cover name used by the Ulster Defence Association, a major loyalist paramilitary group founded in 1971.

D E A R Séamus," Barry wrote, "I apologise for being such a poor correspondent, but I've been working all the hours God sends and then some." Barry put down the pen and stared at the nearly blank page. It would be a comfort to tell his friend about the problem with Barbara—the latest problem with Barbara—but he was a private man.

I'm sure Ursula keeps you up to speed on events in Harold's Cross. We've taken on Breda Cunningham full-time to help my mother and Barbara—another reason why I have to make money. The new baby has everyone on the hop, even Philpott. She does her sleeping in little short naps like a sentry on duty, and when she is awake we are all awake. We lost one of the boarders because of her roaring at night but we shall replace him soon enough. We could not replace Grace Mary. She's an incredible charmer most of the time. If anyone goes missing, they can be found in the nursery where she is holding court.

Sadly my time with her is limited by the need to make a living. I'm about to head north to take scenic photographs for one of the postcard companies, but also to do some work for myself. I've compiled a photographic archive specifically of republican leaders like Ruairí Ó Brádaigh and Seán MacStiofáin—the papers and wire services are always looking for material like that. Since there are rumours of possible changes within the leadership, I want to add those just coming to prominence to my collection.

I plan to start another archive of leading unionists, because whether they accept it or not, they too are part of Ireland. If we want a thirty-two county nation we have to treat it like one, Séamus. When I'm in Belfast I shall call in to you and get your views on the subject. In the meantime, is there anything I can bring you from Dublin? Philpott bakes on Tuesday and Friday.

W H E N Ursula heard the car door slam she wheeled her chair over to the window to watch Barry drive away. A sullen rain was falling so he had switched on the headlamps.

His mother was tired; she had been sitting in the chair since breakfast. Breda was elsewhere in the house, busy with the baby. Grace Mary had a gift for keeping people busy.

Ursula watched the red taillights vanish from sight. *Auto-mobile, that's Barry. Mobile in a motor car and out of one. I hope he appreciates it. Such a simple thing, being able to walk across a room.*

Increasingly uncomfortable, she squirmed in her chair. *Where is that damned nurse? Has she forgotten all about me?*

There had been some talk of giving Ursula a bell to ring so she could summon help if she needed, but she had firmly vetoed the idea. "I would hate to have anyone ringing a bell for me, so I won't do that to someone else."

Another of my many mistakes. I wish to God I had that bell right now.

She wheeled the chair to her bedside and looked longingly at the white sheets and the dear old red-and-white quilt Barry had brought from the farm. Every muscle in her body cried out to lie down.

Every muscle in my body? What about my legs?

She attempted to differentiate among the complaints being received from the outposts. *Shoulders, yes. Back, yes. Buttocks, assuredly. Legs? LEGS???*

Was something stirring in those dead wooden legs? *Concentrate.*

She thought there was a faint echo of sensation, but only for a moment. *I must have imagined it.* Then it came again. A tingle, like tiny ants crawling. Sweat broke out on Ursula's forehead. With an immense effort of will she forced a command down the damaged neural pathways. *Move, damn you. Move!*

"You must be ready to go back to bed now," said a cheerful voice from the doorway. Breda bustled into the room and began smoothing sheets and plumping pillows. A moment later she was lifting Ursula from the chair and swinging her onto the bed.

Breaking her concentration.

"There now, is that not better?" Breda tucked the quilt

under Ursula's chin. "You can have a sleep until time for lunch."

"I don't want to sleep!"

Breda was not listening. She was already on her way back to the nursery.

As he drove up the Dublin–Belfast road Barry was relieved to be leaving Barbara and their problems behind. Yet the sense of relief brought guilt as well. *It's the curse of being Irish,* he thought. *We're afflicted with a deeply penitential version of Catholicism, so we suffer guilt for the most normal human emotions.*

I do everything I can but there's just no pleasing Barbara. It's not my fault.

It's not my fault.

And if it is, I don't know what to do about it except what I'm already doing.

He was working harder than ever, but if he was honest with himself it was not for Barbara's sake, nor even to support his family. Barry was doing what he had always done. Fighting in his own way for the Republic. As the situation in Northern Ireland worsened, he was concerned that the IRA alone would never be sufficient to resolve the problem. He was beginning to agree with Brendan Delahanty. The only option was politics, though that route was fraught with problems of its own.

Years of observing the government at work in the Republic had taught Barry to mistrust the subversive treachery of words. In the mouths of politicians words concealed what they purported to reveal; misleading, distorting, convincing, confounding. Words could lie.

With his candid portrait of Eamon de Valera he had discovered it was possible to uncover the truth of a man no matter what his words said. Now Barry hoped his photographs would give ordinary people, both nationalist and unionist, an uncompromising look at those who were leading them; the men behind the masks.

When he reached Belfast Barry applied for the familiar Long Kesh visitor's pass, adding the names of the men from Cage Eleven whom McCoy had mentioned. He also requested permission to bring a camera to the visiting area.

The official handling the application glowered at him. "You the photographer who took those pictures in the H-Blocks?"

"I am."

"They got a lot of coverage, didn't they?"

"I believe so."

"Maybe that wasn't such a good idea, you know what I'm saying? There was a lot of criticism about the way the protestors came across. You didn't show them as the brutes they are, you made them look . . ."

"I didn't 'make them look' any particular way," Barry said. "The camera only recorded what it saw."

"Permission to photograph denied," the other man snapped. "And you'll have to reapply for your visitor's permit."

W HILE Barry waited to see McCoy he made appointments with Unionist politicians and prominent Protestant businessmen. The invitation to become part of a photographic archive depicting Northern Ireland's most influential individuals met with an enthusiastic response from everyone he approached.

None of them asked if Barry planned to include any Catholics in the collection.

His first call was to a building contractor who lived off the Malone Road; possibly the most desirable residential area of Belfast. Frederick Liggitt was a senior member of his local Orange Lodge.

Founded in 1795, the Orange Order had since its inception been a secret society devoted to the preservation of the Protestant ethic and the demonstrable superiority of Protestants over Catholics, as exemplified by the victory of William of Orange over his Catholic rival, King James II, at the Battle of the Boyne on the twelfth of July, 1690.

The date of that victory, which marked the ascendancy of the House of Orange to the throne of England and of Protestantism to the state religion among the ruling classes of Ireland, was commemorated each year throughout Northern Ireland with almost three thousand Orange parades. Marching triumphally through the towns and villages, celebrating their victory over the evils of the Roman Church as if it had happened yesterday, Orangemen in their bowler hats, bright orange sashes, and tightly furled umbrellas appeared to be a colourful anachronism. In reality they were the tip of the iceberg that had been crushing the life out of the Six Counties since the partition of Ireland.

The "Marching Season" was a month-long nightmare for the Catholics of Northern Ireland.

The Orange Order was the best known of the so-called loyal orders that dominated most social and political life in the north, and were militant about remaining within the United Kingdom. In his archives Barry also planned to include members of the Apprentice Boys of Derry and the Royal Black Institution, but he had decided to begin with an Orangeman. From many sources he had identified Frederick Liggitt as a major financial contributor to loyalism and a potent force behind the scenes.

On Saturday morning Barry parked Apollo at the kerb and surveyed his surroundings. Houses in the Malone Road area were large, and almost without exception built in the Victorian style. Not so much as a scrap of blowing paper was allowed to disturb the beautifully manicured lawns, the precisely pruned shrubbery.

One exception to the Victorian dominance of the neighbourhood was the home of Frederick Liggitt. Although built

of red brick like the others, it boasted crenellated battle-
ments and an armorial scroll carved from marble mounted
over the front door. The brass door knocker—an exact duplicate of the one at Ten Downing Street—gleamed from
constant polishing.

A small, neat woman with tightly permed hair responded to Barry's knock. She identified herself as Mrs.
Liggitt and, with no further conversation, showed him
into a panelled library complete with roaring fire. Silent
as a ghost, she then disappeared.

Liggitt rose from a leather armchair beside the fireplace
and strode forward, hand outstretched. "Call me Fred," he
said in a booming voice. "You're with the *Philadelphia Inquirer,* I believe?" He was a big man with a handsome if
somewhat fleshy face, and a receding hairline. Even in the
comfort of his home he wore his shirt collar buttoned and
his tie knotted.

"The *Inquirer* is one of the American papers that uses
my work," Barry replied smoothly. Philadelphia was safe
enough; if he mentioned the *Boston Globe* Liggitt might
have suspected a taint of Catholicism. "I'm based in
Dublin, though, as I'm sure you can tell by my accent."

"You hardly have any accent."

Barry smiled. His lack of identifiable accent, like his
ability to alter his appearance, was a painstakingly acquired asset. On this occasion he was wearing a business
suit almost as good as the one Liggitt wore, and his
bright hair was varnished to brown with Brylcreem. In
one swift glance he had assessed the other man's height
and developed a slouch that put their faces almost on a
level.

When he reached into an inside pocket and took out a
pen and notepad, Liggitt said warily, "I thought you were
here to take my picture."

Barry kept smiling. "I am, with your permission. My
cameras are still in the car. I realise you are an extremely
busy man, but it would be very helpful if I could chat with

you for a few minutes before we begin the photography—just to get a feel for my subject, if you will."

Liggitt agreed, though he sounded as if he had reservations. Before they could begin his wife reappeared with a heavily laden silver tray. Following his host's lead, Barry waited passively while she carried the tray to a convenient table and arranged the elaborate silver service. Steaming, fragrant tea was poured into thin porcelain cups. "One or two?" she asked with the tongs poised over the sugar bowl. "Cream or lemon?" When both men had been served she proffered a selection of daintily cut sandwiches, then left the room.

Fred, Barry observed, had not spoken to his wife throughout the entire ritual.

The tea was superb.

After asking a few inoffensive questions about Liggitt's background and schooling, Barry casually remarked, "I believe you may know a relative of mine: Mrs. Winifred Speer?"

"Winnie? Oh yes, everyone knows Winnie. She's a real character. Mrs. Liggitt went to boarding school with a daughter of hers—or maybe a granddaughter, I don't remember now—and when the children were younger we bought a couple of dogs from her. I'm sorry to say they weren't properly house-trained. The dogs, I mean, not my children." He laughed, but his eyes were still watchful. "How did you say you're related to Winnie?"

"She's a cousin of my wife."

"Your wife's a Belfast girl, is she?"

"She was born in America, though," Barry said, simultaneously telling the truth while adding a single word that would allow Liggitt to make an erroneous assumption. "Her family was in the automobile business over there."

"Oh yes." Liggitt visibly relaxed. He had Barry labelled. A man married to a wealthy American girl, undoubtedly Protestant, and with impeccable Belfast connections. One of Our Own.

The atmosphere in the library changed from formal to friendly.

When Barry mentioned the Orange Order Liggitt loosened the knot of his tie. "The Order is the glue that holds civil society together in this province," he asserted. "People in the south have a jaundiced view of us, but that's only because they don't know us. They believe everything the IRA tells them. I'm sure you don't do that, Barry," he added with a glint in his eye. "I mean, as a journalist you have to seek the truth."

Barry nodded. "I do indeed."

Fred Liggitt spent the next hour lecturing his guest on the Order and its importance in the greater scheme of things. Barry could not help warming to a man so passionate about his subject. It was like listening to an old-time IRA man extolling the dream of a thirty-two-county Republic.

"Our culture is under attack, Barry," Liggitt stressed, stabbing the air with his forefinger. "Protestantism is based on revealed Scripture and rational thinking, which is the very opposite of Romanism. The pope encourages the working classes to breed like mice while enslaving them through idolatry. In Northern Ireland you see the two forces pitted against each other in a struggle to the death. But make no mistake: right will triumph, thanks in no small part to the Orange Order. The Order is a powerful force for community stability; we will not give way. The people can trust us and they know it. For three hundred years we have been upholding their civil and religious liberties in this province, defending them from the most barbarous attacks. Without us Ulster would descend into anarchy."

Barry listened, nodded, drank tea. Longed to pour a naggin of whiskey into his cup but did not ask. Eventually he went out to Apollo and brought in his cameras. Fred Liggitt posed in front of the fireplace in his library, with one arm stretched along the mantelpiece and a framed photograph of the queen of England next to his hand. A lovely young queen shortly after her coronation, as radiant as a fairy tale princess.

Barry made sure the photograph was plainly visible in the picture he took.

His next call, in late afternoon, was to a house off the Antrim Road in North Belfast; not as imposing as Liggitt's pseudo-baronial, but comfortable and well appointed. There Barry was told at length about the virtues of the Unionist Party, the necessity for one-party governance in Northern Ireland, and the dedication of the brave self-appointed vigilantes who were acting to defend beleaguered Protestants by burning out Catholic neighbourhoods.

His host's wife explained that Catholics proved they were evil every time they opened their mouths because they took the name of the Lord in vain, which God-fearing Protestants never did.

Then she invited Barry to stay for dinner.

The food was delicious, but Barry, whose table was often the platform for passionate debate over anything from politics to the arts, was surprised that there was no dinner-table conversation. The family, which included three teenaged youngsters, ate in near silence. At last Barry said, "You can talk in front of me, you know."

His hostess glanced up. "We don't waste food or talk." She smiled when she said it, to take the sting out of what might otherwise be construed as a rebuff.

During the following days Barry met and photographed other prominent members of the unionist community. Some invited him to their offices. Others preferred to meet him at their homes. No one was willing to see Barry on Sunday, however. The Sabbath belonged to the Lord.

The interviewees were unfailingly polite, eager to get their point across to a journalist with important foreign connections. He listened with mounting incredulity as one man after another earnestly explained to him that the oppressed Catholics of Northern Ireland were responsible for their oppression because they chose to resist. It was never stated in such bald terms but the implication was clear. The perception of Catholics that they were being discriminated against was not based upon fact, but upon myth perpetrated by the Church of Rome for its own evil purposes. The commemoration of 1916 that had been held in 1966 had forced northern Protestants to take up arms. The Civil Rights movement itself was responsible for unleashing a virulent sectarianism that had not been present in the Six Counties before.

At night in his hotel room Barry sorted through the copious notes he had taken. *Can they really believe what they're saying? Can otherwise intelligent people think this is the truth?*

He stopped reading. Lay down with his fingers laced behind the nape of his neck and his long legs hanging off the end of the bed. Stared at the ceiling.

Why not? We believe our version of what happened is the truth.

The ceiling plaster was scored with a multitude of tiny cracks, like the striations running across the limestone surface of the Burren in County Clare. At first glance the Burren looked hopelessly barren, yet thousands of exquisite wildflowers bloomed there every year, and in the winter people from the valleys brought their cattle to graze the rich grass that persisted on the heights.

Chapter Twenty-four

———— ·◦≪≫◦· ————

ON St. Valentine's Day, 1977, Gerry Adams was released from prison.

Convinced that the vast resources and numerical superiority of the British military would make it impossible to drive them out of Ireland through military force alone, Adams had, through his "Brownie" articles, persuaded others that the campaign needed rethinking.

Immediately following his release he was asked by Séamus Twomey of the IRA to head up a commission that would report directly to general headquarters about the possibilities for restructuring the organisation in preparation for "the long war." This presented an opportunity to reinvigorate the republican movement on two fronts: creating a tighter military structure, and introducing a programme of dynamic political action to develop support within the wider community.

ADAMS had left Long Kesh by the time Barry was allowed to visit Séamus McCoy.

"It's a damned shame you missed him," McCoy said, "but he's going to be around, you'll meet him one of these days."

"You're saying he'll be arrested again?"

"Wouldn't be surprised, Seventeen. There's a revolving door on this place, like I told you. You going to see any of the other lads?"

"I hoped to, but I'm not very popular with the prison

officials right now because of my H-Block photos. They were even reluctant to let me visit you, so I'm not pushing it. I don't want to call more attention to myself because . . ."

"Aye," said McCoy. "Sometimes I'm surprised you have the balls to come north at all after you were almost beat to death in Derry that time."

"How many republicans in the Kesh have been almost beaten to death, Séamus? And how many let it change them?"

McCoy grinned. "Point taken. You have to be tough to survive in here. The day they brought me into the Cages I had my first lesson about life in Long Kesh. One of the screws blew up a little red balloon, a child's toy, and turned it loose. A soldier with a rifle stood off to one side waiting. When the balloon had floated so high it was almost out of sight the soldier raised the rifle and blew it to bits. The screw turned to me. `See that, you republican bastard? That's what we can do to you if you even think about making a run for it.' But I've thought about making a run for it every day since then, and—" McCoy interrupted himself with a hard cough.

"Are you all right?" Barry asked anxiously.

The older man sat with his head down for a few moments, then looked up smiling. "We're none of us as good as we were when we came in here, but I'm all right, Seventeen. Don't you worry about me."

Barry did worry, though. Through an act of sheer will McCoy had appeared to regain his health while in prison, if only to spite the authorities. Yet the strongest will had its limits.

Driving back to Dublin Barry found himself murmuring a prayer for his friend. *How many other men and women are praying for Volunteers in prison?* he wondered. *How many of those prayers will be answered?*

Damned few, probably. Seems like God's been turning a deaf ear to the republicans since the Civil War. Does

*that prove we're on the wrong side, or just that we're not
individually good enough?*

*Come to think of it, how good a Catholic am I? About
the only thought I give to Mass is to be certain I'm wearing a fresh collar.*

*My mother believes people need religion in their lives.
Maybe they don't need churches, she says, but they do
need God.*

*My children have been christened in the Church and
they'll have their first communions and their confirma-
tions with Barbara and me right there in the front pew,
looking proud.*

Is that good enough, God?

He shook his head in anger at himself. "Don't be stupid,
Halloran," he said aloud, "you can't bargain with God.
He runs the world to suit himself no matter how we feel
about it."

LIFE went on in Harold's Cross. Barry devoting himself to his work, Barbara busy with the children. Ursula,
in her room, struggling.

She did not let anyone, even Breda, see her attempts to
move her legs. It was like a secret vice to be hidden from
all eyes. In the wheelchair she kept a blanket wrapped
around her lower body throughout the day, so if there was
even the slightest tremor no one would notice.

At night she walked. Ran. Rode her horses again!

Being awake was the nightmare.

Her only escape was in her dreams, when she was with
Ned and Síle and the future was an adventure yet to unfold.

On May third another workers' strike was called in
Northern Ireland. Although Ian Paisley gave the strike his
full support and once again loyalist paramilitary intimidation was employed, this time the strike failed.

Seán Garland proposed a change of name for Official

Sinn Féin. They were to be Sinn Féin—The Workers Party. A few years later this would become simply The Workers Party.

A T eight P.M. on the twenty-sixth of June a seagoing craft of a type unseen on any shores for over a millennium made landfall on Peckford Island, northwest of St. Johns, Newfoundland.[1] The voyage of the *Brendan* was over. Adventurer Tim Severin had proved it was possible that a sixth-century group of Irish monks led by a man called Brendan had travelled four thousand miles from the Kerry Coast to the New World, using medieval technology and a boat made of ox hides.

W H E N the wire services reported the news of Severin's success, Barry Halloran kissed his family good-bye and headed for the southwestern corner of Ireland. In order to follow in Saint Brendan's footsteps, Severin had launched his boat from the mouth of Brandon Creek in County Kerry. Barry hoped to do a photographic study of the isolated site before it was discovered by the world press. He already had a title. "Nine centuries before Columbus the Irish may have discovered America."

G U S T Y Spence was the commander of the Ulster Volunteer Force prisoners inside the Maze. Spence was another man who used his prison time to read, and think. That became apparent when he issued a statement to the loyalists under his command attacking violence as counterproductive and supporting the idea, at least, of reconciliation.

T H E thunder of the old iron door knocker invariably awoke Grace Mary just when she had—finally—fallen asleep, so Barbara had the knocker removed and a doorbell with a musical chime installed.

Philpott swooped upon the discarded door knocker and started to carry it away.

Barbara stopped him. "Where are you going with that?"

"I thought I'd keep it as a souvenir. It was here when I inherited the house; I believe my grandfather bought it."

She shook her head. "You're worse than a magpie, Warren; you keep everything. I don't want an old-fashioned knocker on the door of your flat, it will spoil the contemporary design I established for the mews. Take that thing up to the attics if you like, a lot of your junk's there already."

GRAINY grey twilight had settled over the yellow brick house. Ursula's pain had been unusually bad that day; Breda Cunningham had left an hour earlier after administering a hypo. Ursula read for a little while, then fell asleep with the book still open on the bed. A sudden pounding at the front door startled her awake. She struggled to sit up. At first she did not know where she was. Or even when.

Someone's trying to break in, she thought groggily.

Reaching under her pillow, she took out the Mauser. The pistol was too heavy for her shaking hands. She caught her lower lip between her teeth and tried to steady the weapon as she had been taught to do, holding her right wrist firmly with her left hand. She could not concentrate. Her head was swimming.

A shadowy form appeared at her window and began to raise the bottom pane.

She fired.

THE boarders had lingered late at table. Forgotten cigarettes smouldered in overflowing ashtrays while they engaged in a loud argument about football. Just when tempers were getting out of control, they heard the crack of a pistol shot and the sound of glass shattering.

Philpott ran in from the kitchen. He was deathly pale. "Did you hear that? Is it burglars?"

Upstairs in the nursery Barbara quickly fastened the last safety pin in Grace Mary's nappy and put the baby back in her cot, then headed for the staircase. "What's happening down there?" she called over the balustrade. "Why the hell is Barry never home when something goes wrong?" she muttered as she hurried down the stairs.

A voice cried from somewhere below, "Help, please help!"

Hearing Ursula Halloran call for help alarmed Barbara more than anything. At the bottom of the stairs she jumped from the third step and hit the hall running. Philpott and the boarders had a head start, but with a skilful use of elbows Barbara broke through the traffic jam at Ursula's door.

Barry's mother was across the room from her bed, with the upper part of her body halfway through a shattered window. "Help!" she cried. "Help us!"

Barbara thought someone was trying to kidnap her. She rushed forward and grabbed Ursula around the waist, dragging her back inside.

Ursula screamed in pain.

One of the boarders helped carry her to her bed. The other men congregated at the window to stare down at a dark figure lying on the ground outside.

Ursula's arms and nightdress were smeared with blood. At first glance Barbara could not tell if the cause was the broken window glass or a gunshot wound. "We'll need a doctor for her, Philpott," she called over her shoulder.

"And the police, we have to have the police," he jabbered. He took no action other than waving his hands.

"Bloody damned useless," Barbara said in disgust. "If there's a man in the room will he please go ring a doctor?"

Half a dozen boarders hurried to obey.

"I shot him," Ursula mumbled.

Barbara bent closer. "Shot who?"

"Outside. I woke up and saw him and . . ."

"It's all right now, don't worry. Everything's going to be all right."

Ursula struggled to untangle her knotted thoughts. "I was dreaming about Papa and Mama. Then someone was trying to break in. I thought the Free Staters had come to arrest Papa. Or maybe it was the Black and Tans." She clutched Barbara's arm. "The Tans killed Mama, you know. Caught her and killed her when she was unarmed!" Her eyes rolled like those of a horse about to bolt.

Barbara placed a gentle hand on the other woman's forehead. "Ssshh, ssshh, it's all right, just rest. You were imagining things."

Ursula's glassy eyes steadied; fixed on hers. "I didn't imagine firing my pistol."

"No," Barbara agreed, "you didn't imagine that."

"Or his voice. Just as I shot him he cried out, but it was too late." Ursula was fighting hard to overcome the effects of the narcotic. "Sweet Christ, I've killed Séamus!"

As the last light was fading Séamus McCoy had stood at the front door of the yellow brick house. He could have sworn the door had a knocker; had he not used it a hundred times?

The knocker's absence was disturbing. He wanted, needed, everything to be the same. He had lain on his prison bed night after night envisioning the house, seeing himself walk up to the door, seeing Ursula open it . . .

No, she couldn't do that. But she'll be there when I get home.

Now the knocker was gone.

McCoy had stared at the wooden panel where the knocker should have been, then raised a hand and touched the surface. His fingers detected screw holes badly filled

with putty. When he put his face almost against the panel
he could see that a small section of the wood had been re-
painted. The gloss of the paint did not match the rest of the
door.

Barbara would never allow a half-assed job like that,
he told himself.

He gave the door a gentle shove. It was, like most
doors in Ireland, unlocked during the day. Barbara locked
it herself after all the boarders were home. Barry had his
own key, of course.

McCoy used to have a key to the door but that was before he was arrested. The RUC had taken his personal be-
longings: his watch, his wallet, his spectacles, his keys,
even his rosary and the miraculous medal his mother had
given him. His wallet and spectacles had finally been returned to him, but God alone knew where the rest were.

The door was firmly locked.

He began hammering on it with his fist.

When there was no response he set off around the side
of the house. *They're probably all in the back, that's why
no one hears me.*

Chapter Twenty-five

THE boarders carried the wounded man into the
house. At Barbara's direction they laid him beside Ursula
on the bed—"So we can look after them both at once."

The boarders were bank clerks and shoe salesmen and
minor civil servants; too young to have lived through the
revolutionary years when a man had to know how to deal
with gunshot wounds. They lived in a narrowing world.

Unlike their ancestors, not one of them could build his own house or plough a field to feed his family.

Leaving the nursing to the woman, they gathered in the hall outside.

McCoy's eyes were open but unfocused. His neck and collar were soaked with blood. Barbara bent over him. "Séamus. Séamus? Can you hear me?" When he did not reply she straightened up and shouted, "Warren, is that damned doctor coming?"

The little man hurried into the room, wringing his hands. "I rang and left a message."

"Well call another doctor, you halfwit. I don't care who, just get someone here right away. And call an ambulance too."

"That will cost a . . ."

"I don't care if we have to remortgage the house!" Barbara exploded. "Just do it or I'll break your scrawny neck with my own two hands!"

Philpott fled back to the telephone.

Little Brian shouted from the head of the stairs, "Mammy, Mammy, the baby's crying!"

"I can hear her," Barbara said through clenched teeth.

"Mammy, do you want me to pick her up?"

"God forbid. Just leave her, will you? And get back to bed yourself!" Barbara's voice shrilled upwards. Below the surface lay the jagged edges of panic, like the shards of glass in the shattered windowpane.

Surrendering to panic was an attractive prospect. *But if I do,* she thought, *who'll take care of me?*

No one.

Damn Barry.

Barbara rolled up her sleeves and got to work.

By the time the doctor arrived, two minutes ahead of an ambulance, she had sponged enough blood off of her patients to get a look at their injuries. McCoy's wound was the more serious. He had been shot near the base of the neck. Barbara temporarily stanched the flow of blood with a pad of Ursula's clean handkerchiefs fastened down with adhesive tape. McCoy was conscious but in obvious pain. When he tried to speak the blood welled up again, so she ordered him to be quiet.

Ursula's chest and arms had been lacerated by the glass but no arteries were damaged. Barbara dare not attempt to remove the splinters of glass herself, or give her mother-in-law anything to ease her discomfort. *The mystery is, how did she get across the room to the window?*

That was a question for later. As soon as Barbara was able to turn her patients over to the professionals she ran upstairs to calm her children, leaving Philpott and the boarders to fend for themselves.

B a r r y returned to Dublin in a good mood. By manipulating light and shadow he had taken a number of dramatic pictures of Brandon Creek, which was in itself unremarkable. He was packing up to come home when he was approached by a representative from one of the big American news magazines. After a pub lunch in the nearest village—and talking about Irish history and adventurers and Christopher Columbus until late into the night—Barry had a contract in his pocket. He was to cover Severin's triumphant return to Ireland; he might even go to America to photograph the *Brendan* being prepared for its journey home aboard a cargo ship.

He parked Apollo at the kerb and walked, whistling, to his front door.

Y o u sure know how to make a fella feel welcome," McCoy said. He was tucked up in bed in his old room with his neck and one shoulder swathed in bandages. "Take off the door knocker and if that doesn't stop him, shoot him."

Barry grinned. "Frankly, I thought Ursula was a better shot than that." The doctor had assured him McCoy would make a full recovery. The bullet had nicked his clavicle and exited beside his shoulder blade. Although he would be sore for a while, he could be up in a day or two.

"Why were you trying to get into my mother's bedroom?" Barry asked—still smiling. "Has criminalisation gone to your head?"

"It wasn't like that, Seventeen. I was on my way to the back door when I saw a light coming from one of the windows at the side of the house. I looked in and there was Ursula. I was so damned glad to see her I tried to raise the window to say hello."

"There's usually a lamp on in her room at night," said Barry. "She likes to read for a while before she goes to sleep."

"Do you know when she can come home from hospital?"

"Not for a while, Séamus. She lost more blood than a frail woman could spare and they've given her a couple of transfusions. Besides, they want to keep her in while they run some tests. The doctors are very curious as to how she got from the bed to the window. They say she couldn't possibly have walked—and she doesn't remember.

"Now answer a question for me. How did you get out of prison?"

"A screw just came to the hut and said to collect my things, I was going home. No explanation. That's the way it is up there, no one tells the prisoner anything. But a pal of mine overheard one of the screws tell another one, 'That bastard is too old to be dangerous so we're gonna let him go.' "

"As simple as that?"

"Nothing the prison service does makes sense, they're a law unto themselves. But more men are coming into the Kesh all the time, so I guess they were just hard up for room. I'll tell you something for nothing though, Seventeen.

I hate like hell being thrown out because I'm too old. That hurts. At least in the Cages I was in the Fourth Battalion, I was still part of the Army."

"You could have gone back to the Belfast Brigade instead of coming to Dublin."

"I could have," McCoy agreed. "But I know when I'm over the hill, I didn't need the damn prison governor to tell me. Say, do you know this is the first time I've ever been shot? That's a turn-up for the books."

NINETEEN seventy-seven was the year the United States sent the new Space Shuttle on its maiden flight, perched atop a Boeing 747.

Disco dancing became the newest rage among the young people of Ireland, to the horror of the Catholic Church.

In a major political miscalculation, Liam Cosgrave dissolved the Dáil and called for a general election. A triumphant Jack Lynch swept back into power on the fifth of July.

Widespread accusations of torture were made against the RUC in Northern Ireland, but summarily dismissed.

ON the sixteenth of August it was announced that Elvis Presley, the undisputed king of rock and roll for over twenty years, had died in his home in Memphis, Tennessee.

"The day the music died," mourned Barbara.

Barry tried to console her. "There will always be music."

"Nothing as wonderful as Elvis."

"What about jazz? And opera, you love opera."

"I used to sing opera, it's not the same thing."

"You couldn't have done it if you didn't love it."

"I sang opera because I had the voice for it, that's all. Now I don't have the voice for anything."

"Of course you do, sweetheart. I love to hear you sing."

"Fat lot of good that is to me," she said sullenly.

O N the tenth of October the Nobel Peace Prize was awarded to Mairéad Corrigan and Betty Williams for their work with the Peace People. The award was actually that for 1976, for which they had been nominated by West German parliamentarians, but the nominations had arrived after the closing date.

According to a television survey, many Irish Americans believed the bestowing of the Nobel on the pair would mark the dawn of a new day for Northern Ireland.

One U.S. news magazine even proclaimed: "Woman Power Will Win!"

T H E Yanks see this country through the wrong end of the telescope," Luke told the Usual Suspects.

McCoy said, "Don't let Barbara Halloran hear that, she thinks she's an expert on Ireland."

"No one's an expert on Ireland," Brendan interjected. "Least of all the Irish."

Danny gave an exaggerated sigh. "Here we go again. The Professor's going to be profound."

"I simply believe the situation is more complicated than most people realise."

Barry leaned forward with both elbows on the table. "I agree. According to the so-called experts sectarianism is responsible for all the problems in the north, and I don't mean just institutionalised Protestant sectarianism. We're beginning to hear 'sure there's a pair of them in it.' So, although northern Catholics were almost exclusively on the receiving end of violence until recently, they're as much to blame as the Protestants because now they're fighting back. As for those who aren't churchgoers, if they're nationalists they're labelled as Catholics and if they're unionists they're labelled as Protestants because it's convenient, and they're swept up in the action anyway.

"The British and their apologists portray the conflict as a two-way street with the RUC and the soldiers caught in the middle, heroically trying to keep the peace. Commentators speak of 'ancient tribalism' and 'the religious divide,' to make sure people get the message: 'This is all about taking sides and holding ground and it's a war to the death, so dig in, everybody. Don't give an inch.' "

Barry dropped his voice even lower. Spoke more slowly; made them listen. "In a war someone always wins, even if it's only the arms dealers. Is it possible that the real guilt for what's happening in the north lies neither with one side nor the other, but with forces behind the scenes who're deliberately manipulating a terrible situation for their own gain—just as they manipulated the Treaty that forced partition on Ireland in the first place?"

Brendan sagged in his chair. "If your supposition is true, then politics, which as far as I know is the only alternative to war, is a poisoned chalice. Northern Ireland is a giant chessboard. We're only the pieces; someone else is calling the moves."

"We need another round," Danny decided. Shoving back his chair, he headed for the bar.

Séamus McCoy had settled back into life in the yellow brick house, though not exactly as before. His old room was no longer available; boarders had to be shifted around to accommodate him and he was aware of a certain resentment. Philpott had taken over management duties to justify his possession of the mews flat, leaving McCoy to do the maintenance work—for which Barry insisted on paying him far too much.

McCoy spent part of every day talking to Ursula. She loved to hear what he called his "war stories."

"Back in '69," he would begin, "or it might be earlier. Or later."

"Go on, Séamus, tell me!"

"Back in '69 there were riots in Newry as you may recall. They were meant to distract the RUC from Derry,
which was taking a hammering. The B-Specials came roaring into Newry in Bedford tenders. That's a kind of armoured yoke, y' see."

"I know that, go on."

"The Bedfords were as hot as an oven inside, and the
men all smoked cigarettes, which made it worse. Hell on
wheels, you might say. They parked in a row on the grassy
bank by the canal and everyone piled out to head for the
centre of town, where the riot was.

"The word went out. Within a short time people were
coming up from as far away as Dundalk. While the B-
Specials were busy elsewhere, ordinary men and women
overturned the Bedfords and dumped them into the canal."

Ursula roared with laughter. "You're better for me than
a tonic," she told McCoy.

They never seemed to run out of topics for conversation. The only subject that was forbidden was her state of
health.

"I am what I am," she said, "and that's an end to it."

But it was not. In secret she still struggled with her
body, forcing it to do the impossible.

*I did it once, I walked once. How else could I have got-
ten to the window the night I shot Séamus?*

But how did I do it?

The more she tried to remember and send those same
messages down the highways and byways of her nerves
again, the more miraculous the achievement became in
her own mind.

Sometimes at night she turned her face into her pillow
and wept.

A new craze called Punk Rock arrived in Ireland, high-
lighted by a group called the Sex Pistols rendering their

own unique version of "God Save the Queen." In the Bleeding Horse Barry remarked, "I like it a lot better than the original."

He bought the next round and they toasted the Sex Pistols.

PATSY'S wife—whom the Usual Suspects knew only as a woman of surpassing ugliness—died of a stroke shortly before Christmas. It came as a shock to his friends that he was devastated by the loss.

In a country where most people had nothing, status could be determined by the number of mourners at the funeral. Patsy had notices posted in every obituary section of every newspaper in the capital. "Dearly beloved wife . . . will be missed forever by her heartbroken husband."

Five of the dead woman's eight surviving sons came home from their construction jobs in England. All seven daughters were with their father in the front pew of the church for the Requiem Mass. At graveside Patsy was close to collapse.

Barry, Barbara, and Séamus McCoy piled into Apollo to follow the party back to Patsy's house in Summerhill for the wake. "He must have loved her very much," Barbara commented.

"Don't know," said McCoy, staring out the window. "He never talked about her."

She turned towards her husband. "Do you talk about me?"

Barry looked shocked. "Not in the pub!"

"Well, what do you talk about then?"

"Politics, sports, that class of thing."

"But not your wife and children?"

"Of course not, it's not the place."

"You could invite your friends to our house and talk about politics and sports there."

"In our house?"

"Of course."

"I thought you hated political conversations."

"Well I do, but I'm trying to . . . I mean . . . invite them anytime you like," she finished lamely.

I'm too wise to fall into that trap, Barry told himself.

He watched Barbara out of the corner of his eye as he parked in front of the house where Patsy lived. After she and McCoy got out he carefully locked the car. He doubted if his wife had ever been in a neighbourhood like Summerhill before. Technically it was in the same Dublin as Harold's Cross, but in reality it was light-years away.

Summerhill, the street with the lovely name, lay two blocks south of Mountjoy Square and ran from Portland Row to Gardiner Street, where it became known as Parnell Street. Once the whole area had belonged to Luke Gardiner, a self-made eighteenth-century property developer who had conceived of Dublin as the Second Capital of Empire and set out to make it so. Gardiner and his son, also named Luke, had laid out handsome Georgian residential blocks and broad thoroughfares such as Sackville Street—later renamed O'Connell Street—without realising that nothing is permanent. By the time Ireland freed herself from Empire, much of Gardiner's Dublin had fallen into decay.

Some of the worst slums in the city were those of Summerhill.

Wide-eyed, Barbara took in the coal dust-blackened tenements crowded together as if to keep each other from falling down. The ragged children playing in the street barefoot in spite of the winter weather.

"Your friend lives *here*?" she asked in a tone of disbelief.

Barry's smile was bitter. "A number of my friends have come from here."

At the wake Barry was careful to introduce Barbara to Luke, Danny, and Brendan without mentioning either their politics or the Bleeding Horse Pub. Nor did he describe them as the Usual Suspects.

The tradition established for Irish wakes over many generations was strictly followed. Food and drink were provided in abundance. Anyone who could think of something good to say about the dead woman did so. Then the members of her own sex gathered in the kitchen while the men congregated in the tiny front room to talk about things that really mattered.

Barbara was the only woman who did not adjourn to the kitchen to exchange gossip and household hints. She skirted around the edges of male conversation, trying to pretend she belonged. Her husband's equal.

As drink continued to flow and the shadows gathered outside the windows, one of Patsy's neighbours predicted in a loud voice, "If they ever try to force a united Ireland there'll be another civil war."

"Civil war?" Barry lifted one eyebrow. "There's already a civil war in the north but no one calls it that, because to give it a name would be to admit it exists. Which would nullify it as a threat."

Suddenly Barbara said, "How can anyone threaten people with a situation that's already an accomplished fact?"

All eyes swung toward her; most of them with disapproval. Then they swung back to Barry to see how he would react.

He would not insult her by being patronising. "We on this island are perfectly capable of holding two contradictory viewpoints at the same time, Barbara. With a loaded gun held to our heads we can genuinely be afraid someone will hold a loaded gun to our heads."

"I don't understand."

"Sure you don't, Mrs. Halloran," another man said kindly. "They're brewing tea in the kitchen and we could all use a cuppa; would you not go in and help them bring it out?"

She threw Barry a desperate glance but he would not intervene further. She stalked off to the kitchen. Her departing back was rigid with anger.

McCoy remarked, sotto voce, to Barry, "I'm afraid you let her down, there. She just wanted to be included."

"She's always wanting something I can't give her." Barry sounded exasperated. "I can't make her an honorary man, Séamus."

"One of these days some bright spark will invent a roundy yoke he'll call 'the wheel' and humanity will start to make real progress," McCoy said dryly. "I can hardly wait."

Once it really got going, the wake looked likely to last all night. The Hallorans had small children at home so Barry explained they must leave early. He and McCoy took turns shaking Patsy's hand and clapping him on the shoulder. Then they headed for the door.

Barbara lingered for a moment to speak softly to the bereaved man. Barry turned around, looking for her, in time to see Patsy's face crumple.

With no further word Barbara simply gathered the little man into her arms and pressed his sobbing face against her bosom. Paying no attention to anyone else in the room, she held him while an absolute tidal wave of grief washed over him and gradually receded. At last she released him and smiled down into his face. "You'll feel better now," she said.

Patsy seized Barbara's hand and kissed it.

Barry had never seen his wife make such a gesture; would never have imagined such a response from Patsy. He was amazed and moved and deeply proud.

And he loved her.

Chapter Twenty-six

⟵⬥⟶

O N January 18, 1978, the European Court of Human Rights in Strasbourg found Britain guilty of contravening Article 3 of the European Human Rights Convention by subjecting internees in Northern Ireland to inhuman and degrading treatment.

That same month the Provos unveiled a new weapon during a Bloody Sunday commemoration. The U.S. army's M-60 was a general-purpose machine gun that could fire six hundred rounds a minute and take down a helicopter in flight.[1]

W H A T the IRA considered a war to free Ireland, Britain chose to call a crime wave. The British policy of criminalisation was not limited to the Provisional IRA but extended to the entire movement. The treatment of imprisoned republicans, whether in Ireland or England, became more brutal. Men and women alike were subjected to physical and psychological abuse far in excess of customary prison policy.

Anger grew.

In February La Mon House, a hotel southeast of Belfast, hosted the annual dinner dance of the Irish Collie Club. The jovial atmosphere gave way to horror when an incendiary bomb planted on one of the restaurant windows exploded, sending a huge fireball billowing through the room. As was customary the Provisional IRA had issued a warning about the bomb so that civilians could be evacuated. Unfortunately the men making the call had not been able to find a telephone box in time to clear the hotel.

Twelve people, seven of them women, were incinerated by the blast, and twenty-three more were injured.

The botched bombing was a major public relations disaster for the IRA. A wave of revulsion swept all thirty-two counties of Ireland. In its aftermath the security forces arrested everyone they could find with republican or Provo credentials—including Gerry Adams. He was charged with having been a member of the IRA since his release from Long Kesh the year before, and spent the next seven months in the Belfast's Crumlin Road Prison. The groundwork he had been patiently laying and that he hoped would bring a political dimension to the republican struggle was left in disarray.

By March more than 150 men were "on the blanket" in the Maze, a number that would swell to five hundred by the end of the year. The three H-Blocks originally involved were so full that newcomers to the protest were being put into other Blocks. Protestors were routinely and severely beaten in an effort to make them give up.

They gritted their teeth and endured.

O N the second of April a soap opera premiered on prime-time television in the U.S. It was entitled *Dallas*. The network had little enthusiasm for the programme and at first agreed to run only five episodes.

S PEAKING on RTE, a spokesman for the infant computer industry told the Irish nation, "You missed out on the first Industrial Revolution, but you could be in the forefront of the second."

· · ·

A covert operation was set up by the Garda Siochana to
monitor the actions of a growing number of dissident republican groups operating south of the border as well as
in Northern Ireland. Unwilling to accept the discipline of
the IRA, they were determined to operate in their own
way—which included random criminality and gratuitous
violence.

I N my family," Barry remarked to McCoy, "republicanism was more a faith than a political philosophy. I joined
the IRA to help create a nonsectarian republic where all
the children of the state would be cherished equally.
But the longer the struggle drags on the less we seem to
be the sort of men Pearse would have been proud of."

"Come on, Seventeen; you don't believe that."

"A lot of people will. If you doubt it just look at history.
Ignoring the fact that Sinn Féin was elected by a landslide
to form our first government in 1919, the other political
parties accused them of every crime in the book because
genuine, egalitarian republicanism was a threat to their
own ambitions. It wasn't just a demonstration of Irish begrudgery, it was a calculated attempt to manipulate public
opinion for political advantage. But before it could succeed
we were plunged into the Civil War.

"When the Free State side won—with a lot of British
help, it must be said—the majority of journalists quickly
joined in condemning the republicans. To preserve their
jobs they demonised both Sinn Féin and the IRA with little regard for the truth. It eased off when they thought we
were a spent force, but when we started to recover the accusations began again. Unfortunately now some republicans are playing into their hands by becoming as bad as
they make us out to be. I realise there's a large element
of frustration involved, but that doesn't justify random
brutality."

"You can't accuse the whole IRA of random brutality."

"No, Séamus, but the mud's rubbing off on us. When your average Joe Soaps reads lies in the papers day after day, and hears them on the radio night after night, he's going to believe them because it's easier than finding out the truth. I need to go north and take more photographs of the men in the H-Blocks. When people see with their own eyes what's going on there, what's being done to their fellow human beings . . ."

McCoy was shaking his head. "I don't think they'll let you, Seventeen. Not again. You did too good a job the last time."

"Then what *can* I do?"

McCoy gave him a level look. "You know the answer to that. Do what I'm not strong enough to do anymore. You still have the reputation you won during the border campaign and you're a born leader. Thousands of men would follow you, no questions asked."

Barry's face tightened. "I can't do it."

This was important enough to make McCoy break his rule about not asking personal questions. "Will you tell me why not?"

Barry started to reply; stopped himself. Flashed his old reckless grin instead. "Will you tell me your nickname in the Kesh?"

The question caught McCoy off balance. "That's private, Seventeen."

"Exactly."

McCoy never asked Barry again, but he often thought about their conversation. *Something terrible happened to Seventeen at some stage, and I don't think it was the death of Feargal O'Hanlon, either. I'd hate to go to my grave without knowing the answer.*

I wonder if Ursula knows?

With Séamus McCoy home again to keep her company, and Breda Cunningham on hand to care for her physical requirements, Ursula began to come to terms with her changed life. She would never stop trying to walk again but the imperative was no longer there. She was beginning to accept life in a wheelchair.

Or so she tried to tell herself.

F ROM the time Barry's daughter could walk she was called Trot. Ursula gave her the nickname. "The child's always in a rush," she said, "and trying to be Grace is unfair to a little girl in a rush. Trot describes her better."

And it did.

On pleasant summer days Philpott would pack a box lunch and two flasks of tea. In late morning a small procession would set out from the yellow brick house on its way to the village green. Ursula rode like a queen in her wheelchair, pushed by Séamus McCoy.

At first she had been self-conscious about appearing in public in the chair, but McCoy was so matter-of-fact she soon forgot there was anything unusual about her mode of transport. He walked and she rode and the children toddled along beside them.

The adults never ran out of conversation. Often it was about politics; everything seemed to come back to politics. "I used to be able to stride along like a boy, almost as fast as some people could run," Ursula once remarked. "Even after I bought the Ford I thought nothing of walking into Ennis to the market, or over to Quin to buy a mare. But now . . ." She shook her head. "I'll never forgive the loyalists for that; for making an old woman of me."

"You'll never be an old woman," he said.

But when the chair was parked at the green so they could watch the children playing, he was careful to drape the blanket around her body and legs so the wheels of the chair were not visible.

He knew she was a proud woman.

Brian was under strict orders to hold his little sister's hand at all times. Grace Mary, not yet two years old, had other ideas. She was forever pulling free and darting away, so that McCoy had to abandon the wheelchair and pursue her while Ursula sat laughing.

Why, we're a family! she thought to herself one day. The idea delighted her.

U.s. president Jimmy Carter described Iran under the leadership of the shah as "an island of stability."

Two popes died in swift succession, as did the fifth president of Ireland, Cearbhall Ó Dálaigh.

Polish-born Karol Wojtyla became Pope John Paul II.

Martin McGuinness became chief of staff of the Provisional Irish Republican Army.

And Gerry Adams finally faced trial for IRA membership. The charges against him had been based on a *Panorama* programme broadcast on BBCTV, showing him making a speech at the Sinn Féin Ard Fheis.* (An occasion that could not be televised in the Republic.) During the speech Adams had used words such as "billet" and "war zone," which had been deemed sufficient by the RUC to prove his membership in the Provisional IRA.[2]

The judge who heard the case, Lord Chief Justice Sir Robert Lowry, disagreed. The case was thrown out. Gerry Adams was a free man.

In August Archbishop Tomás Ó Fíaich visited the H-Blocks at the request of Sinn Féin. Afterwards he commented, "One could hardly allow an animal to remain in such conditions, let alone a human being." The archbishop went on to say that the nearest approach to life in the H-Blocks was "the spectacle of hundreds of homeless people living in the sewer pipes of the slums of Calcutta."[3]

*High convention.

FOUR young Dubliners calling themselves The Hype went in search of a record contract. They got the contract and a new name as well: U2.

SEPTEMBER saw a new war begin.

This time England—aka Perfidious Albion, Great Britain, the United Kingdom, the "Ancient Enemy"— was not involved in any way and could not be blamed.

The situation had its roots much earlier in time, and lay much closer to home.

Ursula's explosion of anger disrupted the breakfast table. "Just look at this newspaper!" she cried, waving the offending item in the air. "Did you know that the largest Viking town outside of Scandinavia was found right here in Dublin, at Wood Quay? There are ancient timber streets and house foundations and everything. Hundreds of arte-facts have been discovered and the archaeologists say they haven't even uncovered the entire town yet. But now Dublin Corporation's going to bulldoze the whole area."

Barry put down his fork. "Are you serious?"

"It says so right here."

"I know about Wood Quay, of course; the ruins were first discovered in '69 or '70, and I've been there a num-ber of times as the archaeological work progressed. It's slow going; they have to be very careful and they're al-ways struggling to get more funds. I must have taken a hundred photographs over the years because the place fascinates me for some reason, but I haven't been down there in a long time and had no idea this was in the wind. Hand me that paper, will you?"

With growing astonishment Barry read that Dublin Corporation, the governing body of County Dublin, planned to build a huge new complex of civic offices that would obliterate the early Viking settlement.

A private group called the Friends of Medieval Dublin had been trying to have the signing of the building contracts postponed if not set aside altogether. But the corporation was determined. They had lined up a cadre of experts to support their argument, spearheaded by Michael J. Kelly, head of the Department of Archaeology at University College, Cork. In an interview Kelly claimed that money spent elsewhere would give a much better view of life in medieval Ireland than "this hole in Dublin."[4]

Barry was disgusted. "This country is desperate for money and here we have a ready-made tourist attraction that would bring in tens, maybe hundreds of thousands of people every year, and city government wants to destroy it to put up a monument to themselves? It defies logic."

Barbara reached for another slice of toast, thought of her waistline, and drew back her hand. "It's progress, Barry," she said. "You can't keep every old thing in Ireland; the country's full of old things."

Barry shoved back his chair. "Well, by God . . . I'm sorry, Ursula . . . by God we're going to keep this one!"

By the end of day both he and his mother were members of The Friends of Medieval Dublin.

On the fourteenth of September Barry was among the two thousand people from every walk of society who crowded into the Mansion House, official residence of the city's mayor, to listen to speakers every bit as eminent as Michael Kelly. At the end of the evening they passed strongly worded resolutions to protect the Wood Quay site and have the civic offices built somewhere else.

On the twenty-third Barry took part in a massive protest march calling for the preservation of Wood Quay. McCoy pushed Ursula's wheelchair; she carried her son's camera equipment on her lap. During the march she chatted with a number of other people who felt strongly about the issue, including an impassioned young lawyer called Mary Robinson. "I would have been a good lawyer," Ursula remarked, rather wistfully, to McCoy.

The next edition of *The Irish Times* read "Save It!" above Barry's twin photographs of Wood Quay and the protest march. The editorial went on to point out that the Viking ruins had been designated by the High Court as a national monument, a fact that the corporation was choosing to ignore. The article concluded, "The decision has all the appearance of a deliberate and brutal opting for the uncouth, for the short-term, and to hell with heritage, history, and higher values."[5]

The marchers included leaders of the trade union movement, city councillors, historians, academics, representatives of the Irish Hotels Federation and of Dublin Tourism, and thousands of ordinary men, women, and children—the latter often marching en masse with their school classmates and carrying banners pleading for the preservation of the Viking city. The Gardai estimated twenty thousand people took part. It was the largest protest march to be held in Dublin since the Workers' Strike of 1913.

An Phoblacht—although diametrically opposed to the *Times* politically—also gave front page coverage to the subject. The lead article stated, "Wood Quay barbarism is so very much in Leinster House character."[6]

Ursula agreed. "What else would you expect from Jack Lynch's government? Of course they'll abandon Wood Quay and all it stands for to the building contractors, because those are the men who donate big to Fianna Fáil.

"Remember how easily Lynch abandoned the Catholics in the north? When I was a girl being a republican meant one gave one's word to create a sovereign, independent, thirty-two-county Irish Republic. An oath was binding to the real republicans. They didn't adjust their integrity to suit their self-interest. But this lot . . ."

The three national daily newspapers reported an avalanche of letters to their editors, with ninety-nine percent in favour of preserving the national monument. Met with such a concerted public outcry, various politicians not currently in power made grandiose statements of support

for Wood Quay. The Committee on Culture and Education of the Council of Europe sent a strongly worded tele-
gram to Taoiseach Jack Lynch. Seanad Éireann* opened a
formal debate on the subject of Wood Quay.

Feelings ran even higher when drawings were published
showing the proposed civic offices as designed by architect
Sam Stephenson. They depicted two giant concrete bunkers
reminiscent of World War Two, obscuring the view of historic twelfth-century Christ Church where Strongbow was
entombed. Their squat and sinister appearance was a calculated insult to the historic city beside the Liffey.

"Save Wood Quay!" the nation cried in alarm.

What neither the Irish Senate nor the Irish public knew
was that the government had long since taken the final
decision. The contracts with John Paul & Co. Ltd, Building Contractors, were already signed.

Barbara did not join Barry in his newfound campaign,
although in spite of having two small children to care for,
she was beginning to show signs of boredom. More and
more she relied upon Breda and Philpott for child-minding
while she took up new ideas—hobbies, projects—one after
another, tried them for a while, put them aside, and found
something else.

She bought a pair of canaries and announced her intention to breed the little birds. Then a spider got into the
cage and the female died of fright. Upon losing his mate,
the male stopped eating and soon died too.

"If anything happened to me would you give up eating?" Barbara asked Barry in bed one night.

"Why would I do that?" he asked in all innocence.

She sulked for days.

In swift succession she tried sketching—using the
children as subjects whom she rendered as unrecognis-
able blobs—then furniture refinishing—until the smell of
the chemicals made her nauseous—and next turned to the

*The Senate of Ireland.

homely skill of bread making. Philpott schooled her in the essentials.

On one of the rare days when Barry returned home early he found her alone in the kitchen. He stood in the doorway, transfixed by the sight. Watched her kneading the yeasty dough; smooth, elastic, as sensuous as flesh.

The need rose up in him then. Blind, primordial. He reached for her without thinking; without weighing the consequences. He did not even lock the kitchen door.

SHORTLY before Christmas of 1978 the IRA's new M-60 killed three members of a British army patrol in Crossmaglen.

Chapter Twenty-seven

THE winter of 1978–79 was bitterly cold. Britain was disabled by labour union strikes. Rubbish collectors, health workers, and grave diggers all suspended their services. The situation did not bode well for a parliamentary form of government with no fixed limit to its life span.

IN the Republic of Ireland on the twelfth of February, 1979, Mr. Justice Gannon granted an interlocutory degree restraining Dublin Corporation from proceeding with new construction on the national monument site at Wood Quay. The media reported him as saying, "Wood Quay is of national importance, irreplaceable if destroyed and beyond value in monetary terms."

The corporation appealed.

With very little discussion, the Supreme Court found unanimously in their favour. Dublin Corporation was free to demolish the ruins of the ancient Viking town and build whatever it wanted. The bulldozers moved in the following day to begin destroying history.

The Friends of Medieval Dublin were far from through, however. Once again they took their case to the Council of Europe, hoping to pressure Dublin City Council to take up the cause. The council was an elected body representing one of the three different areas encompassed by the county of Dublin. These three local authorities comprised Dublin Corporation. If the City Council could be persuaded to weigh in behind the effort to save Wood Quay, surely there was a chance?

At least some of the city councillors were willing. When they tried to represent their preservation-minded constituents they ran into a bureaucratic stone wall. If they pushed too hard they received vague threats of personal legal difficulties or the withdrawal of city services. Dublin Corporation was a monolith. Deaf and blind, a law unto itself. Greater than the sum of its parts.

City councillors decided their time would be better spent planning for the next election.

The Friends set out to find and support candidates of their own who would be more sympathetic to Ireland's heritage.

Y o u could run for the City Council," Ursula suggested to her son. "You're just what they need right now, an intelligent man who's interested in history."

"There's only one thing wrong with your idea; I have no desire whatsoever to wade knee-deep in shite," Barry stated flatly. "Forgive my language, Ursula, but that's what politics is. Corrupt and self-serving. Some of them may be idealistic when they go into office but the system gets hold of them and grinds them down, until one's no better than another. A warrior faces you. A politician sneaks around behind your back and puts the knife in when you're not looking. Brendan Delahanty once told me politics is the only alternative to war, but if he's right it's a damned shame. Pardon my language again."

Ursula sighed. "No need. I agree with everything you said, including the profanity."

Barry continued the fight for Wood Quay in his own way, as he was continuing so many fights.

Because he was a warrior.

M ARCH thirteenth was the date when the Republic of Ireland joined the European Monetary System, breaking its link with the British pound sterling.

A month later schoolchildren, exploring rubble the bulldozers had cleared from Wood Quay, found a Viking sword. Barry Halloran's photograph of the sword went out on the international wire services. "Dublin Wants to Destroy Its Own Past," was one of the headlines given the story.

The attention of the Irish public was sharply refocussed on the issue.

The corporation countered the unfortunate publicity it was receiving by claiming that the concept of building centralised civic offices was important to the overall scheme for the city; undertakings had been given to the contractor involved that would result in legal difficulties if they were not adhered to, and finance already allocated to the project would be "wasted" if any alterations were made in the plans. "Taxpayers' money would be lost!" the corporation cried.

I can't be pregnant again!" Barbara wailed.

"Of course you can," said Ursula. "It's the most wonderful thing you can do, bringing new life into the world."

"That's easy for you to say, you only did it once."

"In a way I'm sorry about that now," the older woman admitted. "I think I would have enjoyed having more children—if my life had been different."

"Well, my life was going to be different; I was going to be an opera singer. I never meant to be saddled with all of this." A dramatic wave of the hand indicated the house and all its denizens.

Why does she deliberately make remarks that get up my nose? Ursula wondered. "I'm sorry you look upon us as an inconvenience."

"I didn't mean it that way. It's just that . . . didn't you ever want something so bad you could taste it?"

Ursula gave a faint smile. "I have," she said softly. "But something one desires so much might be the worst thing one could possibly get."

"Not in this case. An operatic career would have given me a wonderful life with all my dreams come true. Now they're lost."

"Dream new dreams," Ursula advised.

"I knew you wouldn't understand."

A British general election on the third of May provided a decisive win for the Conservative Party, returning them to power. Party leader Margaret Thatcher officially became the first female prime minister in British history. She promptly began waging war on the trade unions.

ARCHBISHOP Tomás Ó Fíaich was elevated to the title of Cardinal, making him a member of the College of Cardinals and a prince of the Church.

IN recent weeks there had been a substantial increase in the damage done to Wood Quay. Meanwhile the local

elections had brought in a new Dublin City Council, many
of whose members said they were favourably disposed towards preserving the national monument. The Friends began to have hope.

But first the work on the site must be stopped entirely.

Friday the first of June was a day the defenders of
Wood Quay had been working towards for months. Occupation Day.

"Operation Sitric" was carried out that morning with
military efficiency. An advance party arrived at dawn, carrying the black raven banner of the Vikings. A proclamation
by the poet Thomas Kinsella was read. Promptly at seven-
fifteen A.M. hundreds of men and women came marching
up the quays. The lord mayor was among them, as was a
pair of Alsatian dogs rejoicing in the names of Thor and
Olga. Mothers had brought their children for the occasion.
People had even come from abroad. Members of the Dáil
and the Seanad were also much in evidence, expounding to
the swarming reporters on how much they loved "our nation's great history."

People wore costumes. People sang.

A limited number were allowed access to the site itself.
They entered through a door in the corrugated iron walls
erected by the builders. Blankets were unrolled and
spread on the rubble-strewn earth in the very shadow of
the bulldozers. There was a nip in the air; a reminder that
the elusive Irish summer had not yet arrived. Gas rings
were soon at work boiling kettles for tea.

Writers and academics rubbed shoulders with priests
and labourers, sitting together on the earth where Viking
houses once had stood. The widow of a former president
of Ireland poured tea.

Accompanied by his mother and Séamus McCoy,
Barry was on hand to photograph the event. When they
arrived almost the first person they met was Éamonn
MacThomáis. His last imprisonment had wrought a
change in MacThomáis. He seemed to have shrunken

physically. He greeted Barry's little party with a broad smile, but there were shadows in his eyes that nothing could banish.

He drew Barry aside to have a few words in private.

"Portlaoise has done for me," MacThomáis admitted when no one else could hear. "I don't think I'll ever be the man I was. The worst of it was the abuse I took came from our own. From our own," he repeated; his voice a growl of pain. "The dissidents, the new splinter groups, the men who think they have the right handle on republicanism and the rest of us are wrong. They can call themselves by any name they like but in the heel of the hunt they're outlaws, or what I call outlaws. They refuse to accept authority and make it up as they go along. They're doing the name of republicanism terrible damage."

Barry nodded agreement.

MacThomáis gave a wry smile. "When I tried to talk to them they did me some damage too." He did not elaborate. But Barry could imagine.

He changed the subject. "What's your current take on the Wood Quay situation, Éamonn?"

"It's another example of outlaws doing what they like and to hell with everyone else. We have to do everything we can to stop it. The photographs you've been feeding to the international wire services help. I was just talking to a couple who came all the way from Boston to protest this . . . villainy."

"Will it do any good, do you think?"

"Hard to say. Once I would have told you, 'We can make a difference!' Now I'm not so sure. One of life's little ironies is that might doesn't make right, but neither does right make might. If they are strong enough the bullies win."

"Not if we can help it," Barry vowed. "I'm planning an extended photographic essay on Wood Quay, setting it in context. If I can sell it into the right markets it will add substantially to the pressure.

"You're a Dub born and reared, Éamonn, and you have an encyclopaedic knowledge of the old parts of the city. Do you have the time to take me on a tour of the area around Wood Quay? I want the history of all the little streets and laneways. I know that some of them, like Fishamble Street and Winetavern, date back almost to Viking Dublin."

MacThomáis's glum visage brightened slightly. "I'm your man," he said. "Shall we go now? Will your mother be all right?"

Barry laughed. "She has the best bodyguard in the world." He winked over at McCoy, who winked back.

"Then what are we waiting for?"

Seeing old Dublin through his friend's eyes, Barry took photograph after photograph. Forgetting everything else. Absorbed in the past.

Meanwhile McCoy found a level spot with a view of the site entrance and arranged Ursula's blanket to hide the wheelchair. "It's supposed to be the first day of summer," she remarked, "but that wind would cut right through you."

"I'll bring you a hot drink." He was always happy to find something else he could do for her. "What would you like, tea?"

"See if the pubs are open, I could murder a hot whiskey."

She sat for a time watching the crowd: the participants and the passersby, the committed and the merely curious. *What would the Vikings think if they could see us here?*

Can they?

How many ghosts surround us?

Ursula shivered. *I hope Séamus hurries with that hot whiskey. He's likely to meet someone he knows and start talking and forget all about me.*

When a tall, smartly dressed man with beautifully cut silver hair walked past her, the set of his shoulders looked vaguely familiar . . . and then she recognised him.

"Lewis Baines!"

He whirled. Stared at her a moment longer than good

manners allowed, then bent over her extended hand. "My wild Irish rose. I don't believe it."

The voice that once had thrilled her had no effect on her now, she discovered. His eyes were still—almost—as blue, and his bearing every bit as elegant, but he might as well have been a stranger.

"Did I hear that you were married, Lewis?"

"I was for a while, but she died years ago. In an auto accident."

"Oh, I *am* sorry," said Ursula with genuine feeling.

"And you—are you married?"

"I have a son who's taller than you."

"Does he resemble his father?"

"Very much, in some ways. They both had pointy ears."

"Had?" He was quick, Lewis; *quicker than he used to be,* she thought with vast indifference. "Your husband is dead also? Then perhaps you would care to join me. I'm going back to my hotel for something to eat since this could be a very long day."

"Thank you, Lewis, but I'm waiting for someone."

"Ah." Baines hesitated. "Not me, I gather?"

Ursula laughed.

In the nearest pub McCoy had ordered a glass of hot whiskey and asked the bartender to wrap it in a cloth napkin to hold the heat in. He headed back for Wood Quay, walking carefully and watching where he put his feet so as not to spill the drink. He had almost reached Ursula before he looked up.

She was talking to an exceptionally handsome man.

McCoy stopped in his tracks. Scowled. Then hurried forward to challenge the stranger. No longer watching his feet, he tripped on a broken stone and nearly fell. The napkin caught most of the whiskey, but some splashed onto his shoes.

Ursula was asking Baines, "Do you still have relatives in Belfast?"

"Fancy you remembering that!" He was pleased.

"Seeing you again reminded me, that's all. Some years ago I met a Belfast woman whose maiden name was Baines. She's Winifred Speer now."

"Aunt Winnie! I can hardly believe it. How ever did you meet her?"

Ursula shrugged. "This is a small country, Lewis; we all know someone who knows someone."

"Do you see her often? Does she ever talk about me?"

"I only met her once and you weren't mentioned at all." Looking past him, Ursula flashed her most radiant smile. "There you are, Séamus!" she cried with the warmth one might show to a lover. McCoy felt a flush of heat rise upwards from his collar.

Baines looked from one to the other. Cleared his throat; a small, precise sound. "I see your friend has arrived, Ursula. It was nice meeting you again, but I must be going. Cheerio." He walked away with a very straight back.

McCoy glared after him. "Do you know that man?"

"I do not know that man." Ursula reached for the glass in its sodden napkin. "I never did," she added. "What have you done with my whiskey, Séamus? Drunk it all yourself?"

"Is he . . . I mean, was he—"

"One of the many things I like about you," Ursula interrupted, "is that you never ask personal questions."

McCoy looked down at his shoes. "Aye," he said.

"Good. So let's go get a refill for this glass, shall we? And whatever you're having yourself."

Barbara, with her American penchant for hyperbole, would have said, "One of the things I love about you," and it would have meant nothing. Ursula had said "like," but McCoy knew she meant it.

His heart lifted.

OPERATION Sitric continued. Wars were being fought and won and lost elsewhere, but Barry Halloran kept his focus on Viking Dublin.

On the twenty-first of the month the Supreme Court granted an injunction to John Paul & Co. Ltd. The court warned that the current illegal occupiers of Wood Quay were incurring criminal responsibility and making themselves liable for damages on a massive scale.

By the time their representatives left the court, the bulldozers and rockbreakers were back at work.

Vested interests, which the Irish people had never been willing to tackle head-on, had triumphed again. The new civic offices that would soon glower over the Liffey became a permanent monument to ugliness; an indictment set in concrete of the failure of the nation's leadership at a crucial moment.

ONE of the victims of the Shankill Butchers who had survived an horrific attack was able to identify the members of the gang. They were arrested and all convicted except for Lenny Murphy, who escaped on a technicality. He swiftly assembled a new gang and resumed his campaign of torture and murder.

IN the summer of 1979 two Catholic priests—Father Alec Reid, of the Redemptorist order, and Father Desmond Wilson, a priest in Gerry Adams's home parish of West Belfast—were engaged in the thankless task of seeking to bring peace to Northern Ireland. All Catholics were deemed targets by the loyalist death squads, but these two men, acting independently, reached beyond the Catholic community to offer aid and succour to people of every persuasion. They listened, they talked, and most of all they refused to give up hope.

Amongst some—though by no means all—of the Protestant clergy a similar hope was struggling to be born.

When in July it was announced that the new pope planned a visit to Ireland, Ian Paisley responded with his usual vigour. "This visit is not on, full stop. The pope is Antichrist, the man of sin in the Church."[1]

CLASSIEBAWN Castle, at Mullaghmore, County Sligo, was the summer retreat of Lord Earl Mountbatten, hero of Burma and the uncle of Prince Philip. Here, with minimum security consisting of two members of the Garda Siochana, Mountbatten could relax with family and friends away from the rigid formality of his life in England. He kept a small yacht in the harbour and was fond of fishing and tending his lobster pots; the pleasant pastimes of an elderly man who had long been out of the wars.

In the 1960s the IRA had considered a hit on Mountbatten while he was at Mullaghmore, but the idea was rejected. Mullaghmore was in the Republic. Any member of the British royal family was considered a legitimate target in Northern Ireland, but it was Army policy to commit no violence south of the border.[2]

By 1979 the ongoing violence in the north, with the numbers of casualties continuing to mount, was causing the Provisional leadership to think again. The IRA wanted to strike a major blow against the British; one that would state, once and for all, that this was war. A war the British could end by withdrawing their occupying forces.

The Volunteers of South Armagh were highly skilled in the use of the radio-controlled bomb. Television repair shops provided both the necessary material and excellent cover. Even British Intelligence was forced to admit that the IRA had achieved an exceptional level of skill in this particular area.

The South Armagh Brigade decided to mount an action at Warrenpoint, a Northern Ireland town just across the border from the Republic. They had observed that whenever a bomb exploded in the vicinity of British troops, the soldiers ran to the nearest "hard shelter" to regroup. The plan at Warrenpoint was to set up a smaller bomb beside the road along which a large convoy was due to pass, and plant a larger bomb in concealment at the gatehouse of Narrow Water Castle, one hundred yards away.

Meanwhile another team was assigned to Mullaghmore. Their job was to place a fifty-pound gelignite bomb on board Mountbatten's boat, which was unguarded. The two operations were coordinated to take place at almost the same time; a devastating double attack that in its own way mirrored the double attack on Dublin and Monaghan five years earlier.

On Bank Holiday Monday, the twenty-seventh of August, a unit from South Armagh was manning their detonators just across the river from Warrenpoint. A second team was in place at Mullaghmore Harbour. Mountbatten's boat, *Shadow Five*, was painted in the colours of an admiral's barge. The vivid green hull stood out clearly in the binoculars trained upon it as it slipped its moorings and set out into the bay.

The time was eleven-thirty.

On board the vessel that bright summer morning were the seventy-nine-year-old Lord Mountbatten and six others, including three children—two of them Mountbatten's grandchildren. Watching from the shore was the IRA's "button man" with his finger on the detonator of the hidden bomb.

When the boat was a hundred yards from shore he pressed the trigger.

A massive explosion tore the little yacht and its occupants to pieces.

That same afternoon two IRA men waited across the river from Warrenpoint until a convoy of thirty members of the British parachute regiment came down the carriageway on the opposite shore. They had to pass close to a hay trailer stalled on the road. At that moment the first bomb, which had been hidden in the hay, was detonated.

Five hundred pounds of explosive slammed into the rear of the convoy. Of the nine soldiers in the last vehicle, only two survived.

Ammunition in a burning truck started to explode. Thinking they were under fire, the paras ducked behind their vehicles and began to shoot back. Unfortunately they had no idea where the enemy was, and so fired wildly in every direction. Bullets shattered nearby trees and tore their leaves to ribbons. Other drivers on the carriageway fled for their lives. The hail of futile gunfire lasted until an officer roared an order for the paras to seek the nearest hard shelter.

A command post was swiftly set up at the entrance to Narrow Water Castle. Twenty minutes after the first bomb, a much larger one destroyed the gatehouse. Another eleven soldiers died along with their commander. Smoking debris, bloody clothing, burning straw, mutilated human torsos, and various body parts littered the landscape.

The IRA had killed eighteen British soldiers in one blow, its largest single score ever. The massacre of the hated paras and the killing of a member of the royal family in a single day were a turning point in the undeclared war. As was true with Bloody Sunday, nothing would be the same again.

The death of soldiers in what some perceived as a war was understandable. The murder of a defenceless old man who was also an internationally recognised hero was unforgivable.

PHILPOTT was in the kitchen preparing the evening meal. Ursula was in the parlour, telling the children a story Ned Halloran had told her when she was little. "Once upon another time entirely, when Ireland was a hot dry land and the sun shone until everyone was sick of sunshine, a young man fell under an enchantment. He was a tall short fat thin man, and every woman loved him because every woman saw in him what she most desired. That, however, was not the enchantment."

Barbara walked briskly into the room and switched on the television. "It's time for the six o'clock news and the boarders will be here any minute," she announced, "so we need to clear you out of here."

"This is our house too!" Brian protested.

Then the news began.

ONE of the major wire services sent Barry to Sligo to photograph the Mountbatten assassination scene. Classiebawn's mythic outline silhouetted against a bloody sunset. Debris still floating on the water; occasional bits drifting into shore like scattered memories. Then on to Warrenpoint and a verdant meadow beside a river. Another castle; more debris. More remnants of what had been lives.

When his work at Warrenpoint was finished Barry methodically packed up his equipment and stored it in the boot of Apollo. *Holding on to control.* He drove to a republican-owned pub in the lovely nearby town of Rostrevor and bought three bottles of Irish whiskey. *A bomb inside me ticking; ticking.* Apollo carried him up into the vast, windswept expanses of the Mourne Mountains. "Where dark Mourne sweeps down to the sea," he sang as he drove. He found a place where there was no visible indication that humanity had ever existed, and stopped the car.

The bomb ticking, ticking.

Barry sat for a long time breathing the cool clean air off the sea, and listening to the roar of the silence. Then he threw the car keys into a patch of furze where he would only be able to find them once he was sober again, and started drinking his whiskey.

AFTER the assassination of Lord Mountbatten there was a rush of recruitment among loyalists and republicans as

well. As one loyalist would say years later, "People from
both sides joined the paramilitaries willingly, yet in a way
they were sleepwalking too. It was something they felt
compelled to do because they simply didn't know what
else to do."

O N the twenty-ninth of September Pope John Paul II arrived in Ireland for a three-day visit. The plane that was
bringing him flew right over the Phoenix Park on its way to
the airport. Looking down from his window he saw over a
million people already gathered in the park, waiting to hear
him celebrate Mass.

Barry had offered to take Ursula to the event, but she
declined. "I was there for the papal visit in 1932 and that
was enough. I have memories I would not like to over-
write with new ones."

"What memories?" Barry had asked. He did not expect
her to tell him.

Ursula never lost her ability to surprise. "Of your father. I fell in love with him that day in the Phoenix Park."

A t the end of the Mass the pope made a heartfelt plea
for an end to violence.

Chapter Twenty-eight

DURING the 1970s an internal police reform programme in Britain, code-named "Operation Motorman,"
had uncovered appalling levels of corruption in the Metropolitan Force. Public confidence in the police took a
nosedive. The entire criminal justice system came under
scrutiny as doubts began to be raised about individual
convictions. Prominent campaigns around such cases as
the Guildford Four and the Birmingham Six gained momentum.

BARRY made several trips to England to photograph
protests there.

Patrick James Halloran made his appearance that autumn. For once Barry was present at this child's birth; lit-
erally present, as Barbara suddenly went into labour one
morning while he was still in the house and the baby arrived before anyone could ring for a doctor. Breda officiated at the birth. Ten minutes later she emerged smiling
from the bedroom to put Barry's son in his arms.

He stared down in awe at the little face. Red from crying but startlingly adult in its lineaments. "He looks almost like a grown man," he said to Breda.

She laughed. "Newborns do that sometimes. Folks used
to say you could see the grown-up in the infant, but just
for the first few hours. By tomorrow you'll have no doubt
he's a baby."

"I want to hold him!" Barbara called from the bedroom.

"In a minute." Barry continued to study Patrick James. Everything about him was a marvel. A tonsure of dark hair plastered against his skull. Slightly pointed ears, like his father's: faun's ears. Milky blue eyes staring blankly at a world they could not yet focus upon.

Or were they blank? Barry peered more closely. Caught a glimpse of fading cognizance.

Is he still seeing the world he came from? Is that why he appears so old and wise?

B RIAN had his father's big bones and bright colouring. Grace Mary was a coltish girl with her mother's hazel eyes. From the beginning Patrick had a dark Celtic look about him: not wild, perhaps, yet definitely not tame. A creature born to mountains and forests.

"He's a changeling," was Ursula's comment.

Barbara took umbrage. "What an awful thing to say about a baby! He's mine, mine and Barry's, and nobody else's. Besides, I didn't know you were superstitious."

"*Super*-stitious? I'm not even average 'stitious.' I only believe in what my senses tell me. My *six* senses," Ursula added.

Christening, First Holy Communion, Confirmation— each child in turn would undergo the prescribed rituals. Ursula approved. Long ago she had ceased believing in the institution of the Church but she had never denied it to others. Barry had been raised a good Catholic; a bulwark against the vicissitudes of life, should he choose to employ it.

With three small children in the house Barbara's hours were filled to the brim. Her hours were filled but not the essential Barbara, the woman inside who was composed of dreams and ambitions. Even when she was physically exhausted part of her mind continued to race like a squirrel caught in a cage, frantically seeking a way out.

There must be something else, she told herself again and again.

There was no one to whom she could express her feelings; certainly not Barry, nor any other man. Her only real female friend was Alice Cassidy, whom she had known before she married. Since then she had focussed on Barry and the house—*this awful old house*—and then the children, while life went on without her. It was different for Alice, who had worked for years in Switzer's Department Store in O'Connell Street and expected to be promoted to buyer someday. *She'll have a real career,* Barbara thought enviously. *Travel the world buying clothes and going to fashion shows, while I'm stuck here.*

CHANGES were in the air. In December Charles J. Haughey succeeded Jack Lynch as *taoiseach.*

THE seventies had been a decade of tension, terror, and transformation. With a new *taoiseach* in charge, on New Year's Eve the citizens of the Republic looked hopefully towards a better future.

During the first month of 1980 Charles Haughey appeared on television to inform the Irish people that as a community they were living way beyond their means. This came as a shock to the many who were just barely getting by. Haughey proposed to take a firm hold on the fiscal reins by introducing stringent economic measures. The programme he laid out was punitive but made sense; the first solid economic sense the electorate had heard in years. Even Fine Gael, the party now in opposition, put the national interest ahead of party politics and announced its support. The Church also commended the plan.

Obedient as ever, the Irish people set out to tighten

their belts still more. If it was what their priests wanted it
was what they would do.

Roman Catholicism still was intrinsic to the Irish in the
early eighties. After being central to their society and culture for almost two millennia it was embedded in their
genes. Elsewhere organised religion was beginning to
lose adherents, but not in the Republic of Ireland.

On the seventeenth of February an amateur archaeolo-
gist using a metal detector in County Tipperary found the
eighth-century Derrynaflan Chalice with a hoard of other
gold and bejewelled ecclesiastical objects. The medieval
craftsmanship was of a very high degree, as was the religious devotion that had inspired it.

When the story hit the newspapers Barry immediately
put in a request to be allowed to photograph the hoard before any restoration was attempted. It soon became obvious, however, that a protracted battle over possession of
the rare objects was under way. The State claimed them
as part of the national heritage. The landowners claimed
them as private property. The owner of the metal detector
claimed them as treasure trove.

B ECAUSE 1980 was an Olympic year and Ursula was
keenly interested in the equestrian events, Barry bought a
television set.

"You did that for your mother but you never would for
me," Barbara complained to him.

"I would have, if you had not kept on and on about it."

"How can I know that now?" she asked reasonably.

U .S . president Jimmy Carter announced a boycott of
the Moscow Olympics in reaction to the Soviet invasion
of Afghanistan. Britain and Ireland refused to join the
boycott.

•   •   •

B ARRY photographed the small but hopeful group of
Irish competitors. In spite of having such great riders as the
brilliant Eddie Macken, the nation's show jumping and
three-day event teams would not be going to Moscow. Bord
na gCapall, the Irish Horse Council, had suffered a huge
budget cut and could not fund them.

"I could have saved the money I spent on the telly,"
Barry lamented.

O NE afternoon Barbara left Breda and Philpott in charge
of the children long enough to have a quick lunch with
Alice Cassidy. The two women ate in the café of the department store where Alice worked. The sandwiches were fresh,
the tea was hot. Shoppers—mostly mothers with small
children—sought a brief respite from trying to stretch too
little money over too many necessary purchases, while their
youngsters played at their feet and overturned their shopping bags.

Alice eyed the toddlers wistfully. "Aren't they dotes?"

"You might not think so if you spent all day every day
with them."

"Oh, I would think so, Barbara, I'd be in absolute
heaven. I do wish Dennis would push for a pay rise. Sub-
editors at *The Irish Press* don't make enough to support a
family. If only he had more ambition I could give up my
job and have a baby."

"Ambition isn't everything in a man," Barbara assured
her. "Look at Barry. At last he's making money from his
photography but he's never home anymore, and then
when he is we never go out together, no matter how many
times I ask him. Sometimes I feel like I'll scream if I . . .
I don't know. I just don't know."

"God love you," Alice said sympathetically as she

spooned more sugar into her tea. She was genuinely fond
of her friend, though Barbara had married the man she
used to dream of marrying. Barbara was beautiful and talented and exotic, all the things Alice Cassidy longed to
be. Barbara was a blazing sun while she was a pale moon,
but at least in proximity to the other woman she could
shed a little reflected light.

Besides, Barbara could be fun. She had a wicked sense
of humour and loved a laugh. What a pity that with all her
assets, she did not have the companionship of her husband; the one gift Alice took for granted.

After a few moments she said brightly, "Listen here to
me, Barbara. Dennis and I go dancing at least once a week.
I'll have him ring Barry and invite the pair of you to meet
us at the Stardust one evening. You have built-in child-
minders at home. The Stardust's the most popular nightclub on the northside and they always have great music.
You know how lads are; Barry won't refuse if the invitation
comes from Dennis. The pair of them can natter away
about journalism while you and I find some fellas to dance
with."

The two women conspired by telephone until the timing was right. Barry came in one Thursday afternoon and
remarked that he did not have another assignment until
Monday. "I'll be taking pictures for myself this weekend," he told his wife.

Barbara ran to the telephone.

When it rang an exact fifteen minutes later she called
out in her sweetest voice, "Will you answer that, Barry?
I'm up to my elbows here and Philpott's gone out to the
shops."

T H E Stardust Nightclub was in the working-class neighbourhood of Artane. The locale was immaterial; as soon
as Barbara heard the music she was in her element. Barry's
reluctance to dance was no handicap. Barbara appropri-

ated Dennis just long enough to demonstrate her skills
on the dance floor, and after that she never lacked for
partners.

As they were driving home in the small hours of the
morning Barbara began humming to herself.

Barry smiled. "You really enjoyed that, didn't you?"

"It was wonderful."

"Then would you do something for me?"

"What?"

"If you're in a mood to hum, how about singing?"

"What would you like to hear?"

"Something beautiful," said Barry.

O N the fifth of May a crack SAS* team stormed the Iranian Embassy in London, ending a six-day siege by terrorists demanding the release of political prisoners in
Iran. Nineteen surviving hostages were freed. Four of the
five gunmen who had taken over the building were killed.

B A R B A R A persuaded Barry to take her back to the
Stardust Nightclub several times that summer. He really
did not want to go; it seemed a frivolous waste of time
and the music was too loud. But it was a small price to
pay to keep his wife happy.

"Anything for a peaceful life," he remarked to Philpott.

The other observed, "A lot of married men say that.
Perhaps it's why I've never married."

Barry bit the inside of his lip. He thought he knew why
Philpott had never married. The little man genuinely did
not like women. For a long time Barry had assumed he was
sexually attracted to men, yet he never gave any evidence
of it. He appeared to be one of those rare asexual beings
whose life was composed of other elements. In an earlier

*Special Air Services.

era Philpott might have been an ascetic living in a beehive hut on the Blasket Islands. In the twentieth century he cooked like a professional chef and collected foreign coins.

Barry envied his apparent inner peace.

Most of the crowd who frequented the Stardust were younger than Barbara but she did not care. Their youthful energy was a tonic shot straight into her veins. She would dance with anybody and dance better than anybody. If Barry was watching she danced provocatively to make him jealous.

Eventually they quarrelled about it, of course. But any subject would do. When Barbara bought an abstract painting and hung it on the wall above Lord Nelson's stone nose, Barry asked what the picture was supposed to represent.

"It doesn't 'represent' anything, it's modern art. You wouldn't understand," she added loftily.

"Jack Yeats once said that painting was tactics, not strategy."

"That doesn't make any sense, Barry. Who was Jack Yeats anyway?"

"Only one of the greatest Irish artists, and William Butler Yeats's brother." Barry, who was beginning to lose his temper, could not resist adding, "Don't you know anything?"

"I don't have to when I'm married to a man who knows everything!" she flared.

ALONE in his darkroom after a row with Barbara—yet another row with Barbara—Barry cast his memory back in search of a time when he had neither a simmering anger nor a clenched gut. At first he found nothing to give him comfort. Only years of conflict and struggle. The Struggle. But perhaps earlier . . . the years unrolled like cinema film run backward . . .

. . . to his childhood in Clare.

Ursula when he was small and she was tall. Granda and Auntie Eileen and the Ryan brothers. The fragrance of freshly dug loam in the kitchen garden; the hens clucking about Eileen's feet as she scattered corn from a metal pan; his own small self toddling home across the fields after a day's adventures and finding his mother at the door waiting for him, trying to pretend she had not been anxious about him. His own small self tucked up in his bed at night, snug under quilts frayed by generations of use, listening to the house go to sleep around him. Safe and warm. Eager for tomorrow, when it would all start over again.

Why did I not realise that what I had was as good as it ever would be? But children never do. Perhaps it's human nature to want to escape from Eden.

THE slaughter went on in the north. Catholics and Protestants, civilians and soldiers, students and pensioners. Elsie Clare, a fifty-six-year-old shop worker, died of a heart attack after learning that a close friend of hers had been shot. Her friend recovered.

On the eleventh of October Dr. Rose Dugdale was released from jail in Limerick, having served six years of a sentence for involvement in the Beit art theft.

I wish Barbara and I liked each other," Ursula remarked to McCoy, "so I could be more of a friend to her. She's so edgy and tense I wonder she doesn't take it out on the children. She certainly takes it out on Barry."

McCoy said, "What makes you think she doesn't like you? When she thought you were being kidnapped she went to your rescue without a moment's thought, even though for all she knew she could have been shot dead. If that's not liking, I don't know what is. It's exactly what your son did for his pals at Brookeborough."

Ursula considered his words. Then she put pen to paper

and began writing letters to old acquaintances; reestablishing connections she had allowed to fade away over the years.

They might be useful sometime, and Ursula never wasted anything.

SINCE his latest release from prison Gerry Adams had become politically active again. The republican movement was a complex one with a number of strands. Ruairí Ó Brádaigh, the president of Provisional Sinn Féin, was also on the Provisional Army Council, the governing body of the IRA. The political wing and the physical force element were almost inextricably interlinked by the number of people who belonged to both organisations.

Most mainstream republicans agreed that the need for arms against the British was indisputable. Others hearkened back to the foundation of Sinn Féin, which Arthur Griffith had intended to be a constitutional political party peacefully achieving its goals in the political arena. The two visions of Irish republicanism appeared on the surface to be irreconcilable, yet men and women from both strands worked together for the sake of a free Ireland.

Stresses and strains were inherent in the situation. To make matters worse, with the appearance of more dissident groups calling themselves "republican," the difference between paramilitarism and banditry was disappearing from the public perception. Support was dwindling fast.

The primary concern of the Army Council was to maintain the military momentum that had been building up since Bloody Sunday, and to retain the structures and tight discipline that had evolved through trial and error over many years. The Army Council mistrusted politics, fearing it would corrupt the movement.

Gerry Adams, and a few others who felt as he did, such as Danny Morrison, the editor of the *Republican News,* hoped to see the republican movement restructured through

Sinn Féin in order to reach more people. They recognised that they were in a long war, and a long war must always be a people's war. The work to win the hearts and minds of ordinary civilians began. In the meantime the bombing and shooting continued. On both sides.

Chapter Twenty-nine

O N the twenty-seventh of October seven H-Block prisoners began a hunger strike. They had five demands, which if met would effectively restore their status as political prisoners: 1. no prison clothes 2. no prison work 3. permission for one weekly visit, one letter out, one letter in, and one package in every week 4. free association with fellow prisoners 5. entitlement to remission of sentences where appropriate.

The strike was not ordered by the Army Council but was determined by the men themselves. Deprived of everything that gave human existence dignity, the prisoners felt that all they had left to fight with was their lives. Among them was Brendan Hughes, the current Officer Commanding.

Because the strike might incapacitate Hughes, Bobby Sands took his place as O/C.

Conditions in the northern prisons had been deteriorating all year. Sinn Féin had initiated a campaign known as the H-Block/Armagh Committee, which comprised a coalition of interested groups and attempted to ameliorate the situation. With no support from Dublin they made little headway against the British government.

Gerry Adams was not in favour of using hunger strikes

as a tactic, fearing it would not be effective and lives would
be lost. Two male republicans had died on hunger strike in
England in 1974 and 1976. Two republican women had almost died from force-feeding after months of self-imposed
starvation.

O N the fourth of November Ronald Reagan defeated
Jimmy Carter in the United States presidential election.

L A T E that month three women in Armagh Prison joined
the hunger strike. In the Republic the news was relegated
to the back pages, though Barry bombarded the national
dailies with photographs of the prisons taken from every
angle he could think of to stress the grimness of the situation.

It had long since been decided that he would be allowed no photographic access to the interiors.

G E R R Y Adams was in almost daily contact with Bobby
Sands. The two men were good friends and had much in
common. Sands was by now an old hand in the prison system, but he also was familiar with Sinn Féin, having worked
as a community activist at one stage. As the O/C Sands was
kept informed of all developments. The authorities thought
they had the H-Blocks locked up tight, but they could not
imprison information.

The republicans were resourceful.

In December another thirty H-Block prisoners joined
the strike. The international community was beginning to
take interest—until the eighth of December, when John
Lennon was shot dead in New York.

The murder of the enigmatic and arguably most talented
of the Beatles engaged the news media to the exclusion of
everything else. Little notice was taken the following day

of the first Anglo-Irish summit meeting, held in Dublin between Margaret Thatcher and Charles Haughey. Thatcher acknowledged Britain's "special relationship" with Ireland and agreed to continue with biannual meetings to discuss "the totality of relationships within these islands."

The Irish government hailed the occasion as a historic breakthrough.

B ARRY went to Leinster House, photographed the two prime ministers shaking hands as Thatcher departed, and went home in a bad mood.

"They didn't talk about a damned thing that's really important," he told McCoy.

"How do you know?"

"They were smiling."

As he was getting ready for bed that night Barry began softly humming "Imagine," his favourite of Lennon's songs. Barbara started to sing the words, but they were so painful under the circumstances that he asked her to stop.

She understood at once. And he loved her for it.

Had anyone asked, Barry would have said he loved America. America as he remembered it. Shiny and full of confidence.

What he really loved—as so many Irish people did—was the *idea* of America. Or more specifically the United States: the world's largest democracy and last best hope. Now the man whose songs had epitomised so much of that hope had been shot dead by an American with no hope at all.

I N Northern Ireland other people who felt they had no hope at all continued with the hunger strike. The commitment having been made, all of republicanism rowed in behind them. Personal misgivings were set aside. Ruairí Ó Brádaigh, president of Sinn Féin, announced, "We must bend every muscle, strain every nerve to support the hunger strikers. This is a showdown with imperialism."

Known only to the participants, a secret line of communication code-named "Mountain Climber" was opened between the British government, working through the Foreign Office, and the republican leadership. It involved reactivating a channel first used during the ceasefire of '74–'75. In spite of their public protests that no quarter would be given, the British were growing anxious to end the strike. The international fallout could be horrific if it went on too long.

On the fifteenth of December twenty-three more republicans joined the hunger strike. One of the first strikers, Seán McKenna, was losing his sight and reported to be approaching death. He was wrapped in a blanket made of tin foil to conserve his falling body heat and transported to an outside hospital. Supporters set up a vigil outside the hospital.

B a r r y photographed the scene. Flickering candles, pleading placards. Kneeling women fingering their rosaries and sombre men standing with downcast eyes.

Time slipped; slid.

It was a cold, dark November morning in 1920, during the War of Independence, and he was standing outside Mountjoy Prison. Within those walls Volunteer Kevin Barry, only eighteen years old, was about to be hanged for taking part in an attack on a bread lorry delivering rations to British soldiers. He personally had not shot anyone, but he was the only member of the attack party to be captured.

Over two thousand people had gathered outside the jail to pray for him. Tenement women with ragged shawls tightly drawn around their thin shoulders; local businessmen in their dark suits; Maud Gonne MacBride, beloved of William Butler Yeats. Some carried flickering candles.

Women knelt in the muddy road fingering their rosaries.
Sombre men stood with downcast eyes.

A warder came out and pinned a typewritten notice on
the wall: "The sentence of the law passed on Kevin Barry,
found guilty of murder, was carried into execution at eight
A.M. *this morning. By order."*[1]

According to his executioners young Kevin had died
calmly, almost cheerfully, praying for both his friends
and his enemies as the hangman pulled the hood over his
head.

Afterwards Michael Collins grimly promised there
would be "no more lonely scaffolds."

Barry Halloran shook his head, trying to clear it. When
he looked around he was in Belfast again.

What the hell just happened?

O N the following day seven more republican prisoners
joined the hunger strike.

Cardinal Ó Fíaich issued a personal appeal to Margaret
Thatcher, asking her to intervene. He also called on the
protestors to give up their strike, in the name of God.

Through the Foreign Office, the British government suggested that a compromise could be reached. They promised that a document setting out the details of a proposed
settlement, which would at least partially meet the strikers'
demands, would be sent to the men inside the prison as
soon as they came off the strike. The outside leadership
had dealt with the British government in this way before
and had little reason to trust them. But time was running
out. They passed the word along to the hunger strikers and
their families. Believing that a deal was on its way from
London, Seán McKenna began accepting nourishment in
hospital.

On the nineteenth of December the hunger strike was
called off.

When the British were sure the strike was over, they

reneged. The concessions that had been promised to the republicans were withdrawn in a major, and ultimately tragic, breach of faith.

Bobby Sands summed it up. "Next time we'll have to go all the way."

A T the end of the year the northern death toll for the Troubles was two thousand and rising.

T H R O U G H December and into January Bobby Sands did everything he could think of to persuade the British to go ahead with their commitment. It was no use. London had gone deaf. At last he sent word to Gerry Adams that he intended to initiate a second hunger strike. Adams tried hard to dissuade him. On behalf of Sinn Féin he wrote, "We are tactically, strategically, physically and morally opposed to a hunger strike."[2]

But he was not in the H-Blocks.

Anyone who was not in the H-Blocks at the time could not fully understand just how terrible it was.

I N 1981 the rural quiet of County Tyrone was ruptured by gunfire on the sixteenth of January when Bernadette Devlin McAliskey and her husband Michael were seriously wounded in a loyalist attack on their home at Derrylaughan.

Five days later the IRA killed Sir Norman Stronge, former speaker of the Stormont Parliament, and his son, then bombed his house, Tynan Abbey.

On the sixth of February Ian Paisley took five journalists to a remote location in County Antrim. There Paisley addressed five hundred followers whom he described as "The Third Force," which was prepared to resist to the death the process of a united Ireland. Speech concluded,

Paisley returned the journalists to Belfast to spread the word.

O N the night of February thirteenth the Stardust Nightclub in Artane was hosting the final of a disco-dancing contest. Although all of the dancers and most of the audience would be considerably younger than she was, Barbara was eager to go.

"I have an assignment down in Waterford that will take some time, so I probably will stay overnight," Barry told her. "But there's no reason why you can't go to the club on your own. When Ursula could walk she went everywhere on her own."

"Well, that's Ursula, isn't it? If I went by myself people would think I couldn't get a man to go with me."

"Then why not ask Séamus?"

"You must be joking. They'd think I'd come with my father, and I'm not *that* desperate."

"Why do you care what people think?"

"Don't you?"

"Not particularly," said Barry.

H A R O L D ' S Cross was too far from Artane for Barbara to hear the shriek of the fire sirens.

The Stardust had been packed to capacity when a fire broke out behind the stage. As the frightened crowd tried to escape they found most of the exits had been locked to keep anyone from coming in without paying. Panic broke out. People were trampled. Bodies piled up at the doorways.

In the early hours of St. Valentine's Day the Stardust was totally destroyed. Forty-eight young people died and over two hundred were injured. Some parents lost more than one child in the inferno. Friends and families were devastated.

Barry had returned home in the morning to find Barbara in near hysterics. "I rang and rang the Cassidys but no one's home. Were they at the Stardust, Barry? Were they?"

He put his arms around her. "Of course not, sweetheart. I'm sure they're all right."

He was not sure at all.

They were both hugely relieved when Alice rang a few minutes later from her mother-in-law's house, where they had been visiting overnight. When she heard Barbara's voice Alice exclaimed, "We were afraid you might have gone to the Stardust!"

Barbara, caught between laughter and tears, replied, "We were afraid you had!"

Not everyone received such good news. The nation's newspapers put out special editions listing the names of the dead together with dramatic pictures of the burnt-out club and rows of sheet-covered bodies in the morgue. But no photograph could adequately express the agony of desperate parents who rushed from one hospital to another, only to discover that the face they sought was under one of those sheets. Nor could a camera convey the horror of the smell that lingered over the ruins of the Stardust.

Barry Halloran did not join the other photographers covering the story.

Barbara might have been one of those charred bodies under a sheet.

FIANNA Fáil was holding its Ard Fheis that weekend. Party leader Charles Haughey ordered an adjournment as a mark of respect. But this was Ireland; there was never a shortage of political commentary. Several newspapers carried a quote from Ian Paisley: "The *taoiseach* will never get his filthy venomous hands on Northern Ireland!"[3]

•   •   •

O N the first of March a second hunger strike began in the H-Blocks, led by Bobby Sands.

The five demands of the protestors were the same as before. Although there were some private misgivings among *taobh amuigh*—the outside republican leadership—about the tactic, they gave the strikers their support. The willingness of the men in the H-Blocks to sacrifice themselves if necessary for the greater good of their fellow republicans was recognised as the ultimate symbol of solidarity.

O N the fifth of March Taoiseach Charles Haughey announced the establishment of Aosdána, an academy of the arts created to publicly honour those of distinguished achievement in literature, music, and the visual arts. A burse of four thousand pounds per annum would be awarded to members whose earnings were not sufficient to allow them to devote their full-time energies to their creative work.

That same day the MP for Fermanagh/South Tyrone died unexpectedly of a heart attack. There would have to be a by-election to replace him.

O N the sixth the *Irish Independent* announced that a tract of land on O'Connell Street had been purchased from the Estate of George Pentland, an Englishman, by the Department of Posts and Telegraphs. For £3000 the Irish people at last had acquired the ground upon which stood the General Post Office, the most visible icon in the nation. There in 1916 a schoolmaster called Pádraic Pearse had read the Proclamation of the Irish Republic, and brave men subsequently had fought and died to make Ireland free.

The transfer of ownership passed almost unnoticed. In contrast to its original passing into English hands, the land was not seized by force of arms and no abuse of power was used in its conveyance to the State.

• • •

MEANWHILE Sinn Féin was moving fast to enter a candidate in the upcoming by-election. Bobby Sands was seen as the ideal candidate.

THAT spring the Grand National Steeplechase enjoyed one of its most heart-warming victories ever. Jockey Bob Champion, who had fought and won a battle against cancer, came home ahead of the pack on Aldaniti, who had been given up as a cripple. Even hardened racegoers who had bets on other horses stood and cheered the pair.

ON the ninth of April Volunteer Bobby Sands, with an address in the H-Blocks and 30,492 votes to his credit, was elected MP for Fermanagh/South Tyrone, defeating Unionist Harry West and becoming the newest member of the British Parliament.

The prisoners in the H-Blocks had smuggled in radios to allow them to follow the elections results on BBC. Bobby Sands' triumph was not broadcast on RTE in the Republic because of Section 31.

Unionists were baffled by the outcome. A shocked Harry West said, "I never thought the decent Catholics of County Fermanagh would vote for a gunman."[4]

They genuinely could not understand why their Catholic neighbours would vote for their enemy, the IRA, any more than they could understand the motivations behind the hunger strike.

For the prisoners, continuing the strike to its inevitable conclusion was a last-ditch, despairing effort to die with dignity as opposed to dying with none.

At 1:17 A.M. on the fifth of May, 1981, IRA Volunteer and MP for Fermanagh/South Tyrone Bobby Sands died in the H-Block prison on the sixty-sixth day of his hunger strike.

During the preceding week Sands' condition had been steadily deteriorating as he slipped in and out of consciousness. His condition was reported as critical. He had lost all feeling in his mouth and gums and could hardly talk. His eyesight was rapidly failing. His skin had become so thin that he had been placed on an improvised water bed to keep his bones from breaking through.

There had been two major attempts to bring the strike to an end in time to save his life. The first had been an intervention by the European Commission on Human Rights. The second took the form of a visit to Sands by the pope's private secretary, Fr. John Magee.

After both of these attempts Bobby Sands, Francis Hughes, Raymond McCreesh, and Patsy O'Hara, a member of the INLA, had reaffirmed to their relatives their intention to go all the way if necessary.

Although twenty-eight Labour MPs had signed a parliamentary motion calling on the British government to negotiate with the prisoners, Labour's Northern Ireland spokesperson Don Concannon called on Sands on the first of May to tell the dying man that Labour would not support the hunger strikers' demands. It was a final touch of cruelty.

Bobby Sands had spent the last two days of his life in a coma, with his family constantly at his bedside as his breathing became more and more laboured. And finally stopped.

The silence in the tiny concrete cell was louder than all the noise in the world. Although he had been against the strike, Father Denis Faul, the Maze prison chaplain, wept openly.

As if an electric shock had galvanised Belfast, within a few minutes of Sands' death republican women all over the city began banging on the pavement with metal bin lids.

The international journalistic community leaped into action. Floodlights were set up outside the forbidding walls of the Maze and miles of television cable were snarled like tangles of sea serpents on the tarmacadam.

A small green Austin Healey raced up the Dublin–Belfast road. When Barry arrived at the Maze he was met by a huge sign that proclaimed: "Photography of All Kinds Within the Prison Is Strictly Prohibited."

Barry turned around and headed back to Belfast. For the first funeral.

S ANDS' death had been expected for days, but the sense of shock was profound both north and south. Thousands of people reacted immediately, gathering in prayer vigils or marches to express their outrage. In the Six Counties barricades were erected in the streets as crowds fought fierce running battles with the RUC and the British army. The capital of the Republic was brought to a standstill when a huge crowd spontaneously gathered in O'Connell Street to hold a silent vigil in the rain.

After being released from the prison Sands' body was taken to his home in Twinbrook. Thousands of mourners gathered to file past his open coffin. To gaze in awe at the emaciated face; the blind eyes, once so bright and merry, firmly closed. The coffin was flanked by an honour guard composed of members of Óglaigh na hÉireann,* Na Fíanna Éireann,† and Cumann na mBan.‡ The following day the coffin, draped with the Irish tricolour, was carried the short distance to St. Luke's Chapel.

From there on Thursday afternoon the funeral cortege began its four-mile journey to Millbrook Cemetery. A lone piper played a song that had been written in the H-Blocks:

---

*The Irish Volunteers; Irish name of the IRA.
†The Warriors of Ireland; Irish republican youth corps.
‡The Society of Women; republican women's organisation.

I'll wear no convict's uniform, nor meekly
serve my time,
That Britain may call Ireland's fight
Eight hundred years of crime.

A crowd estimated at over one hundred thousand people heard the IRA fire three volleys over the flag-draped coffin. It was the largest funeral in Ireland since that of Terence MacSwiney, the mayor of Cork who died on hunger strike against the British in 1920.

At graveside Gerry Adams officiated at a ceremony that began with the playing of "The Last Post." Owen Carron, who had managed Sands' election campaign, gave the funeral oration.

Seven-year-old Gerald Sands helped to shovel soft earth onto his father's coffin.

B ARRY Halloran took photographs that were reproduced around the world and brought tears to the eyes of people who hardly knew where Ireland was.

W E thought there was no way Britain would let an MP die, but we were eejits," a stunned Volunteer told a reporter at the funeral. "Maggie Thatcher could and did let him die."

The republicans had failed to take one crucial fact into their calculations: Margaret Thatcher understood neither Ireland nor republicanism.

Months after ordering the executions of the leaders of the 1916 Rising, General Sir John Maxwell had been still pondering the events. He had learned much about Ireland since those desperate days when he arrived fresh from England with a set of orders and a sense of urgency.

As he eventually wrote, "The rebellion in Ireland was

a direct result of the British government shamelessly pandering to a small minority of Protestants in the north-east corner of the predominately Catholic island."[5]

T H E Irish were a people over whom symbolism had always exerted a powerful influence. The symbolism of the hunger strikers—gaunt, bearded Christ-like figures wrapped in blankets and willing to sacrifice themselves for a cause—was irresistible. With the death of Bobby Sands, people who had been lukewarm or even antagonistic to-wards republicanism became deeply emotional about the men·in the H-Blocks.

B A R R Y determined to stay in Belfast until it was over— however it ended. He could not afford to spend a long, indeterminate time in a hotel, so he began staying with a series of friends in the republican community, mainly the Falls Road area.

There was only one subject of conversation. In the Falls it was as if life were being held in abeyance while death loomed over the Maze.

O N the eighth of May Volunteer Joe McDonnell took Bobby Sands' place on hunger strike.

Father Faul began meeting with the mothers of the hunger strikers to encourage them to take their sons off the strike.

On the twelfth Volunteer Francis Hughes died.

The rioting that had begun with the death of Bobby Sands increased. There was a major upsurge of IRA at-tacks on British and RUC installations. In Dublin the Gardai used batons to beat back a protest march headed from the GPO to the British Embassy. At the same time in the north, fourteen-year-old Julie Livingstone was killed by a plastic bullet fired by a member of the British army.

The RUC hijacked Hughes' funeral cortege as it passed through West Belfast on its way to his native Derry, forcing it to go by a much longer route. A member of the RUC openly spat on the coffin; an act captured in newsreel footage.

Martin McGuinness gave the funeral oration for Hughes. "His body lies here beside us but he lives in the little streets of Belfast, he lives in the Bogside, he lives in East Tyrone and Crossmaglen. He will always live in the hearts and minds of unconquerable Irish republicans. They could not break him. They will not break us."

Chapter Thirty

ON the thirteenth of May an attempted assassin shot Pope John Paul II while he was blessing a crowd at the Vatican. In the Republic of Ireland people flocked to their churches to pray for him. Catholics in Northern Ireland did the same, though somewhat less openly.

McCoy suggested, "I'll ring for a taxi, Ursula, if you'd like to go to the Pro-Cathedral to pray for the pope. That seems to be where most folks are headed."

"Are you offering to go with me?"

"I am of course, you'll need me."

"Would you go on your own without me?"

"Probably," he replied. "I have a lot of people to pray for."

Ursula began counting on her fingers. "Raymond McCreesh, Patsy O'Hara, Joe McDonnell . . . ring for that taxi, Séamus. We'll both pray for the boys in the Maze."

OBLIVIOUS to gunfire, the ten-tonne, six-wheeled Saracen armoured car was not oblivious to a thousand pounds of explosives concealed in a culvert near Raymond McCreesh's house in South Armagh. All that was left of the Saracen was one of its tyres and the armoured turret. Five British soldiers died.

That same day twelve-year-old Carol Anne Kelly was walking home from the corner shop within hailing distance of Bobby Sands' house in Twinbrook when four British army Land Rovers came speeding up the road. The crack of gunfire startled the child but it was already too late; she had been fatally hit by a plastic bullet travelling at 180 mph.

ON the twenty-first of May Raymond McCreesh died in the early hours of the morning. Patsy O'Hara followed within hours. The two men had been born within days of each other in 1957.

O'Hara's sister said later, "As he was dying his face just changed, he had a very, very distinct smile on his face which I will never forget. I said, 'You're free, Patsy. You have won your fight and you're free.' "[1]

IN Dublin Charles Haughey, who had been under relentless pressure to call a general election—and had failed to make headway with the European Commission on the matter of the hunger strike—dissolved the Dáil. He announced that the election would be held in three weeks, the shortest notice allowed by law.

In spite of the physical difficulties involved—the Republic made no allowances for handicapped voters—Ursula planned to cast her ballot. She had no illusions about the electoral process, however. "During the last election," she told McCoy, "promises were flung about like snuff at a wake."

A T Raymond McCreesh's funeral Mass one of the celebrants called attention to a speech given by the pope in 1979: "Violent means must not be used to change injustices. But neither must violent means be used to keep injustices."

T H E governor of Long Kesh, Stanley Hilditch, had promised O'Hara's family that his remains would be delivered to the town of Omagh, from whence the funeral cortege could begin. At four-thirty in the morning a telephone call from the RUC told the grieving relatives they had better come for Patsy's body before daylight. When they opened the coffin they found the young man's body had been mutilated. By persons unknown.

On the night following the two deaths there was more rioting in the streets. The RUC in O'Hara's native Derry responded with a hail of plastic bullets that killed Harry Duffy, an innocent bystander, and injured a number of others. In the Ardoyne district of Belfast Paul Lavelle, aged fifteen, was left in a coma after being struck by the bullets.

Five British soldiers were killed in an IRA ambush at Altnaveigh, South Armagh.

But international support for the hunger strikers soared.

Behind a solid wall of concrete resolute young men were dying. The British meant the Maze to be the breaker's yard that would destroy the republicans but they would not break.

Demonstrations were held every day in the United States. Thousands marched through the streets of New York, protesting the deaths of McCreesh and O'Hara. Large demonstrations were also held in Australia, Norway, France, Portugal, and Greece.

Cardinal Ó Fíaich pleaded with Margaret Thatcher. "How many more Irish men must go to their graves inside and outside the jail before intransigence gives way to a constructive effort to find a solution?" the cleric wanted to know.

There was no response.

In the United States Senator Edward Kennedy condemned the British policy. The Boston City Council renamed the street upon which the British consulate was located "Francis Hughes Street." The Irish in America understood the meaning of symbolism.

In the by-election that followed Sands' death, Volunteer Owen Carron, who had been his campaign manager, succeeded him as MP for Fermanagh/South Tyrone.

Despite Margaret Thatcher's public intransigence, British government officials continued communicating through back channels with the republicans. Negotiations between Gerry Adams and the government appeared to hold out some hope of a breakthrough. In the tension between political strategy and the armed struggle, a seismic shift began to take place in the foundations of republicanism. Although it was not apparent at the time, the first tentative steps had been taken toward a peace process.

After the fourth hunger striker died a secret proposal that granted most of the strikers' demands was put forward to the IRA. The outside leadership told the British, "Go into the prisons with this and if the hunger strikers accept it, we shall."[2]

Then Joe McDonnell died—and the strikers themselves refused any further negotiations.

·   ·   ·

B ARRY Halloran's moody yet insightful photographic coverage of the situation in the north was in constant demand from the news services and was having a huge impact abroad. But he longed to go back to Dublin. Every death was a heavier stone on his heart. He wanted to see his children and make love to his wife and talk politics with Ursula and old times with Séamus and do anything but stand around outside the Maze waiting for someone to die.

He stayed.

The men inside were staying.

I N June Barry did return to Dublin in order to vote in the general election. Like his mother, Barry always voted. Great men had given their lives so that he could.

Fianna Fáil won seventy-eight seats in Dáil Éireann to Fine Gael's sixty-five, giving neither party a sufficient balance of power to rule the country alone. Barry explained to young Brian, "In this situation the *taoiseach* can be chosen from either side, and it will then be up to him to form a coalition government."

Brian was growing up amongst people who read books and followed the news, so it was not surprising that he asked questions. His parents, Barbara included, did their best to answer them, but he always had more. Intelligent questions.

Trot was different; she was all action. Ursula was beginning to talk about leaving the farm to her in her will. The breeding of thoroughbred racehorses was becoming a serious business in Ireland. Experts were beginning to claim the country would soon rival Kentucky in its production of quality bloodstock. "I can just see my granddaughter becoming the first female owner of an Irish racing establishment," Ursula said.

As for Patrick James, it was hard to predict how he would turn out. That dark, fey look . . .

Although Barry went into considerable detail about the political situation with his son—*Perhaps I'm telling him more than he wants to know*—he himself was not interested in who would become *taoiseach*. From Barry's point of view something more historic was taking place. Quietly, without fanfare aside from the election posters Sinn Féin had put up, two republican prisoners in the H-Blocks had been elected to Dáil Éireann.

There were boisterous celebrations in the Bleeding Horse.

The following morning Barry drove Apollo to Paudie Coates' garage. As always he had a list in his head. Fill up the petrol tank, check the oil, water for the battery, air for the tyres. New windscreen wipers. Laugh at Paudie's latest jokes. Then back to the house for his suitcase and cameras, and a reporter's spiral notebook crammed with notes, many of them taken from Séamus McCoy.

Barry hoped to meet Gerry Adams, among others, on this trip, and he had been doing his homework.

He gave Philpott last-minute instructions, hugged his children, spoke for a few minutes with his mother, exchanged a rueful shake of the head with McCoy, and braced himself for the most difficult farewell of all—one that never got easier.

Barbara followed him out to the kerb. "Would it make any difference if I begged you not to go?"

"We've been over this so many times, sweetheart. It's my job."

"But it's getting more dangerous all the time. I watch the news programmes and they scare me to death. They're all crazy in Northern Ireland, Barry. Anything could happen to you, and then what would *we* do?"

I wonder how many men around the world have similar discussions with their women? "I'll be all right," he assured her. "The people in the north aren't crazy, just angry, and I know how to take care of myself."

The tawny eyes flashed a warning. Barbara was on the

verge of losing her temper for real. If an open quarrel erupted he could not drive away and leave her; he might not have a marriage when he came back.

I might not have a marriage now.

"You know how to take care of yourself," she repeated sarcastically. "I suppose that's why you walk with a limp when you're tired: because you're so goddamned good at taking care of yourself."

"It won't happen again."

"You can't promise that. You're so damned selfish, you and your stupid photography."

"I'm sorry you feel that way, but if I didn't have my work I might . . ." He caught himself in midsentence.

They stood staring at each other.

"I hate you, Barry Halloran! I really truly hate you!" She flew at him with balled fists and began pounding his chest.

There was nothing to do but take her back in the house and try to repair the fractures in their relationship one more time, in the only way that always worked with Barbara—for a little while.

The effects were never lasting.

Catching both her wrists in one hand, Barry held her pinioned while he lowered his mouth to hers. When he kissed her she tried to bite him. He turned his head away and spun her around to face the house. "We're going inside. Now."

"I won't go anywhere with you!" She arched her back and tried to break free.

He forced her into the house and up the stairs ahead of him, fighting all the way. "Be quiet," he admonished. "What will the others think?"

That was sufficient to subdue her long enough to reach their bedroom. As soon as they were inside he closed the door and turned the key in the lock.

"I hate you," hissed Barbara. "Hate you hate you hate you!"

"Of course you do," he said.

Barry tried to be gentle. Knowing how strong he could be when he was angry, he tried desperately to be gentle. Barbara fought as if her life were in danger. With the restraints he placed on himself it was an uneven struggle.

Just when he thought she might actually throw him off, she relaxed abruptly. He felt her body go soft beneath his and her thighs part. "Please don't go to Belfast again," she whispered.

"I must go." His heart was pounding, though not with the exertion of their struggle. Heat was rising from her in waves.

Barry was intensely alive on two levels at once. The cognitive man was already in the car, driving north. Checking items off lists. Preparing interviews with those who were taking serious risks; planning photographic layouts that might show the first cracks in the monolith.

Meanwhile the primordial man—and who was to say which was the truer Barry—was submerged in the senses. Touch, taste, smell. Writhing flesh. Irresistible pressure and great surging sweetness that obliterated everything but itself, sweeping him into the heart of the exploding universe.

For one brief moment the two Barrys came together. And knew what it was all about.

He left for Belfast much later than he had planned. Barbara, with her lips swollen and her hair tumbling around her shoulders, stood in the doorway to wave good-bye.

A populist tide engendered by the hunger strike was sweeping through Irish republicanism. The armed campaign on which so many had pinned their hopes would continue, but would have to allow for a new dimension: the involvement of ordinary people. To this end republicans were initiating an "Armalite and Ballot Box" strategy, signifying the intention to contest future elections.

Sinn Féin had become a player.

Introducing a political element into mainstream republicanism was never going to be easy. It required a very delicate tightrope act. The IRA would have to be carefully brought along step by step by someone whose credentials were accepted as impeccable by the Army Council—experienced veterans who, for good reason, deeply mistrusted the whole political process.

Gerry Adams had worked his way up through the ranks, serving Irish republicanism ably in a number of ways. He had the trust of the Army Council—for as long as he could maintain it—which was the vital key to the process.

Belfast-born Adams came from a large republican family, and had fought hard to overcome a youthful stammer. He had started attending Sinn Féin educational classes when he was seventeen—the year he left school to help out the family by bringing home a pay packet. He found employment as a bartender in a Belfast bar owned by a Catholic but frequented by Protestants. Adams mingled easily with people from both religions. Belfast was not yet as savagely divided along sectarian lines as it was about to become.

Like most young men Adams was more interested in girls than politics—until 1964, when Ian Paisley's temper tantrum about the Irish flag flying at the Sinn Féin office in Belfast caused the RUC to break into the office and tear down the tricolour. Within a matter of days Gerry Adams had joined the Sinn Féin Party.

On the party's behalf he organised a summer camp south of the border in County Leitrim to give boys in the area something to do and keep them out of trouble. As a republican activist he also was increasingly involved in the expanding conflict that would be known as the Troubles. Catholics became targets simply because of their religion. Friends of his were shot and killed. Over fifteen hundred northern Catholics fled across the border into the Republic in July of 1970, becoming refugees in their own land.

In August of 1971 British soldiers had thrown Gerry Adams' father down the stairs of his house and dragged him off to jail. His family lost their home when it was occupied by paratroopers. Theirs was a common story in Northern Ireland; one more pebble thrown onto the waste ground of injustice.

In October of 1971 Gerry Adams' young wife miscarried after two of their close female friends were shot dead by British soldiers.

Enough pebbles can build a mountain.

Gerry Adams' republican activities had put him high on the arrest list. After months on the run, in March of 1972 he was seized and taken to a British interrogation centre. While one soldier shouted questions at him others kept kicking the chair out from under him. He was repeatedly punched in the head. Various methods, such as suddenly hurling heavy metal food trays onto the floor behind him, were employed to unnerve him. He was new to this sort of intimidation and did not know what to expect, but he soon found out. He could hear men in other cubicles being reduced to a state of terror by the attacks against them.

In Adams' case this included having an apparent madman threaten him with a bloodstained hatchet, and being forced to stand spread-eagled against a wall while he was systematically beaten. The worst of the damage was inflicted on the kidneys and between the legs.[3]

Afterwards Adams was interned on the *Maidstone,* one of Britain's notorious prison ships. The cramped, rusting hulk was filthy and dangerous but well guarded. Being moored at a dock in the heart of loyalist East Belfast provided an additional deterrent to republican prisoners hoping to jump ship.

They had found another route to escape. By organising a well-publicised food strike at the exact moment when the old Stormont regime was being replaced by an English cabinet minister, they had brought attention to the dreadful conditions of the *Maidstone* and forced her closure. The prisoners, including Adams, had been transferred to Long Kesh. Where he began thinking about the situation in new ways, and writing the "Brownie" articles.

On the thirtieth of June Garret FitzGerald, the anti-republican leader of Fine Gael, became *taoiseach* of the Republic of Ireland. Charles Haughey found himself leader of the opposition.

Martin Hurson of the East Tyrone Brigade did not have a lot to say for himself aside from making jokes; he was a happy-go-lucky sort of fellow who never seemed to take anything seriously. But there was one thing he took seriously. Commitment.

On the thirteenth of July, Hurson, aged twenty-four, died in the Maze after forty-six days on hunger strike.

Five days later the Gardai in Dublin narrowly prevented another large and angry H-Block protest from reaching the British Embassy. There were violent clashes between police and protestors.

At the end of July Pat Quinn's family took him off hunger strike—against his wishes. Barry sought and gained permission to take a few informal photographs of his relieved family. They were filled with praise for Father Denis Faul, and his efforts to intervene in the strike. "He's a great man for helping a lame dog over a stile."

The other strikers continued, though there was a sense that something vital had been damaged. "It's a breach in the dam," said a veteran Volunteer whom Barry interviewed in a republican pub on the Falls Road. "Some of the families just don't understand."

"Can you blame them? Suppose Pat was your son."

"Suppose he was yours."

The first eight days of August brought three more deaths: Kevin Lynch of the INLA, Kieran Doherty, who had been elected in the Republic as TD* for Cavan/Monaghan, and Thomas McElwee.

The British media claimed the hunger strikers were being manipulated "by outside control" for publicity purposes. The Church worried that it would be blamed.

Barry Halloran understood the mentality of the strikers better than either the British media or the Catholic Church. He knew no one could manipulate them.

He was intensely proud of them.

B REANDAN MacCionnaith, an Irish Catholic, attempted to blow up the British Legion Hall in Portadown.[4] Fortunately no one was killed.

B ARRY was told there would be no difficulty about meeting Gerry Adams—except Adams' life had become a marathon of meeting people; talking, listening, explaining, negotiating, starting over again. "He'll have to be caught on the hop," said Billy Keane.

In West Belfast Barry was staying with Billy Keane and his family, which included Billy's wife Carmel, their five children under the age of nine, Carmel's widowed mother Anne, and Billy's younger brother Eddie, a gangly youth who spent his days hanging around street corners, hurling stones and profanity at the soldiers. There were few jobs in Northern Ireland for young men like Eddie. The future presented two possibilities: getting arrested or being shot by the security forces for some real or imagined infraction of the law. Eddie had one advantage. His brother had signed him up for Sinn Féin classes, which meant he would get an education.

Barry knew the Keane family through Séamus McCoy. Carmel was the aunt of one of McCoy's friends from

Teachtai Dála: parliamentary delegate.

Long Kesh. Everyone in the tightly knit West Belfast community was related to everyone else in some way. Every grief, every death, was shared.

It was Billy Keane who finally was able to arrange for Barry to meet Gerry Adams.

The meeting took place in an anonymous kitchen in a safe house. Leaning across a table spread with a patterned oilcloth, two tall men shook hands. Both were casually dressed, with open collars. Elsewhere in the house children were playing. Street noises came through the thin walls. The woman of the house provided tea and biscuits before saying, "I'll leave you to it then, shall I?"

Not all women would leave the men to it. Those like Marie Drumm and Bernadette McAliskey took part in policy-making decisions and manned barricades.

And got shot.

Across the table Barry surveyed Gerry Adams. He had seen a couple of photographs taken in Long Kesh, showing a tall, slim, dark-haired man with a heavy beard and aviator-style glasses. The beard was neatly trimmed now. It suited Adams' long face; a keen, intelligent face that looked younger than its thirty-three years until one noticed the lines around the eyes. Watchful eyes.

"I'm surprised we didn't meet before now, Barry," Adams said. He had a distinctive Belfast accent, sharper than Séamus McCoy's. Thanks to government censorship people in the south had never heard that voice. "I know all about you through our mutual friend Séamus."

Barry laughed. "Not *all* about me, I hope."

"Enough. You're something of a legend among republicans."

"You're fast becoming one yourself."

This time Gerry Adams laughed. "Jaysus, I hope not."

Time was limited; Adams was supposed to be somewhere else in an hour, but he did not rush the interview. He listened as much as he talked, questioning Barry about his own ideas for bringing a resolution to the problems in

Northern Ireland and paying close attention to the answers. Adams was articulate but careful in his choice of words, with a dry, self-deprecating wit and an impressive knowledge of Irish history—uncommon in Northern Ireland, where only English history was taught in the schools. "You have time to do a lot of reading in prison," he explained.

Barry liked him.

By the time the two men stood up again, and shook hands again, he had taken several good photographs of Gerry Adams and begun to think that just maybe there was hope for the future.

RECOGNISING the influence Gerry Adams had with other republicans, members of the clergy began pressuring him to go into the H-Blocks and tell the hunger strikers to give up. He refused. The pressure increased; became a form of psychological torture. He still refused. "What you are asking me to do is go to a lifelong friend on his deathbed and tell him I'm not with him. My answer is no."

The last man to die was Michael Devine, better known as Micky, who was the leader of the INLA in the prison. From his cell in the H-Blocks he had written a letter to Cardinal Basil Hume. The English cardinal had dismissed the hunger strikes by characterising them as violence against one's own body for the sake of publicity.

In part, Devine's letter read: "Have you ever been dragged from a dirt-infested cell to have your head forcibly shaved? Have you had metal tongs inserted into your back passage searching for something that never existed in the first place? I'm prepared to bet this torn smelly blanket I'm wearing that you can't remember the last time you were beaten unconscious . . . or the last time you were forced to eat your own vomit. I would suggest you investigate the violence of your fellow countrymen who are responsible for driving their victims into near-insanity. The H-Block hunger strike is not a publicity stunt; it is a last desperate cry for help."[5]

Devine received the last sacraments on Tuesday, the eighteenth of August. He lived until Thursday morning.

Ten young men had died agonising deaths, and it was obvious that Margaret Thatcher would let as many more die as cared to sacrifice themselves. Those who tried to appeal to her in private described her as being as stony-hearted as she appeared in public.

On the third of October the six remaining hunger strikers ended their protest. Their families had announced they would intervene to save their lives. A statement issued by the prisoners blamed "Mounting pressure and cleric-inspired demoralisation," and concluded that "it is a physical and psychological impossibility to recommence a hunger strike after intervention."[6]

BARRY Halloran photographed each of the ten graves individually, then arranged them in a collage forming a stark landscape. His accompanying text read: "These young men desperately wanted to live but believed something else was more important. They died for a dream of freedom—and trying to protect others from what they had undergone."

The pictorial statement was not published anywhere in the Republic.

However the hunger strike had soured the Republic's "special relationship" with Margaret Thatcher. Ever since the Arms Trial Charles Haughey's political career had been the subject of controversy. Now he put it at risk again by sending out feelers to the IRA about the possibilities for developing a peace process.

·   ·   ·

IN the Bleeding Horse the Usual Suspects gathered to hear Barry tell about the hunger strike. He had returned to Dublin sick at heart and did not want to talk about it, but they insisted.

"You were right there on the front lines, Seventeen," McCoy said to open the conversation. "You know what it was really like."

"No one knows what it was really like, and I wasn't on the front lines. I was no more than a hurler on the ditch."

"You'd've gone on the blanket if you were in the Kesh. You'd've been on hunger strike."

"I probably would have," Barry acknowledged. "For all the good it did."

Brendan said, "More good than you may realise. Until the first striker died and the story hit the headlines around the world Ireland was just a dot on the map to most people. Now we're real to them. Our struggle is real. And Margaret Thatcher has perfectly demonstrated the arrogance and cruelty of the imperial mentality. She's alienated friends her government could ill afford to lose."

Danny spoke up. "You think so? She didn't alienate Garret FitzGerald. He did fuck-all to save those lads."

"Not for the first time," Patsy interjected. "Jack Lynch sat on his backside after Bloody Sunday, remember?"

Remember, remember, Barry thought, staring down at the water rings on the table in front of him. *How many times do we have the same conversation? We endlessly re-plough the ground we've ploughed to death already.*

"I don't understand people like that," said Luke. "Still sucking up to the British after all they've done to us . . ."

Séamus McCoy set down his drink. "Let me tell you something. When I was a wee lad in Belfast we lived in a very tough neighbourhood on the edge of Tiger's Bay. The people across the road dug with the other foot, if you take my meaning. Their lads were a lot bigger than our crowd too. After a few hard thumpings we learned to stay out of their way and just go on about our business. We even began to think they'd got it right, so we tried to walk like they did and talk like they did.

"Countries are much the same, Luke. Little ones are influenced by bigger ones. The Republic is bigger in size and population than Northern Ireland, but if you throw in the rest of Britain we're tiny. It was a miracle of God we ever beat the British at all, and people down here still tip-toe around them. Some even try to be like them. It's only human nature to want to be on the winning side."

Patsy stroked his jaw contemplatively. "Can't change human nature. Me oul' woman used to say that and she's right so."

"But we can change the way we think," Barry responded. "It's the only hope we have."

"What do you mean by 'change'?" asked Luke.

"What do you mean by 'we'?" Danny wanted to know.

"Change means being willing to consider new ideas, even if they're unpalatable. We is us; all of us. The Provos, the civilians, the nationalist politicians—both Sinn Féin and the SDLP—and . . ."

Luke snorted. "Don't expect anything from the Social Democratic and Labour Party, they're only lip-service nationalists."

Barry rounded on him. "Do you know that from personal experience?"

"Not from personal experience. But every dog in the street knows it."

"That," said Barry firmly, "is where change begins. We have to forget what 'every dog in the street' knows. We're not dogs, we're Irish men. If we want our grandchildren to grow up in a united Ireland we have to start making it happen now."

Brendan peered at him from beneath his bushy brows. "This doesn't sound like you at all, Barry. Just who have you been talking to?"

Chapter Thirty-one

⸻ ✦ ⸻

In November Ian Paisley declared, "My men are ready to be recruited under the Crown to destroy the vermin of the IRA. But if they refuse to destroy them, then we will have no other decision to make but to destroy the IRA ourselves. We will exterminate the IRA!"[1]

In the second week of December two Sinn Féin leaders, Gerry Adams and Danny Morrison, took part in a phone-in programme broadcast over LBC, a radio station in London.

The programme was not carried in the Republic.

Because of his inflammatory remarks in Northern Ireland the U.S. State Department revoked a visa it had granted to Ian Paisley.

Nineteen eighty-one wound down to a close. As the Christmas decorations went up, posters depicting the hunger strikers still clung to lampposts. Men and women on their way to the nearest IRA recruiting station or Sinn Féin office saluted them. Public support for Irish republicanism had never been so strong.

January of 1982 was the coldest in living memory. Ireland had its first significant snowfall in almost two decades. Cars skidded off roads and trees broke beneath the weight of snow cover. Taoiseach Garret FitzGerald was out of the country on holiday. Acting in his stead, Tanaiste

Michael O'Leary slipped and fell on his way to government buildings, seriously injuring himself.

The country ground to a halt.

Barry took Brian and Trot to frolic in the snow in the Phoenix Park. In the photographs he took that day he began looking for small details that possessed a beauty of their own aside from the larger context. Like his daughter's glossy eyelashes, each one a separate work of art. When he managed to capture a single snowflake frozen on the bonnet of his car, he punched the air like a child let out of school.

"Why did you do that, Da?" Brian wondered.

Barry grinned. "I just stopped Time."

In the glittering winterscape of the Phoenix Park he had discovered a brief freedom. By narrowing everything down to one tiny detail and making that his sole focus, he could escape the conflicting thoughts about a much larger issue that were pulling him in two directions.

Barbara dismissed Barry's photographic miniatures as "artsy-fartsy." Yet one day when she picked up his latest photograph, showing the eyes of a tiny kitten peering over a child's naked toes, she smiled. Barry saw her touch the glossy surface of the photograph with her fingertips as if to stroke the kitten.

And he loved her.

A T the end of the month loyalist leader John McKeague was shot dead by the INLA.

Northern Ireland also proved fatal to the dreams of entrepreneur auto manufacturer John DeLorean. He was forced to close his Belfast plant and the business went into receivership, consigning the avant-garde DeLorean motor car to history. DeLorean was arrested in Los Angeles and charged with possessing cocaine.

In the Republic the coalition government was brought down over the issue of tax increases on beer, petrol, and cigarettes, taking Garret FitzGerald down with it.

On the ninth of March Charles Haughey returned to power, becoming *taoiseach* for the second time.

Eᴀʀʟʏ in April a white paper entitled *Northern Ireland: A Framework for Devolution* was published by the British government. It proposed the election of an Assembly to consist of seventy-eight members, who would then work to reach agreement on the establishment of a devolved government for the Six Counties.

Gerry Adams and Sinn Féin gave the idea a cautious welcome.

The Ulster Unionist Party opposed it from the beginning.

Before the Assembly bill could be readied for Parliament war broke out in the Falkland Islands, three hundred miles east of Argentina. Argentina claimed sovereignty over the islands but that claim was disputed by the British, who were using them as a base to administer a colony composed of a whole cluster of islands in the South Atlantic. Negotiations to resolve the dispute had been under way for years until Argentina finally had despaired of reaching a political solution and went on the attack.

Margaret Thatcher immediately declared a war zone of two hundred miles around the Falklands and sent a British task force steaming eight thousand miles to do battle. Her premiership, which had been undergoing heavy weather at home, was greatly strengthened by the fact that suddenly she was "a war leader."

The reaction in Ireland was somewhat different. Charles Haughey, recalling Britain's colonial past in his country, denied Thatcher his support.

Relations between the two countries soured still further. Thatcher announced "no commitment exists for Her Majesty's Government to consult the Irish government on matters affecting Northern Ireland."[2]

· · ·

CHARLES Haughey proceeded to appoint Séamus Mallon, the deputy leader of the Social Democratic and Labour Party in Northern Ireland, to the Seanad. The Republic's Senate had very little actual power; that rested with the Dáil. But the gesture was huge, a pledge betokening the future of a united Ireland. Expressed politically.

MARTIN McGuinness gave up his position as chief of staff of the Provisional IRA to devote himself to politics.

THE massive British force that slammed into the Falklands proved overwhelming. Argentinean planes succeeded in sinking two British destroyers and two frigates, but the defenders were helpless against a vastly superior force. The British soon established a beachhead and surrounded the Falklands' capital, Stanley, on the thirty-first of May.

On the fourteenth of June Argentina surrendered. The Falklands War was over. The final casualty count was seven hundred Argentinean dead, compared to British loses of 250. Aside from that nothing much had changed—except Margaret Thatcher had acquired a new nickname: The Iron Lady.

ALONE in her room one morning before breakfast, Ursula felt a distinct tingling in her feet. She started to call out to Breda but changed her mind. Closing her eyes, she concentrated on moving her toes beneath the bedcovers.

Did they? I can't tell.

She flung aside the covers and watched her feet intently. Surely that was a twitch, a slight flexing of the toes. Using both hands, she lifted one of her legs over the side of the bed. Then the other. *I can feel the floor under my feet. I can!*

Don't get your hopes up, she warned, even as a flood of images poured over her: herself standing, herself walking, herself strolling along beside Séamus McCoy, the two of them laughing together over a private joke. The two of them . . .

"You should have waited for me," Breda said from the doorway. "I was just coming to help you get dressed."

O n June eighteenth Lord Gowrie, minister of state at the Northern Ireland Office, said, "Northern Ireland is extremely expensive on the British taxpayer . . . If the people of Northern Ireland wished to join with the south of Ireland, no British government would resist it for twenty minutes."[3]

U r s u l a schooled herself to awaken an hour before anyone else in the house. In that private time she renewed her struggle to walk. She was sure she was making progress, though not enough for the doctors to accept. It was a matter of "infinitessimalism": the name she had given to Barry's photographs of tiny details. Tiny details painstakingly connected to other tiny details added up to a whole picture.

A whole woman.

Maybe I shall even ride again. And teach Grace Mary.

I n July an IRA bomb exploded in London's Hyde Park as a detachment of the Blues and Royals trotted by on their way to the Horse Guards' Parade. Two guardsmen were killed instantly and seventeen spectators were injured. Seven horses lay dead in the road. Another horse, called Sefton, would recover after an eight-hour operation to remove shrapnel.

Two hours after the first bombing a second charge was detonated under a bandstand in Regent's Park, killing six members of the Royal Green Jackets army band.

URSULA was deeply shocked. "They killed *horses*!" she kept saying over and over again, as if she could not believe it.

McCoy tried to explain, using all the clichés about war, but she brushed them aside. "We never did things like that, we never waged war on women and children and innocent animals."

"Maybe you just don't remember," he suggested gently.

"Oh, leave me alone!"

THE 1982 winner of the Eurovision Song Contest was "A Little Peace." Ireland did not send an entry to the contest that year.

At a Falklands remembrance service in London, Archbishop Runcie said, "War has always been detestable."[4]

But war was in the air.

Poland was under martial law.

Meanwhile a revolution of a different kind was sweeping Ireland—the video revolution.

MOST people down the country still did not have television sets, but in Dublin, as Barbara told Barry, "Everyone's buying video players, even the Cassidys."

"So you're campaigning for one too?"

"Your mother could watch those old movies she loves,"

Barbara replied virtuously. "They're coming out on video. VHS, not Betamax. Alice says Dennis says VHS is the way to go."

Barry responded with his most successful defence: saying nothing.

Barbara fumed for several days before taking her case to Ursula.

"I've had a long nonversation with your wife," Ursula told Barry later. "It would be more productive to talk to the dog."

"We don't have a dog."

"That's what I mean," his mother said. "Barbara wants a video player and tried to persuade me to ask you for it. I told her I had absolutely no interest whatever in the latest gadgets but she wouldn't listen. She simply doesn't listen, Barry."

"Tell me about it," he sighed. A few days later he bought the machine. *Anything for a quiet life,* he thought with a sting of self-contempt.

Talk in the Bleeding Horse began to centre around the possibility of a new Northern Assembly. Amongst the Usual Suspects opinion was divided. Barry, Luke, and Brendan said they were in favour. Danny, Patsy, and Séamus McCoy were opposed.

Barry found himself in the position of arguing for a point of view with which he was not—totally—in agreement.

"We have to take a serious look at the political option," he told the others. "Northern Protestants reject the idea of a united Ireland because they're afraid we will treat them as they've treated us. The only way to convince them otherwise is through peaceful dialogue, it certainly can't be done at gunpoint.

"Secondly we have to address the deep distrust unionists feel for nationalists. They've been deliberately infected with it for generations by those in power, and it will probably take more generations to overcome the damage. But they have to be peaceful generations. Which brings us back to that word 'peaceful.' "

"With the loyalists beating the drums of war every step of the way?" scoffed McCoy. "I don't think so."

"That's where leadership comes in, Séamus. Not military leadership, but political leadership."

"You're daft, Seventeen. I never thought I'd hear you talking like this."

Am I daft? Barry wondered.

MEANWHILE the Troubles continued in Northern Ireland. Shootings, beatings, bombings. Too much blood on too many streets, while ordinary people did their best to raise their children and pay their bills. Life had to go on in the midst of death.

Death which attacked in the midst of life.

Danny went as suddenly as a candle is snuffed out. The man from Kerry dropped dead when he was attacked by his own heart one Thursday afternoon in Harcourt Street. None of the Usual Suspects had even known he had a heart condition.

At Danny's funeral a tricolour was draped on the coffin. The church was almost full. "He must have had a lot of friends," Barbara whispered to Barry. "He didn't talk about himself much," her husband replied.

Afterwards the remains were taken to Mount Jerome Cemetery for burial. Three uniformed Volunteers wearing black masks suddenly emerged from amongst the mourners at graveside. Barbara gasped and cringed against Barry. The gun party raised their rifles to fire a volley over the grave, then melted back into the crowd and disappeared.

Barbara was shaken. "It's like . . . like a military funeral."

"It *is* a military funeral," Séamus McCoy told her. "With full honours."

O N the thirteenth of September Her Serene Highness Grace Kelly, princess of Monaco and descendant of the Kellys of Mayo was involved in a fatal automobile crash on the Riviera.

W I T H the passage of time Ursula could see more and more of Ella Rutledge Mooney in Barbara. She did not physically resemble her elegant grandmother, but she had many of her ways. Her quick light step. Her perfectionism. Even her insistence on the social niceties. If one of the children referred to someone as "he" Barbara would cry, "He! He! Who's 'he,' the cat's dinner? Call a person by his name."

So my dear Ella lives on in a new generation, Ursula thought. Although the knowledge gave her comfort, sadly it did not make Barbara herself any easier to like.

I N the autumn the INLA successfully planted a bomb at the offices of the Ulster Unionist Party. The resultant explosion caused extensive damage.

"So much for politics," Séamus McCoy commented with some satisfaction.

T H A T autumn Lenny Murphy, the psychopathic leader of the Shankill Butchers, was killed by the IRA. Members of the Belfast Brigade drove to the house of Murphy's current girlfriend in the Upper Shankill. They found Murphy outside. The Volunteers, who were armed with a 9mm submachine gun and a .38 special, did not waste time in dialogue. They opened fire, hitting Murphy with twenty-six rounds and killing him instantly.

·   ·   ·

Barry Halloran sold several photographs of Murphy to the wire services, but refused to furnish pictures of the man on a slab in the morgue.

On the twentieth of October an election was held for a new Northern Ireland Assembly—the first election to be contested by Provisional Sinn Féin. The SDLP won fourteen of the seventy-eight seats but previously had announced it would not take them, maintaining the republican tactic of abstentionism. The Ulster Unionists took twenty-six seats to the DUP's twenty-one.

By winning 10.1 percent of the poll Sinn Féin claimed five seats, though they also planned to abstain from taking part in the Assembly. Two of those elected were Gerry Adams and Martin McGuinness.

Sinn Féin's surprisingly good showing in the election caused consternation among the British establishment. Claiming that the republican movement was a criminal conspiracy with no support amongst the ordinary people was no longer possible.

There were demands from the more moderate amongst the unionists for Sinn Féin to cut its ties with the IRA.

"How can we even think of decoupling the IRA from Sinn Féin," Barry asked the Usual Suspects, "when the nationalists have nothing else to protect them? The unionists have the British government stoutly on their side, plus the RUC as their military wing. While the British government turns a blind eye the RUC openly colludes with loyalist murder gangs. If they weren't at least a little afraid of IRA retribution, God knows what they might do to our people."

The northern elections were not uppermost in the minds of politicians in the Republic. In November Charles Haughey's government collapsed following a wiretapping scandal involving the telephones of journalists, amongst others.

Meanwhile three unarmed Volunteers were shot dead by the RUC at a checkpoint near Lurgan. Their deaths sparked claims that the police and army were pursuing a "shoot to kill" policy, and requests that the Irish government demand accountability from Britain.

The following month Garret FitzGerald reclaimed the prime ministership of Ireland.

O N the sixth of December seventeen people were killed by an INLA bomb at the Droppin' Well Pub in Ballykelly. In the House of Commons Margaret Thatcher said, "This is one of the most horrifying crimes in Ulster's tragic history. The slaughter of innocent people is the product of evil and depraved minds and the act of callous and brutal men."[5]

W H E T H E R Barbara liked it or not, political discussions had become a fixture in the yellow brick house. Even the most transient boarder had an opinion about what should be done in Northern Ireland, though none were as articulate, or as convincing, as Barry Halloran.

"Maybe I'm just getting old," McCoy said to Ursula on one of their outings together. The weather was cold and grim but neither could stand being indoors a minute longer. "Maybe I'm just getting old," he repeated—hoping she would disagree—"but it's hard for me to imagine republicans going into politics. Can you see me sitting down around a conference table with men who hate my guts? And me hating their guts too!"

Ursula reached back to pat his hand. "I know, Séamus. But it may never happen; Sinn Féin and the SDLP aren't taking their seats in the Assembly."

"Not now they're not, but I have an itchy feeling at the back of my neck."

"My son seems to think it might be a good idea."

McCoy stopped pushing the wheelchair and crouched down beside it. "Does he? For sure? I don't know about that. Your son's a born soldier: he's strong, disciplined, and clever. When a man like that goes into the Army he finds what he was made for. Seventeen couldn't possibly do a one-eighty; I know him too well."

"Does anyone ever really know anyone else?"

"I know him," McCoy averred.

During the Christmas holidays Barry paid a call on Éamonn and Rosaleen MacThomáis and their young family. "Do you not miss being editor of *An Phoblacht*?" Barry asked his friend.

"Yes and no. I enjoyed the work but the unpaid holidays weren't so good."

Rosaleen said, "We were all happier when he started making those films for RTE; you know, his walking tours around Dublin."

"I've bought them all on video," Barry assured her. "Tell me, Éamonn, do you still learn the news before anyone else?"

"I still have my sources, if that's what you mean."

"The other day I heard through my sources that a body had been dumped near the Tyrone border. Shot through the back of the head."

MacThomáis nodded. "I can confirm that. He was an informer."

Barry's expression was grim. "Well placed, was he?"

"Well enough. MI5."

Conversations like this tore Rosaleen's heart. Excusing herself, she went to make the tea.

A T Christmas it had become a Halloran tradition for every member of the family and any guests who were in the house to take part in the entertainment. Barry usually recited a poem—and it was usually Yeats. Barbara sang;

requests a specialty. McCoy kept the boys enthralled with selected, carefully edited anecdotes from his own experiences. Trot preferred to hear the stories her grandmother had learned in her childhood.

For Christmas 1983 Ursula gave Brian a framed copy of the Proclamation. "Your father used to be able to quote this by heart," she said, casting a meaningful glance in Barry's direction.

"I still can. Shall I recite it for him?"

"I want him to read it for himself," she replied, "but first he must understand what it is.

"Brian, this document was the Irish Declaration of Independence. Your mother's people have theirs enshrined in Liberty Hall in Philadelphia, I believe." For confirmation she glanced at Barbara, who shrugged. History had never been one of Barbara's strong points.

Ursula continued. "The Proclamation was written by Pádraic Pearse, with a few suggestions from James Connolly and Thomas MacDonough. It was printed on an old hand press in the basement of another Liberty Hall right here in Dublin, which was trade union headquarters. A print run of twenty-five hundred copies was intended, but because the machinery was dilapidated and paper was scarce they were barely able to print a thousand. Pearse read the Proclamation aloud under the portico of the GPO on the day the Rising began. Copies were pasted up all over the city.

"My uncle Henry was in Dublin that Easter Monday. He took down two copies of the Proclamation and kept them. I think he gave one away, but when I was a little girl he still had the other one. Sometimes he would unfold it—carefully, because the paper was not of good quality—and read it to me."

Brian's eyes were huge. "What happened to it? Can I see it?"

Suddenly Ursula was very tired. "I don't know what

happened to it. Things . . . simply disappear, as years go by."

"Do people do that too?" Patrick wanted to know. "Simply disappear?"

"Sometimes," his father told him.

Chapter Thirty-two

···········✥···········

ALTHOUGH Barry was trying to throw light on the situation in Ireland with his photographs, he was painfully aware that no camera could capture the crucial, subterranean details. Plans were being formulated far from the actual battlefields. Deals were being made in unlikely places and among unlikely people. There were secrets that might someday come crawling out like maggots.

Maggots in the cells in H-Block 5. Not lice, but maggots so big and fat they crunched under a man's feet. The limit of a man's horizon was six paces up and six paces down. Orders from the O/C were printed in minuscule writing on cigarette papers and hidden in a man's anus.

The terrible legacy of inhumanity.

Yet life went on. On St. Stephen's Day Ursula began teaching Patrick to read. Grace Mary had a fall on her new roller skates and chipped a tooth. By the sixth of January—*Nollaig na mBan*, the Women's Christmas, when traditionally the husbands did the work in the house—Brian was talking about the next All-Ireland to be held in Croke Park.

He had discovered the GAA.

In Northern Ireland the oppression of a rigidly Calvinist society had resulted in an explosion of Protestant violence aimed at those even more vulnerable—the Catholics. The situation in the Republic was markedly different, in spite of the fact that the south was, for most of the nineteenth and twentieth centuries, a repressed society dominated by the Catholic Church. Thanks to the farsightedness of its founders, the Gaelic Athletic Association provided young men with an acceptable physical outlet for their frustration. Like the warriors of old, young Celts went out to challenge their opponents in honourable battle.

At nine years old Brian Halloran knew the names of all the heroes of the GAA, both hurling and football.

Ursula made sure that Trot knew the names of the great racehorses.

O N the seventh of February, 1983, six heavily armed Iranian divisions crossed the border into Iraq. A full-scale war had begun.

F E B R U A R Y eighth was bitterly cold in County Kildare, but the thoroughbred stallion Shergar was warm under layers of blankets. His roomy loose box was piled knee-deep with golden straw. Irish-bred Shergar, who had won the prestigious Epsom Derby and been named European Horse of the Year in 1981, was owned by a large syndicate headed by the Aga Khan. With his splendid pedigree and glittering career on the race track Shergar was worth millions. Upon retiring the horse from the track the Aga Khan could have sent the stallion to any one of his many breeding farms. Instead he had chosen to keep him in Ireland as the star of Ballymany Stud, just outside the village of Newbridge. His decision had been a catalyst to attract still more horse breeders to Ireland.

Shortly after eight-thirty that evening a gang of masked men forced their way into the cottage of Ballymany's head

groom, Jimmy Fitzgerald. By holding his family at gunpoint they forced him to lead them to Shergar. It was
breeding season, which meant the horse was even more
highly strung than usual. The ancient imperative was
coursing through his veins.

IN their bedroom Barry Halloran watched Barbara at her
dressing table, brushing her hair. Mindlessly he rose from
his chair and walked over to her. Put his hand on her
shoulder. Felt the warmth of her skin and the ancient imperative.

WITH Fitzgerald at hand to keep him under control,
Shergar allowed himself to be loaded into a horse van.
Fitzgerald was blindfolded and forced into a different car.
After being driven around Kildare for several hours, he
was dumped unharmed within seven miles of Ballymany.

Shergar vanished as if the earth opened up and swallowed him.

The news sent shock waves through the international
racing community. When a telephone call demanding a
two-million-pound ransom was received, the Aga Khan
refused to pay. "It would put the lives of every valuable
horse in Ireland in danger."

Although they had no proof, the Gardai said they suspected the IRA. "The ruthless efficiency of the operation
is typical of that organisation," they stated.

URSULA was livid with anger. "If the IRA did this I'm
through with them! First the Horse Guards and now this.
It's unforgivable."

"We don't know it was the IRA," Barry said. "It could
just as easily have been the UVF. You know from personal

experience what ruthless efficiency that crowd's capable of. This wouldn't be the first time a loyalist gang's committed an atrocity just to get the IRA blamed for it; it happens more often than you can imagine."

Ursula wanted to believe him.

UNTIL 1983 a padlocked gate had been the only security most farms employed. Following Shergar's kidnapping the level of security was drastically increased. But for him it was too late.

There was a flurry of phone calls from people claiming to have him, or know where he was, but they came to nothing. In spite of one of the largest searches ever held in Ireland, no one ever saw Shergar again.

FOR racehorse owners like the Aga Khan money was no problem, but Garret FitzGerald's government was struggling with a moribund economy and high unemployment. Well-educated young people were emigrating in their thousands. Barry Halloran knew how fortunate he was. When the wire services or television producers needed still photographs of anyone or anything in Ireland, they contacted him first. No other freelancer north or south had archives to equal his. Combined with the rental income, his career was keeping the Hallorans solvent. At the end of the month after the bills were paid there was even a bit left over.

"You really are becoming a capitalist," he told the face in the mirror. Then he laughed. *No chance, I'm not even fashionable; I don't have a mullet.*

The mullet was the latest fad among young Irish men. The bizarre hairstyle was a close cousin of the Americans' "Mohawk" and consisted of a ridge of hair standing bolt upright along the centre of an otherwise shaven skull. Proudly sporting mullets, boys only slightly older than Brian Halloran happily posed for snapshots that would cause them massive embarrassment when viewed years later by their hysterically laughing children.

"If you ever come into this house with a mullet," Barbara warned her son, "I personally will shave every hair off your head."

He believed her.

Because Barry was so often away from home, the role of disciplinarian had fallen on Barbara. She was conscientious about it and tried to match the punishment to the crime. The most severe penalty involved a stunted willow tree that grew behind the mews. If one of the children really went too far, such as talking back to an adult, he or she was given an old pocketknife of Barry's and told to go out and cut a switch from the willow tree. Having to be the instrument of one's own punishment made a profound impression, and hurt much worse than three lashes of a willow switch applied to bare legs.

B ARRY, wake up. Something's wrong."

Barry came out of a deep sleep to find Barbara tugging at his shoulder. "What do you mean?" he asked groggily.

"I have the most terrible pain. Here, put your hand on my stomach. Feel that? It's like labour pains only worse, so much worse. Help me!"

By the time they reached the hospital she was bleeding copiously.

"Did you know your wife was pregnant, Mr. Halloran?" asked the doctor on duty.

"Pregnant? I . . . no, I didn't know that. And I don't think she did either, or she would have told me."

"She's lost the child, I'm afraid," the doctor said. "A miscarriage this early in a pregnancy is usually not dangerous for a woman, but in your wife's case I think we should call in a consultant. There appears to have been rather severe damage to her womb at some stage. Her last child was born at home, I believe?"

...

"He was born at home. It happened so fast we didn't even have time to come to hospital, but she was fine when her doctor saw her afterwards."

"I see. A woman that big and strong can have very powerful contractions, Mr. Halloran. She may have damaged herself internally at the time, and it's only showing up now."

"Will she be all right?"

"We'll take the best possible care of her," the doctor said reassuringly.

U 2's big hit of the season was "In the Name of Love."

B A R B A R A came home from hospital thinner and paler, but otherwise all right. There would be no more children, however. "I don't know what I did wrong!" she said to Barry.

"You didn't do anything wrong, sweetheart. The doctors explained it's just one of those things that happens sometimes. They would have saved your womb if they could, but . . ."

"But. But. Life would be perfect but. Oh, Barry, I'm so sorry!"

He gathered her into his arms and held her with all the tenderness he possessed.

J U N E saw the Conservative Party win a resounding victory in the British general election, returning Margaret Thatcher to power. Barry Halloran went to Northern Ireland to photograph the candidates there. Amongst those winning seats in the Assembly were John Hume of the SDLP—and Gerry Adams.

One journalist had written, "All Gerry Adams has to do is not get killed and he can't lose."[1]

ON the fifth of August evidence given in a Belfast court by informer Christopher Black—a self-confessed bully, perjurer, robber, and failed assassin—led to sentences totalling more than four thousand years being given to twenty-two members of an IRA cell.

The Usual Suspects talked of nothing else for days. Between them they devised methods for "taking care of" Black that would have put the Inquisition to shame.

IN September, after a bitter and divisive campaign, two-thirds of the voters in the Republic opted for adding a "pro-life" amendment to the Constitution.

Barbara was still depressed about the miscarriage. "There's no point voting for life if you can't give birth any-way," she said to Ursula.

"One should always vote for life," the older woman replied. "No matter what."

THE big political news in Northern Ireland was Gerry Adams' election as MP for West Belfast, replacing a man who had held the seat for seventeen years.

BARRY Halloran decided to update his photographs of Adams, who obviously would be in the news for the fore-seeable future. By the time he returned to Belfast there was a more explosive story to cover. He could not photo-graph the central figures involved, however. Like Shergar, they had vanished.

ON the twenty-fifth of September thirty-eight members of the IRA had escaped from the escape-proof H-Blocks.

One man who had repeatedly tried to escape, not only from Long Kesh but from every prison in which he had ever been held, was Gerry Kelly. An unsuccessful attempt to escape from the Cages had landed him in the Blocks, where he was put into H7. The Block contained 125 prisoners, most of them in their twenties, serving sentences ranging from a few years to life. Many but not all of the men were guilty of the charges against them. They were guilty of being republicans.

The escape was organised as tightly and thoroughly as a military procedure. Less than half of the prisoners in H7 had any idea what was going on and it had to be kept that way. The larger the number who knew, the greater the chance of premature discovery.

Or an informer.

At two-thirty on Sunday afternoon there had been several Provos in or near the Circle. Even on Sunday the prisoners were assigned cleaning duties. Those in the Circle that day were chewing gum to calm their nerves.

While Gerry Kelly was operating the bumper—a cleaning machine used on the floors—Brendan Mead engaged senior warder George Smylie in conversation about a problem he was having with another prisoner. Mead asked if they could go into the office where it would be more private. Robert George, the acting principal officer, was sitting behind his desk in the office but paid little attention to them. Lately the prisoners had been bringing more and more of their problems to the senior warders. It was considered a sign of improving prison relations.

Gerry Kelly pushed the bumper toward the communications room. Bobby Storey and Tony McAllister approached the officers' mess as if to clean it. Seán McGlinchey and Rab Kerr were in place at opposite ends of the Block, between two gates that gave access to two wings each. Then Brendan "Bik" McFarlane headed towards the hall area that gave access to the entire Block.

Timing was crucial. The signal was given.

In the warder's office Mead produced a gun and ordered both men to hit the deck. The other conspirators leaped into action. Within ten seconds they had taken control of the Block. Ninety minutes later, thirty-eight republican prisoners, including leading figures in the IRA, had made it to the outside world. They headed in as many different directions and disappeared.

It was the biggest jailbreak in Europe since World War Two.

A huge manhunt began at once. Some prisoners were recaptured immediately, others were caught later. Some were never caught at all.

L I K E the 1981 hunger strike, the Great Escape marked a high point in the republican struggle. The operation seriously embarrassed the Thatcher government, which thought it had destroyed the morale of the H-Blocks.

Séamus McCoy reacted to the first news of the escape like a schoolteacher whose students had garnered huge honours. "Oh, those boyos!" he exclaimed gleefully.

"But how did they do it, Uncle Séamus," Brian kept wanting to know. "How did they *do* it?"

No details were available. An immediate media clampdown had been ordered. The residents of the yellow brick house had to wait until Barry finally came home, ten days later. The information he gave them was sketchy; obtained, he said, secondhand, through a number of contacts.

"There is—or was, I'm sure they've closed it by now—a machine shop for the prisoners in the Kesh," Barry related. "Metalworking was part of the whole 'arts and crafts' programme. With enough time and experience, and our lads had plenty of both, they simply made guns for themselves. The Belfast Brigade and other friends on the outside supplied backup. Everything was planned to the tiniest detail, though on the day, of course, there were bound to be some slipups. It was an amazing achievement anyway."

Escape. The word haunted Ursula. *Escape. They did the impossible, they escaped. They were not willing to serve out their sentences in prison. How did Barry describe the cells in the Blocks? Six paces by six paces? Not much smaller than my room here.*

My life here.

I want to go home," said Ursula.

Chapter Thirty-three

Barry frowned. "What are you talking about, Ursula? You are home."

"Your home. My home is in Clare."

The conversation was taking place early in the morning when Barry stopped by her room, as he often did, on his way out. She was sitting up in bed with a cardigan slung around her shoulders and her hair still unbrushed. Pillow creases lined her cheek. "Next May it will be ten years since Talbot Street," she said. "It's high time I went home."

Barry put down the holdall he was carrying. He was used to Barbara ambushing him on his way out but Ursula had never done so before. "I don't understand what you're talking about."

"You've been wonderful," she said. "You've done everything you possibly could for me. But this isn't *my life,* Barry, can you understand? This is *your* life. I need to have my own again before it's too late, and that means going back to the farm."

Barry was worried. *Does she know something she's not telling anyone? Is that sixth sense of hers warning her?*

"Mother," he said—choosing the unfamiliar title deliberately—"you couldn't possibly live on your own at the farm."

"I shall employ a companion." The set of her features told him the matter was already decided.

He progressed from worry to alarm. "There are too many practical problems to even consider it. If you're homesick for Clare I can certainly understand, but . . ."

"I've already spoken with Paul Morrissey on the phone and told him I was moving home. He will have everything ready for me by the time I arrive. The farm is turning enough profit to support me, so I won't need any help in that respect. I can even install one of those mechanical lift gadgets to take me up and down the stairs in the wheelchair. There are good doctors in Ennis and a good hospital too, so that's covered. I hope you will all come to see me often. And be happy for me?" she added hopefully.

Barry sat down on the foot of the bed. "You're really serious about this, aren't you?"

"I am serious."

His churning brain tried to come up with an argument she would accept. "But what about your grandchildren?"

"I love them to bits and shall miss them very much, but they're going to have their lives to live too. Bring them every time you come down, so Trot can learn the horse business. They will love visiting their Nana on the farm because it will be different, and much nicer than paying duty visits to an old woman living in a room that smells like an old woman."

"You don't spend all your time in here. You go all over the house, you even go out."

"Within limits," said Ursula.

"You can go wherever you want to."

"Fine. I want to go to Clare."

Barry postponed his drive to Belfast and went to talk to Barbara.

Alone in her room, Ursula dressed herself with the clothes Breda had laid out for her the night before, and got into her wheelchair. She sat at the window, gazing out. Seeing a different landscape.

The light in the morning is so beautiful at home. Atlantic light. I love the sound of horses chewing their grain in the barn, and the smell of the hay. Even if I never walk again I want to look out of my own windows and see the green fields waiting for my feet.

Even if I never walk again.

Ten years. Everyone thinks it's hopeless by this time. Maybe it is. But I'm certain it's hopeless if I stay here where nothing more is expected of me.

Looking out at the streets of Dublin, she saw the rolling hills of Clare.

I have to go home.

W H A T did you do that put this notion into her head?" Barry demanded of his wife.

"Nothing. I didn't know anything about it until this minute."

"You must have upset her somehow. I know you two aren't the best of friends, but . . ."

Barbara resented the accusation. "Everything that goes wrong around here is not my fault! Maybe Ursula just wants to go home."

"You'd like that, wouldn't you?"

"I . . . I honestly don't know. I'm used to her. And there are times when we like each other. You're right, we'll never be the best of friends, but that's just how it is. She's your mother and she's welcome to stay here for as long as she wants."

"That's the problem," Barry said. "She doesn't want."

He went back to Ursula's room for another conversation.

He found her sitting in her wheelchair with the blanket over her lap, staring out the window. For a moment she seemed unaware of him.

"Mother?"

That unfamiliar word again. She turned towards him. "What is it?"

"I was thinking about a companion for you, in case you do go to Clare. Plenty of people are looking for work. If we take our time and don't rush into this, maybe we can find a strong young woman here in Dublin who will . . ."

"There's no 'in case' about it," she replied with asperity. "And I don't want a high-strung young thing, I want Breda Cunningham. She's low-strung and we get along. I've already spoken to her about it. Her family's scattered to the four winds and she thinks she would like to live down the country. She was born on a farm, did you know that?"

"When did you discuss this with Breda?"

"Yesterday."

Barry was irked that he had not been the first to know. "And Séamus, I suppose you told him too?"

"Not yet." In truth she was not eager to tell McCoy she was leaving. Of them all, he was the one she would miss most.

Sensing her reluctance, Barry thought, *That might be the solution. She and Séamus are very close, maybe he can persuade her to stay.*

He found McCoy mending a broken shutter. "Go talk to my mother, Séamus."

"Right now? What about?"

"A certain decision she's made. I hope to God you can talk her out of it."

Puzzled, McCoy put his hammer aside and went to Ursula's room. When he knocked at the open door she knew at once who had sent him, and why. *I'm not ready for this,* she thought, steeling herself.

She tried to sound very casual as she outlined her plans to McCoy. He was seriously taken aback, but knew her too well to try to argue. She was like her son once her mind was made up. "Breda's going with you?"

"She is."

"Why not take me instead?"

Ursula could not help smiling. "You know yourself, Séamus; in this country unmarried women don't have unmarried men as nurse-companions."

He had rehearsed the request that sprang to his lips a hundred times, but never found the perfect moment. This was certainly not perfect; too rushed, too fraught, not good enough by half for Ursula Halloran, who deserved champagne and roses. Yet, "Marry me!" he blurted.

She blinked; recovered. "That's very gallant of you, Séamus, but it's really not necessary. Breda and I will do just fine, and there is a shower of big strong Morrissey men across the fields if I need them."

"I'm not trying to be gallant, I mean it. I want to marry you."

She searched his face. That dear face she knew so well. He did mean it. His whole soul was in his eyes.

Keeping her own face rigidly impassive, Ursula began struggling to move her legs beneath the concealing blanket. Her feet. Just one toe. Only yesterday there had been a tingle . . . or maybe that was the day before. Or maybe it was only wishful thinking.

Move, will you. Move! If ever I'm going to have a miracle let it be now.

McCoy was terrified by his own audacity. *Under fire,* he thought, *a man can find courage he never knew he had.*

Time seemed to stop. Tiny beads of perspiration formed on Ursula's forehead.

If it's that hard for her to make a decision, maybe I'm in with a chance.

Ursula felt her life balanced on a knife edge as it had been almost ten years ago, when she turned towards Talbot Street instead of going on to Clerys. Then she did not know what might lie ahead; now she did.

With all the willpower she possessed she made one final, desperate effort.

Nothing happened. Nothing at all.

She gave McCoy her most radiant smile. "I am far too fond of you, Séamus, to lumber you with a broken wreck like me. Besides, you're a city man, you would be lost in deep country where the nights are silent and the stars are close enough to touch. Stay here with Barry, he needs you."

She continued to hold the smile as if it did not hurt. Hurt terribly.

I did everything I could," McCoy duly reported to Barry, "but your mother's determined. Maybe I even made it worse."

"Rubbish. But thanks for trying anyway. You know, if this had happened six or seven years ago I wouldn't have been so surprised. But when she made no effort to leave I thought it was because of the children—or because she wanted to stay close to the doctors who knew her case. What do you suppose triggered it now?"

I n November the first formal meeting between the prime ministers of Ireland and Britain took place at Chequers, the country residence of the British head of state. After promising to help Ursula move to Clare as soon as he returned, Barry flew to England to photograph Garret FitzGerald and Margaret Thatcher. When the two appeared together after their meeting their body language indicated that matters were improving between their respective governments.

Upon returning to Ireland FitzGerald claimed that Thatcher had accepted his analysis of the Northern Ireland situation. He further announced that his proposals for the future government of the province would be presented to cabinet for approval, and then sent to the British.

H E ' S going to learn the hard way," was the unanimous opinion of the Usual Suspects.

O N the thirteenth of November Gerry Adams, MP for West Belfast, was elected president of Sinn Féin at the annual Ard Fheis.

B A R R Y insisted that his mother have a full-scale checkup before returning to Clare, and get the doctors' approval for the undertaking—if possible. "Even if they say no I'm going," she assured him.

"I know that. But do it for me, will you?"

S I T T I N G beside him in the familiar passenger's seat of Apollo, with her wheelchair crammed into the boot, Ursula watched the Dublin streets glide past. There had been a time when she would have said she loved her birthplace.

Now she just wanted to leave and never see it again.

Talbot Street, Talbot Street. How long does one have to live to forget the worst nightmare?

The waiting room at the hospital was full, as usual. A nursing sister regretfully informed Barry that it might be an hour or more before the consultant could see them. "I'll be all right," Ursula told him. "Why don't you . . ."

"Go get the newspapers," he finished for her.

"You've been with Barbara too long, you're beginning to interrupt the way she does."

As Barry left the waiting room an old woman sitting to Ursula's left leaned forward. "He's a big 'un, ain't he?" The accent was northside Dublin.

"My son," Ursula said proudly.

"You must've fed him good."

Ursula turned to look at her. The woman was at least ten years older than herself, with skin as wrinkled as crumpled newspaper. Poverty was written in every line, but her face was alight with the typical Dublin desire to talk.

"We were lucky," Ursula replied. "My son grew up on a farm where we had enough to eat."

The other grinned, revealing a scant snaggle of yellow teeth clinging to her upper gums like stalactites in a cave. "You was lucky, missus. When I was a young wan we lived in Railway Street and slept ten in a bed, so we did. The only protection the women in the tenements had to keep from having more children was to not sleep with their husbands. Every evening, rain, hail, or blow, they'd gather in the doorways wrapped up in their shawls and talk. Talk about the weather, yer wan up the street, yer wan down the street, the young wans—anything. Anything to keep them occupied until the children came down to say 'The Da's asleep.' Then the women'd head upstairs to their beds."

"That was a hard life," Ursula commented. Dimly remembering.

"Mountjoy Square was not far from us," the old woman went on, warming to her topic. "That's where the rich people lived. English people and want-to-be English people and the like. They had poor Irish girls living in their attics to do the housework. More often than not a son of the family would give one of them girls a big belly. The poor crayture would give birth in the attic, and then a closed carriage would come driving down Gardiner Street and her ladyship would lean out the window and beckon to the women sitting in the doorways. 'Will you take a baby?' she'd say.

"Mammy never took one, she said she had too many already. But other women did. They'd take the poor thing because they knew a bit o'money came with it. Some even got money all the years the child was growing up. Lots of tenement children were reared with brothers and sisters who wasn't really their brothers and sisters but it never made no difference. There was always a new baby squalling and they just took it for granted.

"Sometimes when they got older they'd notice that 'brother' had a different look to his face than the rest of the family, or different coloured eyes, or . . . like you, missus, a fine set of white teeth like you never saw in the mouth of a child of the tenements." She shook her head, bemused by memories. "Will you take a baby, missus?" she murmured again.

Ursula sat as if turned to stone.

T HE doctors see no obstacle to her going back to the farm," Barry reported when they got home. "After all this time her condition's considered stable, and she won't be alone. So I guess we'll have to let her go. She's made up about it, of course. At least I think she is. With Ursula you can never be sure. She's been awfully quiet since we left the hospital."

B ARBARA planned a farewell dinner with all of her mother-in-law's favourite foods. And no eggs. Several close friends were invited, including Paudie Coates and Éamonn MacThomáis. The conversation was lively and Barbara made no attempt to diminish its political content; in fact she encouraged it.

This is Ursula's night, she'll be gone tomorrow.

Sometime before the pudding was served the talk came around to the role of women in modern society. Barbara perked up; here at last was a subject that interested her.

"I don't understand why more Irish women don't have careers. If I even mention going back to singing I'm treated like a freak."

"That's not true," Barry said.

"No? In America I'd be encouraged, but not over here."

"I've never tried to discourage you from having a singing career. I love to hear you sing."

"So do I," McCoy added.

"And how am I supposed to have a career with three children clinging to my skirts?"

"They hardly 'cling to your skirts,'" Barry replied.

"Well, I have to be here for them all the time; it amounts to the same thing."

For once Ursula took Barbara's side. *I might as well, I'll be out of here tomorrow.* "I think she should resume her career," Ursula said. "In fact, she owes it to the rest of us.

"The Proclamation of the Irish Republic was deliberately phrased to give women equal rights with men. Our first government after independence, the Sinn Féin government, wrote the new Constitution along the same lines. Then came the Treaty that led to the so-called Free State in which women would never be free again. When de Valera rewrote the Irish Constitution he wrote us out. We were dismissed from any serious consideration by such phrases as 'the inadequate strength of women' and 'women's place in the home.' We'd won the vote in 1918 but that was the last political triumph for Irish women. From then on we were meant to be domestic slaves; a slavery sanctioned and encouraged by a patriarchal Church that demanded we bear all the children we could so we'd have to stay at home. Just to make certain, the Marriage Ban specifically denied married women the right to salaried employment."

Barbara exclaimed, "That's awful, I didn't know that!"

"You're getting too excited, Ursula," Barry murmured under his breath. Her cheeks were very flushed.

She ignored him. "Yet Irish women had fought side by side with the men of 1916! Curiously enough, Eamon de Valera was the only commanding officer who had no women with him. What does that tell you? Women were an active part of that first government under Sinn Féin. In the Free State, however, those same women were marginalised.

"If women were wise enough not to marry, at least they still had personal autonomy. But the government went out of its way to make sure their voices were not heard in any meaningful way. The only women who were allowed into even the lowest realms of political life were the widows of Free Staters who would sit with their hands folded and their eyes cast down and agree with anything the men wanted.

"Things are no better now. If Barbara wants to have a singing career, or go into politics, or join the Gardai for that matter, I think she jolly well should!"

Ursula flung her head back and swept the table with her eyes. Daring any man to contradict her.

"Whew," said Paudie Coates. Whose wife had been left at home to mind the children.

On the seventeenth of December an IRA bomb exploded outside the exclusive Harrods department store in London. Six people were killed, including three police officers, and more than ninety were injured.

With a heavy heart, Barry flew to London to photograph the scene.

Subsequently the IRA issued a statement saying the Army Council had not authorised the attack, and expressing regret for the deaths.

Chapter Thirty-four

—————•◦∞◦•—————

IN the 1980s the control and direction of loyalist death squads became a key item in Britain's strategy for Northern Ireland. Up to fifteen percent of the Ulster Defence Regiment, ostensibly dedicated to keeping the peace and protecting the people, was involved in these squads.[1]

The Force Research Unit of the British army, together with the RUC Special Branch, reorganised, armed, and directed a number of unionist paramilitaries. Within a few years of receiving new weapons smuggled into the Six Counties by British agents, loyalist murder gangs had increased their capacity to kill by three hundred percent.

Politicians, civil rights activists, election workers, and human rights lawyers all became targets. Through a network of paid agents the British government identified troublemakers it wanted disposed of and guaranteed the assassins would have a clear run at them. Special Branch made sure that any subsequent investigations were cursory and the killers were never brought to justice.

British Intelligence justified collusion as "taking the war to the IRA."

NINETEEN eighty-four was the year George Orwell cursed.

On a bitterly cold January day a fifteen-year-old schoolgirl called Ann Lovett was found in a pool of blood at the grotto of the Blessed Virgin on a small hill outside the town of Granard. Her arms were covered with bruises where

she had gripped them in the birthing agony. By her side
was the pair of scissors she had brought to cut the umbil-
ical cord. On a moss-covered stone at the foot of the
statue lay her tiny baby boy. The girl was rushed to hospital but died of exposure and haemorrhaging.

A referendum on abortion had taken place halfway
through her pregnancy. Although the "Swinging Sixties"
were already a generation in the past, Ireland had turned
thumbs down.

When the Ann Lovett story appeared in the newspapers
the shock to the nation was intense. Here was the truth
behind the hypocritical veneer of Holy Catholic Ireland.
People were moved to tears by the tragedy—but not really surprised. Emotionally crippled by the arrogant, un-
forgiving morality of their Church, generations of Irish
men and women had lived in denial of their own sexuality
and its consequences.

Slowly at first, then like a dam breaking, other women
began to reveal secrets they had kept hidden for years.
They told of rape and incest, of love betrayed, of concealed pregnancies and nightmarish births in hidden
places and babies buried in battered suitcases. Pain and
shame and grief. Broken hearts and wrecked lives.

BREDA Cunningham made certain that Ursula saw a
doctor in Ennis General Hospital on a fairly regular basis.
As Ursula had long since discovered in Dublin, people
stranded on the beaches of hospital waiting rooms loved
to talk.

One day she encountered a woman of her own generation, a spinster named Sophie Sinnott who had been born
on a country estate north of Dublin, a place called Willow
Park. "We had a big cut-stone house with three stories plus
the attics," she reminisced, "though I was never allowed
into the attics. Of course there was a basement too, the

kitchen and laundry were down there. I never saw them either, that was the servants' territory."

"How many servants did you have?"

"Let me think." She began ticking them off on her fingers. "There was the butler, the housekeeper, the parlour maid and the upstairs maid, two ladies' maids—my mother said no lady could ever have enough maids—the cook, the kitchen maid, and a girl in the scullery."

"To care for how many people?"

"My parents, my brother Jack, and myself and my sister Elisabeth. But we always had a lot of guests too," she added hurriedly, as if suddenly realising that the size of the staff required justification.

"Did you employ anyone else?" Ursula asked.

"My goodness yes. The outside staff included the chauffeur—he was married to the housekeeper—the head groom and a couple of stable boys, and two men in the dairy. We always kept eight or ten cows to supply the family with milk. Jack used to boast that he could drink a cow dry all by himself."

The mention of horses had brought a sparkle to Ursula's eyes. "Did you ride?" she asked when the other woman paused for breath.

"No, but my father and Jack went out with the hunt two or three times a week."

"As a girl I had the most wonderful horse," said Ursula. "He was called—"

"Oh, really?" Sophie Sinnott interrupted. "I'm nervous of horses, they're far too big. What was I saying? Oh yes. There was a full-time carpenter at Willow Park to see to the maintenance." She gave an aristocratic sniff. "You know, it's impossible to hire a carpenter for even an hour's work these days. They make more than doctors and they're busy littering the landscape with ugly boxes of houses that all look alike." The spate of words slowed; stopped. She peered at Ursula as if seeing her for the first time. "Are you sure you want to hear all of this, my dear?"

Ursula gave a wry smile. "I find it fascinating. My girlhood was very different from yours; it's hard to believe we were living on the same planet, never mind in the same country. The Ireland I grew up in was bone-poor, subsistence level. We never knew there was such a thing as a butler."

"Everyone in our set had servants," Miss Sinnott replied. "How could one possibly manage without them? With a country house like ours—though we had a town house in Dublin too, of course—a head gardener and his apprentice were essential, as was a kitchen gardener. The kitchen garden was walled to keep neighbouring boys from stealing the apples. We grew our own vegetables there on the estate; we were practically self-sufficient. One could spend weeks without ever leaving the grounds. Our light and heat were supplied to the house by a gasometer. It never failed. My father was very proud of that."

Ursula recalled the paraffin lamps and turf fire of her childhood. They had never failed either. "How did the gasometer work?" she wondered.

"I'm not exactly sure, I never had to concern myself with such things. I believe the gas was pumped to the house under pressure, using a system of weights that some of the outside staff winched up by hand. But country houses are impossible to keep warm, you know. All those high ceilings and acres and acres of windows."

"How dreadful for you," said Ursula, suppressing a smile. "Did your family do any farming at Willow Park? Aside from the kitchen garden, I mean?"

"Oh yes, the demesne was expected to pay for itself. We had forty or fifty acres under tillage and several large fields where we raised cattle for market. The drover would leave in the afternoon with a dozen or so bound for Dublin. All livestock travelled on foot in those days, you know; there was none of this fancy motorised transportation for cows and pigs. The drover would have to run ahead of the cows for a while to keep them from ducking through open gates and gaps in the hedge, but once they began to tire they were more manageable. They would reach Dublin early the next morning and be herded through the streets before the traffic grew heavy."

"When I was a small child I saw cattle driven through the streets of Dublin on their way to the slaughterhouses," Ursula remarked. "They looked so anxious and bewildered; I felt sorry for them."

Sophie Sinnott raised her sparse eyebrows in surprise. "Did you really? Why?"

"Because they didn't know what was about to happen to them, I suppose."

"Oh, my dear, none of us ever knows what's about to happen to us."

McCoy was hardly himself after Ursula's departure. When the phone rang in the hall he was always the first one there, hoping it was a call from the farm. He was immensely cheered by a newspaper article on the twenty-fifth of January. "Listen to this!" he announced at the dinner table. "Yesterday the Northern Ireland Office agreed to a request by the City Council of Londonderry to change its name back to the original Derry, as taken from the Irish. *Daire*, meaning Oak," he elucidated for the benefit of those who did not have Irish.

In March Gerry Adams was arrested while trying to calm a potentially violent situation that had developed after the RUC tried to take an Irish flag from Sinn Féin election workers.[2] Adams and two colleagues were summoned to appear before a magistrate in the courthouse in Belfast on March fourteenth. During the lunch recess they left the building together with a friend. As they drove away in search of fish and chips a volley of gunfire rang out. The car windows shattered.

Three men were hit by rifle fire. In an assassination attempt by loyalist paramilitaries, Gerry Adams took five bullets. The most serious was in his back.

Rushed to hospital, he walked in despite his wounds. Belfast republicans organised a round-the-clock vigil at the hospital. Still in pain but recovering, Adams checked himself out after five days and resumed his work on behalf of the party.

THE house seemed strangely empty with Ursula gone. Barbara constantly complained about the amount of work that had fallen on her shoulders since Breda was no longer available to do it.

Barry was thankful for his own work, which kept him out of the house. It seemed as if every month brought some new report on Northern Ireland from some official body or commission, contradicting one another, irritating northern politicians who did not agree, and coming no closer to providing a solution. The New Ireland Forum stated that Ireland was one nation and that Britain was ultimately responsible for partition by refusing to accept the democratically expressed wishes of the majority of the Irish people.

The Haagerup Report, adopted by the European Parliament, rejected any idea of a British withdrawal from Northern Ireland and said there was no possibility of a united Ireland in the foreseeable future. However it did call for a power-sharing government and an integrated economic plan.

In the June elections for the European Parliament there were eight candidates for the three Northern Ireland seats. Among those running were the DUP leader Ian Paisley, Ulster Unionist John Taylor, John Hume for the SDLP, and Danny Morrison for Sinn Féin. Paisley, Taylor, and Hume were elected, but Morrison had increased the Sinn Féin vote by fifty thousand over the previous European election.

Afterwards Morrison stated, "Electoral politics will not remove the British from Ireland. Only armed struggle will do that."[3]

FOR the privileged few in Ireland there was a radical new development in residential design. They were having "en suites" installed: a private bathroom adjoining a bedroom, instead of the customary one bathroom for an entire house.

"We could build an en suite off your bedroom," McCoy suggested to Barbara.

"I'd love it, Séamus, but we could never afford it."

"Are you sure? Seventeen seems to be doing all right. The other day he was talking about buying a car to replace Apollo."

"His car is a business expense; an en suite is a luxury."

"But you'd love it," he reiterated.

She didn't say no.

SEVERAL members of the IRA and the INLA were murdered by loyalists under circumstances that made collusion with the security forces embarrassingly obvious. Newspaper headlines in both Ireland and Britain used phrases such as "Shoot to Kill" and "Police Cover-up." The British government was forced to act. John Stalker, the recently appointed deputy chief constable of Greater Manchester, was assigned to make enquiries.

Upon his arrival in Belfast Stalker was given a chilling warning by John Hermon, the chief constable of the RUC: "Remember, Mr. Stalker, you are in the jungle now."[4]

·   ·   ·

IN May the Soviet Union announced plans to boycott the Olympic Games in Los Angeles, just as the United States had done to them in 1980. The world's leading athletes were caught in an international tit-for-tat.

PRESIDENT Ronald Reagan paid a four-day visit to Ireland. He and Mrs. Reagan were warmly welcomed in the village of Ballyporeen in Co. Tipperary, from which his Irish ancestor had emigrated.

BARRY Halloran joined the scrum of reporters and photographers surrounding the U.S. president. Private opinion amongst them seemed to be divided about Reagan. Some saw him as a joke, a Hollywood cowboy whose good looks had carried him a long way; an example of America's preoccupation with the superficial. Others suspected a keen intelligence behind the amiable facade. Barry fell into the latter category. As part of his "homework" he had read some of the essays Reagan published on policy issues, both domestic and foreign. He did not agree with everything the man said, but he agreed with the way he said it. That positive, grittily optimistic attitude was severely lacking in Ireland.

Except, perhaps, in a very few.

AS a city, Galway was celebrating its five hundredth birthday, so Barry drove down to take photographs. It would be his first trip in the new car—the new used car, as he jokingly described the black, four-door Ford. It was only two years old, which made it new enough on Irish roads dominated by old bangers.

Parting with Apollo was difficult for Barry, but when he traded it in to Paudie Coates his friend promised he would not sell the Austin Healey again. "There's no market for old sports cars in this country, to be honest," he told Barry. "Sure we'll keep it here at the garage and if your missus ever wants it, she can take it out."

"Séamus talked me into building an en suite for her," Barry said laughingly. "Don't tell her about the car too, at least not for a little while. It might give her ideas above her station."

"Your mother did that months ago," Coates replied.

Before Barry left for Galway he urged McCoy to join him. "We can try out the new car, you'll enjoy that. We'll open her up on the N7. I'll be going by way of Ennis so we can call on Ursula."

"Can't do it, I'm afraid."

"And why not?"

"I've started work on that bathroom for your wife. The plumbing's in a right state and she will be too if I don't get it finished double-quick."

"Barbara's lived this long without being able to step out of bed and into the shower, another week won't kill her."

"I know, but I promised her I'd finish it so I will."

"Séamus, is there some reason why you don't want to visit Ursula? Every time I go down there I invite you to come with me and every time you find some excuse."

"Perhaps I don't want to say good-bye to her again. I said it once the day she left Harold's Cross, and that's enough."

Barry was puzzled. "You don't have to say 'good-bye' at all. She's not going anywhere, you can see her anytime you want to. If you don't drive down with me there's always the train."

"I know." McCoy gave his friend a long, thoughtful look. "You said good-bye to the Army years ago, Seventeen—for your own reasons, and I'm not asking about them—but would you like to have to do it again?"

·   ·   ·

T H E British Conservative Party announced it would hold its annual conference in the seaside resort of Brighton in early October. The Grand Hotel was to be the venue. Three weeks before the conference a member of the IRA, dressed as a workman, casually entered the hotel and planted twenty pounds of explosives behind a panel in the bathroom of room 629. Pat McGee set the timer for twenty-four days later, when the government's high command would all be in residence, and casually strolled out again.

The bomb went off at 2:54 A.M. on the twelfth of October; the culmination of a bloody four-year campaign by the IRA on the "British mainland." The massive explosion ripped open the hotel. One of the Grand's huge Victorian chimneys collapsed and went crashing through seven floors. Five people were killed and more than thirty were seriously injured.

Prime Minister Margaret Thatcher escaped the assassination attempt, but the bathroom in which she had been only two minutes earlier was destroyed.

The IRA issued a chilling statement aimed directly at Mrs. Thatcher. "Today, we were unlucky. But remember— we only have to be lucky once. You have to be lucky always."

T H A T was good work, that bomb," Patsy said at the next meeting of the Usual Suspects. "I'd like to meet that fella and shake his hand, he's a hero in my book."

Abruptly, Barry's brain presented him with a snapshot of Talbot Street, 1974. A yellow-haired man with a pock-marked face was sprawled on the pavement with his chest and belly torn open. There was a puzzled expression on his face, as if death were a door he had walked through by mistake.

Barry felt his stomach clench. "I was an engineer in the IRA," he said, trying to keep all emotion out of his voice, "which means I built bombs for them. But don't call me a hero. Life isn't worth living if we don't face up to who we really are and what we really do. I may be many things, but I refuse to be a coward."

Brendan cleared his throat. "While watching the battle of Fredericksburg, a glorious victory for the Army of the Confederacy, General Robert E. Lee said, "It is well that war is so terrible; we should grow too fond of it."

Barry threw him a grateful glance. "You understand, then?"

"I understand that what's happened in Ireland since partition has done terrible damage to this country and its people, morally as well as physically. And it grows worse day by day. The old truisms are vanishing.

"When I was young the republicans were heroes and the British were the enemy. That is no longer a given. We have a partitioned country that calls itself a republic, but our government and a sizable percentage of the population remain cringingly subservient to Britain, and the republicans have become the enemy. We haven't changed, yet everything else has."

"The republicans are changing too," Barry told him.

"For good or ill?"

"It's too soon to tell."

RECESSION was biting deep. Woolworth's closed its Irish branches. Women who had worked behind the counter at Woolworth's ever since they left school suddenly found themselves unemployed—and there were no jobs to be had.

Barry photographed the customers waiting for the doors of the main store in Dublin to open for the last time. Huge price reductions had been widely advertised. "One person's disadvantage is another's advantage," one woman laughed as he was taking her picture.

The following day, Barry put an ad in the papers looking for a housekeeper.

America was static, dumbing down; drowning in its own

excesses. By contrast, Europe as a single entity was a long-held dream finally on the verge of realisation and there was tremendous interest in its potential. The Old World demanded a nimble mind and a solid knowledge of history—and a Swiss passport was even more useful than an Irish one.

Barry Halloran was receiving more assignments than he could cover. "If we hire a housekeeper to be here all day, every day, you could go back to singing," he told Barbara.

IN the north, DUP councillor George Seawright said of educating Catholic children, "Taxpayers' money would be better spent on an incinerator and burning the whole lot of them. The priests should be thrown in and burned as well."[5]

RONALD Reagan was reelected as president of the United States in November.

The Sunday Press published a story claiming that Margaret Thatcher had asked civil servants to draw up documents on repartition in Ireland, and they had refused.

On the seventeenth of November a two-day summit meeting between Margaret Thatcher and Garret FitzGerald on the question of Northern Ireland began. Barry flew to England to take photographs. Afterwards Thatcher told the press, "A united Ireland was one solution. That is out. A second solution was confederation of the two states. That is out. A third solution was joint authority. That is out. That is a derogation from sovereignty."[6]

FitzGerald described her behaviour as "gratuitously offensive."[7]

·   ·   ·

BARRY returned from the airport to find Barbara in tears.

"Séamus has left us!" she wailed, flinging herself into her husband's arms. "What am I going to do?"

Chapter Thirty-five

------------◆∞◆------------

BARRY had a sense of déjà vu. "You mean he's gone back to the Army again? I don't believe it; I thought he'd given up after Long Kesh."

"Not the Army, I only wish it were. He's emigrated."

"He's what? Sweet Jesus; where to?"

"America," Barbara sobbed. "He left here almost as soon as you did the other day, I'm surprised you didn't see him at the airport."

"We would have been at different gates," Barry replied automatically. "But why?"

"He didn't say. I saw him coming down the stairs carrying an old suitcase and when I asked where he was going, he said, 'Boston.' He kissed me on the cheek and the next thing I knew he was out the door. You could have knocked me over with a feather."

Barry was astonished. "I didn't even know he had a passport."

"Would they let him enter America?" Barbara wondered. "With his background?"

"There are ways," said Barry. "And I suspect our Séamus would know them all. Or know how to find out."

The children were upset; they loved their "Uncle Séamus." Barbara, surprisingly, was disconsolate. She had never realised how much she relied on McCoy until he was gone. "He was like the father I never knew," she confided to Barry.

He understood all too well.

Christmas in the yellow brick house was subdued that year, only slightly cheered when a card arrived from America showing a snowy scene on Boston Common, and bearing a brief greeting from McCoy. "Miss you all and will write soon," he promised.

O n the eleventh of March, 1985, Mikhail Gorbachev assumed leadership of the Communist Party in the Soviet Union.

With the encouragement of U.S. president Ronald Reagan, relations between the world's two superpowers began to improve.

Dear Seventeen,
I'm well settled in Boston now. You would be surprised how many of us are over here—or maybe you wouldn't. An old pal of mine from Belfast Brigade has married a local lass, a widow with a grown family and a house down near the harbour, so I'm stopping with them at present. I can look out the window and imagine the famine ships sailing into Boston all those years ago, bringing our people to the new world. I wonder if they felt then the way I feel now.

I should have told you what I was planning but I hate good-byes. Don't worry about me, I have enough money for now. You always paid me too much and I didn't have anything to spend it on anyway. If I need more another old pal of mine who manages a pub off Commonwealth Avenue said he would give me a job as a bartender. Gerry Adams started that way.

Barry telephoned Ursula and read the letter to her. She was relieved and infuriated at the same time. Relieved that they had heard from Séamus at last; infuriated that he had not written to her first, or at least at the same time. With an effort of will, she kept both emotions out of her voice. "He doesn't say anything about his health," she pointed out. "What will he do if he falls ill again?"

"Barbara tells me there are all sorts of health schemes over there that we don't have here, and Boston has superb hospitals."

"But America's not a socialist country, Barry. They don't take care of simply everybody. An undocumented alien, and I'm sure that's what Séamus is, could have a hard time."

That's just what I needed, Barry told himself after he hung up the phone. *Something else to worry about.*

A N Air India 747 exploded off the Irish coast on the twenty-third of June. Search parties flocked to Ahakista, County Cork. Of the 329 people aboard, all were feared dead. Sikh extremists were suspected.

U R S U L A Halloran, who once rose before first light, now lingered in bed in the mornings, waiting for the little German music box whose rendition of "O Donnell Abu" opened the RTE broadcast day at six A.M. This was usually followed by a commercial extolling a remedy for fluke, a parasite in livestock.

When Barry drove down to see her he reported, "Now that his adult teeth have come in we took Pat to the dentist for his first checkup. You'll be pleased to hear that they're strong as granite and not a cavity. Of the three children, he's the only one to inherit yours."

"I'm not surprised," said Ursula.

She had been badly hurt by what she perceived as Mc-Coy's defection, though she never admitted it. When she finally received a letter from him he sounded contrite.

"I guess you're mad at me and I don't blame you," he wrote. "I should have talked to you before I left. But there wasn't anything to say. I did not tell anybody I was going but I had my reasons. You of all people understand them."

At the end of the letter he gave a telephone number where he could be reached in case of emergency. "Over here they have fancy new telephone systems now, and phone calls cost pennies instead of pounds. But I know the Irish telephone still costs the earth, so don't ring me unless you have to." ·

"It's about time that man wrote to you," Breda Cunningham said indignantly. "Did he explain why he left Ireland?"

"It wasn't necessary."

Breda shook her head. "I never did understand that man. I liked him, but I didn't understand him."

"Many would not," said Ursula. She folded up the letter and put it in the little tin box with the "Brownie" articles.

O N the fourth of June a member of Sinn Féin was elected chairman of the Fermanagh District Council with the support of the SDLP.

June fourteenth was marred by the explosion of a thousand-pound IRA bomb in Belfast city centre, causing widespread property damage.

On the twenty-ninth of the month Patrick Magee, an Irish republican, was charged in London with the murders resulting from the Brighton bombing.

B ARBARA and Barry put the children on the train that summer to spend two weeks in Clare. Breda collected them at Limerick Station in Ursula's old car, which she referred to as "the Antique." Drunk with freedom, the children squirmed like puppies during the drive to the farm. "Are we there? Are we almost there?" They burst into the house, into the parlour where their grandmother waited for them with open arms, like a gale of fresh air, and began jabbering excitedly to her about the train journey and school and friends and . . .

"Slow down there," Ursula admonished. "My ears don't hear as fast as they used to."

For a fortnight the youngsters dwelt in an Ireland which once had been home to the vast majority of Irish children. Cows, chickens, pigs, a well for water, an outdoor toilet (there was a lot of hilarity about that), stacks of turf to burn in the cavernous kitchen fireplace on chilly nights, trees to climb and streams for wading and long tall summer grass in which to lie and dream and make daisy chains. And chores to do as well; Ursula made certain they understood the responsibilities that went with freedom.

She personally introduced her granddaughter to every horse on the place, calling each one by name. It was not Trot who fell in love with the farm, however, but Patrick.

Dark, fey Patrick, who spent all of his time either with the horses or wandering alone through the countryside, listening to music only he could hear.

In July Bob Geldof launched Live Aid at Britain's Wembley Stadium. Barry Halloran was on hand to photograph the event, though he was almost lost in the sea of television photographers. But his pictures were important. Ireland proved to be the highest per capita donor for famine relief.

Viking artefacts found during the excavations at Wood Quay went on exhibition at the National Museum, attracting huge international attention. Barry photographed them too; trying not to think about the defeat they represented.

Cork City celebrated its five hundredth birthday.

French secret agents blew up the Greenpeace vessel *Rainbow Warrior* in Auckland Harbour.

As for Northern Ireland—a total of twenty-nine prison officers had been killed; ten men had starved to death in prison for their political beliefs; violence and sectarianism were still rampant.

Yet the horror chambers of the Maze had created the fragile key to begin unlocking a peace process. The secret channels for negotiation between all the parties involved remained in place.

J U L Y saw violent clashes between the police and loyalists in Northern Ireland over the loyalists' insistence on their right to march through Catholic areas.

At the end of the month the BBC refused to transmit a programme called "At the Edge of the Union," which featured an interview with Martin McGuinness. Journalists went on strike over the decision. For the first time in its history, the BBC World Service went off the air.

In early autumn John Stalker submitted an initial report of his enquiry into the RUC's "shoot to kill" policy.

But the big international news story of the year broke on the first of September when the *Titanic* was found. The wreck of the huge luxury liner that sank in April of 1912 finally was located on the floor of the Atlantic Ocean, some four hundred miles south of Newfoundland, by Robert Ballard and a team of explorers.

"My grandfather Ned Halloran was on the *Titanic*,"* Barry told his fascinated children. "He was one of the lucky ones, he was rescued."

"Did he see a lot of people die?" Brian asked eagerly.

Barry was amused. "You're a bloodthirsty scamp, aren't you?"

"Well, did he?"

*See *1916* by the same author.

*   *   *

O N the fifteenth of November Barry was at Hillsborough Castle in County Down to photograph something that, for once, truly could be described as an historic occasion in the history of Northern Ireland. In spite of the obvious difficulties between them, Margaret Thatcher and Garret FitzGerald met to sign the Anglo-Irish Agreement, giving republicans the right to put forward their views and proposals for the future of Northern Ireland.

At an Ulster Clubs rally in Larne, Ian Paisley expressed his reaction: "If the British government force us down the road to a united Ireland we will fight to the death. This could come to hand-to-hand fighting in every street in Northern Ireland. We are on the verge of civil war. We are asking people to be ready for the worst and I will lead them."[1]

T H E latest hit song was Paul Brady singing "The Island," with the line "Up here we sacrifice our children to feed the worn-out dreams of yesterday."

W H E N the Anglo-Irish Agreement was debated in the Dáil, Fianna Fáil strongly opposed and voted against it. Yet ten years later, when he was party leader and *taoiseach,* Bertie Aherne would describe the Agreement as having been "a shaft of light in a time of despair."[2]

S É A M U S McCoy sent a Christmas package to Harold's Cross containing a small, carefully chosen gift for every member of the Halloran family and Philpott too.

In Clare, Ursula received the most beautiful Christmas card she had ever seen, accompanied by a new hardcover edition of *Julian*. Breda's gift was a box of Vermont Maple Sugar Fudge.

• • •

DESMOND O'Malley, a former government minister, had been expelled from Fianna Fáil because he refused to support the party's policy on contraception. By the end of the year O'Malley was at the head of a new political party, the Progressive Democrats. More liberal than the Soldiers of Destiny, they promised a genuine republic that would encourage pluralism and free itself of the shackles of the Catholic Church.

With the typical Irish penchant for acronyms, overnight the party became known as the PDs.

O'Malley possessed a rugged integrity that seemed to augur well for his new party, but there was one problem. He was an intellectual. As fellow politician Michael D. Higgins stated from personal experience, "To be an intellectual in Irish politics is more of a handicap than being a pervert."

ON the tenth of January, 1986, Ian Paisley said, "No today, no tomorrow, no forever," to the Anglo-Irish Agreement.

"I wish he would be more specific," Ursula quipped during a telephone conversation with Barry.

WHILE Paisley was inveighing against the Agreement, Father Alec Reid, a Redemptorist priest based in Belfast, contacted Charles Haughey to ask if he would meet personally with Gerry Adams. Haughey declined to do so at that time, fearing political consequences because of his role in the Arms Crisis.[3] However, he asked his adviser, Martin Mansergh, to keep in touch with Father Reid, and Haughey himself met with Cardinal Ó Fíaich at his home in Kinsealy to explore the possibilities for creating a peace process.

Another northern politician entered the picture when Haughey conferred with John Hume of the SDLP.

Meanwhile, Gerry Adams continued to push for an end to political abstentionism on the part of republicans. To succeed he would have to convince some of the most hard-line elements within the IRA; the real "hard men."

The task ahead was daunting.

O N the twenty-eighth of January the U.S. space shuttle *Challenger* exploded on launch, killing all seven aboard, including a young schoolteacher who had trained for the mission so she could share the great adventure with her students.

W H E N Barry returned to the house Barbara did not need to ask where he had been; she had a very good idea. He had gone to church to pray for the dead.

She asked anyway, to show him she was interested. "Did you get Mass?" Once she would have said, "Did you go to Mass?" but it was a reflection of her gradual assimilation that she automatically used the Irish phraseology.

He replied with a sombre nod.

I N March Easter Monday came and went, unremarked in the Republic. Alone among the free nations of the earth, Ireland officially ignored her birthday yet again. The Troubles had hijacked the glorious past, replacing memories of an earlier IRA fighting a clean fight against overwhelming odds with more recent images of masked and hooded terrorists.

B A R R Y was well aware that his wife was restless. The children were growing up; becoming separate entities. The new housekeeper, very thankful to have a job, was a hard worker and Barbara found herself with time on her hands. Too much time.

Never one to suffer in silence, Barbara complained to everybody she knew—one of whom was Rosaleen Mac-Thomáis, who mentioned it to her husband. Who spoke to someone at RTE. Who rang Barbara and asked if she would like to come in for an audition. "A mutual friend tells me you have a beautiful voice, and we're always interested in finding talent."

I N Dublin, Eircell, Ireland's first mobile phone company, was established to general scepticism.

North and south, male and female, people were wearing shoulder pads and watching television. British soaps like *Eastenders* and miniseries from America, such as *Mistral's Daughter*, captured a family's attention the way Mass used to do.

O N the twenty-sixth of April an undercover SAS unit near Roslea wounded, captured, and summarily executed Volunteer Séamus McElwaine, who had played a pivotal role in the successful 1983 escape from the H-Blocks.

As O/C to the Fermanagh Easter Commemoration held the year before, McElwaine had said, "We call on all republicans to unite, to put petty bickering and old grudges behind them, and we emphasise that no one has the right to carry on campaigns of vilification or division."[4]

B A R B A R A Halloran, wearing a new outfit bought especially for the occasion, was fifteen minutes early for her interview at Radio Telefís Éireann. The RTE complex at Montrose, on Dublin's south side, comprised several modern buildings that might have been designed to serve as factories if broadcasting proved to be a flash in the pan.

The receptionist behind the desk smiled when Barbara said rather breathlessly, "I think I'm early."

"You're American, aren't you?"

"Well, yes."

"That's why you're early then. Sit down over there, someone will come for you."

MONSIGNOR James Horan, who presided over the shrine to the Virgin at Knock, County Mayo, had long dreamed of establishing an airport at the little town of Knock to facilitate the devout. In 1981, against considerable opposition and sheer disbelief on the part of the majority, the monsignor had broken ground for his airport.

By 1986 commercial flights were taking place between Connaught Regional Airport, Knock, County Mayo, to Rome. Monsignor Horan had proved that in the last half of the twentieth century miracles could still happen if one had enough faith.

AS Barbara was leaving RTE she met the monsignor on his way in for an interview. She returned to Harold's Cross alight with news. "I'm going to be a continuity girl!" she crowed to Philpott, who was unimpressed.

"What's that when it's at home?"

"You know, I'll introduce programmes on the radio. Well not introduce them exactly, but sort of say they're coming up."

"Oh." Philpott returned to basting the chicken.

Barry was away. Barry was always away. But Alice Cassidy was within reach of a telephone, so Barbara rang her at Switzer's, where she had recently been promoted to department manager. Alice was holding a meeting of her

sales staff when the phone rang, and resented being
interrupted—particularly when she heard Barbara's news.
She said peevishly, "Are you not a little old to be any sort
of a 'girl'?"

Barbara had not expected spite from her faithful acolyte.

Chapter Thirty-six

April 26, 1986

NUCLEAR DISASTER IN THE UKRAINE
REACTOR EXPLODES AT CHERNOBYL NUCLEAR
FACILITY. MASSIVE FIRES RAGE. NUMBER OF
CASUALTIES NOT YET KNOWN.

THAT spring yet another breakaway group of dissident republicans emerged. Following the pattern of their
predecessors, they gave themselves a name meant to im-
ply that they were the true heirs of the Volunteers of 1916.
They called themselves the Continuity IRA.

In Northern Ireland John Stalker was removed from
his two-year investigation into the RUC shoot to kill policy. No specific reason was given to the public and no report of his was published.

When a divorce referendum was introduced by Garret
FitzGerald's government, polls showed the public supporting the proposed constitutional amendment by two to
one. Then thousands of priests took to their pulpits to in-
veigh against such pure godlessness. The family would

be destroyed, they asserted. And even more tellingly—particularly to Ireland's tens of thousands of male farmers—the land would be divided and pass out of their control.

The referendum failed.

Since 1982 the Irish national debt under the government of Garret FitzGerald had doubled. The tax rate for a single person earning more than ten thousand pounds a year reached a crippling sixty-five percent.

Emigration was still draining the country, though unlike earlier generations, now it was the well educated who were leaving. Tanaiste Brian Lenihan was criticised for commenting, "Ireland just isn't big enough for all of us." But it was true.

I'M so lucky," Barbara wrote to Isabella Kavanagh, "to have a job in broadcasting. Continuity is only a beginning but it will lead to greater things. I shall have to do some networking first, of course, because Ireland is all about who you know and who you can impress, but that's the easy part. Before you know it I'll be singing on the Late Late Show. I'll have them send you a tape."

Barbara sealed the envelope and pressed the stamp down with a determined thumb.

SHE worked hard at her new job, concentrating until she had expunged every trace of American twang from her radio voice. Her diction was perfect, her inflection correct.

No one complimented her on it. No less was expected.

She and Barry grew farther apart. Initially he had been happy about her new job because she was happy about it, but when the career she had envisioned did not immediately materialise she took her dissatisfaction out on him.

He began finding excuses to stay away from Harold's

Cross, only returning at night to spend time with the children before locking himself into his darkroom and working until he felt certain Barbara was asleep.

A t Christmas the Halloran children were excited by the arrival of McCoy's package, which was becoming an annual event. Brian bought a tinfoil star with his own money, inscribed it "Séamus," and hung it on the tree.

E arly in 1987 the Finn Gael/Labour coalition led by Garret FitzGerald collapsed. It was replaced by a Fianna Fáil government under Charles Haughey, who thus became *taoiseach* for the third time, equalling the record of Eamon de Valera.

The new government set out its stall with a series of radical proposals designed to turn the economy around and change the face Ireland presented to the world. Foreign companies willing to locate in Ireland were lured with a ten percent corporate tax rate. Creative artists were invited to live tax-free in Ireland to found "a new Byzantium." An entrepreneurial spirit unknown in Ireland before began to come to life.

A t Loughgall, County Armagh, the East Tyrone Brigade planned an attack on an unmanned RUC station in the middle of the town. They hijacked a digging machine to use in crashing a bomb into the empty station.

They did not know their security had been compromised; perhaps by an informer, perhaps through electronic eavesdropping.[1]

At the crucial moment an ambush party consisting of both soldiers and RUC men opened fire from four separate positions. Eight Volunteers were killed, effectively wiping out most of the East Tyrone Brigade. Four civilians, including a woman and her child, were injured in the withering fusillade. One man died.

I N June the conservatives in Britain won yet another general election. Margaret Thatcher began a third term as prime minister.

S P E A R H E A D E D by Charles Haughey, work began on a new Financial Services Centre to be built in Dublin's rundown dockland area. Haughey hoped the centre would spur an upturn in the country's economic fortunes, but also, with its stunning modern design of glass and steel, would begin the revitalisation of Ireland's shabby capital.

"This is all going to cost money," people in the streets and pubs moaned to one another. "And Mother Ireland without a pot to piss in or a window to throw it out of. It's mad, I tell you."

The public criticised, complained, begrudged. Every step was met with massive resistance. Yet throughout the summer a new and different vision of Ireland slowly began to rise along the quays, hidden behind hoardings plastered with advertising posters.

At the same time and under the same government, what remained of Georgian Dublin was being sold off to the developers to be demolished.

B A R R Y decided to revisit an earlier project—his photographic archive of Dublin's fast-disappearing streetscapes from another era. *Best salvage what I can before it's all gone. The Irish have never had a reputation for architecture; our finest houses and public buildings were part of our colonial legacy. But they were built on*

Irish land using Irish labour. And they're ours now. We should be saving them.

IN July the Greek government announced a state of emergency when over seven hundred people died during a heat wave. Temperatures continued to soar.

ONE morning in August Barry set out to photograph the derelict Georgian town houses surrounding Mountjoy Square. As usual, Barry had done his homework beforehand. It was important to have the history to accompany the pictures.

Mountjoy Square was set on a plateau north of the Liffey, taking advantage of a stunning downhill vista of Dublin with the mountains to the south. In 1014 this high ground would have offered an unimpeded view of land and sea in all directions. According to tradition this was where Brian Boru had pitched his command tent for the Battle of Clontarf—and where he was slain in his hour of triumph.[2]

Mountjoy had once been celebrated as the most beautiful of Dublin's squares, surrounded by houses of classic elegance. Former home to many of the Ascendancy. Despised symbol of Empire.

Part of Ireland.

Poverty-stricken and in an advanced state of decay, Mountjoy Square was still part of Ireland. A sad testament to the failure of the Irish to succeed in their own land. *The Irish have no reputation for architecture,* Barry thought, *yet they have a great reputation for poetry. Why could the two not somehow be married?*

He went from one building to another, photographing lovely architectural details like the last few curls on a dying woman.

One house in particular stopped him in his tracks. He could not say why. But he stood in front of it for a long time with his feet firmly planted on the broken paving. And the ground beneath.

"Here," he said aloud. For no particular reason. "Here."

A visit to the estate agent whose name was on the faded "For Sale" sign assured him there were no sitting tenants in the house; no tenants of any kind. "Except for the rats," the agent said with a laugh. "It's been on our books so long I thought it would fall down before we sold it. But I have to say, you can get the house for a song and a dozen more like it, if you want. No one's buying property. Are you thinking of renting out flats? That's all those old places are good for: tenements."

B A R R Y spent a sleepless night adding up columns of figures; chewing the end of the pencil; striking through and starting again. *You think you have enough until you find out you need more. How much is "enough"?*

The following day he visited a splendid marble edifice whose three-sided, colonnaded front faced onto College Green. The bank occupied the former home of the Irish Parliament, dissolved with a stroke of the pen by the Act of Union with Britain in 1800.

A conversation with the bank manager ensued while sweat puddled unseen in Barry's armpits. The manager was less than encouraging about a venture into Ireland's severely depressed property market. "Very risky for a private individual, Mr. Halloran; very risky indeed. Perhaps you would be better off investing the same amount in shares—bank shares, for example?"

Barry assumed his most confident air and engaging grin. "We can talk about that some other time. Right now I feel like taking a bit of a risk; after all, it's my money. But . . . ah . . . we don't have to discuss this with my wife, do we?"

The bank manager tapped a finger against his nose. "No need to bother the women with business they don't understand, eh? Eh?"

There followed days of waiting. Then a flurry of activity: solicitors to contact, papers to sign.

And at last she was his. His and the bank's. A derelict house on Mountjoy Square. A grand old Georgian girl with tall windows—boarded up—and a graceful fanlight—broken—over what remained of an imposing front door. Three floors over basement littered with rubbish and peeling paper and smelling strongly of urine. Piles of rags in the corners where squatters slept at night. A roof that leaked and blocked chimneys and stairs that were unsafe to climb, though the remaining banisters were elegant.

The house in Mountjoy Square became Barry's mistress, his secret passion that he confided to no one. Hugging the knowledge of her to his heart, he laid plans to reclaim her beauty.

In a rubbish skip in Marlborough Street Barry noticed part of an old front door. The timber was too rotten to be of any use, but a massive knocker and striking plate, discoloured with age, were still attached. Barry used brute force to tear them free. That evening he spent hours in his darkroom with the door closed, working with wire wool and metal polish.

Until the big brass knocker gleamed like gold.

NORTHERN republican and political activist Alex Maskey was shot in the stomach when he answered a knock at his front door. The would-be killer had long since departed the scene by the time the RUC arrived.

ON the sixteenth of October a massive storm—which had been predicted by Ireland's Meteorological Office but not by forecasters in Britain—swept across England, killing seventeen people and leaving a 300-million-pound trail of destruction.

Three days later a storm of a different sort struck as the bottom fell out of world financial markets. Headlines in New York proclaimed "Black Monday!" Fifty billion pounds were wiped off the London stock market.

The value of Irish bank stocks plummeted.

BARRY drove to Mountjoy Square and parked in front of his house. He just sat looking at her and smiling to himself.

ON the first of November French authorities seized a huge arsenal of weapons being shipped from Libya aboard the *Eksund,* bound for Ireland—and the IRA.

The eighth was Remembrance Day, when Britain commemorated those who had fought and died in two world wars. Poppies were worn in British lapels as lilies were worn by Irish republicans at Easter. While marchers were assembling for the annual Remembrance Day parade in Enniskillen, County Fermanagh, an IRA bomb exploded in a disused school.

Gordon Wilson, aged sixty, and his daughter, Marie, a nurse, had been attending the ceremony. They were buried in an avalanche of wreckage. Father and daughter held hands and tried to comfort one another as they waited for rescue. Wilson kept asking his daughter if she was all right, and she said she was. But the fifth time he asked she replied, "I love you, Daddy."

She died five hours later on a life-support machine, one of the eleven people to die that day. Sixty-three had been injured, some critically.

The statement Gordon Wilson made at the hospital was as stunning as the bomb itself. He publicly forgave his daughter's killers. "I shall pray for those people tonight and every night."[3]

W I T H a heavy heart, Barry drove to Fermanagh to photograph the scene of devastation in Enniskillen. There was still blood on the ground. Dark, drying. Crying out.

It wasn't supposed to be like this. We were not supposed to be like this. Why isn't Séamus here to talk to when I need him?

In the midst of so much ruin, no one paid much attention to a tall man who seated himself heavily on a broken slab of cement and covered his face with his hands.

F A T H E R Alec Reid had arranged a secret meeting, to be hosted by Cardinal Ó Fíaich, between Charles Haughey, Gerry Adams, and John Hume of the SDLP. In spite of Enniskillen Haughey held his nerve and went ahead with the meeting.

T H E usual package arrived from McCoy at Christmas, crossing in the mail with packages to McCoy from Dublin and Clare. In the package to McCoy Barry included photographs of the children—"Look how they are growing!"—and a photograph of the house on Mountjoy Square. "I bought this as an investment and am fixing it up, but don't tell Barbara. It's to be a surprise. Wish you were here to help."

He sent the same picture and message to Ursula, but without the sentence wishing she could help.

The telephone in the hall rang on Christmas Eve. "Barry, it's your mother. I need an explanation for that photograph you sent."

"I thought the picture and note were self-explanatory."

"But of all the houses you might have bought, why Mountjoy Square? Do you realise I once lived just across the square in Gardiner Street? That's where I was going the day the bomb . . ." She swallowed hard. "Tell me: why are you keeping this a secret from Barbara?"

"I told you, I want to surprise her."

"A house is not the sort of thing a man keeps secret from his wife. A mistress, perhaps, but not a house."

Barry smiled.

Chapter Thirty-seven

ON the first day of January, 1988, Dublin began the official celebration of its Millennium—ignoring the fact that the first settlement on the south bank of the Liffey had been a small Christian community built long before the Vikings arrived at Wood Quay in the early ninth century.

On the eleventh of the month John Hume, leader of the SDLP, had a secret meeting in Belfast with Gerry Adams of Sinn Féin. They hoped to find common ground for an all-Ireland settlement of the northern question. The meeting had been arranged by Father Alec Reid, who had acted as mediator in various republican feuds.

The two men planned to have further meetings whenever possible.

DESPITE compelling evidence that the six men convicted in the 1974 Birmingham pub bombings were innocent and the forensic material had been fabricated by the police themselves, on January twenty-eighth the Court of Appeal in London upheld their convictions.

The following month Ian Thain, a private in the British army and the only man ever to receive a life sentence for murdering a Catholic in Northern Ireland, was allowed to walk free after serving only two years in jail. During that time the army had kept him on its active service rolls with full pay, and welcomed him back to his old regiment upon his release.

Days later a British soldier shot Aiden McAnespie in the back, in broad daylight, at a security checkpoint. McAnespie, who was on his way to a Gaelic football match, was a popular and well-known member of Sinn Féin. He also was unarmed.

THE Progressive Democrats drafted a suggested new constitution for the Republic, dropping any constitutional claim to Northern Ireland and deleting any reference to God.

IN the Bleeding Horse, Brendan was contemptuous. "The PDs have been intimidated to the point of cringing subservience."

Luke disagreed. "I don't think it's intimidation. They're courting the political support of all those West Brits who still long in their heart of hearts to be part of Mother England."

"What about dropping God from the Constitution? How do you explain that?"

"God's going out of fashion," Luke said flatly.

Patsy was not listening to either of them. As far as he was concerned, political discussions were going out of fashion too. There had been too many for too long and it did not help. Nothing helped.

He stared morosely into his glass.
The conversation dwindled and died.

A T a UDA press conference in Belfast a spokesman read aloud a statement from the UFF that claimed that "innocent Catholics" had nothing to fear from them.

The item was carried on the six o'clock news the following evening. Later, in the Bleeding Horse, Brendan said, "Was there not some American soldier who claimed the only good Indian was a dead Indian?"

Barry Halloran set down his glass and leaned forward.

His days were consumed either by his photographic career or the house in Mountjoy Square, where he was needed to supervise plumbers and electricians and carpenters when he could get them to come—Ireland being notorious for the laxity of its labouring force—or doing the work himself. His evenings with the children were not always idyllic; they were totally disparate personalities. Brian was a typical fifteen-year-old boy, rebellious and secretive, with more energy than he could use. On the verge of puberty, Trot was a giddy butterfly with skinned knees. Patrick, his father observed to his grandmother on the telephone, was sui generis. "I can't find the key to him, there's no one like him."

On this particular March night, lonely for a different kind of company, Barry had driven to the Bleeding Horse. *It hasn't changed*, he had thought with relief as he entered the familiar door. *That's why pubs are so great. Not the drink, not even the conversation. Just the fact that they exist unchanged, a fragment of the past caught like sheep's wool in a thornbush.*

"If you're implying the loyalist paramilitaries think the only good Catholic is a dead Catholic," Barry said to Brendan, "I'm sure that's true; at least for some of them. But there's a large element of follow-my-leader in any crowd." A simile from his own rural past occurred to him. "Danny could tell you: if a bellwether goes through a gap in a hedge the rest of the flock will too."

Luke cleared his throat. "Danny's not here anymore."

"I know that." Barry picked up his glass again. Took a long, slow drink.

"What d'ye hear from Séamus?" asked Patsy.

"Not a lot, he's keeping busy."

"Séamus always was a great one for keeping busy." Barry took another drink.

"And your mother?" queried Brendan. "How is she?"

"Still getting along well."

Brendan nodded. "Strong woman, your mother."

"She is that." Barry set his glass down. Watched the slow dust of time settle over the table.

O N the authority of Prime Minister Margaret Thatcher, by the sixth of March a large team had been assembled in Gibraltar, the British colony at the southern tip of Spain. It consisted of twelve members of Britain's Special Air Service, a bomb disposal squad, a score of surveillance specialists, several senior officers in MI5, and an Army Legal Services lawyer. The team was hunting three known members of the IRA, using information gleaned through MI5, MI6, the RUC, and Irish and Spanish police forces.[1]

According to a highly placed informant, possibly within the Gardai itself,[2] the Volunteers—Seán Savage, Daniel McCann, and a young woman, Mairéad Farrell—allegedly were coming to Gibraltar to bomb British fortifications there. The official purpose of the SAS team and their support group was to arrest the three.

It was a typical March afternoon on the peninsula, slightly warmed by that Africa-tinged wind that sometimes comes sweeping across the Strait to caress the famous Rock.

Unaware that their every move was being watched, Farrell and McCann parked a red Ford Fiesta a few hundred yards from the border that separates Spain from Gibraltar, then simply walked across into the town.

Meanwhile the SAS, according to their own testimony, had already spotted Savage's white Renault 5 parked in the town. They could not explain how it had entered Gibraltar undetected. No effort had yet been made to arrest him, nor to examine the car.

After meeting in the town, the Volunteers walked together toward Winston Churchill Blvd. Gibraltar was swarming with casually dressed visitors like themselves, and locals going about their own business. Farrell and her companions sauntered along, chatting together. Three young people out for a day in the sun.

Something must have alerted them. Savage split off from the other two, but it was too late.

A police siren sliced through the air, sending shock waves up the nervous system. Then the staccato of gunfire. As he fell, Seán Savage might have heard the screams of children in a nearby playground.

Farrell and McCann were already being cut to pieces by bullets on the footpath north of him. Farrell was shot five times in the face and a further three times in the back, from a distance of less than five feet.

None of the three was armed.

Neither of their cars contained any explosive device or part thereof.

Within half an hour the first of a mounting cacophony of news reports was issued from London. The IRA had tried to blow up the Rock of Gibraltar. The IRA had engaged in a running gun battle threatening the lives of hundreds of innocent people. British security forces had, at great risk to their own lives, disarmed one or several huge IRA bombs.

As it happened, no car bomb was found until the next day—at the resort of Marbella, miles away. It could just as easily have belonged to ETA, the Basque separatist organisation.

The press in London had a field day. This was as big as Thatcher's victory in the Falklands. An article in the *Daily Express* carried a photograph of Mairéad Farrell with the caption "Queen of Terror, Weaned on Hate!"[3]

Shocked and grieving relatives of the slain republicans set off for Gibraltar to identify their loved ones and bring them home for burial. The process took the better part of three weeks. Under heavy political pressure, the various commercial airlines discovered they could not rearrange their schedules to fly the bodies back to Ireland.

After Sinn Féin succeeded in raising twenty-five thousand pounds to pay them, a British firm agreed to do the job using a private jet.

When the bodies of the Gibraltar Three arrived at Dublin Airport, Barry Halloran was amongst the thousands of people waiting on the tarmac, in a driving rainstorm, to welcome them home. Many of those who waited were not republicans; just the plain people of Ireland. Who had long memories.

Television cameras carefully avoided showing the size of the crowd.

The coffins were taken from the plane to the airport mortuary, where a priest said the prayers for the dead. Draped with the Irish tricolour, the three coffins were then placed in hearses and began the long drive home, followed by mourners and members of the press.

A s he drove north Barry could feel the anger in himself building.

Shot them in cold blood. A woman too. Shot them lying on the ground. Blew her face off. Left her family with that to think about.

Barry's knuckles were white on the steering wheel.

.   .   .

EMOTIONS in the north were running almost as high as they had during the second hunger strike. When the cortege crossed the border it was met by a veritable army of security forces. As they passed through Protestant areas the procession was pelted with bricks, bottles, and obscenities. The security forces made no effort to intervene. But when a howling horde ran toward Barry's car he rolled the window down and aimed his camera at them. "Smile, please!" he called jauntily.

They turned and ran the other way.

It was common for republican funerals in the north to be hijacked. Since the onset of the Troubles, time and again members of the RUC had blocked funeral processions, pulled mourners off the road, even refused to allow access to churches and cemeteries. This time was no different. The police closed the main road into Belfast to all but the hearses and the cars carrying the immediate families. Strenuous efforts were made to convince everyone else to go back. Preferably all the way to Dublin.

Barry Halloran knew Belfast too well to be misdirected. Through a series of lightless laneways and claustrophobic little streets where boarded-up windows watched like blind eyes, he made his way into the city and checked into one of his usual hotels.

He did not ring home to tell Barbara he had arrived safely. He never rang Harold's Cross from a hotel in Northern Ireland anymore. Instead he placed a prearranged phone call from a public phone box to a neutral acquaintance, and had that person notify Barbara.

British army listening posts, bristling with the latest electronic eavesdropping equipment, were in place all along the border and on the taller buildings around Belfast and Derry.

THE RUC had promised the relatives of the Gibraltar Three that they would be buried in peace, provided the

IRA refrained from firing a volley of honour over the graves. On the afternoon of March sixteenth the funeral cortege set out for Milltown Cemetery in West Belfast. The procession following the hearses stretched for almost a mile. A lone piper playing "The Minstrel Boy" was almost drowned out by the noise from a British army helicopter hovering directly overhead.

The world's media was in attendance too. Reporters and photographers fought ordinary mourners for every scrap of available space. But the assembled crowd recognised Barry Halloran; he was one of their own. They let him pass.

The day was bitterly cold, but it always seemed cold in Milltown Cemetery. The republican dead who lay in their soldierly ranks did not sleep at peace. Not yet.

Barry had brought only one camera. He was wearing it on a strap around his neck, partially concealed by the overcoat he never buttoned. He would take pictures later; not now. The ancient Irish reverence for the ceremony of committal to the earth was deeply ingrained in him.

A number of people were already waiting around a fresh grave roped off by a yellow cord. A grave large enough to hold three coffins. As Barry approached, Gerry Adams acknowledged him with a minute nod. So did Martin McGuinness. With a few exceptions, the leadership of both Sinn Féin and the IRA was in Milltown Cemetery that day.

Barry had photographs of both Savage and Farrell in his republican archives, but not of McCann. None of the three had been personal friends of his yet he knew them well. Knew the forces that motivated them and the dream in their hearts.

Dreams were harder to kill than people.

How many more gravesides will I have to visit? Which will be the final one that brings people to their senses at last? Will I even live to see it?

Concentrating on dark thoughts, Barry paid no attention to a man who stood by himself at the far edge of the funeral plot. The man was wearing a heavy anorak and had blunt, brutal features, yet there was a dreamy look on his face. A distracted look, as if listening to inner voices. He scanned the crowd, then fixed his eyes on Adams and McGuinness. His expression changed. Focussed. Reaching into his anorak, he took out two hand grenades.

A swift flicker of movement in the cold still air.

Barry had trained himself to observe small details at the periphery of vision, and was aware of the grenades being hurled even before his brain identified them. Instinctively he grabbed the woman standing nearest him and threw her onto the ground, covering her with his body.

Two grenade blasts sounded almost simultaneously. Shrapnel tore through the assembled crowd. While people were still screaming and falling, their assailant produced an automatic pistol from another pocket and began pulling the trigger convulsively.

This was not an ordinary crowd; many were Volunteers who had seen action before. It was only a couple of seconds before they hurled themselves after the man with the gun.

He was already trotting towards the nearest road. "You Orange bastard!" someone shouted after him.

Barry scrambled to his feet and helped the woman to hers. "Are you all right?"

"I am all right," she replied shakily. "But I think I owe you my . . ."

Barry did not wait to receive her thanks. He set off with the others in pursuit of the attacker.

Chapter Thirty-eight

BARRY'S long legs covered a vast amount of ground with every stride, but some of the younger men had a head start. They pelted after the shooter who turned on them several times, cursing and firing his pistol. "Catch me if you can, you Fenian fuckers!" he screeched hysterically. From the depths of his anorak he drew a second pistol and began firing that too.

His pursuers dodged behind gravestones, then resumed the chase.

While the gunman ran on, two men zigzagged towards him from near the cemetery gate, hoping to cut off his escape route. He did not see them until they were almost upon him. With yet another mad scream Michael Stone squeezed off a shot at Thomas McErlean. The bullet smashed through the young man's shoulder and into his chest cavity.

McErlean fell, fatally wounded, just as Barry's bad leg gave out on him and he pitched forward. The ground rushed up to meet him. He felt something like a hammer blow to his chest.

"Are you shot?" someone shouted down at him. Gritting his teeth, he shook his head and struggled back to his feet. He hobbled to the cemetery wall and leaned against it, swearing with frustration.

The camera on its strap had been beneath him when he fell facedown on the ground. He gave it a tentative shake. Something rattled.

"I curse that man from a height," Barry growled under his breath.

Meanwhile the object of his curse had reached the road and was trying to flag down passing motorists. No one would stop for a wildly gesticulating madman. He turned back towards his pursuers, fired at them again, and hurled one last hand grenade.

Then he dropped his weapons and began strolling down the road as if he had not a care in the world.

The enraged crowd swept out of the cemetery after him. They had begun chanting. "IRA! IRA! IRA!"

Barry tried to follow but his leg would not cooperate. Only his spirit ran with them. Closing on the gunman. Seizing him, throwing him into the back of a car, beating him viciously, and then dragging him out and hurling him to the pavement where he was pummelled with fists and stones and kicked again and again until the police finally arrived.

THE video camera proved its worth that day. No still photograph could match the shocking immediacy of the violent "home movie" scene in Milltown Cemetery that was broadcast on television that night.

The murderer in RUC custody was identified as Michael "Flint" Stone, who described himself as "a dedicated, free-lance loyalist paramilitary," and wanted to know "How many of the bastards did I get?"

Three of his pursuers had been shot dead. Only one of them was a member of the IRA. Neither Gerry Adams nor Martin McGuinness was hurt, but scores of men, women, and children had been injured.

BACK in his hotel, Barry was badly shaken. He went into the tiny toilet-and-shower cubicle—advertised as "en suite" to justify the price of the room—and leaned heavily on the basin while he eyed himself in the mirror.

"Sick bastard," he observed. He might have been referring to Stone.

He turned on the cold water in the shower to full volume and stepped under it. His skin was impervious to the icy water. All he could feel was the fire in his soul.

Sleep was impossible. Sometime before dawn he took a sheet of hotel stationery from the bedside locker and began writing a letter.

Dear Séamus,

You may or may not hear what happened in Belfast today; I don't know how much Irish news you get in America. What you do receive is probably filtered through the BBC, so it will be one-sided. But there is no way the murders in Milltown Cemetery can be disguised as anything other than what they were.

There was almost another murder outside, on the road. If I had been able . . .

Barry stopped writing. Wadded up the sheet of paper and took out another one.

Dear Séamus,

You may have made the right decision in leaving Ireland, just as Barbara's grandfather did after the Civil War. Tonight I feel almost hopeless about the situation here. Almost. But I cannot turn my back on this country.

Today I saw a graphic illustration of what hate can do to a man. Hate is our real enemy, Séamus. Whatever our political or religious affiliations, we in Ireland are being tyrannised by our own hatreds.

We have to sit down and talk to one another. There simply is no other way. The impetus is not likely to come from people like the man I saw in Milltown Cemetery today. It will be up to the republicans to take a leading role in making the peace, just as we have taken a leading role in making the war.

We must avoid woolly adjectives, abstract philosophy, and waffle. As you know, northern Protestants are plainspoken people who recognise waffle a mile away. Celtic circumlocution only increases their distrust.

I believe the economic factor is the single most powerful force at our disposal for convincing them of the value of a united Ireland. Right now the Six Counties are the poor relations of Britain, living—to put it bluntly—on handouts. More than forty percent of their employment comes from the civil service. Such a warped economy cannot help but warp its people. And they are good people, Séamus; most of them. I really believe that.

What we need to do is talk simply and believably to ordinary men and women, not to the politicians. For decades the politicians have contributed nothing constructive, merely exacerbated the situation.

Lastly but by no means least, if a British identity remains important to northerners we must demonstrate that we are prepared to except their Britishness without qualification, as part of the society of modern Ireland. To see that this is what the founders of the Republic originally intended, we need only go back and read the 1916 Proclamation again. Patrick Pearse said it all, better than I ever could.

Barry signed the letter before reading it again.

Do I really believe all this? I have to. What else is there?

The distance between rational thinking and primal emotions seemed very great indeed.

A few days later two British soldiers drove a car straight into the funeral procession of Volunteer Kevin Brady, one of Michael Stone's Milltown victims. Whether the intrusion was by accident or design no one would ever know. The infuriated mourners dragged the pair out of the car, beat them savagely, stripped them naked, and shot them at close range.

Father Alec Reid arrived in time to give artificial respiration to the soldiers, but it was too late.

P A N Am Flight 103 was blown up by terrorists over Lockerbie, Scotland, killing 259 people on board and eleven on the ground. Libya was strongly suspected.

Y E T the year was not without its lighter side. In June a sculpture depicting an unnaturally elongated woman reclining in a fountain was installed in Dublin's O'Connell Street. Designated as "Anna Livia" in honour of the River Liffey, she was promptly renamed by the locals. Her new titles were exemplars of Dublin wit. "The Whoor in the Sewer" and "Anna Rexia" were two of the best.

Barry photographed her from all angles.

More and more of his time was being spent in Dublin. It was emotionally harder for him to go north; to cover the stories that never seemed to stop. The deaths, the beatings, the brutalisations. Names and faces were almost interchangeable. They were all human beings and they were all suffering.

B E L O W the surface hope was stirring. The Hume-Adams meetings continued. Secret contacts among various factions, including the two governments, remained in place.

H O P E was beginning to put out tiny green shoots elsewhere in the world as well. As 1989 approached a tyranny was crumbling.

On a grey November day Barry Halloran photographed the flag of the Union of Soviet Socialist Republics hanging limply on its flagpole in front of the embassy. Under the leadership of Premier Mikhail Gorbachev, the winds of change were sweeping across eight and a half million square miles.

Ursula had predicted a new flag would be hanging from that pole before too long.

CHRISTMAS in the yellow brick house was brightened by the presence of Ursula and Breda Cunningham. Barry had refused to take no for an answer. The children were delighted with their grandmother's company. Barbara privately complained to Barry, "They behave so well when she's around. It's insulting, really. Why don't they act like that for me?"

"Because you're here all the time and they only see their grandmother on special occasions."

"I'm not here all the time! I'm a working woman, I have a job. A *career*," Barbara stressed.

She made every effort to get along with Ursula during the holidays. Ursula did the same. Both women were uncomfortable, with a nagging sense that things could be so much better, if only.

Ursula had brought the Christmas present she already had received from Séamus McCoy. On Christmas Eve she opened the gaily wrapped package and found a small crystal globe containing a snowball scene. Turned upside down, it created a miniature blizzard that delighted the children. "Until you can visit me in Boston," McCoy had written on the accompanying card, "here's a bit of Boston for you."

Until you can visit me in Boston.

Ursula turned her wheelchair so no one could see her face and busied herself neatly refolding the wrapping paper; neatly smoothing the ribbon to use again.

BEFORE she returned to the farm, Ursula took Barry aside. "When are you going to tell Barbara about that other house of yours?"

"When it's ready. I only work on it as the money comes in because I don't want to go any farther in debt, but one of these days I'm going to drive her up to the front door and hand her the key. It's what her mother wanted for her all those years ago. I'll never forget how disappointed Isabella was when she saw this house instead."

"Why are you trying to please someone else's mother?" Ursula asked sharply.

"I'm not, I'm trying to please my wife. Do you want to see the house? We could drive over there before I take you back to Clare. You could show me where you used to live."

Ursula gave a barely perceptible shudder. *We're not meant to go back; surely the bomb taught me that.* "I don't think so, Barry, but thank you for asking. Right now I'm just homesick for the farm."

Pat overheard her final words. "Can I go too, Nana?"

She smiled. "You have to go back to school, little man."

"But school is *everywhere!*" the boy cried, throwing wide his arms as if to embrace the world. "Like wind and grass and God."

"We may have an agnostic here," Barry remarked.

Ursula said, "We may have a druid."

N I N E T E E N eighty-nine began badly. On the twelfth of February a Belfast solicitor, Pat Finucane, was eating dinner with his family in the kitchen of their home in a middle-class area in North Belfast. Finucane was well known for defending republicans. His brother Séamus had been involved with Mairéad Farrell; the two had even set up a home together. But that was before the killings on the Rock.

It was almost seven-thirty when two masked men wearing camouflage jackets burst into Finucane's house through the unlocked front door. Finucane started towards the glass door that separated the kitchen from the hall. The intruders shot him in the chest and stomach. In front of his wife Geraldine and their children, they then fired eleven more bullets into their victim as he lay dying on the floor. A ricocheting bullet struck Geraldine in the ankle. The children were unharmed—physically. The trauma of that day would remain with them all their lives.

The assailants made a clean getaway. At the time, no one was identified for the murder and no arrests were made. Once again people spoke of state-sponsored assassinations and a governmentally sanctioned shoot-to-kill policy targeting republicans and their supporters.

No official enquiry was undertaken aside from the basic forensic examination carried out at the scene. Although there had been a recent spate of strongly anti-republican comments by representatives of the British government, London denied responsibility for any actions that might have precipitated or encouraged the murder.

UNTIL you can come to Boston. Keeping her efforts secret even from Breda, Ursula once more began trying to reactivate her dead legs. Every instinct told her it was far too late.

Every instinct told her she must not give up.

She kept McCoy's glass globe beside her bed so she could see it every morning as soon as she awoke.

IN May tens of thousands of Chinese students flooded into Beijing's Tiananmen Square to protest the policies of their government. Within a few days their ranks were swelled to over a million by ordinary men and women joining the protest. On Sunday, the fourth of June, the government sent in the troops.

The massacre that followed was dubbed Bloody Sunday by the international news media.

Barry briefly considered putting together a photographic essay on three Bloody Sundays—two in Ireland and one in China—then discarded the idea. *All joy is the same, but no pain can be compared with any other pain.*

Dear Urṣula,
Here I am again, with no big news to report. Which is all right with me. I have plenty of time to read and I still like Boston. I think you would too. My only problem is a chest cold that keeps coming back on me. A pal of mine said I should go to Arizona because the climate there is good for a bad chest.

IRELAND experienced its hottest summer in years. Sunny days uninterrupted by even a hint of rain brought people out in the thousands. Many had to be treated in hospital for sunburn and heat exhaustion before the rain returned, melting the burning sky and pouring ozone-scented rain over the thirsty land.

PAUL Morrissey continued the practical management of the farm, but Ursula was increasingly involved in its day-to-day operations. The electronic lift installed in the stairway gave her slow but reliable wheelchair access to every part of the house, and a ramp had been built to allow her to take the chair outside.

There were days when she could forget, for a while, that she was handicapped. But not at night. And not first thing in the morning. Those were the times when she fought to regain what had once been hers.

·   ·   ·

In Dallas, Texas, Isabella Kavanagh was killed in a car crash. The telephone shrilled in the hall of the yellow brick house late at night. Barry was not yet home and Philpott had long since gone to bed. Barbara was alone when she took the call.

"Mom would have hated dying on the Lyndon Baines Johnson Expressway," she said to Barry later. Much later, when he finally came home. Long after the first shock; after the silent, lonely tears. "She always voted republican, you know. I mean American republican, not Irish republican," Barbara added hastily.

"I knew what you meant," said Barry. With his arms around her.

He accompanied his wife to Dallas for the funeral. The city had changed almost beyond recognition since his visit in the late fifties. Numerous skyscrapers rose from the flat prairie to stab the innocent sky. Some of the buildings appeared to be gold-plated.

"I have to go back to Ireland after the funeral," Barry said, "but you can stay on here for as long as you want. I'm sure you and your sister have some catching up to do."

"Not much, we were never that close and our lives are very different now. I think I'd rather go home when you do, Barry. People in America talk too loud."

Once they were back in Ireland Barbara resumed her life as if nothing had happened. The children grieved more for the grandmother they had never known than Isabella's own daughter appeared to do. She, the drama queen who made huge emotional issues out of trivia, kept her pain hidden.

Sometimes Barry glimpsed it in her eyes. When he tried to comfort her she shrugged him off. "Nothing's wrong, just leave me alone."

The songs she sang to herself when she sat at her dressing table brushing her hair changed. No longer the latest pop hits, but the operatic arias which had first captivated

Barry. They belonged to a time when her mother was still alive and love and success were a promise waiting in the future.

Trot loved hearing her mother sing. "Teach me the words," she pleaded.

"It's opera, and it's Italian."

"I don't mind, I can learn it. Please teach me!"

Barbara tried, but her heart was not in it. Opera was hers, had always been hers. She was not ready to pass on what she considered her greatest gift.

Trot began teaching herself from the radio. Ráidió na Gaeltachta, transmitting from Galway, did not always come through very clear, but she was a persistent child and loved the Irish ballads they often played. The first time Barry heard his thirteen-year-old daughter sing "My Lagan Love" she stopped him in his tracks. Trot had her mother's voice.

In August the UDA shot dead twenty-eight-year-old Loughlin Maginn and then boasted about it, claiming he was a member of the IRA. To support this they produced classified British Intelligence documents in their possession that identified Maginn as a "suspected" Volunteer.

The media scented blood. Investigative reporters, a relatively new phenomenon in Ireland, began developing networks. By late autumn thousands of British Intelligence documents would be uncovered in the hands of loyalist paramilitaries.

On the seventeenth of October it was announced that corruption proceedings were being instigated against the police involved in the convictions of the Guildford Four. Two days later three of the four were released. One remained in jail because he was still implicated in another case; his conviction was subsequently quashed.

·   ·   ·

BECAUSE Barbara was not using her bereavement to make emotional claims on him, Barry felt more tender towards his wife than he had in a long time. He began coming home earlier and trying to find conversational topics that would be of interest to her.

He was not aware there had been a chill between them until it began to thaw a bit.

Barbara loved to talk about her career. She always referred to her job in RTE as "my career." Only once did Barry make the mistake of reminding her, "My mother had a career in RTE too." Several days passed before Barbara was responsive again. Barry thought seriously about telling her of the house in Mountjoy Square but decided against it. The house was too big a bargaining chip. It must be saved for the future.

THE news story of the year took place in November.

On the ninth of the month the partition of Berlin came to a end. The infamous Berlin Wall separating the two halves of the divided city was breached after almost three decades.

Since 1961 the Wall and the 860-mile-long border shared by East and West Germany had allowed the development of two dissimilar Germanys; one prosperous, the other struggling under Communist dictatorship. People caught trying to escape East Germany were shot dead by border guards.

When the changes taking place in the Soviet Union began to affect its satellites, Hungary had been amongst the first to reflect them. A new, more liberal regime had opened the border between Hungary and Germany.

Once walls started coming down the momentum was hard to stop. Czechoslovakia was the next country to grant free access to West Germany through its border.

East Berlin's Communist Party spokesman announced that East Germans would be allowed to travel directly to

West Germany. West German chancellor Helmut Kohl hailed the decision as historic and called for a meeting with the East German leader.

The plain people of Germany would not wait. Hundreds converged at crossing points along the Berlin Wall. Bowing to the inevitable, the Communists gave permission for the gates to be opened from the eastern side. Eager crowds surged through to be embraced by jubilant West Berliners on the other side. Within hours huge chunks had been torn out of the wall. Berlin then gave itself a week-long party of fireworks and champagne.

IF it can happen there it can happen here," the Usual Suspects told one another. "It's only a matter of time."

Chapter Thirty-nine

———◦∞◦———

TIME," Barry wrote to McCoy on New Year's Eve, "is doing two things simultaneously. When I look at the kids it's whizzing by. Ursula would be furious to hear me call them kids, but that's what everyone calls children now so I do too. We have to move with the times. Just look at Germany.

"Yet time is standing still when it comes to Northern Ireland, Séamus. I used to pop into the car and drive up there two or three times a week, but I don't bother anymore. How many pictures of bloody people lying in the street does anyone need to see?"

•   •   •

THE salient events in the northern struggle were taking place more and more out of the glare of the media. Barry was aware of many of them and followed them with acute interest, exchanging each scrap of information he obtained with Éamonn MacThomáis, but there was nothing he could cover with his camera. No photograph could illustrate the struggle of men fighting their prejudices. Men who, on the republican side at least, were trying to imagine the impossible: moving the armed struggle into the political arena.

Yet tiny step by tiny step it was happening. Guided by progressive thinkers such as Gerry Adams, the republican movement was beginning to focus less on what it was against and more on what it was for.

How do you really feel about going the political route?" Barry asked MacThomáis. The two had met in a republican pub—not the Bleeding Horse—close to Glasnevin Cemetery.

Barry sometimes visited the cemetery for his mother's sake and his own. Laid flowers on the graves of Ned and Síle Halloran in the republican plot. Tried not to think of Milltown.

"The same way you do, I suspect," MacThomáis replied to his question. "I'm torn. I have no faith at all in politics but the bomb and bullet don't seem to be getting us anywhere either."

Barry said, "There are a lot of hard-liners in the Army who can't accept anything else."

"I know that. According to the experts they'll never come around."

Barry raised a cynical eyebrow. "The people who claim to be experts on republicanism are the very people the republicans don't talk to."

.   .   .

Nineteen ninety was Ursula Halloran's putative eightieth birthday, and a banner year for news.

In May Cardinal Tomás Ó Fíaich died in France of a heart attack during a visit to the Marian shrine at Lourdes. Gerry Adams and Martin McGuinness attended his funeral, as did Taoiseach Charles Haughey; Peter Brook, secretary of state for Northern Ireland; and Hugh Annesley, chief constable of the RUC.

That same month David Trimble of the Ulster Unionist Party won the Upper Bann by-election with a majority of fourteen thousand votes. Barry drove north to take his photograph.

In the larger world there were other major news items, including the official reunification of Germany and Mikhail Gorbachev receiving the Nobel Prize for Peace.

In the Republic the media campaign against the IRA, encouraged by politicians in both major parties who feared any resurgence of genuine republicanism, was intensified. "IRA" had become a blanket term for any violent or criminal individual or group, with the result that the acts of such individuals or groups were automatically assumed to be politically motivated. Any member or suspected member of the IRA was a criminal. Any member of Sinn Féin was an evil person intent on destroying democracy and replacing it with the Communist conspiracy.

By now the plain people of Ireland had become so conditioned to this characterisation that they accepted it without question.

Almost.

Thousands of file photos were searched to insure that pictures of known republicans presented the worst possible image, depicting them as "shady" or "dangerous." Only those that lived up—or down—to a certain standard were shown to the public, either in newspapers or on television.

When a civil servant arrived at Barry's front door with a request to examine his archives he slammed the door in the man's face.

DURING a press conference in New York, Nelson Mandela was asked about the IRA. The vice president of the African National Congress replied, "Every community is entitled to fight for its right to self-determination."

His statement was denounced by every political party in Ireland—except Sinn Féin.

BARRY'S income had reached a level where it grew almost without his help. Rental income still formed a substantial portion, but no week went by without requests for material from his extensive archives. He taught young Brian his filing system and put the boy to work filling requests and mailing out invoices. Brian thrived on the responsibility. Soon he began contacting papers and periodicals on his own, with suggestions for photographs they might like to use.

Barry was able to speed up the restoration process on the Mountjoy Square house. The work had been much more extensive than he originally anticipated. A new roof had been essential, which had led to taking down and rebuilding the chimneys. Then the floors with their rotting timbers had needed replacing. Every job took at least twice as long as it might have because the work was done a bit at a time, but now the structural repairs were complete.

Replumbed and rewired, the old Georgian girl was internally healthy again.

Another year at the most for the cosmetic work, Barry thought, *and it will be ready for us. Barbara will want to choose the interior colour scheme herself, so the final painting will have to wait until she sees the place.*

Sometimes at night he lay in bed beside his wife and tried to imagine the look on her face when she saw her new home for the first time. *It's too bad her mother will never see it.*

I N the Irish presidential election Mary Robinson, barrister and member of Seanad Éireann, was selected by the Labour Party as its candidate. "A woman for president? Ridiculous!" the Usual Suspects scoffed. But she touched a chord with the people. In November she became Ireland's first woman president and invited the world to "Come dance with me in Ireland."

When she took up residence in Arras Uachtaráin, the President's House in the Phoenix Park, Mary Robinson gave orders that a lighted candle must always be burning in the window. Its purpose was to guide the children of the Irish Diaspora, the exiles to Britain and America and Australia and New Zealand, back home.

O N the second of August Saddam Hussein, president of Iraq, invaded Kuwait. In Aspen, Colorado, U.S. president George Bush was conferring with British prime minister Margaret Thatcher. Mrs. Thatcher told him, "Remember, George, I was about to be defeated in England when the Falkland conflict happened. I've stayed in office for eight years since that."[1]

T H A T autumn Barry was in his own home, busy in the darkroom, when Philpott knocked timidly at the door one morning. "Can I come in?" he asked in an odd voice.

"Is the red light on?"

Philpott looked up at the bulb over the door. "It is not on."

"Then come in of course. What's wrong?"

The little man was actually wringing his hands. "The police, I'm afraid," he stammered. "They're here."

Barry brushed past him and went out to the hall.

They had not waited for an invitation. Three men in plainclothes were already entering the parlour while two more were on their way up the stairs.

"What the hell do you think you're doing!" Barry shouted.

The power in his voice and the sheer size of him made them pause.

They were all big men themselves, though a little thick around the middle. Barry automatically assessed his chances against them. The physical activity of working on the Mountjoy Square house was keeping him very fit. *I could take down a couple at least, even if I am out of practice. And if my leg would hold up.* He had no real intention of fighting them, but the knowledge was satisfying.

Years of experience resurfaced in an instant. Barry knew just what to do in this situation and how to do it. Standing very still, he folded his arms and waited with a closed face. Just waited. Letting them read him; his quiet intensity, his total self-confidence.

The officer in charge briefly produced his identification, then put it back in his pocket.

"Special Branch," Barry confirmed.

The man nodded.

"That gives you no right to search my house."

"We do have the right to search your house, or anywhere else that may pertain to terrorist activities."

"Terrorist? You must be joking; I'm a photojournalist."

"We know what you are," the officer replied evenly. "Do you have chemicals on the premises?"

"I do of course, I just told you: I take photographs for a living and develop them myself. In fact I was in my darkroom when you burst in here."

"Perhaps you had best take me to your darkroom, Halloran."

Barry did not respond. Did not move the slightest muscle, nor bat an eyelid. Just waited. The big clock in the hall ticked on.

Beneath Barry's flinty gaze the officer felt like an insect pinned to a cork. "Mr. Halloran," he amended.

THE Special Branch operatives remained in the yellow brick house for over four hours, while Barry alternated between icy anger and grim amusement. He laughed outright when one of them asked him about the stone nose under the bell jar. "It's a phallus," he lied.

The policeman looked blank.

"Phallus. Latin word; it means a penis."

"Oh."

"My grandfather modelled for it," Barry claimed.

The other man stared at the piece of stone.

"Big man, my grandfather," said Barry.

When Barbara came home from work he met her at the door.

"Special Branch is in here," he told her in a low voice. "Don't say anything to them, I'll deal with it. Just sit down in the parlour and wait until they leave."

"But the children will be home from school soon!"

"I'll send them to their rooms. They'll be all right, we'll all be all right. Just do as I tell you."

Barbara was less upset than Philpott, who was distraught. "Never in my life," he kept repeating. "Never in my life! I'll have to give my notice, I can't stay here. I can't stay here."

"You can of course," Barry assured him. "This has nothing to do with you."

The men from Special Branch would not tell him what they were looking for. They found nothing that would

link him to the IRA—neither his weapons nor Ned Halloran's notebooks.

All the while they were searching the house Barbara sat
on the couch in the parlour, except for two brief excursions
to the bathroom. At first Barry was impressed by her composure. Then he noticed the guilty way she glanced at him
when she thought he was not looking.

When the police finally left the house, he faced her.
"You know something about all this, don't you?"

"Of course not! I was as surprised as you were."

"You may have been surprised, but not as much as I
was. You'd better tell me what's behind this, Barbara."

By the way her pupils dilated he knew he was right. He
took a step closer, looming over her. It was not a tactic he
had employed with the men from Special Branch because
it would make no difference, but it had a profound effect
on his wife.

She would not meet his eyes. "Well, I may have said
something I shouldn't have."

"Said what? To who?"

She chewed her lip. "Inside in RTE. You know how it
is, we all got to talking . . ."

"I do not know how it is, Barbara. Tell me."

"Well, I mean . . . you know how hard I've been trying
to make an impression. I just couldn't get anyone important to notice me. Not really, not as a person who might
be important in her own right. Then one day in the can-
teen when a couple of the higher-ups came in I happened
to mention your notebooks."

"You *what*?"

She was instantly defensive, pulling her shoulders forward as if to protect herself from a blow. "I told them
about your notebooks with the lists of IRA contributors.
They were really impressed."

A muscle jumped in Barry's jaw. "Did you bother to explain that those notebooks were fifty years old or more?"

"I don't remember; I suppose I did." Wide-eyed innocence.

"You don't remember? Do you have any idea what you've done?"

"I didn't expect the police to come looking for them, if that's what you mean. I thought, well"—a dismissive gesture here—"I guess I thought those old books might make an interesting documentary or something. And the people upstairs would be grateful to me."

His voice was flat, weighed down by the effort to hold his temper. "Barbara, the names in those old books belonged to men and women who have living children and grandchildren. And unlike you, some of those younger people have been raised in the republican tradition."

Comprehension dawned in her eyes. "Do you mean they're still supporting the IRA? Is that why you kept the notebooks a secret?" Her voice shrilled in outrage. "Are you raising money for those terrorists? Admit it, damn it, I know you are!"

Turning on his heel, he left her standing there and retreated to his darkroom. His plundered darkroom, where every bottle and box had been opened and at least seven rolls of undeveloped photographs exposed to the light.

He flung himself onto a stool and sat there trying to cope with the awful sense of betrayal.

After a while Barbara knocked at the door.

I should have switched on the red light. Not that it makes any difference now.

"Barry, let me in. Please, I have to talk to you."

He did not answer.

"I wasn't trying to make trouble, really I wasn't. I just didn't think."

You just didn't think.

"I'm sorry for what I said. I know you aren't active in the Army anymore—that's right, isn't it?—so there seemed to be no harm . . ."

Her voice trailed off.

She stood on one side of the locked door while he sat on the other. Neither spoke.

After a long time he heard her walk away.

BARRY stayed in his darkroom until the house was quiet. The evening meal had been served, his children had gone to bed, even the boarders had retired. Barbara no doubt was upstairs in their bedroom. Her bedroom.

Walking on the balls of his feet, he made his way to the secret closet he and McCoy had prepared together long ago. Silently he gathered up his weapons and Ned's notebooks. Silently he carried them out to his car.

And drove away.

He returned for breakfast in the morning but he did not speak to Barbara. He managed to act normally towards the children, though once or twice he saw Patrick slant a speculative look in the direction of his parents. As soon as they left for school Barry went upstairs and began packing his things.

Barbara followed him. "What are you doing?"

"What does it look like I'm doing?"

"You can't leave me! What about the children?"

"I'm not officially leaving; this is divorce Irish style. I'll spend my nights someplace else, but I'll be here as much as I can for the children. If you play your part well enough they may not even realise we've separated, at least not for a while. You can do that, can't you? It seems to me you're a pretty good actress."

She began to weep. Her tears did not move him.

The six P.M. news reported, "Acting on a tip from an undisclosed source, yesterday the Gardai searched the home of a known republican in Harold's Cross. It has been hinted that an arrest is imminent."

Barbara wrote out her resignation and mailed it in to RTE.

. . .

O N November twenty-second, Margaret Thatcher re-signed. The Iron Lady was replaced as prime minister and leader of the Conservative Party by her former protégé, John Major.

Chapter Forty

I N December the IRA called a three-day Christmas ceasefire.

C H R I S T M A S was relatively normal in Harold's Cross, though by now all three Halloran children were aware that something was wrong between their parents. So was Ursula, who regretted she had made the difficult journey to Dublin.

"We're going to go home early," she told Breda. "It's too cold here."

"It's probably even colder in Clare," the nurse said.

Ursula shook her head. "I doubt that seriously."

She was careful to take McCoy's Christmas present to her, and his card, back to the farm from which she had brought them.

E A R L Y in 1991 a series of heavy storms swept across Ireland, causing massive flooding and widespread power outages. Fourteen people died.

On the fifth day of the new year IRA incendiary bombs destroyed a factory and six shops in the Belfast area.

The following month an IRA mortar was fired into the garden of 10 Downing Street. It landed within yards of the room where John Major, the new prime minister, was holding a cabinet meeting. No one was injured, but the meeting was relocated in the basement.

One morning a member of the Royal Ulster Constabulary appeared at the Sinn Féin office in Belfast, claiming he was a journalist and had an interview booked. When the duty press officer said there was no such interview planned, the RUC man emptied his weapon into the unarmed occupants of the office and calmly walked out. He left three men dead—including a young father who had just come to the office with his two-year-old son, seeking advice about a domestic problem.

Northern media attention ignored the plight of the victims, preferring to focus on the RUC officer. According to them he was the victim. He was described as a hero who had "simply lost his head." Nationalists were blamed by inference for the killings, it being claimed that the "stressful situation" in which the officer was working was solely responsible for his mental breakdown.

The three Irish nationalists who went into their graves were mourned only by their families and friends. Nothing was said in the media about the stressful conditions in which they had lived for their whole lives.

Within days, UFF gunmen murdered five nationalists, including a fifteen-year-old boy, at Sean Graham's bookie shop on the Ormeau Road. Nine others were seriously wounded. The attack took place in broad daylight only a few minutes after a pair of RUC Land Rovers that had been parked across from the shop for most of the day finally drove away. The killers were never caught. No one was charged.

It became a tradition for members of the Orange Order parading down the Ormeau Road to tauntingly wave five fingers in front of Sean Graham's shop.

MARCH third saw four Catholic men shot dead when members of the UVF attacked a pub in Cappa, County Tyrone.

Eleven days later the Birmingham Six were freed after spending sixteen years in prison. The latest appeal against their convictions had been granted when it was proved that the scientific evidence against them was seriously flawed. The Appeals Court also accepted that the police had beaten their confessions out of them.[1]

"Terrorists Released!" screamed headlines in the unionist newspapers.

In May Danny Morrison, former publicity director for Sinn Féin, was convicted along with seven others of false imprisonment. They had been holding an RUC informer captive.

BARRY had prepared a small apartment for himself on the ground floor in Mountjoy Square. It was a convenient location from which to work on the house, though he no longer felt any urgency about completing the task. Nor knew what he would do with the place when he did.

In the basement he had set up a new darkroom. Elsewhere in the house he had replicated the secure hiding place in Harold's Cross, and stored his weapons and the notebooks.

A man of powerful sexual appetites, he missed Barbara very much—physically. Even his anger did not dampen his desire. He had spent a lifetime developing iron self-control, and he put it to use. He could go to Harold's Cross every evening and spend time with his children, speak in a civil tone to his wife, observe her full curves and creamy skin and those amazing tawny eyes—and then return to Mountjoy Square.

To lie awake at night, remembering her body and her skin and those tawny eyes.

When he thought about the bitter words Barbara had flung at him—which he often did, the way the tongue will continue to torment a sore tooth—he understood why she had said those things. She knew his soul, even if she did not understand it. Just as he knew hers.

We're chalk and cheese, he muttered to himself.

He was not guilty of "raising money for terrorists," though she probably would never believe him. She had known perfectly well what she was doing when she told an outsider about the notebooks. In retrospect she was sorry, as she always was when she was caught doing something she shouldn't, but that had not changed her true feelings about the IRA.

And somehow he did not care anymore.

Y O U R leg moved? Show me!" Breda demanded.

Ursula gripped the arms of the wheelchair and concentrated until sweat burst out on her forehead. "Just a minute; just a minute now . . . I can do it again."

And she did.

T H E U.S. launched Operation Desert Storm in Iraq, claiming the purpose was to liberate Kuwait. The Gulf War was broadcast on television, live and in colour. As millions of people watched day after day the war became entertainment rather than a news event.

O N the sixth of August, 1991, Tim Berners-Lee, a computer research scientist, posted an item on the

Internet that made public his creation, the World Wide Web.

And the world changed.

ACCORDING to the 1991 census of Northern Ireland, Catholics comprised 38.4 percent of the population. The figure might have been slightly skewed by the fact that a number of those questioned refused to admit to belonging to any organised religion at all.

And the number of murders committed by paramilitary organisations continued to grow, and grow. By the end of the year ninety-four more people would have died due to the Troubles.

IN November Sinn Féin held its Ard Fheis in Dublin. By a unanimous vote Dublin City Council refused Sinn Féin the use of the Mansion House, where other political parties frequently held their annual conferences.

Although he was not a member of Sinn Féin, Barry Halloran attended the Ard Fheis. He met old friends, took numerous photographs, and talked to everyone who would talk to him.

One of these was an elderly Frenchman who had retired to West Cork; a self-proclaimed socialist who recently had joined the party. Barry was interested to meet someone who had chosen to move into Ireland instead of out of it.

During a break for lunch the two men enjoyed a long conversation over the worst coffee Barry had ever tasted. He found himself boasting about his Swiss passport. "I'm a true European," he remarked.

The other man said, "The Americans and the British have no understanding of what it means to have one's homeland overrun by a foreign power. We French do. We also understand resistance very well indeed. In France we do not describe the IRA as terrorists. For us, the terrorists were those who collaborated with the Nazis.

"Shall I tell you about the spirit which fuels resistance? During the last days of the occupation of Paris, when we were still fighting at the barricades, we were joined by a small boy, a street urchin. He insisted that he wanted to fight for Paris too, but we would not give him a weapon. He was, after all, a *petit enfant*. Or so we thought.

"The little boy found a hand grenade somewhere and came trotting back toward us, proudly holding up his trophy. He was only a few metres away when a band of men carrying a Nazi flag entered the street. The little lad whirled around to throw his grenade at them. At that moment my comrades recognised them as fellow members of the Resistance who apparently had found their own trophy, and shouted a welcome to them.

"Tragically, the lad had already pulled the pin on his grenade. There was nowhere he could throw it without killing fellow members of the Resistance. I saw him take one deep breath, then, in the bravest act I saw during all that terrible war, the little fellow tucked the live grenade into his belly and curled himself into a ball around it, taking all the damage himself."

O N the fourth of December Charles Haughey met with John Major in Dublin. The two prime ministers agreed to meet twice a year thereafter.

W H E N Philpott answered the doorbell he saw Barry standing on the steps with a suitcase in either hand. "I've come home in time for Christmas," he said. "Don't ring Barbara, though. I'll tell her myself when she gets home from work."

"She's not at work. She quit her job at RTE a year ago."

"Sorry?"

"Didn't she tell you?"

"She did not tell me." Barry stepped into the house and put down his suitcases. "Do you mean she's been keeping it a secret all this time?"

"I don't think it was meant to be a secret; we all knew. I just assumed you did too."

"Who was that at the door?" Barbara called from the top of the stairs. She started to come down. Seeing Barry, she halted. "Why did you ring the doorbell instead of using your key?" Then she noticed the suitcases. She hurried the rest of the way. "Are you ready to apologise at last?"

"I don't apologise," he said.

She threw back her shoulders and lifted her chin. "Well, neither do I! Especially when I'm right. Do you think you can just waltz back in here anytime you choose?" She was trying hard to sound angry; trying to keep him from realising how thrilled she was that he was back.

"I do not think that, Barbara, which is why I rang the doorbell. I am asking if I may return."

Philpott scuttled off towards the kitchen.

Barbara already knew her answer, but she would not make it easy. "Why should I take you back, Barry?"

"Why should I stay away any longer?" he countered. "We've both made our points, have we not?"

The marriage did not resume where it had left off. Barbara insisted on what she called a "trial period," during which Barry was to sleep in another room. Now she was the one who lay awake at night. Thinking of him. Feeling him so close to her, only a few paces away. Wondering why she had ever let things go so far in the first place.

Home again, Barry slept soundly.

In Clare Ursula could barely sleep for excitement. She was planning a Christmas surprise for the family. Barry had promised he would drive down to collect herself and Breda a few days before Christmas.

•   •   •

O N the twenty-third of December the IRA again announced a three-day ceasefire—shortly after a series of IRA incendiary devices disrupted trains in London.

A s he had done so many times before, Barry lifted his mother into his car and stowed her wheelchair in the boot. Breda Cunningham did not say a word; let him help his little old crippled mother while she watched—with a twinkle in her eye.

Ursula's eyes were twinkling too.

The drive to Dublin was still wearying, though slightly more comfortable now that Barry had a bigger car. "Do you ever miss Apollo?" his mother asked.

"If I was going to miss that old car I never would have let it go. Which I didn't," he added with a chuckle. "Apollo's available for Barbara whenever she wants it."

"Does she drive to work?"

"She gave up her job at RTE almost a year ago."

Ursula turned in her seat so she could see his face. "Why did you not tell me?"

"I suppose I'm inclined to keep things to myself. I learned it from you after all."

In the backseat of the sedan, Breda Cunningham gave a snort. "It's easier to get information from a fence post than from your mother."

Ursula let a few more miles roll by before quietly asking Barry, "Have you told Barbara about . . . you know?"

By which he understood that his mother had never confided the secret of the Mountjoy Square house to Breda. "Not yet," he replied.

"Is it to be a surprise Christmas present, then?"

"She hasn't done anything to merit a present that big," he said brusquely, keeping his eyes on the road.

Oh dear, thought Ursula, *they're still quarrelling then.* The children had not mentioned it when they came to visit during the summer, but she knew. Ursula always knew things.

When the car pulled up in front of the yellow brick house the children ran out to meet them. "How tall they've grown since the summer!" Ursula cried.

"You have to expect changes," said Barbara.

On Christmas Eve morning the Hallorans opened their presents beside the tree. Patrick had become the official postman, reading aloud the name of the recipient, followed by the name of the sender. When all the presents had been identified Ursula said, with some surprise, "Is there nothing for any of you from Séamus?"

"Not yet," Patrick confirmed.

Tiny cold feet tracked across Ursula's heart.

"How about you?" Barry asked her. "Did you bring your present from him?"

"It had not arrived when I left."

"Speaking of presents," Barbara chimed in, "open that one next, Ursula." She indicated a beautifully wrapped package. "I picked it out especially for you."

On cue, Trot burst into a chorus of "The Spanish Lady." The package contained a large Spanish shawl made of silk. Barbara explained, "It's for you to drape over your lap when you go out in your chair."

Ursula caught Breda's eye. "Now," she mimed.

Breda bent down to make sure the chair's locking device was fastened.

Ursula took a firm hold on the arms of the chair. Leaned forward.

Stood up.

There was an astonished silence.

Ursula took one tentative step before her legs began to tremble. Barry leaped forward to catch her. "Mother," he said.

·　　·　　·

I N hospital that afternoon the doctor was able to confirm that Ursula really had regained the use of her legs. Not totally, but to a degree. "Some spinal cord damage does heal," he admitted. "We just don't know how or why."

"I can explain the why part," said Ursula. "I've been planning a trip to Boston to see an old friend of mine and I wanted to walk up to him in the airport."

As they were leaving the hospital Barry suggested, "You should ring Séamus and tell him the good news straightaway. It may be a while before you can actually walk again, but he'll want to know."

"You call him for me," said Ursula. In a small voice.

He placed the telephone call as soon as they returned to Harold's Cross. "Transatlantic phone lines are jammed at the moment," the operator reported, sounding regretful. "Please try again in half an hour."

Eventually the phone rang somewhere far off, in America. A disembodied voice announced, "We are sorry, but the number you have dialled is not in service."

Chapter Forty-one

A FTER working his way, with a combination of charm and guile, through various layers of the American telephone system, Barry learned that Séamus McCoy's telephone had been disconnected in August. The final bill had been paid in full at that time. The telephone company had no forwarding address for Mr. McCoy. Thank you for calling AT&T, Mr. Halloran.

Barry was worried. "Séamus may be in trouble," he told

Ursula. "I'm going over there to bring him back as soon as I can book a seat on Aer Lingus."

"You don't know where he is."

"Not yet, but there are people who will; our people. I'll find him."

Ursula laid a hand on her son's arm. "Don't try. If Séamus had wanted us to know he would have told us himself." Her gaze slid past him, fixing on a faraway place. "We always have cats at the farm," she remarked with seeming irrelevance, "to keep down the rats. Plain, unassuming cats who go about their business and ask no quarter from anyone. Cats have great dignity, Barry. When one of them feels the time has come to die, it goes off to die alone."

Barry's heart constricted. "You don't think . . ." He could not finish the question.

Ursula offered him hope she did not have herself. "Give it time. If Séamus wants to get in touch with us, he will."

Barry and his mother did not mention their concerns about McCoy to the rest of the family. "There'll be time enough when the holidays are over," they told each other. "Perhaps we'll have heard from him by then."

They had not, however. And Ursula was anxious to get back to the farm.

Barry argued, "Now that you've begun your recovery you should stay here in Dublin, so you can be close to specialists who can help you. You won't find a neurological team in Ennis, I already checked."

"I got this far without them," Ursula said. "I'll go the rest of the way on my own too."

She was adamant. So the suitcases and the wheelchair and Breda went back into Barry's car, the good-byes were said, and they set out for Clare. Barry could not help noticing how much more colour there was in his mother's cheeks after they crossed the Shannon River.

Before he left the farm Ursula, leaning heavily on his arm, managed to take four steps. She was not as jubilant

---

as one might have expected. "Whatever your problems with Barbara," she told her son, "resolve them sooner rather than later. Remember that life is very short, and of all wounds, regret most lacerates the heart."

"Ursula, you're not . . ."

"Don't look so worried. All things considered, I'm in amazing health. My problem is, I have too much life left over."

B Y 1992 the programme for Social Partnership that Charles Haughey had introduced in 1989 was beginning to show effects, although unemployment was still running at two hundred thousand and the young were still emigrating. The concept of having the trade unions work with the government, rather than against it, was taking time to develop, but its acceptance coincided with the arrival of increasing development funds from the EU.

Perhaps there was hope for the future.

O N the twenty-second of January former UDA intelligence officer Brian Nelson pleaded guilty to five charges of conspiracy to murder, as well as fifteen charges of possessing information that could be useful to loyalist paramilitaries. The charges of murder were then withdrawn. Nelson was sentenced to ten years in prison on the conspiracy charges. He would be out in a much shorter time.

A disgusted Brendan Delahanty told the remaining Usual Suspects, "There you see how the northern security forces protect themselves from justifying their actions."

I N February, after becoming embroiled in a wire-tapping scandal involving several journalists, Charles Haughey

resigned as *taoiseach*. He had led Fianna Fáil for eighteen
years. The new *taoiseach* was Albert Reynolds, a former
country music promoter who owned a pet food business.
Unlike his controversial predecessor, who had risen from
middle-class origins to become—as one of Haughey's
many enemies would one day admit—"a natural aristo-
crat," Reynolds was and always would be one of the plain
people of Ireland. He was also a self-made millionaire who
understood that the best way to get things done was to do
them himself.

I'M going to miss that old rogue Haughey," Ursula admitted.

Breda said, "You're a bit of a hero-worshipper, aren't
you?"

"I know it's unfashionable these days, like patriotism
and fidelity. But I believe in heroes, Breda. The very fact
that you sneer at the concept proves how badly we need
them. Our heroes have feet of clay because they're human; otherwise we would crucify them. We did it before."

Yet she was not as contemptuous of organised religion as
she had been in her youth. Sometimes in her wheelchair and
sometimes leaning heavily on Breda Cunningham, but walking, Ursula Halloran had begun attending Mass. Not weekly,
and certainly not daily like the deeply devout, but two or
three times a month. The rituals of her faith that she had
scorned for so long were like a pair of well-worn shoes. She
found herself sinking back into them with a sense of home-
coming.

The Volunteers in the early IRA, like Ned Halloran,
had been Irish men of their time; so deeply religious that
they blessed every operation before undertaking it. The
1969 split in the Army had devastated them, and the tur-
moil that followed had left many behind. Somewhere
along the way the Catholic Church had left Ursula behind

too—perhaps through its oppressively patriarchal attitude towards women.

But if she was honest with herself, and Ursula tried always to be honest with herself, she loved the fragrance of incense.

You get no credit for giving me my legs back, she silently told God from the middle of the second pew. *I did it myself, and it was bloody hard work too. You should have rewarded me instead of taking Séamus.*

Sitting on the bench beside her, Breda rattled her rosary beads.

But I won't hold that against you, Ursula continued. *Maybe he was in so much pain that he wanted to go and you were doing him a favour. Death isn't the worst thing in the world.*

While the service droned on she indulged herself in imagining how things would have been if the major decisions of her life had gone the other way.

But they didn't. What is, is.

THE Republic was rocked by revelations that the popular bishop of Galway, Eamonn Casey, had fathered a child with an American divorcee, Annie Murphy. It would prove to be the first chink in the fortress of the previously unassailable Catholic Church in Ireland.

Ireland's High Court refused to permit a fourteen-year-old girl identified only as "Miss X" to go to Britain for an abortion. The verdict, which became notorious as "the X Case," subsequently was overturned by the Supreme Court as Catholic values began to lose their stranglehold on Irish culture. Allegations of cruelty by members of religious orders perpetrated on children in their care were followed by outright accusations of pedophilia. Within a few years the Church would no longer be a major moral force in the lives of most Irish people.

Ireland was not the only place where institutions were under fire. Los Angeles was hit by race riots. Two days of looting, mayhem, and murder followed the abuse of a black man, Rodney King, by police. The abuse had been captured live on a video camera.

I n the early morning of July fifth, Kieran Patrick Abram, a Catholic from West Belfast, was on his way to his home off the Falls Road. A group of loyalists had been lying in wait for a Catholic—any Catholic. When Abram appeared they attacked him with wooden bats spiked with nails. The victim, whom a pathologist later described as "moderately intoxicated," was unable to defend himself, and died.

The judge hearing the case said, "It is an unfortunate and all too familiar aspect of life in Northern Ireland that the days leading up to the twelfth of July are fraught with violence and confrontation. Hatred and antagonism are aroused and the rituals surrounding what is supposed to be a celebration awaken and encourage those feelings."

The Orange Order was highly critical of the judge's remarks. In a statement issued by the Grand Orange Lodge of Ireland they stated, "Some of the judiciary have a reputation for making silly remarks, but an attempt to blacken the cultural, religious, and political expression of a people, and to relate it to a horrific killing, is not only obviously inaccurate but grossly offensive."[1]

M a n y unionists, and more specifically the loyalists, were not interested in conflict resolution. They only cared about consolidating their version of a Protestant identity that they perceived to be inextricably interwoven with the British culture. Yet it was not the religious aspect of that identity that they sought so grimly to retain, for the means they used had nothing to do with Christianity.

Barry felt sorry for them. Bereft of the tattered trappings of power they had flaunted for three hundred years, these staunch defenders of a long-extinct Union were beginning to learn how it felt to be dispossessed in a land they honestly believed was theirs.

A meeting of the Intergovernmental Conference in London decided that talks in Northern Ireland with an eye towards establishing a long-term and peaceful political arrangement in the province must be resumed.

Albert Reynolds agreed. The new *taoiseach* began making some exploratory overtures on his own towards the parties involved.

On the twenty-ninth of April political talks resumed at Stormont.

As summer approached, the tentative peace process, or at least the exploration of the possibility of a tentative peace process, developed several strands. British and Irish politicians met one another; members of Northern Ireland's political parties, with the exception of the DUP, met one another; even a few members of the various paramilitary organisations met one another. There was talk. There was rancour. There was mistrust.

But connections once established were not broken.

THAT spring the IRA bombing campaign in Britain hit a spectacular economic target by blowing up the Baltic Exchange in London, creating a staggering billion-pound insurance bill.

"One bomb in London is worth a hundred in Belfast" came back to haunt British ears.

And behind the scenes, in quiet rooms, the talking went on.

·   ·   ·

JOHN Major claimed his fourth successive victory to again lead the Conservative Party.

Ireland won the Eurovision again, with Linda Martin singing a song penned by Johnny Logan: "Why Me?"

And Eamon Casey resigned as bishop of Galway.

ON the fourth of September Peter McBride, eighteen, the young father of two small children, was stopped by the British army in Belfast. An identity check showed that he was not wanted by the police; a body search proved he was carrying no weapons. The attitude of the soldiers, however, was so aggressive that the frightened young man broke and ran. Guardsmen Mark Wright and James Fisher chased him and shot him in the back, killing him.

Although they were convicted of murder and given a life sentence, the British Army Board decided the two soldiers could continue in the army under an "exceptional circumstance" clause, describing the murder as "an error of judgement." Guardsman Fisher subsequently was promoted.

FOREIGN investors were beginning to take notice of the Republic of Ireland's favourable tax rates for new businesses.

Several large American firms opened branches in Ireland.

Developers began, cautiously at first but with increasing confidence, building new housing estates.

New car sales increased.

The National Roads Authority began building new motorways to allow the inhabitants of the new housing estates to get to their new jobs.

AN objective person travelling south from Northern Ireland would have noticed that the roads south of the border were beginning to look better than the roads north of the border. The ability to be objective was not, however, in the remit of leading unionists.

Fortunately it existed elsewhere. John Major's government was actively courting the republicans, sending as many as nineteen separate messages to the Sinn Féin leadership through various backchannels.[2] In 1992 the messages focussed on the Adams-Hume talks, which Sinn Féin called "the Irish peace initiative."

However Sinn Féin and the larger republican community remained dubious about the possibility of doing business with the British government. Every tenuous step must be analysed, criticised, and presented to the Army Council. Sinn Féin was becoming the accepted voice of the new republican movement but the Army Council was still the muscle.

And the muscle continued to be exercised.

T H E big obstacle when it came to restoring some form of internal government in Northern Ireland was, at least in Ian Paisley's opinion, centred around Articles 2 and 3 of the Irish Constitution. Paisley refused to consider any form of rapprochement with Irish nationalists as long as they retained a constitutional claim to the Six Counties.

"We'll never give it up," MacThomáis averred.

"What if that's the price of peace?" Barry asked.

MacThomáis folded his arms. "We'll never give it up."

Barry, who went everywhere and listened to everyone and had something of his mother's intuitive understanding of currents beneath the surface, was not so sure.

With the break in his marriage something had been broken in him. He now knew that nothing was set in stone. If peace eventually came—when peace eventually came—it would not be the peace the republicans had fought and died for, but an imperfect peace constructed of compromise. No glorious victory. No clear-cut moment when all the loose ends were tied up and everything made sense.

No.

Peace would be the peace of the scarred and broken body that gradually healed enough to go on living.

But isn't that itself a form of triumph? Look at Ursula. The flames of adversity that can destroy have only made her stronger.

Will make Ireland stronger.

Barry desperately wanted to believe that.

PRINCE Charles and his wife Diana separated.

A fire destroyed part of Windsor Castle.

Elizabeth, queen of England, declared 1992 had been her "anno horribilis."

STEP by step, Barry and Barbara tried to repair their damaged relationship. He brought her little gifts. She took a genuine interest in his photography. They worried together about Séamus McCoy, from whom no letter came. They congratulated each other on the achievements of their growing children.

They slept in the same bed again. And sometimes there was passion.

Barry courted passion not only for the physical release it bestowed, but for the freedom it granted from mental tyranny. The perpetual motion picture theatre that was the human brain, showing reruns of events one would far prefer to forget.

Chapter Forty-two

November 4, 1992

T H A T month, as a meeting of the Anglo-Irish conference
was being planned, the Unionist Party withdrew from the
talks process. After two years and a cost of over five million pounds, the latest efforts to get everyone to sit down together and discuss Northern Ireland's problems had failed.

W H E N the telephone in the hall shrilled its two-ring
bell tone as he passed by, Barry lifted the receiver and answered in his customary way: "Halloran here."

"Halloran here too," said a laughing voice.

"Ursula? Where are you? Are you in trouble, do you
need me to . . ."

"All I needed you to do was answer the telephone so I
could be certain my new mobile was working properly."

"Your new *what*?"

"Mobile phone," she replied smugly. "It's a handy device, every forward-thinking person should have one. My
number is 088 something; I have it written on a piece of
paper in my pocket anyway. Ring me whenever you like,
but don't talk too long. This costs money."

When the conversation ended her son went looking for his wife. "Ursula's bought herself a mobile phone, would you believe it? I can remember when she wouldn't even buy a fridge."

O N the sixteenth of December Sir Patrick Mayhew, former attorney general and newly appointed Northern Ireland secretary of state, said that British soldiers could be withdrawn if the IRA ended its campaign, and that Sinn Féin might then be included in the governmental process.

Eight days later the IRA called another three-day cease-fire.

T H A T Christmas the Dublin middle class noticed that it had a bit more money to spend than in the past. They began to make small, rather nervous jokes about the onset of a "Celtic Tiger Economy." It could not be true, of course; everyone knew Ireland was poor, always had been and always would be. But it was fun to dream about.

Barbara Halloran bought purpose-made Christmas gift wrap for the first time since her wedding.

O N the thirty-first of December the UDA issued a statement promising to intensify its campaign "to a ferocity never imagined."[1]

I N January the single European market came into effect.

A F T E R Patrick Shields and his son Diarmuid were murdered by the UVF in County Tyrone, Diarmuid's girlfriend committed suicide because she could not accept his loss.

In March a UDA gang shot dead four Catholic workers in Castlerock. On that day two of the possible three routes taken by the workmen, who travelled together in a van, had been closed in advance by the RUC. Following the only road left open, the workmen arrived at Gortree Place—where the gunmen were waiting for them.

IN England the Grand National entered history as the Grand National That Didn't Count. The greatest steeple-chase in the world had difficulties from the beginning, when the horses were called back after a false start. The race barely got under way again when a flagman began waving his red flag to signal another halt. By that time the full concentration of the jockeys was on the race ahead and they did not notice. A number of horses completed the four-mile course over thirty daunting fences—only to have their jockeys and owners learn that the entire race had been disallowed.

ON the twentieth of March the IRA planted two bombs in litter bins at the Gold Square Shopping Centre in Warrington, Northern Ireland. Two little boys died: Jonathan Ball, age three, and Timothy Parry, age twelve, causing a wave of revulsion.[2]

Timothy Parry's father Colm expressed his family's gratitude for the many messages of sympathy and support they received. Subsequently he and his wife were instrumental in founding the Timothy Parry Trust Fund, which was established to promote greater understanding between Great Britain and the two parts of Ireland.

AFTER their second meeting in two weeks, Gerry Adams and John Hume issued a joint statement. "The Irish people as a whole have a right to national self-determination. This is a view shared by a majority of the people of this island, though not by all its people." They continued by saying, "As leaders of our respective parties we have told each other that we see the task of reaching agreement on a peaceful and democratic accord for all on this island as our primary challenge."[3]

W H E N Alfred Reynolds was reelected by the Dáil as *taoiseach,* Barry took his photograph in Leinster House—standing in front of a portrait of Patrick Pearse.

Following Des O'Malley's resignation as head of the Progressive Democrats, Mary Harney became the first woman to lead an Irish political party. Barry photographed her too.

Later he invited Barbara into the darkroom to help him decide amongst the negatives of the new PD leader. "Pick the one that makes her look prettiest," Barbara said.

"Male politicians can be handsome, Barbara—take Bill Clinton for instance. Or even Ronald Reagan. But being 'pretty' would be a definite liability for a female politician in Ireland."

"I don't see why. What if I ran for office, would you tell me not to look my best?"

"I'd tell you not to waste your time," he said.

She flounced out to the kitchen to listen to the Irish pop group, The Cranberries, sing "Linger" on the radio.

A E R Lingus began direct flights between Dublin and the United States that summer. All planes were no longer required to stop at Shannon. Chambers of Commerce from Kerry to Galway worried that huge amounts of tourist business would be lost, but Ursula was delighted. She rang Barry to say, "This will make it easier for buyers to come over here and look at my horses!"

"I'm surprised you're still so involved with the business end of things," he told her.

"What do you want me to do, sit in my chair and knit? I don't have to because Breda's taking up knitting instead. Between us we have this whole Old Woman business covered."

T H A T summer Israel and Palestine signed a peace agreement that gave Palestinian areas in the disputed territories limited self-rule.

For the first time, the Republic of Ireland under coach Jack Charlton qualified for the World Cup of Soccer. The nation went soccer-mad.

And Barry finally decided there was nothing left to be done to the house on Mountjoy Square.

He walked through it one more time, bottom to top. Smelling the fresh plaster, noting the coats of magnolia paint that created a neutral backdrop for the gracious, high-ceilinged rooms. His mind peopled those rooms with his family and his friends.

If you make a dream come true what do you have left to wish for?

He could not bear the thought of another family living in the house, because in some ways it was very much his own personal place, just as the farm was his mother's. But there were too many fault lines remaining in his marriage. To bring Barbara here, with all the attendant upheaval, might reveal them and crack the whole thing open again.

He compromised. He put the house with an estate agent to let as office space—retaining one apartment on the top floor for Barry Halloran.

T H E area stretching from Derry city along the northern coast through County Derry to North Antrim was under the control of a single UDA brigade. The territory included both rural and urban communities whose one unifying aspect was the fact that they all were subject to the whims of a highly organised paramilitary group who colluded with state forces to maintain a reign of terror.

Terrorism was not limited to Ireland. Six people were killed in a bomb attack on the World Trade Center in New York.

AFTER John Hume had a private meeting in London with John Major, he made a public statement. Hume said he did not "give two balls of roasted snow" for the people who were criticising his continuing discussions with Gerry Adams.

IN October nine people—two of them children—died in Belfast when the IRA bombed a chip shop in the Shankill. Halloween night brought more horror when two loyalists entered the Rising Sun bar in the village of Greysteele, County Derry; a pub frequented by Catholics. Stephen Irwin and Torrens Knight,* both members of the Ulster Defence Association, shouted "Trick or treat!" Knight, holding a shotgun, then stood guard at the door while his partner sprayed the pub with bullets. Nineteen were seriously injured; eight died.

The gun attack took place within view of an RUC barracks, yet the killers appeared unconcerned about any surveillance. After making their getaway they even returned to the scene of the crime, driving slowly past again for a second look.

No law officer stopped them.

*In 2006 Knight was exposed as having been an RUC Special Branch agent. Although convicted of a total of twelve UDA murders, he was paid £50,000 a year through a bogus Special Branch account.

• • •

THAT month a total of twenty-seven men, women, and children in Northern Ireland died as a direct result of the Troubles, the greatest number in any month since October of 1976.

In November John Major said that terrorists would have to be persuaded to end violence unconditionally. In the media his words were widely reported as claiming, "The IRA have to end violence unconditionally." No mention was made of the loyalists.

As a result of the long-running Hume-Adams talks, on the fifteenth of December 1993 Albert Reynolds and John Major jointly issued the Downing Street Declaration, agreeing to a peaceful and constructive policy on Northern Ireland and committing both governments to its implementation.

The people of the Republic were divided in their reactions. The very fact that Gerry Adams had been partly instrumental in bringing about the step forward was seen by many as sinister. The Troubles had enforced a revisionist view of history. Driven by political expediency disseminated through the media, Irish people were embarrassed by their patriotic past and nervous of republicanism in general.

The Fianna Fáil Party no longer publicly described itself as the republican party.

PROSPERITY was no longer a distant dream for the middle class in the Republic of Ireland. There really were jobs that paid good money. Foreign companies were clamouring for highly educated young people.

At first slowly, but with gathering momentum, the queues of the unemployed at the Social Welfare offices shortened. New department stores and shopping centres opened. The plain people of Ireland were becoming less poor.

Sprawling housing estates sprang into being around Dublin; every house as identical as if cloned, but *new*. Some people actually bought new cars, with or without the complicity of their banks. The plain people of Ireland were becoming financially comfortable.

Credit cards proliferated, and with them the desire for more. More of everything! Some of the plain people of Ireland were becoming wealthy for the first time in centuries.

Ireland, once the Poor Man of Europe, was moving up the scale of national wealth. People referred to the Celtic Tiger with growing pride.

Emigration slowed, reversed, became immigration as the children of the Irish Diaspora began returning home to take part in an economic miracle—bringing their skills and abilities with them.

I N January of 1994, and despite objections from John Major's British government and the U.S. State Department, President Bill Clinton granted a forty-eight-hour visa to Gerry Adams following intense lobbying on the part of prominent Irish Americans.

Even this achievement was a mixed blessing. The republican movement was once more dividing itself: the theorists versus the practical. The split was ideological, but with their guns and bombs the latter, the dedicated physical force men, were reacting to a physical situation and not a political situation.

The bombings and shootings continued in the north.

On both sides.

But the Irish government announced that the order which banned representatives of Sinn Féin from appearing on radio or television would not be renewed.

As Gerry Adams had become more prominent in the political news Ireland's national television service could hardly ignore him, but had reached a farcical compromise. Until 1994 film of Adams had been shown with his voice dubbed by another actor.

Now the people of the Republic heard the man himself. His unmistakable Belfast accent; his thoughtful, articulate speech. Neither strident nor bellicose, he did not engage in the name-calling that was so much a part of northern politics. He talked about sacrifice and possibilities.

Gerry Adams speaking rationally to them from their television screens was a bit of a shock to the plain people of Ireland.

I N May President Mary Robinson was greeted by Queen Elizabeth II at Buckingham Palace. It was the first official contact ever between an Irish president and a British monarch.

A month later Mrs. Robinson was viciously condemned north and south for shaking hands with Gerry Adams during a private reception for community leaders in West Belfast.

T H E Heights Bar, a Catholic pub in Loughinisland, had purchased a big new television set to allow its patrons to watch Ireland play Italy in the World Cup. On June eighteenth the crowd was enjoying the game when three men entered the bar wearing balaclavas and boiler suits and carrying guns. They opened fire on the crowd, killing six men, then made their getaway in a red car that had been waiting outside.

Six weeks later a holdall belonging to the RUC was accidentally discovered by sanitation workers. It contained three balaclavas, three boiler suits, three sets of gloves, and three pistols.

When the getaway car used in the attack—a distinctive Triumph Acclaim—was found and identified by a number of witnesses, it emerged that the automobile belonged to an RUC Special Branch agent who was also a member of the Mount Vernon UVF and an explosives expert. After taking custody of the car the RUC destroyed it. No forensic evidence was retained.[4]

L A T E R that summer IRA veteran Joe Cahill was granted a U.S. visa to prepare Irish Americans for the possibility of a sustained IRA ceasefire.

When Cahill returned to Ireland Barry was on hand at the airport to take his photograph. The grand old man of Irish republicanism looked tired.

"We're all tired," Éamonn MacThomáis remarked later. "Do you really think there could be a longer ceasefire?"

"Do you?" Barry retorted.

"I'd like to think so—and then again I wouldn't. Not unless it really accomplished something."

"A ceasefire alone won't bring about a united Ireland, Éamonn."

"What will?"

"I wish to God I knew. Sometimes I think I'm mistaking politics for real life," Barry said ruefully, "and idealism for common sense."

The two old friends sat in a deepening twilight and pondered on possibilities.

They both knew that with the passage of time sensibilities had become eroded. Men who had joined the Army to protect Catholics and/or reunite Ireland had changed their focus to conducting an all-out war against the British. British Intelligence agents who had been recruited "to help save lives in Northern Ireland" also accepted the premise of war that justified any sort of behaviour, no matter how brutal or immoral.

Barry knew how to recognise the hard men; the real hard men. They lived in a place back behind their eyes where no one else could go. In spite of what the general public had been led to believe they constituted only a tiny percentage of the Provisionals. The real hard men gravitated to the splinter groups, which pursued a more militant policy.

E UROVISION 1994 was held in Ireland, which won the award for the third consecutive year with a song called "Rock and Roll Kids." But what everyone would remember was the entertainment during the interval. An original musical production called *Riverdance* used haunting music and lighting effects to introduce a breathtaking spectacle of precision tap dancing. *Riverdance* combined the traditional with the contemporary to create a new dimension in Irish dance—making it, for the first time, sexy.

W HEN the *Irish Press* leaked plans being drawn up in Dublin to encourage the British government to acknowledge the legitimacy of the goal of Irish unity, Ulster Unionist MP David Trimble stated flatly, "The Unionists will not be party to the marginalisation of the unionist community."

O N the fifteenth of August John Bruton, the leader of the Fine Gael Party, stated unequivocally that in his opinion Sinn Féin could play no part in the political process in Ireland until the IRA called for a total cessation of violence.

Both the Ulster Unionists and the DUP promptly made similar statements.

R IGHT now they're talking as if all they want is a ceasefire, but supposing they get it," MacThomáis said to Barry. "Will the unionists raise the bar and demand something more, and something more, until there's nothing left to give and it still won't be good enough for them?"

Barry drove north. He could not say what in particular impelled him, but he *knew*. He was on hand to take the historic photograph when Gerry Adams announced that he had met with the Army Council and been told that conditions existed for moving the peace process forward.

Chapter Forty-three

RECOGNISING the potential of the current situation and in order to enhance the democratic peace process and underline our definitive commitment to its success the leadership of Óglaigh na hÉireann have decided that as of midnight, Wednesday, 31 August, there will be a complete cessation of military operations. Others, not least the British government, have a duty to face up to their responsibilities. It is our desire to significantly contribute to the creation of a climate which will encourage this. We urge everyone to approach this new situation with energy, determination, and patience."

FOR Barry, the road ahead shone like a river. Ursula was less sanguine about the future. "The Volunteers have been so convinced they would win the Six back through their own efforts, and now it looks like it's not going to happen that way. It's so anticipointing."

As usual, Barry understood what she meant. "Anticipation will probably turn into disappointment a hundred times more," he told her, "but we're going to get there. We are."

Denis Bradley, who helped negotiate the IRA ceasefire

by serving as a link between the Army and the British government, had been the curate who gave last rites to three dying men on Bloody Sunday.

The announcement by the IRA of an open-ended cease-fire was greeted by celebration in nationalist areas of the north, and by almost immediate scorn from unionists and loyalists, who pronounced it a lie and a trick.

It was not.

The Army's guns fell silent.

O n the first of September a Catholic man was killed in Belfast by the UFF.

Five days later, after a meeting in Dublin, Albert Reynolds, John Hume, and Gerry Adams issued a joint statement: "We are at the beginning of a new era in which we are totally and absolutely committed to democratic and peaceful means of resolving our political problems."

I n October of 1994 the loyalists, led by Gusty Spence, also called a ceasefire.

T h e materialistic influence of the Celtic Tiger was cre-ating an apolitical generation of young people whose in-terests centred on what they could buy and who would be impressed by it, but Barry's children had been raised in a house where the news was still the most important pro-gramme of the day. No matter what they were doing, they were home at six in the evening and gathered around the television.

"Does it really mean there's going to be peace in the north?" Trot asked her father.

He was careful with his answer. One must not lie to one's children. "What it means is, there are brave men who are willing to risk it."

He knew the threats that had been made against Adams, McGuinness, and other members of the Sinn Féin leadership—and not just from the unionist side. As Barry told his children, the dissident republican groups were also determined to silence the voice of peace.

"But why?" Patrick wanted to know.

"Because when men have fought very hard for a very long time, it can be hard for them to give it up. They may have learned to define themselves by war. They may even enjoy it."

Trot said, with the vast superiority her sex enjoyed over mere males, "That's ridiculous, how can anyone enjoy war? If women ran the world it would be different."

"What about Boadicea?" challenged Brian. "What about Margaret Thatcher? They were *warriors*!"

"Da's a warrior," Patrick said loyally. "You were in the Army, weren't you?"

Barry nodded. "I was in the Army. For a long time."

"Why aren't you in the Army now then?"

Against his conscious will, Barry's gaze slid past his children. Looked back at a faraway place.

Why did I never return to active service? God knows I had adequate reason. I would have given anything to go up the road with Séamus when he was seeking revenge for Ursula.

He knew the answer well enough. Had carried it hidden inside him for so many years. There are secrets of conscience and secrets of the heart, and this was both.

Barry longed to be alone in the cool clarity of a summer dawn in Clare. To wait, holding his breath, for the first sweet distant music of birdsong that affirmed the unbroken chain of life. To escape from his memories of 1957 and the Brookeborough Raid.

But they were right there where they had always been, just below the surface. When he let his guard down they came flooding back.

After abandoning his post to be with his company, Barry had vaulted over the tailgate of the lorry that brought them to Brookeborough. At that moment a snapshot was forever burned into his brain. Inside was a scene from a slaughterhouse. On the bullet-riddled walls of the truck blood was splashed as high as a man's head. Seán South sprawled motionless across the Bren gun. Beside him lay Paddy O'Regan, gasping with pain. Phillip O'Donoghue sat cross-legged with his face bathed in blood. Seán Garland's trousers were soaked with it, though he was still on his feet.

Barry's best friend, Feargal O'Hanlon, lay on his back. A bullet had smashed his femur. Blood fountained in spurts from a severed artery.

The driver of the lorry threw it into gear and tried desperately to get the injured men away. A single constable ran after them, shouting, "Come back, you fuckin' Fenians!"

Kneeling beside his friend, Barry saw Feargal's eyes go blank.

Barry gave a terrible cry and leaped to his feet with his rifle in his hands. Just beyond the tailboard was the constable in hot pursuit.

Barry shot the man in the face. The thunder of the rifle rang through his living bones.

And he loved it.

God help me, I loved it. Loved the power of watching another man's face bloom into a terrible red flower for an instant before it dissolved into a bloody mush.

What sort of man did that make me?

Appalled by the feelings he had discovered in himself, Barry had set the rifle aside and chosen a different weapon. The bomb.

He could build a bomb and be miles away when it went off; he did not feed the monster inside him by watching death take place.

Then he learned that a bomb had killed his father, and a

different bomb had crippled Ursula, and he was left with no weapon. Only the terrible knowledge that a killer lived in his skin.

He had dedicated the rest of his life to holding that killer at bay.

I N what might have been peace, in what would have been peace if there was enough goodwill on both sides, Northern Ireland waited to see what would happen next.

In the Republic the economic boom continued. New middle-class housing estates blossomed around Dublin and overflowed into the countryside, devouring farmland. "Bungalow bliss" became a euphemism for unchecked growth.

As identical characterless houses began to spring up like toadstools in Clare, and especially around Galway, with no infrastructure to support them, Ursula was scathing in her denunciation of the government's lack of forward planning. "Our so-called politicians are the cream of Ireland," she complained to Breda, "rich and thick. And they're getting rich by selling off the country!"

"They say growth is good for the country. All this building is creating jobs and we have to have jobs."

"We have the sort of government that would urinate down your neck and tell you it was raining," Ursula replied scornfully. "I'll make a prediction about the new millennium. You're going to see politicians using weapons of mass deception against their own people as never before."

The Millennium. People were beginning to use that term, half eagerly, half fearfully. It was approaching like an express train, just a few years down the tracks.

And the IRA ceasefire was holding.

Changes were coming thick and fast; too fast for Ursula, she sometimes thought. Throughout her life she had been a rebel, a modern woman consciously breaking free from the tradition-hobbled past. Now she was beginning to feel overwhelmed by them. "Ours was the first house on our road to get electricity," she told Breda. "In fact I know of one or two old farmers who still refuse to have their houses wired. Maybe they have the right idea."

FOLLOWING Albert Reynolds' resignation after the government failed to deal with a scandal involving clerical pedophilia, on the fifteenth of December John Bruton of Fine Gael became *taoiseach* at the head of a coalition government with Labour. The wealthy Meath landowner was bitterly opposed to both Sinn Féin and the IRA.

THE cubs of the Celtic Tiger, two generations from tenement stock, four generations away from the bog, were reinventing themselves.

They began drinking Château Rothschild in posh hotels and patronising exclusive art galleries, invitation only. Buying Mercs and Beamers, chatting on their mobiles, doing deals over the Net, maxing out their new credit cards, indebting themselves to the bank for half a lifetime in order to buy a million-pound house whose actual worth in terms of bricks and mortar was only sixty thousand.

Ursula Halloran, a onetime child of the tenements who had reinvented herself, understood the Tiger's cubs very well.

"Now Ireland has its own clambering class," she remarked one cold afternoon. A fire was blazing in the parlour where the Hallorans, replete with one of Philpott's lunches, had gathered to enjoy the blinking lights on the Christmas tree. Their number was reduced by one; Brian had departed to take a present to his girlfriend, amidst derision from his siblings.

Barbara said, "What do you mean by clambering class?"

"People scrambling over one another in their haste to get to the top," Ursula replied.

Barry was amused. *There she sits with her glass of straight whiskey and her mobile phone. Not a lady; something finer than that. A person of easy quiet manners and great steadiness of character, like all the best-bred people.*

His mind became a runaway horse, careening here and there, beyond reason. *I could take us all to live in Mountjoy Square. Ursula and Breda too. The entire Halloran clan, looking like we belong in this new Ireland.*

Glancing up, he saw Barbara watching him. Reading the faint frown stitched on his brow. "What?" she mouthed silently.

"I'm just going to get another drink," he told her. "Do you want one?"

Before she returned to Clare, Brian proudly showed his grandmother his new computer. "It's great," he told her. "You should buy one, Nana. I've put all our accounts on it."

Not all our accounts, Barry said to himself. Thinking of the house on Mountjoy Square, and the separate bank account he had established for its rental income. The money was earmarked to pay off the mortgage. When that was done . . .

"Somewhere along the way," Ursula said, warily eyeing the computer, "my machinery's slowed down. The more modern technology I see the older I feel. I'm sure computers make everything easier and faster and so forth and so forth, but I like to keep everything simple and manageable. What if I learned to rely on a computer and the electricity went? All it takes is one bad storm and a tree falling across wires someplace. I can replace the electric lights with lanterns and keep the house warm with a good big fire in the fireplace, but how could I run the farm if I couldn't get access to the financial accounts and the breeding records?"

"That's old-fashioned thinking," her oldest grandson informed her. "Men have walked on the moon, don't you know that? And it took computers to do it."

That night in bed Barry told Barbara, "When I listen to

the kids sometimes I feel positively ancient. I was born in 1939; before penicillin, frozen foods, credit cards, and contact lenses. During my youth we never heard of instant coffee, much less pizza. There were no Italian restaurants in Ireland and no Chinese takeaway. No yoghurt. We thought fast food was what you ate during Lent. To us, a Big Mac was a large overcoat.

"I predate transistors, videos, and computers. When I was a boy hardware referred to nuts and bolts and software wasn't a word at all. We knew nothing of split atoms, laser beams, microwave ovens, or word processors. We didn't even have ballpoint pens.

"If we described a person as gay we meant they were the life of the party. Grass was something to mow and pot was what our mothers cooked in. Coke was what people kept in the coal shed. As for heroin . . . well, Constance Markievicz was a heroine. Or Maud Gonne.

"Were we deprived? We didn't think so, we thought we were the modern generation. We didn't have most of the things our children think are essential these days."

Barbara put a sympathetic hand on his shoulder. "But you could drink the water without putting chemicals in it," she said. "And the air you breathed was clean."

I N January of 1995 John Bruton and Dick Spring of the Labour Party held their first formal meeting with representatives of Sinn Féin. The two sides were wary with one another. Shortly afterwards, a meeting between Sinn Féin and officials of the Northern Ireland Office was cancelled when Sinn Féin learned the room had been electronically bugged.

A Framework for Accountable Government in Northern Ireland was published by the NIO in February, proposing a Northern Assembly consisting of about ninety elected members representing all the political parties.

The unionists reacted with horror. John Major made a

conciliatory speech in the House of Commons. Sir Patrick Mayhew subsequently repeated the unionists' demand for IRA decommissioning.

In March the Ulster Unionists announced that they rejected the framework document in its entirety.

Yet progress continued, like grass growing through broken pavement.

The White House announced that Gerry Adams would be allowed to raise funds in the United States. He was also invited to attend President Clinton's St. Patrick's Day reception, which outraged the British prime minister.

AND the Millennium drew closer.

A bomb outside a government building in the U.S. state of Oklahoma killed 168 people. Timothy McVeigh and Terry Nichols were arrested and charged with the atrocity.

Irish poet Séamus Heaney won the Nobel Prize for Literature.

Irish pop group Boyzone had a chart topper with "Love Me for a Reason."

TIME was telescoping. Barry was increasingly aware of the fact. The many things he had once planned to do with his life had faded into distant dreams. He was able to drive past the house on Mountjoy Square—which now housed two insurance agencies and a charity that wanted to keep its location secret—without feeling any pangs.

From time to time he visited his apartment on the top floor and looked out at the city stretched below him. Wondering what Brian Boru would have made of it all.

One morning he stayed in bed longer than usual, wondering where his energy had gone. When he finally dressed and went down to the kitchen he found Barbara laughing.

"What's so funny?" he asked.

"I was just listening to one of those morning chat shows," she told him. "A feisty little old lady rang in to take the Dublin postmaster to task because the tricolour doesn't fly over the General Post Office on the weekends. She was very exercised about it. She said, 'If JCPenney right next door can fly the flag on Sunday why can't the post office? Men and women died for the right to fly that flag.' The presenter asked her if she had people in the GPO in 1916, and you know what she said? She said, 'We *all* had people in the GPO!' " Barbara laughed again.

Barry did not laugh. "She was right, Barbara. Every person enjoying the benefits of living in Ireland today 'had people in the GPO in 1916.' "

She started to say something; met his eyes; thought better of it. *Sometimes it's easier to let it go,* she told herself, *than fight over every tiny little thing.*

I N July Sinn Féin pulled out of talks with the British government when the subject of decommissioning was brought up, pointing out that it had not been on the table when the IRA called their ceasefire.

A second divorce referendum was put to the Irish public. In spite of dire predictions by the Church that farmers would lose their land and the family as a unit would be destroyed, the referendum narrowly passed.

"Ireland just entered the twentieth century," Ursula Halloran commented. "A little late, that's all."

I N the autumn David Trimble of the UUP met with President Clinton in Washington to put forward the unionist view.

Back in Ireland another version of what had come to be

known as "the way forward" was proposed. Invitations were issued to all parties to participate in intensive talks about the future of the north, with former American senator George Mitchell in the chair.

On the thirtieth of November Bill Clinton became the first serving president of the United States to visit Northern Ireland. Accompanied by his wife Hillary and daughter Chelsea, he arrived in Ireland to a rapturous welcome. They spent a day in Northern Ireland before moving on to Dublin, where eighty thousand people jammed into College Green to cheer the man who had taken a hand in the Northern Peace Process.

His obvious interest in and understanding of the situation impressed northern nationalists, but the unionists were dismissive.

As if his recent visit to Washington had never taken place, David Trimble stated, "We are not prepared to negotiate the internal affairs of Northern Ireland with a foreign government."

ALTHOUGH very little appeared to change on the surface, those who kept statistics observed that in the year just past only nine deaths in Northern Ireland had risen directly from the Troubles.

Chapter Forty-four

————◆◇◆————

"How can it be 1996 already?" Barbara asked indignantly. She was sitting at her dressing table, staring into the looking glass at a largely imaginary spiderweb of wrinkles. "Look at me," she said to Barry. "I'm old."

He looked.

She was not.

"Don't be ridiculous," he told her. "And what difference does changing the calendar make anyway?"

"It makes a lot of difference to a woman. When she's young a day is a year. When she's old a year is a day."

"That sounds like something my mother would say." He expected Barbara to take offence but she did not.

"Your mother's a wise woman, Barry."

"If she were wiser she would come and live with us instead of insisting on living at the farm. She really is old, you know. We figure she was born around 1910, so . . ."

"I can count." Barbara kept studying her reflection. "When I'm that old do you suppose one of our children will want me to live with them?"

"You'll never be old," said Barry. He knew the lines expected of him by now.

"Yes, but if I *was*."

He took her in his arms and showed her how young she was.

THE Mitchell Report was published in January of 1996, specifying six principles of nonviolence for entrance into all-party talks. British prime minister John Major rejected the report. Irish republicans were bitterly disappointed that the British government had failed to live up to its commitments.

The IRA ceasefire came to a violent end on the ninth of February, shortly after the leadership released a statement that said in part, "The cessation created an historic challenge for everyone. Óglaigh na hÉireann rose to the challenge. The British prime minister did not."

At seven that evening bombs in Canary Wharf, London, destroyed part of the financial district and killed two people.[1] The very fabric of the city had become an unstable geology where massive buildings might suddenly leap out into the street.

IRA violence was back on television screens in a very big way.

In March Bill Clinton bluntly refused to meet with Gerry Adams, who was in the U.S. on a six-day visa.

MAY saw elections held in Northern Ireland to select representatives to all-party talks. Sinn Féin polled a record vote. The following month, after increasingly hostile demands from the DUP, Sinn Féin was barred from the all-party talks.

"Sometimes the bullies win," Barry regretfully told his children. "With people like that it's all duck or no dinner."

GERRY Adams announced that Sinn Féin would agree to the Mitchell Principles, but gave no indication of a renewed IRA ceasefire.

VERONICA Guerin, an investigative journalist for the Sunday *Independent,* was working on a series of articles exposing the leaders behind Ireland's rapidly expanding drug gangs. On a bright June day Guerin was driving home after an appearance in court connected with a traffic offence of her own. When she stopped at a red light on the Naas Road a motorcycle pulled up beside her. Seconds later the crusading journalist was shot dead at point blank range by the cycle's pillion passenger.

W H E N Teilifís na Gaeilge, the Republic's first Irish language television channel, began transmission from Galway, Ursula Halloran sent three dozen red roses.

A N increasingly confident Republic was gathering in its lost children. The immigrants were coming home. In spite of the hysterical denials of the unionists a united Ireland was indisputably the future, if only as a result of demographic change.

Yet both the British and the Irish media continued to complain about terrorists. IRA terrorists, as if there could be no other kind.

In a highly polarised Northern Ireland there was more than enough terror to go around. People were dying again.

W H Y can't someone stop the terrorists?" Barbara moaned when the latest northern atrocity was splashed across the evening news.

"Stop the terrorists?" Barry shook his head. "You've got it wrong way round. People don't suddenly wake up one morning and say, 'I think I'll go plant bombs and shoot civilians.' What you call terrorists act out of desperation resulting from injustice and oppression, Barbara. It takes a long time for the rage to boil over, but as long as those causative factors remain the problems will continue. Remove the causative factors, work with sincerity and honesty to develop trust, and you will eliminate terrorism."

To his surprise he realised she was really listening to him rather than arguing with him.

Barry still took the requisite photographs and compiled the stories that interested him. But it was an act of self-preservation to distance himself to some degree from the political arena. He could not keep on breaking his heart over every false hope, every crushing collapse.

Éamonn MacThomáis understood. Since his last time in prison Éamonn had tried to build a new life for himself. He now conducted guided tours of the old Irish Parliament building—Barry Halloran's bank—across from Trinity College.

"You're one of the few people in this country who's actually making a living out of the past," Barry told him with a touch of envy.

"Someday it will all be valuable. We'll grow up and start caring about who we were and where we came from."

"You're still an optimist, Éamonn."

"Perhaps I am," the other agreed. "But not as much as I used to be."

In her sixties Ursula had thought often and sometimes obsessively about death. In her eighties the subject rarely crossed her mind.

"As soon as I faced the fact there was going to be no reprieve for wonderful special Me, I was able to concentrate on living," she told Breda Cunningham while the two were in the kitchen, doing the washing up together.

The other woman laughed. "So here you are at my mercy."

"If you think about it, we are all at one another's mercy," said Ursula. "What sort of life is it for you, being a paid companion?"

Breda laughed again and wiped her hands on her apron.

"Och sure, it's the other way round. You're my companion, Ursula. I'd rather be here with you any day than sitting in some drab little room in Dublin."

"Barry's trying to get me to move back there, you know."

"I know. He tells me. But I tell him, 'As long as the two of us rub along so well together and we're both in the whole of our health, why change?' "

THE latest Northern Ireland Assembly at Stormont, which had been established in 1973 and collapsed and restored more than once in the interim, was in trouble again. In the June elections the balance of power shifted somewhat, with the nationalist parties—Sinn Féin and the SDLP—gaining votes, though not enough to make a major difference. But it was enough to arouse the ire of the DUP. Their foremost representative took to the airways to hurl a number of vague but vicious charges at the nationalists.

Programmers in radio and television did not invite his victims to come in and defend themselves.

THERE were deep divisions in the unionist electorate in general. The only thing they could agree on was that they all hated Sinn Féin—which kept on winning more votes among the plain people of the north.

AMONG the loyalist paramilitaries in the north an on-and-off ceasefire condition had existed for some time. It was off when the IRA was quiescent; it was on again the moment the Army looked about to retaliate.

BARRY Halloran drove north again in September to photograph David Trimble and Gerry Adams having the first official meeting between a Unionist and a Sinn Féin leader in more than seventy-five years.

Afterwards Barry parked his car on the long avenue leading up to Stormont and waited for a heavy bank of cloud to pass away. He wanted a sunlit photograph of the huge statue of Sir Edward Carson, founder of the Ulster Unionists, which dominated the avenue. Arms outstretched as if he would embrace and control the north for a thousand years.

While Barry waited he noticed a small black figure on one of those arms. He quietly got out of his car and walked closer. The figure resolved itself into a tiny robin, watching with cocked head as he approached.

Barry went back to his car, installed a telephoto lens on one of his cameras, and took a picture of the robin instead.

It made him feel better.

THAT autumn the British government received a fresh set of proposals from Sinn Féin. The party asked that its representatives be allowed immediate admission to all-party talks in the event of a ceasefire.

The words "in the event of a ceasefire" sounded hopeful.

The DUP immediately announced that a ceasefire would not be enough. They now demanded full decommissioning.

BARRY rarely called in to the Bleeding Horse anymore. The years were taking their inevitable toll. Brendan had quietly died in his sleep, Luke had gone to Manchester to live with his married daughter, and Patsy had Alzheimer's disease and did not recognise himself, much less an old friend.

Occasionally Barry met Éamonn MacThomáis in one of the other republican pubs, or even outside the Bank of Ireland, and they talked about whatever the current situation was. It was always the same and yet it was not, and both men knew it. They were waiting.

Ireland was waiting.

At least once every time they met, Barry asked Éamonn, or Éamonn asked Barry, "Do you think we'll live to see a united Ireland?" And the other man always replied, "We will of course."

By now neither believed it. The years were taking their toll on them too. *Life is such a lonely battle,* Barry thought, *with the absolute certainty that in the end, you lose. But doesn't that make the battle itself more important? Real heroism lies in taking the blows with head held high, fighting on with all the courage one possesses in a doomed but valiant cause.*

Neither man ever said the reunification of Ireland was a doomed but valiant cause. Neither man could afford to believe that.

I N spite of her lion's heart, Ursula was aware that her body was increasingly frail. As frost blurs the view through a windowpane, the passage of time was beginning to blur the sharp edges of the world around her. Her memories were a scrapbook bulging with clear, unfading snapshots. Compared to their bright reality the present seemed less important.

When she realised this was happening she gave herself a good talking-to.

One of the Clare newspapers sent a features writer to the farm to request an interview with Ursula. He explained, "I'm doing an article on people whose lives have spanned the twentieth century, and I know my readers would be interested in your story."

"I don't have a story, young man," she said with asperity. "I have a *life*."

The next day she ordered a computer and arranged to be connected to the Internet.

Looking back across the span of her life, she was surprised she had not recognised its unifying theme long since. Like links of a chain, one element joined the distant past with the breathtaking present.

Morse code had been responsible for the rescue of Ned Halloran from the *Titanic,* so he subsequently could rescue her from dire poverty and, undoubtedly, a short and miserable existence.

Journalism had educated and defined Henry Mooney, who in turn had given Ursula an education that sustained her throughout life.

An early career in radio had allowed her to go far beyond provincial boundaries. Television had extended her horizons still farther. With the advent of the Internet her world would enlarge beyond all imagining. The twentieth century would be remembered as the Age of Communication.

And Ursula Halloran was truly its child.

Ireland was, in many ways, a totally different country from the one into which she had been born. Even the people were different. Ursula remembered when the so-called hard men were truly hard, scrawny from undernourishment in childhood; wiry and sinewy with the need to fight for existence on a very basic level. "You'd see more meat on a seagull," was a comment applied to them. Now little rolls of fat marred the waistlines of those who thought of themselves as hard men.

Barry had begun collecting a new photographic archive. He was photographing and interviewing those same hard men, talking about the peace process.

"I fully appreciate how much you want action," Barry would say to them, "and how little faith you have in the British government. Your deepest desire is for us to go back into battle until Ireland's united again once and for all. But that's not going to happen—at least not through physical force. Don't look at me like that; I'm just being realistic. The time for violence is over, if there ever was an appropriate time for violence. We have no choice now but to go the political route.

"The Sinn Féin leadership won't always be able to say what you want them to say. Given their relationships with the various parties involved, not least the IRA, there are times when they have to be . . . ah . . . *muted* in their responses. In politics a man can't always tell the truth, or not the whole truth, even if he wants to. That's just how it is. We have to keep all the balls juggling in the air without dropping any of them. And it's damned hard to do."

He always finished by saying, "No matter how hard it is, we have to get tomorrow right."

BESIDE him in the passenger seat, Barbara was laughing. "Where are you taking me, Barry? Why do I have to wear this scarf over my eyes? Is this some sort of game, or what?"

"Just a little farther now, there's something I want you to see and we mustn't spoil the surprise." *Remember that life is very short, and of all wounds, regret most lacerates the heart.*

"Here we are. You can take off the blindfold now."

"An office building?" She looked puzzled. "I don't understand. Do we have business here?"

"We have property here. We own this place."

"You must be joking."

"Not about something as valuable as this; the market for property in city centre is beginning to climb. I bought this old house several years ago and have been fixing it up with an eye to making it into a home for us."

"But offices . . ."

"On leases. If you like this house we can let them expire and move in ourselves."

Barbara stared at Barry's old Georgian girl. She was elegant now, fully restored and the finest house in the street.

Among her neighbours, many of whom were still dilapidated if not derelict, she shone like a diamond.

I wish Mother could see this! Barbara thought.

Barry took her on a conducted tour, pointing out temporary walls and partitions that could easily be removed to make the building a private residence again.

"But it's huge, Barry! We'd have to have servants, and where do you get servants these days?"

"We needn't occupy all of it," he assured her. "We could keep the ground floor as offices for the sake of the income, which is not inconsiderable. Even if we persuade Ursula and Breda to join us we would still have plenty of room."

"We'll ask Ursula when she comes up at Christmas," Barbara decided. "If they want to live here with us you can start tearing up those leases."

"It doesn't work quite that way, they have to run out in the normal course. But the longest only lasts until the end of 1999."

"The Millennium," Barbara whispered.

Chapter Forty-five

THEY were almost back in Harold's Cross before she lost her temper.

"How dare you keep it from me all this time! Spending all that money. And staying away from the children . . ."

Here we go, he thought. "I never stayed away from the children. I stayed in the new house, or rather the new old house, when you and I were separated because I had to stay somewhere. But I always wanted to be with you."

"If that was true you would have shared this with me from the beginning."

How could he explain so she would understand? He parked the car and turned to face her. "Barbara, you had your singing career. That was *yours*. No, don't say anything, I know it didn't turn out the way you wanted, but it was personal to you. Your voice, no one else's. Maybe I felt like that about the house. I wanted something that was personal to me."

"How could a mansion in Mountjoy Square be personal to you?"

"I have no idea," he replied honestly. "Nor did I intend to keep it a secret. Things just worked out that way."

She turned away from him; stared out the window. "Things always work out other than the way we intend."

She sounded sorrowful rather than angry, so he tried again. "What about the house, sweetheart? Would you like us to live there?"

She gave a shrug. "I don't care. No. I mean I'll think about. There's no rush, is there?"

"There's no rush," he said.

ANOTHER bitter divorce referendum was too close to call on polling day. The final result was a vote for divorce by only 50.3 percent, one of the narrowest margins in Irish history.

WHEN *The Irish Press* closed down, Ursula grieved as if for a death in the family. "Eamon de Valera founded that newspaper," she told Barry over the telephone. "I can't believe it's gone."

"I thought you were anti–de Valera."

"I never said that," she replied indignantly.

.   .   .

THE peace process was thrown into disarray when British Prime Minister John Major demanded a statement of surrender from the IRA. However Sinn Féin used all its influence to sustain the ceasefire.

In December the head of the International Body on Decommissioning, former U.S. senator George Mitchell, invited submissions from all parties on arms decommissioning. Sinn Féin actively engaged with the IBD, hoping to resolve the impasse in the peace process.

IN March of 1997 Ted Kennedy called for an immediate and unconditional resumption of the IRA ceasefire. May elections brought the Labour Party back to power in Britain, and in Northern Ireland returned Gerry Adams and his party colleague, Martin McGuinness, as MPs.

The new prime minister, with a strong mandate for change, was an energetic young man called Tony Blair.

Blair appointed Dr. Mo Mowlam as Northern Ireland secretary. One of her immediate priorities was to work towards the restoration of the IRA ceasefire, and to include Sinn Féin in multiparty talks about the future.

She arrived complete with a built-in reputation as a hardhead. Barry remarked to Éamonn MacThomáis, "I like hardheads. It's easier to do business with them than with people who deal in platitudes and warm fuzzy feelings."

IN the Republic a carefully selected handful of government representatives attended a brief ceremony in Arbour Hill on the anniversary of the 1916 Rising, which otherwise went unremarked.

Except by republicans.

ON April twenty-seventh a Catholic man, Robert Hamill, was kicked and beaten by a loyalist mob in Portadown.

Several on-duty members of the RUC were sitting in a police car in plain sight of the attack. They made no effort to intervene. Hamill died of his injuries on May eighth.

THE signs were hopeful when in June Bertie Ahern of Fianna Fáil replaced the strongly anti-republican John Bruton as *taoiseach*. At least Ahern came from a republican background.

BARRY Halloran took the obligatory photograph of the new *taoiseach* in his new office, in front of a portrait of Patrick Pearse.

On the third of July Bertie Ahern held his first meeting with Tony Blair. The Northern Ireland situation was very much on the agenda. Both men were determined to progress towards a peaceful solution.

A letter sent to Martin McGuinness from the British government on the ninth of the month stated that Sinn Féin could participate in peace talks without any decommissioning of IRA weapons, provided the Mitchell Principles were followed.

On the twelfth of July two Protestant teenagers were wounded by an IRA sniper when they wandered too close to the demarcation line between Catholic and Protestant communities.

On the fifteenth an eighteen-year-old Catholic girl in County Antrim was shot dead by the LVF while visiting her Protestant boyfriend.

The following day, the text of an Ulster Unionist document proposing full IRA decommissioning was presented to both the British and Irish governments. The DUP, which had not drawn up the paper, was unhappy and threatened to withdraw from further negotiations.

Ignoring this development, a joint statement from John

Hume and Gerry Adams welcomed what it called "considerable progress" in the peace process.

O N the nineteenth the IRA announced a restoration of
the 1994 ceasefire.

M o Mowlam said she would monitor republican activity during the next six weeks to determine if Sinn Féin
would be admitted to the all-party talks scheduled for
September.

Mowlam did not fit any known political mould. There
was no doubt that she was highly intelligent, but she was
also down-to-earth, straightforward, and possessed an irrepressible sense of humour in spite of the fact that she
had recently undergone brain surgery for cancer. Dealing
every day with life and death, she retained the ability to
take nothing too seriously.

Irish people north and south loved nothing more than a
good story. They began collecting Mo Mowlam stories.

On one memorable occasion she opened a meeting with
Tony Blair and Ian Paisley by propping her feet on the
table, flinging off her wig, and saying to Paisley, "Hi, babe.
How's tricks?" For perhaps the only time in his life, Ian
Paisley was speechless.

T h a t summer Hong Kong was returned from British
rule and threw itself a huge party to celebrate freedom
from the Empire.

Chris Patten, the former governor of the former Crown
colony, returned to Britain to begin drafting proposals for
revamping the RUC in Northern Ireland.

·   ·   ·

IN July there was huge trouble over the issue of Orange parades during the Marching Season. Drumcree became a byword for organised unionist bigotry while world television cameras watched, revealing the insanity of the Irish once again. Within sight of Drumcree Church marchers with stony faces and bowler hats spewed hatred for their fellow man—as long as he was Catholic.

Barry was not present to photograph the scene. He had taken the children to the farm in Clare. While they were entertaining and being entertained by their grandmother, he gave himself a little holiday by driving over to Lough Derg to fish.

He loved the lake that lay between Clare and Tipperary. It was unpredictable; dangerous. In five minutes it could go from serene tranquillity to thunder and lightning and storm-tossed waves.

If Barbara were a lake she would be Lough Derg.

ON the twelfth of August Martin McGuinness of Sinn Féin and Ken Maginnis of the Ulster Unionist Party participated in a debate on BBC television. Barry made certain that his children watched.

Brian pointed out the good points and the bad points of each man's argument.

"Don't tell me you want to be a politician," his mother teased.

His eyes flashed. "I don't know just what I'm going to be. But whatever it is, I'll win."

TWO weeks later Mo Mowlam told the *Belfast Telegraph* that she did not necessarily define "consent," meaning the consent of the people to Irish unification, in a geographic sense.

Assuming that by this she meant if the majority on the

island wanted unification it would happen, the members of the UUP in the British Parliament described Dr. Mowlam as "hostile."

On the following day she told the House of Commons she accepted the IRA ceasefire as genuine, and invited Sinn Féin to participate in all-party peace talks at Stormont.

On the ninth of September Sinn Féin signed the Mitchell Principles and joined the other parties at Stormont. Barry photographed Gerry Adams, Martin McGuinness, and Gerry Kelly on the front steps of the imposing building.

The UUP and other unionist parties withdrew from the talks for the day.

"Decommissioning is going to be the stumbling block, all right," Éamonn MacThomáis agreed with Barry. "Every time we start to get somewhere one of the unionist parties will pull that rabbit out of the hat again. But I know the Army, there's not a chance in hell they'll give up their arms again, even if they bury them twelve feet deep in the ground. You just can't be defenceless when you live with people you can't trust."

"It always comes back to trust, doesn't it?" Barry said wearily.

When do you put aside a lack of trust and just get on with it?

A T the end of August Diana, the former princess of Wales, was killed in an automobile crash in Paris.

T H A T autumn Mo Mowlam announced that internment was to be removed from the statute books.

I N the Republic tax receipts were nine hundred million pounds more than expected. Ireland Inc. was in business.

· · ·

THE republican splinter groups were in business too. In spite of the Provo ceasefire the dissidents continued their warfare against northern loyalists and anyone else in the Protestant community who looked like an easy target.

In October the Continuity IRA put a bomb through the letter box of David Trimble's constituency office.

BARRY and Éamonn stood on the O'Connell Street Bridge, looking down at the murky waters of the Liffey. "It breaks my heart," Barry said. "When I was growing up we still had old IRA men who had fought in the War of Independence and carried their ideals in their eyes. They were tough and hard; they'd had to be. But they were men Pearse and Connolly could have been proud of. Now it's all changed. There's a faction that seems to be more interested in perpetuating the Army for its own sake than in accomplishing what the Army was founded to achieve."

DURING St. Patrick's Day meetings in March of 1998, Bill Clinton called on David Trimble to engage in a face-to-face meeting with Gerry Adams.

MO Mowlam paid an extraordinary visit to the Maze prison to have face-to-face talks with both republican and loyalist prisoners. Afterwards, the paramilitaries announced they would support the peace process.

EASTER fell in April that year; a cold, wet, snowy April in Northern Ireland. The massive hulk of Stormont looked even more bleak than usual. Representatives from the Irish and British governments must have felt a certain foreboding as their cars swept up the long drive.

After sixty-five hours of negotiation that lasted from Spy Wednesday to Good Friday—frequently accompanied by the raucous background of Ian Paisley's followers bellowing insults—an agreement seemed to be within grasp. At the last moment David Trimble could not bring all of his Unionist Party along with him. Then Bill Clinton made good on his promise to help in any way he could. In a three-way conference between the president of the United States, the *taoiseach* of Ireland, and the prime minister of the United Kingdom, a strategy was hammered out that the Ulster Unionist Party was willing to accept.

And the Good Friday Agreement was signed.

Or, as the unionists persisted in calling it, the Belfast Agreement.

April tenth, 1998, Barry carefully printed on the back of each of the photographs he had taken. Most of the men were smiling, though some of the smiles looked pained.

B ARRY returned to Dublin in an emotional state somewhere between euphoria and dread. The high resulting from the signing of the Agreement, with its built-in optimism and promise for finally bringing a peaceful solution to the northern situation, was intense.

Yet all the years of brutal experience were piled onto the other side of the scale.

In spite of all the nay-sayers, the stops and starts, the lies and counterlies, and an almost total lack of trust on both sides, somehow they've done it. Brave men who had their lives repeatedly threatened because of their actions have done the impossible.

Everything came back to the matter of trust. One must trust that somehow it would work and there really would be an end to the violence.

A rainbow in the northern future.

A thirty-two-county republic where all of its children are cherished equally.

ON the twenty-fifth of April a young Catholic man called Ciarán Heffron was shot six times through the head by members of the Loyalist Volunteer Force as he walked through Crumlin, Co. Antrim. Heffron was on his way home from university to visit his seriously ill mother.

During a drunken loyalist party in Antrim a videotape was made on which the killers described explicit details of the murder. The tape eventually was sent to the Northern Ireland public prosecutor's office, but no charges were ever brought.

IN May IRA informer Sean O'Callaghan claimed in his book that the IRA had kidnapped Shergar. According to him they had been unable to control the horse, and the animal injured itself and was dead within four days.

Ursula had not bought the book; she heard the story on the news and promptly rang Barry.

"I don't believe a word of it," she said stoutly. "How can you trust a person like that? An *informer,* someone who sells out his own for money!"

Barry was amused. "Does this mean you're a republican again?"

"I always *was* a republican!"

ON the fifteenth of August a three hundred-pound car bomb in the town of Omagh killed twenty-eight people outright, including a pregnant woman, and injured hundreds more. The RUC had received a warning ahead of time but had been given the wrong location for the bomb.

The Provos strenuously denied planting the bomb. Speaking for Sinn Féin, Martin McGuinness said he was appalled and disgusted, adding that it was an indefensible action.

Three days later a newly emerged dissident group calling itself the Real IRA admitted responsibility for the Omagh bomb.

On the twenty-second of the month the INLA announced a complete ceasefire.

Sometimes there was one grave too many.

ONCE Fianna Fáil had claimed to be "a broad church," a republican, populist party as envisioned by Eamon de Valera, representing all of the people of Ireland. No longer. Since the seventies the culture of corruption had bitten deep. Property developers presented brown envelopes stuffed with cash to politicians who unhesitatingly accepted them—and in some cases demanded them. Fianna Fáil supplanted Fine Gael as the party of the rich, furiously building more golf courses and marinas and luxury apartment complexes, while schools rotted away for lack of funds and sick people waited on hospital trolleys for beds that were not there.

PAUL Morrissey looked embarrassed. "I've been offered so much money for my farm I just can't turn it down, Ursula. We're going to sell out and move to Galway. The twins are at the university there . . . you know . . ." He spread his hands, silently begging her to understand.

Chapter Forty-six

------·«◦≪◇≫◦»·------

IN spite of her best intentions and all of Breda's help, Ursula could not remain at the farm without the support of the Morrisseys. The effort was physically beyond her. She spent several days trying not to face the inevitable, then at last rang Dublin.

"Ursula's going to lease out the farm to someone else," Barry told Barbara. "She asked me if we still want her to live with us."

Barbara stood very still. Savouring the reins of power in her hands. It was not as totally satisfying as she would have expected. "Where?"

"Anywhere you like," he said.

BARRY telephoned his mother. "You have two invitations."

"Two?"

"You can live here with us in Harold's Cross, or we can all move up to Mountjoy Square. For reasons best known to herself, Barbara's decided to leave the choice up to you."

Ursula began to laugh.

She laughed so hard she could not get her breath and Breda had to take the phone away from her. "We'll ring you back," she told Barry hastily.

She helped Ursula to bed and put a cold cloth on her forehead. The laughter had passed but Ursula was still pale; she appeared disoriented.

"What in the name of all the saints is wrong with you?" Breda asked anxiously.

"Life goes in a circle." Ursula sounded bemused. "Did you know that? Isn't it funny?"

"Are you coming down with something? Are you delirious?"

"Barry says we could live in Mountjoy Square if we wanted to but I don't want to. I wouldn't like it and you wouldn't either. So we're going to live in Harold's Cross again."

Breda gave her a sedative, waited until she was asleep, and then telephoned Barry.

W H E N they were packing up her things Barry found a number of letters to Ursula from Henry Mooney. He did not usually read other people's letters, but he could not resist.

"The military defeat suffered by the republicans in 1923," Henry had written, "encouraged rational men to look in another direction—politics. The militant force people hated him for it, but Eamon de Valera rightly foresaw there was no other way to get back the Six Counties which Britain had coerced away from us in the Treaty.

"As a trusted friend, rather than as a journalist, in August of 1924 I attended a two-day meeting of present and former republican deputies of the Dáil. Mary MacSwiney kept the minutes. There was a hot discussion about whether or not the republicans, as heirs of the legitimately and constitutional elected first Dáil which had preceded the Civil War, were in fact an emergency government de jure. Sean McEntee pointed out that since they were not now the government de facto they had no power over the life and property of citizens of the state.

"De Valera concurred, adding—and I think these were his exact words—'We can have no sanction of force.' He said that criminality was something the republicans could not deal with on their own, except by public opinion and expulsion. On the second day of the meeting he stressed, 'We will not permit or sanction any executions.' Con Markievicz backed him up. Her words were, 'If we attempt to execute a man for common murder we should be acting as a junta.'

"De Valera had a final warning for the IRA. He said if the Army made any attempt to take life, he and his fellow republicans in the Dáil would disclaim all responsibility and regard the Volunteers responsible for the killing as traitors.

"Harsh words indeed, Precious, especially coming from a commandant in the Easter Rising. In retrospect, I realise that he was staking out the moral high ground for Irish republicanism. Surely we can be militant without being militaristic. As long as the movement stays within the law, avoiding both the hypocrisy of the Free Staters and the cynical manipulations of the British government, sooner or later the people of Ireland will reclaim what they have lost. I truly believe that. I am only sorry I will not be there to see it."

In faded pencil in the margin of the letter, Barry recognised his mother's handwriting. "You will be here, Henry. You'll see it through my eyes, or Barry's, or the eyes of his children."

PREPARING for what she anticipated would be the last big change in her life, Ursula managed to summon a spirit of adventure. At least on the surface, for others to see.

When everything was almost ready she paid a long visit to the barns, spending the day with the horses. Trying to inhale their very essence into herself to sustain her through all the days to come.

On the last day, the absolutely final day, Ursula watched as the favourite bits of furniture and other possessions she was keeping were loaded into a removal van. Barry and Breda were with her but she was hardly aware of them.

Presences at the periphery. The farm was at her centre; would always be at her centre.

She insisted on going into the house one final time, alone. Slowly, painfully, she made her way up the stairs, her fingers spidering along the wall for support because she refused to hold on to the stair rail. *This will be the last time I put my foot on this step. And this is the last time I shall see my bedroom with the view out across the fields.*

She peered into the dusty looking glass on the dressing table. "I turned into an old woman while I wasn't looking," she told her reflected image. She scrutinised the frown stitched between her eyebrows, which had turned white. And her deeply pleated upper lip. "No laugh lines, though. Perhaps I didn't laugh enough."

The good bones that had been her genetic gift remained, more beautiful than ever with the flesh pared away. Hers was a face one might see on the statue of an heroic female figure: Maeve of Connacht, or Constance Markievicz.

"I shall look like that in my coffin," Ursula said aloud. "Good. No one will pity me."

HAVING read Henry's letter, when Barry returned to Dublin the first thing he did after Ursula and Breda were settled in their new rooms was to drive to Mountjoy Square.

The door to the private apartment at the top of the elegant staircase had a beautiful antique crystal doorknob, but also a very modern combination lock. It rather spoiled the effect, Barry thought sadly.

His weapons and Ned's notebooks were where they had always been, safe in the private hideaway he had constructed for them. He picked up the rifle and held it for a long time. Letting his body remember. Daring the beast to surface.

It was under control now.

He laid the rifle aside and picked up the last of the notebooks to read again the very final entry, scrawled when Ned was almost blind:

"De Valera was both right and wrong. So was Collins. So were we all. That is little comfort now."

ON the first of January, 1999, the Republic of Ireland took its place with ten other countries in the European Union.

In July five hundred thousand Irish men and women bought shares in Telecom Eireann when the communications company was floated on the stock market. The government had heavily promoted the deal, but within a short time the share price began to fall dramatically, never to recover.

ANOTHER Northern Ireland solicitor who had defended republicans was blown to pieces in a car bomb. Rosemary Nelson had been only a few yards from her home when she was murdered by loyalist paramilitaries.

No one was arrested or charged with the crime.

HUNDREDS of thousands fled Serbian aggression in the Baltic country of Kosovo.

MO Mowlam was replaced as Northern secretary by Peter Mandelson in October 1999.

The British and Irish signed an agreement by which Articles 2 and 3 of the Irish Constitution was changed.

And former *taoiseach* Jack Lynch was buried in his native Cork.

A television programme shown on RTE, entitled "States of Fear," exposed to a shocked nation the incredible amount of physical and sexual abuse that had been suffered by children in state institutions run by the religious orders.

As with every other news item of interest, there was considerable discussion of the programme in the yellow brick house. Ursula said she had always suspected it. Barbara said it could never happen in America.

Breda said it was probably still going on and always would, and people had to forgive and forget.

"Forgive and forget," Barry echoed. "That's where it goes wrong. Forgetting solves nothing, it only sweeps the dirt under the carpet to reappear some other time, maybe at the worst possible time. We must forgive and remember."

I N December Chris Patten published his long-awaited report on policing in Northern Ireland. His detailed observations were acute and his cogent suggestions were widely praised. If strictly followed, they would bring an end to any question of RUC collusion with loyalists, creating a just system to replace generations of institutionalised sectarianism. The report was then put in some bureaucrat's bottom drawer and forgotten. But the step had been taken. The suggestion that a way forward was possible now existed.

Somewhere over the horizon there was a glimmer of hope; of peace.

T H E Irish government sent a free Millennium candle to every household in the Republic with instructions to light it at midnight on December thirty-first.

.   .   ..

B ARRY invited every friend he could think of to join them for a huge pre-Christmas party in the yellow brick house. "There would have been more room in Mountjoy Square," Barbara pouted.

On Christmas Eve he gave her a topaz ring the colour of her eyes.

She held it up to sparkle in the lights from the tree.

In those same lights Ursula glimpsed the pattern of her life in its entirety, stretching from past to future.

Young Brian, gifted with his father's great energy and fine mind, would become a captain of industry in the new Europe. Grace Mary, no longer "Trot," had a singing career ahead of her that her mother would envy.

And Pat would inherit the farm. Her will had been rewritten and signed. Pat with his darkling eyes and faun's ears would spend his life amidst the scenes she loved, and perhaps someday he would find a girl with a rebel heart to share them with him.

T HE very last present that Patrick handed out that day was to his father. "This is from my mother. She says it's always been yours."

The package was flat, and stiff with cardboard. When Patrick laid it in his hands Barry felt something akin to an electric shock. He glanced up to find his mother and his wife watching him closely.

There were tears in Ursula's eyes and her arm was around Barbara.

Barry opened the package. It contained Henry Mooney's copy of the Proclamation of the Irish Republic.

I N her room that night Ursula took out a fresh sheet of creamy paper and began to write a letter.

Dear Papa,

How strange to think that I am almost ninety years old! What astonishing years they have been. We never knew the exact date of my birth but that does not matter. Ireland made me, and my death, when it comes, will be in Ireland. I want to be waked at home for three days and nights. I want the tricolour on the coffin at my funeral and a grave in Glasnevin Cemetery with the patriots.

Over the last months I have observed my eyesight slowly dimming. Sounds are growing muffled. I welcome each subtle change that launches me towards a new adventure. I am fading out of life; fading into death like the changing of the seasons.

When my vision is clear again I shall look upon a different world. But please God, let it still be Ireland!

ON New Year's Eve Barry took Barbara to the apartment at the top of the house in Mountjoy Square. "We'll have a great view," he promised.

They stood together looking out over the city. Just for a moment she leaned her head on his shoulder. Barry knew the future with her would be turbulent. But he would not trade it for anything.

PRECISELY at midnight hundreds of thousands of Irish men and women lit their candles to welcome the new Millennium.

Ireland bloomed with stars.

26 September, 2005

Amongst the IRA weapons decommissioned and put forever beyond use as of this date was a short magazine Lee-
Enfield .303 rifle made during the First World War. The
old rifle was fitted with a small brass plate proclaiming its
place of manufacture: "Winchester Repeating Arms Co.,
New Haven, Connecticut."

THE PROCLAMATION OF
POBLACHT NA H EIREANN.
THE PROVISIONAL GOVERNMENT
OF THE
IRISH REPUBLIC
TO THE PEOPLE OF IRELAND.

IRISHMEN AND IRISHWOMEN: In the name of God and of the dead generations from which she receives her old tradition of nationhood, Ireland, through us, summons her children to her flag and strikes for her freedom.

Having organised and trained her manhood through her secret revolutionary organisation, the Irish Republican Brotherhood, and through her open military organisations, the Irish Volunteers and the Irish Citizen Army, having patiently perfected her discipline, having resolutely waited for the right moment to reveal itself, she now seizes that moment, and, supported by her exiled children in America and by gallant allies in Europe, but relying in the first on her own strength, she strikes in full confidence of victory.

We declare the right of the people of Ireland to the ownership of Ireland, and to the unfettered control of Irish destinies, to be sovereign and indefeasible. The long usurpation of that right by a foreign people and government has not extinguished the right, nor can it ever be extinguished except by the destruction of the Irish people. In every generation the Irish people have asserted their right to national freedom and sovereignty; six times during the past three hundred years they have asserted it in arms. Standing on that fundamental right and again asserting it in arms in the face of the world, we hereby proclaim the Irish Republic as a Sovereign Independent State, and we pledge our lives and the lives of our comrades-in-arms to the cause of its freedom of its welfare, and of its exaltation among the nations.

The Irish Republic is entitled to, and hereby claims, the allegiance of every Irishman and Irishwoman. The Republic guarantees religious and civil liberty, equal rights and equal opportunities to all its citizens, and declares its resolve to pursue the happiness and prosperity of the whole nation and of all its parts, cherishing all the children of the nation equally, and oblivious of the differences carefully fostered by an alien government, which have divided a minority from the majority in the past.

Until our arms have brought the opportune moment for the establishment of a permanent National Government, representative of the whole people of Ireland and elected by the suffrages of all her men and women, the Provisional Government, hereby constituted, will administer the civil and military affairs of the Republic in trust for the people.

We place the cause of the Irish Republic under the protection of the Most High God, Whose blessing we invoke upon our arms, and we pray that no one who serves that cause will dishonour it by cowardice, inhumanity, or rapine. In this supreme hour the Irish nation must, by its valour and discipline and by the readiness of its children to sacrifice themselves for the common good, prove itself worthy of the august destiny to which it is called.

Signed on Behalf of the Provisional Government,

THOMAS J. CLARKE.

SEAN Mac DIARMADA. THOMAS MacDONAGH.
P. H. PEARSE. EAMONN CEANNT.
JAMES CONNOLLY. JOSEPH PLUNKETT

Notes

CHAPTER TWO

1. *An Phoblacht,* September 1, 2005.
2. *Ruairí Ó Brádaigh,* p. 163.

CHAPTER FOUR

1. *Bloody Sunday in Derry,* p. 72.
2. *The Fingal Independent,* February 4, 1972.

CHAPTER FIVE

1. *Revolutionary Underground,* p. 3.
2. *A Chronology of Irish History Since 1500,* p. 257.
3. *Orders for the Captain?,* pp. 18–22.

CHAPTER SIX

1. *Daily Ireland,* October 19, 2005.
2. *The Troubles,* p. 251.

CHAPTER SEVEN

1. *The Mitrokhin Archive,* p. 501.

CHAPTER NINE

1. *RTE,* June 24, 2005.

CHAPTER TEN

1. *Peace in Ireland: The War of Ideas*, p. 197.
2. British State Papers released in 2004.
3. *The Skerries News*, July 2005.
4. *An Phoblacht*, September 1, 2005.

CHAPTER ELEVEN

1. *A Chronology of Irish History Since* 1500, p. 260
2. *Lost Lives*, p. 356.

CHAPTER TWELVE

1. *Interview with Rosaleen MacThomáis*, February 20, 2006.

CHAPTER THIRTEEN

1. *The Troubles*, p. 127.
2. *Hostage*, p. 106.

CHAPTER FOURTEEN

1. British State Papers, released in 2004.
2. *The Dublin and Monaghan Bombings*, p. 13.
3. British State Papers, numbers 8 and 9, released in 2005.

CHAPTER FIFTEEN

1. *The Dublin and Monaghan Bombings*, p. 33.
2. *The Baron Report*, published by the Irish government in December 2003.
3. *Le Monde*, May 20, 1974.

CHAPTER SIXTEEN

1. *Northern Ireland: A Chronology of the Troubles*, p. 93.
2. *On the Blanket*, p. 158.

CHAPTER SEVENTEEN

1. From a personal interview with Rosaleen MacThomáis.
2. *Northern Ireland: A Chronology of the Troubles,* p. 92.
3. From personal letters of Ruairí Ó Brádaigh, released to the public in 2005.

CHAPTER EIGHTEEN

1. British State Papers, released in 2005.
2. Irish State Papers, released in 2005.
3. *Northern Ireland: A Chronology of the Troubles,* p. 100.
4. *Out of the Maze,* p. 11.

CHAPTER NINETEEN

1. *An Phoblacht,* July 2004.
2. *The Shankill Butchers: A Case Study of Mass Murder,* p. 67.
3. *The Shankill Butchers: A Case Study of Mass Murder,* p. 94.

CHAPTER TWENTY

1. *Provos,* p. 200.
2. *The Killing of Pat Finucane,* p. 43.

CHAPTER TWENTY-ONE

1. British State Papers, released in 2006.
2. *Armed Struggle: A History of the IRA,* p. 312.
3. *Northern Ireland: A Chronology of the Troubles,* p. 113.
4. *On the Blanket,* p. 228.
5. *Daily Ireland,* October 28, 2005.
6. *Man of War; Man of Peace,* p. 143.
7. Excerpts from the writings of Bobby Sands.
8. *Man of War; Man of Peace,* p. 142.
9. From a government-guided tour of the Maze in 2006.

CHAPTER TWENTY-THREE

1. *2RN and the Origins of Irish Radio*, p. 11.
2. *Lost Lives*, p. 696.

CHAPTER TWENTY-FOUR

1. *The Brendan Voyage*, p. 252.

CHAPTER TWENTY-SIX

1. *Hope Against History*, p. 143.
2. *A Secret History of the IRA*, p. 173.
3. *Hope and History*, p. 8.
4. *Viking Dublin Exposed*, p. 39.
5. *The Irish Times*, September 23, 1978.
6. *An Phoblacht*, September 30, 1978.

CHAPTER TWENTY-SEVEN

1. *The Irish Troubles*, p. 193.
2. *A Secret History of the IRA*, pp. 174–75.

CHAPTER TWENTY-NINE

1. *Kevin Barry and His Time*, p. 165.
2. *Before the Dawn*, p. 290.
3. *The Irish Times*, February 14, 1981.
4. *The Irish Troubles*, p. 611.
5. *1916: The Man Who Lost Ireland*, RTE documentary broadcast in April 2006.

CHAPTER THIRTY

1. *An Phoblacht*, May 25, 2006.
2. Danny Morrison interview broadcast on RTE, May 5, 2006.
3. *Before the Dawn*, pp. 190–91
4. *Orangeism: The Making of a Tradition*, p. 349.

5. *The Irish Hunger Strike,* p. 569.
6. *Northern Ireland: A Chronology of the Troubles,* p. 157.

CHAPTER THIRTY-ONE

1. *An Phoblacht,* September 1, 2005.
2. *Northern Ireland: A Chronology of the Troubles,* p. 165.
3. *Phrases Make History Here,* p. 194.
4. *Chronicle of the Twentieth Century,* p. 1207.
5. *Northern Ireland: A Chronology of the Troubles,* p. 168.

CHAPTER THIRTY-TWO

1. *Marxism Today,* March 1984, p. 3, article by Alan Murdoch.

CHAPTER THIRTY-FOUR

1. British State Papers, released 2006.
2. *Hope Against History,* p. 20.
3. *Magill,* September 1984.
4. *Stalker,* p. 30.
5. *An Phoblacht,* September 1, 2005.
6. *The Times (London),* November 20, 1984.
7. *Northern Ireland: A Chronology of the Troubles,* p. 185.

CHAPTER THIRTY-FIVE

1. *An Phoblacht,* September 1, 2005.
2. *The Independent,* October 23, 2005.
3. *Short Fellow,* p. 331.
4. *An Phoblacht,* May 25, 2006.

CHAPTER THIRTY-SIX

1. *The Killing of Pat Finucane,* p. 52.
2. *Dublin as a Work of Art,* p. 110.
3. BBC News, November 9, 1987.

CHAPTER THIRTY-SEVEN

1. *Fatal Encounter,* p. 67.
2. *The Tribune,* March 12, 1988, article by Veronica Guerin.
3. *Fatal Encounter,* p. 86.

CHAPTER THIRTY-NINE

1. *The Family,* p. 495.

CHAPTER FORTY

1. *Northern Ireland: A Chronology of the Troubles,* p. 245.

CHAPTER FORTY-ONE

1. *Lost Lives,* pp. 1291–92.
2. *The Fight for Peace,* p. 246.

CHAPTER FORTY-TWO

1. *Northern Ireland: A Chronology of the Troubles,* p. 270.
2. *Endgame in Ireland,* p. 79.
3. *Irish News,* April 26, 1993.
4. British State Papers, released 2006.

CHAPTER FORTY-FOUR

1. *Endgame in Ireland,* pp. 203–015.

Periodicals consulted:
The Irish Times
Irish News
Cork Examiner
Irish Independent
Sunday Independent
The Times (London)
Connacht Tribune

Belfast Newsletter
Belfast Tribune
An Phoblacht
Life
Time
Magill

Bibliography

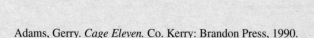

Adams, Gerry. *Cage Eleven.* Co. Kerry: Brandon Press, 1990.

———. *Before the Dawn.* Co. Kerry: Brandon Press, 1996.

———. *The Politics of Irish Freedom.* Co. Kerry: Brandon Press, 1986.

Anderson, Brendan. *Joe Cahill: A Life in the IRA.* Dublin: O'Brien Press, 2002.

Andrew, Christopher, and Vasili Mitrokhin. *The Mitrokhin Archive.* London: Allen Lane/Penguin Press, 1999.

Ballard, Robert D. *The Discovery of the "Titanic."* London: Hodder and Stoughton, 1987.

Bell, J. Bowyer. *In Dubious Battle: The Dublin and Monaghan Bombings.* Dublin: Poolbeg Press, 1996.

———. *The Secret Army: The IRA from 1916.* Dublin: Academy Press, 1972.

Beresford, David. *Ten Men Dead.* New York: Atlantic Monthly Press, 1987.

Berners-Lee, Tim. *Weaving the Web*. London: Texere, 2000.

Bew, Paul, and Gordon Gillespie. *Northern Ireland: A Chronology of the Troubles*. Dublin: Gill and Macmillan, 1999.

Bourke, Richard. *Peace in Ireland: The War of Ideas*. London: Pimlico Press, 2003.

Bradley, John, editor. *Viking Dublin Exposed*. Dublin: O'Brien Press, 1984.

Brown, Terence. *Ireland: A Social and Cultural History, 1922–1985*. London: Fontana Press, 1985.

Campbell, Brian, editor. *Nor Meekly Serve My Time*. Dublin: Sinn Féin Publications, 2006.

Clayton, Pamela. *Enemies and Passing Friends: Settler Ideologies in Twentieth Century Ulster*. London: Pluto Press, 1996.

Collins, Tom. *The Irish Hunger Strike*. Dublin: White Island Press, 1986.

Colley, Dudley. *Wheel Patter: Memories of Irish Motor Sport*. Dublin: Loft Publications, 2003.

Conroy, John. *Unspeakable Acts, Ordinary People*. New York: Alfred A. Knopf, 2000.

Coogan, Tim Pat. *The IRA*. London: Fontana/Collins, 1987.

———. *On the Blanket*. Dublin: Ward River Press Ltd., 1980.

———. *The Troubles*. London: Hutchinson, 1995.

———. *Wherever Green Is Worn*. London: Hutchinson, 2000.

Curtis, Liz. *Ireland: The Propaganda War*. Belfast: Sasta, 1998.

Davies, Nicholas. *Ten-Thirty-Three: The Inside Story of Britain's Secret Killing Machine in Northern Ireland*. Edinburgh: Mainstream Publishing, 1999.

Devlin, Bernadette. *The Price of My Soul*. London: Pan Books, 1969.

Dillon, Martin. *The Shankill Butchers: A Case Study of Mass Murder*. London: Arrow Books, 1990.

Dillon, Martin, and Denis Lehane. *Political Murder in Northern Ireland*. London: Penguin, 1973.

Doherty, J. E., and D. J. Hickey. *A Chronology of Irish History Since 1500*. Dublin: Gill and Macmillan, 1989.

Doherty, Paddy. *Paddy Bogside*. Dublin: Mercier Press, 2001.

Dunne, Derek. *Out of the Maze*. Dublin: Gill and Macmillan, 1988.

Dwyer, T. Ryle. *Short Fellow*. Dublin: Marino Press, 1999.

Eckert, Nicholas. *Fatal Encounter*. Dublin: Poolbeg Press, 1999.

English, Richard. *Armed Struggle: A History of the IRA*. London: Macmillan, 2003.

Faulkner, Brian. *Memoirs of a Statesman*. London: Weidenfeld and Nicolson, 1978.

Ferriter, Diarmaid. *The Transformation of Ireland, 1900–2000*. London: Profile Books, 2004.

Garland, Roy. *Gusty Spence*. Belfast: The Blackstaff Press, 2001.

Garvin, Tom. *Preventing the Future*. Dublin: Gill and Macmillan, 2004.

Girvin, Brian. *From Union to Union*. Dublin: Gill and Macmillan, 2002.

Gladstone, Parnell, Davitt, and Others. *The Irish Question*. New York: Ford's National Library, 1886.

Haddick-Flynn, Kevin. *Orangeism: The Making of a Tradition*. Dublin: Wolfhound Press, 1999.

Holland, Jack. *Hope Against History*. New York: Henry Holt, 1999.

Howard, Paul. *Hostage*. Dublin: The O'Brien Press, 2004.

Kearns, Kevin C. *Dublin Pub Life and Lore*. Dublin: Gill and Macmillan, 1996.

Kelley, Kitty. *The Family*. New York: Doubleday, 2004.

Kelly, James. *Orders for the Captain?* Dublin: James Kelly, 1971.

———. *The Thimble Riggers*. Dublin: James Kelly, 1999.

Lincoln, Colm. *Dublin as a Work of Art*. Dublin: O'Brien Press, 1992.

McCann, Eamonn. *Bloody Sunday in Derry*. Co. Kerry: Brandon, 1992.

McDonald, Henry. *Trimble*. London: Bloomsbury, 2000.

McKay, Susan. *Northern Protestants: An Unsettled People*. Belfast: Blackstaff Press, 2000.

McKittrick, Kelters, Feeney and Thornton. *Lost Lives*. Edinburgh: Mainstream Publishing, 1999.

McPhilemy, Seán. *The Committee: Political Assassination in Northern Ireland*. Niwot, Colo.: Roberts Rinehart, 1998.

Major, John. *John Major: The Autobiography*. London: Harper-Collins, 1999.

Mallie, Eamonn, and David McKittrick. *Endgame in Ireland*. London: Hodder and Stoughton, 2001.

———. *The Fight for Peace*. London: Heinemann, 1996.

Mercer, Derrick. *Chronicles of the Twentieth Century*. London: Longman Chronicle Communications, 1988.

Mitchell, George J. *Making Peace*. Berkeley: University of California Press, 2000.

Moloney, Ed, and Allen Lane. *A Secret History of the IRA*. London: Penguin, 2003.

Mowlam, Mo. *Momentum*. London: Hodder and Stoughton, 2002.

Mullan, Don. *Bloody Sunday: Massacre in Northern Ireland*. Dublin: Wolfhound Press, 1997.

———. *The Dublin and Monaghan Bombings*. Dublin: Wolfhound Press, 2000.

O'Brien, Justin. *The Killing of Pat Finucane*. Dublin: Gill and Macmillan, 2005.

Ó Broin, Leon. *Revolutionary Underground*. Dublin: Gill and Macmillan, 1976.

O'Callaghan, Sean. *The Informer*. Dublin: Corgi Books, 1999.

O'Clery, John. *Phrases Make History Here*. Dublin: O'Brien Press, 1986.

O'Donovan, Donal. *Kevin Barry and His Time*. Dublin: Glendale Press, 1989.

Pine, Richard. *2RN and the Origins of Irish Radio*. Dublin: Four Courts Press, 2002.

Pringle, Peter, and Philip Jacobson. *Those Are Real Bullets, Aren't They?* London: The Fourth Estate, 2000.

Reagan, Ronald. *Reagan in His Own Hand*. New York: The Free Press, 2001.

Redmond, Adrian, editor. *That Was Then, This Is Now: Change in Ireland 1949–1999*. Dublin: Central Statistics Office, 2000.

Rose, Richard. *Governing Without Consensus*. London: Faber and Faber, 1971.

Ryder, Chris. *The RUC: Force Under Fire, 1922–1997*. London: Mandarin, 1997.

Sands, Bobby: collected works both published and privately owned.

Severin, Tim. *The Brendan Voyage*. New York: McGraw-Hill, 1978.

Sharrock, David, and Mark Devenport. *Man of War; Man of Peace*. London: Macmillan, 1997.

Sinn Féin. *Sinn Féin: A Century of Struggle*. Dublin: Sinn Féin
    Publications, 2005.

Stalker, John. *Stalker*. London: Harrap, 1987.

Taylor, Peter. *Provos*. London: Bloomsbury, 1997.

Tiernan, Joe. *The Dublin and Monaghan Bombings and the
    Murder Triangle*. Dublin: Joe Tiernan, 2002.

Toolis, Kevin. *Rebel Hearts*. London: Picador, 2000.

Townshend, Charles. *Ireland: The Twentieth Century*. London:
    Arnold, 1999.

Walsh, Dermot P. J. *Bloody Sunday and the Rule of Law in
    Northern Ireland*. Dublin: Gill and Macmillan, 2000.

White, Robert W. *Ruairí Ó Brádaigh: The Life and Politics of
    an Irish Revolutionary*. Bloomington: Indiana University
    Press, 2006.

Wood, Ian S. *God, Guns, and Ulster*. London: Caxton Publica-
    tions, 2003.

Other Sources:

"Paisley's Progress," television documentary, BBC4, March 23,
    2004.

Personal interviews on RTE as given in endnotes.